CONSCRIPT

Scott Bartlett

Mirth Publishing
High River

Cover art by Tom Edwards (tomedwardsdesign.com)

Library and Archives Canada Cataloguing in Publication

Bartlett, Scott

Conscript (Paperback Edition) ; Scott Bartlett; illustrations by Tom Edwards

ISBN 978-1-988380-55-1

Contents

Chapter 1

Po was guiding his power loader toward the next shipping container when something caught his eye:

Tanner, the new guy, had just sent his last load up to the magtrains that ran through the giant cylinder's center...

...and was now rushing toward the same container as Po.

That wouldn't have meant much, except for Tanner's obvious haste. Po had only known Tanner for a few days, but already he had the impression the guy was no over-achiever. Maybe not a complete slacker, sure, but since he'd started working the Docks a few days ago, he'd done nothing beyond the bare minimum required.

Not that I blame him, Po thought. *I do the exact same thing.* Po never, ever exerted himself beyond what he needed to do to keep his job. Why break your back for the company that had enslaved you before you were even born?

Either way, Tanner's behavior seemed highly unusual. The W-200 Powered Loader—the workhorse of the solar system—was slaved to its operator's movements, with sophisticated subroutines designed to dampen any inefficient or involuntary inputs from the controller, a system that usually resulted in a smooth ride.

But Tanner was fresh out of the five-week training period required to operate one of the mechs, and he still hadn't learned to let the machine lead his movements...at least, not at the speed he was trying to operate it at right now. The W-200 lurched sideways as he navigated around a stationary crane arm, nearly toppling his machine as he did.

Po grinned, then sped up his own gait. Unlike Tanner's mech, his surged confidently forward, since he knew to keep his movements steady and conserved.

At first, Po had been fine with letting Tanner reach the container first, to let him process it for transport elsewhere in the asteroid colony. But then, a few things had clicked into place in his head.

It had been almost two months since the last time someone had been caught rerouting shipping containers, to be accessed by smugglers at a new destination. Yes, the "new destination" was always just another Equipoise Metals warehouse, and so usually the change went unnoticed, since the company always recovered the rerouted cargo.

But this time, a supervisor had decided to check the container's total mass, and found that seventy kilos of...something...had gone missing.

What it had been was anyone's guess. Probably Joy, Spike, or some other synthetic tweaked to let its user pass drug tests. It didn't matter, though. The dock worker who rerouted the container had clearly been working with the Obsidian Angels to keep contraband flowing through Psyche Station, and they'd sacked him for it...which was almost as good as a death sentence, on Psyche.

Now, as Po watched Tanner struggle desperately to reach the shipping container first, he felt sure he was looking at the Angels' newest agent planted among the dock workers. Which meant that container held something valuable. Something that could mean a lot of coin to Po—and to his mother and his brothers and sister.

He was always looking for the angle that would help pay down their colossal debts, and now here it was. A gift from the stars, just waiting for him to pluck it up. He only needed to reroute the container somewhere safe, a place only he would know.

And I won't be stupid enough to alter its total mass either. I'll just replace whatever the contraband is with something of the same weight.

Fear jolted through him, and a small voice tried to warn him that messing with the Obsidian Angel meshmind might be a bad idea. *Fortune favors the bold,* he told the voice, pushing it away.

This was for his sister.

Tanner didn't have Po's experience when it came to piloting the W-200, but he *was* a lot closer, having dropped off his last container at an elevator a lot nearer the ship they were unloading.

Po was gaining on him steadily, but as the distance closed to twenty meters, twelve meters, two meters...Tanner did something unexpected. He threw his mech sideways into Po's path.

With a gasp, Po yanked back on his handgrips, which threw his body forward against the mech's roll cage. For an excruciating few seconds, he felt sure he was going to fall forward into Tanner's mech, possibly wrecking one or both of their machines in the process. But his loader regained its balance just in time, barely avoiding a collision.

"Are you crazy?" Po yelled. Damaging the mechs like that would have been sure to get them both fired, not to mention adding to Po's already towering generational debt. But all he could hear was Tanner's laughter, which faded as the other mech pulled away.

The insane maneuver had demonstrated something to Po: Tanner could afford to lose this job. This wasn't his real job, anyway. He was an Obsidian Angel, and Angels he'd meshed with would take care of him no matter what happened to him here.

But Po would be ruined if he got fired. And Tanner had been willing to exploit that.

Gritting his teeth, Po shoved one handgrip while swinging the opposite foot forward. His mech once again broke into a run, this time much faster than before.

The final stretch to the waiting shipping container was about a hundred meters of relatively open space. Here, Po adopted a new strategy. Knowing he could move much faster than his opponent, he swung around in a wider arc, eliminating Tanner's ability to force a collision but still gaining ground.

And in the final stretch, Po overtook the other worker's mech, swinging around the container to slide his grippers into its brackets from the other side.

He locked eyes with Tanner triumphantly, who met his gaze with a menacing leer. Po thumbed the buttons at the tops of his handgrips, which lifted the container from the scuffed metal floor. With that, he strode past Tanner, his motions smooth and easy.

"Hey, Abbato," Tanner called as Po strutted by him—or at least, as much as it was possible to strut inside a mech carrying a three-ton payload. "Po Abbato, right?"

Something in his voice made Po pause.

"I wonder what your mother would think of you taking the sort of risks you just took with company equipment. She's on Level 3, Cylinder 22, right? South end? Maybe I should pay her a visit, get her thoughts on it all. I doubt your sister would think much of it, either. Your poor, sick sister." Tanner's voice carried a mocking note.

My mother and sister. He's threatening to tattle on me to my mother and sister. Which meant he wasn't really threatening to tattle. No, Tanner was an Obsidian Angel, and violence was his bread and butter. This wasn't a threat on Po's job, but on his family.

Except, it was worse than that, wasn't it?

Someone in the meshmind knows who I am. And where I live. Why? Tanner didn't need to be the one who'd acquired the information. It would be enough that someone else in his meshmind had. If they knew it, Tanner knew it.

Slowly, Po lowered the shipping container to the floor, then retracted his grippers.

"Have it," he muttered. With that, he stalked away, to await the next container to be unloaded from the docked ship.

***

At the end of his shift, Po dismounted his loader, stored it in its charging alcove, and checked his rads on the way out. The light turned green on the scanner, indicating he was still well within the limits Equipoise Metals considered acceptable for its employees. He gave the rad detector's mottled plastic case a slap, then headed for one of the hatches leading out of the Docking Cylinder.

The Docks extended outside of the asteroid proper, meaning they didn't have the usual meters of rock protecting workers from the ever-present threat of radiation. Instead, a layer of compressed hydrogen acted as the Docks' shields, doubling as a fuel reserve for sale to ship captains looking to top up.

The hydrogen worked just as well, but Po's mother clung to her superstitions about it.

"You wouldn't catch me dead working in one of the outer tubes," she liked to say. She worked as a mineral analyst, in a cylinder nestled deep within Psyche, near one of the entrances to the core mines. "You never know how that's going to affect you, later on down the line."

Po would just shake his head when she talked about it, saying nothing. Rosa Abbato was a chronic worrier, and even if he managed to win an argument about hydrogen being just as good as rock for radiation shielding, she'd only start nagging him about something else.

She knows I don't have a choice, anyway. So why say anything at all? Equipoise needed him at the Docks, so that was where they'd keep him. End of story.

He heaved a sigh as he clicked on his electromagnetic boots by stamping each one twice, then entered the microgravity hub connecting the Docking Cylinder to one of the commercial districts that flanked the Docks on either end. After four years of working in the Docks—first as an apprentice mechanic fixing the loader mechs, and these past two years as an operator—he still hadn't decided whether he'd rather be at work or at home at any given moment.

He turned the question over in his mind as he traveled down the right side of the wide boulevard, just another working stiff in a flood of Equipoise Metals employees fresh from their shifts. His stride was halting as he waited for each boot to make secure contact with the floor before pulling his rear foot away from the steel surface with a jerk. The last thing he needed was to be seen flailing wildly for one of the overhead handles after breaking contact with both his magnets.

Home had always been unbearable, but it was a different *type* of unbearable ever since he'd gotten his father arrested for nearly killing his mother. Sometimes he felt like Rosa resented him for doing that, which still seemed crazy to him.

As for Lorenzo, he *definitely* resented it.

"What did you think you were gonna accomplish, exactly?" His brother's voice echoed through his thoughts. "You took everything he owed and dumped it right on our heads."

Which was true, but it had also stopped Luca Abbato from borrowing any *more* against his children's future wages.

It's better, this way. Lorenzo just doesn't want to see it. Which was no surprise.

At the threshold between the hub and the cylinder that held the dockside market, Po switched off one magnet with a flick of his ankle, then pushed off with that foot, disengaging the other and leaping onto the rotating surface with a practiced motion.

The cylinder had a standardized diameter of 600 meters, meaning it spun at just under two revolutions per minute to simulate one G on its lowest level. There were railed moving platforms you could take that would match you to the cylinder's rotational speed, but using one of those would make him look like a wuss to the other workers, and besides, he'd long ago mastered the art of making the transition without stumbling.

He hadn't been inside the commercial district for five seconds when a cop-bot made a beeline for him, its stiff gait straight out of the uncanny valley.

Great. Now I have this thing to deal with.

"Excuse me, sir. I am an Equipoise Metals Security Robot, designation five-alpha-three-seven-hotel-zero, responsible for Cylinders One through Nine. Can you confirm that you are Po Angelo Abbato, son of Luca Abbato and Rosa Abbato?" Its red eyes blinked in time with its words, while its black slit of a mouth remained impassive. The thing's crowded features and squat, cylindrical head were meant to make it look cute and disarming, but Po had seen these things on the hunt. Most times, they took their targets down before they made it even a quarter of the way down a tube, and they weren't very gentle about it, either.

"That's me," Po answered, studying the bot warily.

"Very well. You have been selected for a pat-down search. Your selection was made using authenticated random selectors, and it is my duty to assure you that it is free of human failings, limitations, prejudice, corruption, negligence, or laziness."

"What a relief."

"Do you consent to a pat-down?"

"Do I have a choice?"

"If you decline, it will be noted on your company file."

Po sighed. "I consent."

"Very well. I will now proceed with the pat-down. Please hold out both arms parallel to the floor, and spread your legs as wide as you are able to comfortably."

Po assumed the position, and the robot proceeded to make contact with every inch of him—starting with his tousled brown hair before moving to his face, patting everywhere with its claw-like adjustable silicon hands. He tried to imagine what it might take to successfully conceal contraband inside his exposed skin, but he guessed it *would* be possible, with the right prosthetic makeup.

He distracted himself by taking in the market beyond, which seemed more gaudy than usual, with multiple rainbow banners stretched across every lane, and holographic posters adorning almost every surface. Nearly every merchant he saw wore a costume, from various historical periods.

Oh, right. Tomorrow's Landing Day.

Like any self-respecting asteroid mining colony, Psyche had three annual holidays, all kept using Earth's calendar year: Discovery Day, Probe Day, and Landing Day. They were pretty self-explanatory.

For Psyche, Discovery Day fell on March 17th, and it celebrated the day the Italian astronomer Annibale de Gasparis first discovered the asteroid in the Naples sky in 1852. January 31st was Probe Day, marking the day an unmanned spacecraft first visited the asteroid and confirmed that it was the iron core of a planet, whose outer crust had been stripped off by a collision with...something else.

But August 9th was Landing Day. Seventy-nine years ago today, the first colonists had landed on this rock—Po's great-grandfather, Alessandro Abbato, being one of them. He was the one who'd first agreed to Equipoise Metals' family debt scheme, putting the Abbatos in the mess they were still living with three generations later.

Like most stations and colonies, Psyche had no officially recognized holidays other than those three days. The Global Equity Accord—GEA, pronounced gee-uh—discouraged the promotion of any religious or national holidays, claiming it alienated people who didn't celebrate them. But Po felt pretty sure he knew the real reason behind that particular policy. GEA wanted everyone as divided as possible, with little in common with each other. That lowered the chances of anyone banding together and opposing their rule.

At last, the bot finished. "Thank you for your valued patience and cooperation," it said, its voice pitched slightly higher than before, which Po had heard was a subtle way of rewarding and reinforcing compliance. "Please expect further delays while traveling the station's public areas during the next twenty-nine hours and forty-three minutes. Heightened security measures are being implemented to curtail an expected spike in illegal activity during the holiday."

With that, the bot stalked away without so much as a fare-thee-well. *Probably seeking its next victim.*

"Nice to see you too," Po muttered.

But instead of continuing through the press of people thronging the merchants' stalls, all clamoring to see what goods might be on sale for Landing Day, he lingered, then finally glanced back into the section he'd just left, where the last dock workers were trickling out into the commercial district. A group of five people he didn't recognize emerged from the microgravity hub, one of them stumbling as he stepped out onto the spinning cylinder.

Freighter crew members, probably, visiting Psyche Station for what seemed like it could be the first time, by the way a couple of them were gawking like tourists. Po scowled at them, distantly aware of the envy that licked at the back of his mind like tongues of flame. He'd never left Psyche in his life, not even once.

The bot had given him an idea. If the station would be crawling with it and its groping amigos until Landing Day was over, then it was unlikely the Obsidian Angels would risk recovering their contraband from the rerouted shipping container until the holiday had ended.

Which meant if Po could find out where it had gone, he could safely get to it before they could. And as long as he could dodge the security bots with his newfound treasure, he could make a lot of crypto selling it—coin that would go a long way toward paying down the debt his father had taken out on him and his siblings.

He'd need help dodging the bots. But finding out where the container had been sent came first.

Luckily, he knew just who to ask.

Chapter 2

"Po," Dempsey said when he entered the Docks' Brain, blinking owlishly at him through grubby glasses. "Oh, don't tell me. You've come to collect on that favor, haven't you?" He squeezed his eyes shut, rocking back in his office chair. "I'm bracing myself."

Po chuckled at the scrawny man, whose graying hair always stuck up in tufts on both sides of his head, like a wolverine's ears. Not that Po had ever seen a wolverine—that wasn't an animal that made it out of Earth's gravity well very much, if it ever had. But he'd seen photos of them on the system nets.

"Relax, Demps. It's not going to be that bad."

Dempsey opened his eyes again and regarded him warily, as if hesitant to buy into Po's reassuring tone.

The favor in question came from the time Po had covered for the old guy, when Dempsey's wife had come storming up to him as he'd left the zero-G hub after a particularly long and grueling shift.

"Abbato," she'd said. "Young Abbato."

"Ma'am," Po had answered.

"You tell me the truth, boy. Did Aiden miss his shift yesterday?"

Po had spent a couple seconds considering the question. In fact, Dempsey *had* gone missing for the day, and a less experienced tech had needed to step in to oversee the Brain—making sure that the incoming and outgoing ships docked and decoupled on schedule, timing their comings and goings so as not to disrupt Psyche's orbit and spin.

"No, ma'am," Po said after a brief hesitation. "Ol' Dempsey was in there the whole time. Brought us all coffee on our lunch break, actually."

The coffee part had probably been a bit much, and she'd narrowed her eyes to scrutinize Po with clear suspicion. But he'd held his own under her searching gaze, and finally she'd spun on her heel with a huff, marching off through Cylinder Two, and nearly bowling over a merchant in the process, who was even skinnier than her husband.

Why had Po lied? He didn't know really, other than because he could, and he'd smelled trouble in it for Dempsey if he hadn't.

Well, he'd been right. It turned out Demps had been on the bender to end all benders, and had forgotten about work altogether. Instead he'd hit the midtown casinos and gotten lucky enough that he only found himself a few hundred E-coins in the red—otherwise he would have had a lot more explaining to do to his wife.

The shift supervisor hadn't been too happy about Dempsey missing work without calling in, but what was he going to do? No one came close to Demps when it came to making sure the docks ran smoothly, and this had been the first time he'd ever let his drinking affect his attendance. So it had gotten brushed under the rug with Equipoise Metals.

But more importantly, he'd escaped the wrath of his wife. When Dempsey had found out Po was his savior, "I owe you one" were the first words out of the grateful man's lips.

"You sure do, Demps," Po had shot back, straight away. "You sure do."

"Well, out with it, boy," Dempsey said now, his tone just as grim as before. "What do you want from me?"

"Just a quick peek at the container routing logs. No questions asked."

Dempsey's bushy eyebrows knitted together. "Now, why would you be wanting that?"

"What part of 'no questions asked' are you having trouble with?" Po shook his head. "Look, if anyone does ask, I was worried I sent one of my containers to the wrong place and wanted to double check. But no one's going to ask." *If the managers were that attentive, they'd catch a lot more smugglers.*

Muttering under his breath, Dempsey rose from his chair and crossed the control room to a console in the corner. He slid into the seat, tapped an access code into the interface, then stood. "She's all yours," he said, sounding resigned as he returned to his usual spot.

"Thanks, Demps. Told you it wouldn't be that bad." Po lowered himself into the corner chair and took over the console. It took just a minute of searching to locate Tanner's work logs, and then a few seconds' scrolling to find the timestamp he was looking for.

Gotcha.

Tanner had sent the container he'd been so fixated on all the way to a processing warehouse in Cylinder 29, close to where Po's mother worked. The payload had had time to arrive and be sorted, so the log had been updated with the aisle and shelf information, too—the container's current exact location—along with when it would be processed—three days. More than enough time for Po to get in, extract the goods, replace them with something else, and get out.

He didn't need to worry about updating the cargo manifest of the ship the container had come in on, since the contraband wouldn't be listed on it anyway. All he needed to concern himself with was the container's total mass. As long as that stayed the same, he'd be in the clear.

"Thanks, Demps," Po said, standing up. "We're even, now."

"We are?" Dempsey dragged the back of a hand across his brow. "You know, you were right. This could have been a lot worse. I *expected* it to be a lot worse."

"You shouldn't build things up so much in your head." Po grinned as he crossed the room toward the Brain's exit. "How long you been worrying about what I might ask you for?"

"Ever since you seemed so cranked up by the idea of me owing you a favor."

Po shook his head, still grinning. "Well, try to avoid any more benders, would be my advice."

With that, he pressed down on the hatch's heavy bar, throwing his shoulder against it to push it open.

And locked eyes with a GEA Marine in full combat armor, standing guard outside a newly arrived gunship.

Po stiffened, momentarily paralyzed by the sight of a Marine on Psyche. His eyes wandered past the ship, where he saw a platoon's worth of them forming up, with the guy in charge up front, speaking to them in a voice too low for Po to make out.

What are they doing here? The last time Marines had visited the station had been before he was born, to prepare a defense against a Scourge attack that had never materialized.

The fact the attack hadn't happened wasn't surprising: as far as anyone knew, the last time the Scourge had attacked any human colony or outpost had been over a century ago. Sure, they might have hit an interstellar colony ship. But those were all way out of real-time com range, and besides, the solar system itself hadn't been attacked again. A lot of people believed it never would be.

The first Scourge invasion had set humanity back by at least a century, with the total destruction of Ceres—along with its thriving mining colony, the only one of its kind at the time—being the most devastating blow. But humanity had rallied, banding together in a rare moment of unity to blast the Scourge fleet into oblivion.

"Fleet" was maybe a strong word. No one believed the alien ships had belonged to anything more significant than a scouting force, and those scouts alone had nearly put an end to the human race. But they'd also probably taken two centuries to reach Earth from where GEA astronomers thought their homeworld was.

If Po had been in the Scourge's shoes, and his scouts dropped off the map without a trace, he wouldn't be in too big a rush to send any more forces after them. *There have to be easier targets out there for them to invade.*

The Marines were probably here to clamp down on what their overseers saw as unacceptable levels of opposition on Psyche Station. It wouldn't be the first time they sent in an occupying force, using some tall tale of a Scourge attack to justify their presence. And it wouldn't be the last.

***

He managed to make it to his home in Cylinder 22 without suffering any more random searches.

Word had traveled fast about the Marines' arrival, and walking through the market he'd heard snatches of conversation speculating why they might be here.

Most of it seemed to center around the Scourge, and whether the Marines' presence meant they would attack. Po felt surprised to hear people buying into the possibility the aliens might actually show up. His parents had always been cynical about that, believing that GEA only used humanity's old enemy to scare people into submission.

"Do people really think the Scourge are coming back?" he asked a Chinese lady wearing a brown-bordered yi with her hair drawn tight in a top bun, at the stand where he often picked up noodles after a long shift.

"Well...." she answered in unaccented English, then shrugged. "There *have* been strange sightings, lately. Near Vesta, and over Russia and Egypt. Craft that can do things none of ours can. Things that violate the laws of physics. There are vids going around."

"What else is new?" Po said. People had been seeing things like that since at least the twentieth century. None of it had ever led to anything, and besides, Scourge ships hadn't seemed capable of anything all that out of the ordinary—they'd just been better at everything human ships could do. "Listen, those vids are probably fake. A psyop."

"A psyop? By who?" She raised her eyebrows, as though daring him to say it.

"I can think of at least a couple possibilities." He shook his head. "No one ever worries about an attack from the aliens already living in our system, do they?"

"The Nibirans? Or the Emplor?"

"Take your pick. People spent about five minutes wondering how a rogue planet just so happens to be perfectly angled to be 'caught' by our sun. Or how we can miss an entire planet for centuries, and then suddenly discover it one day, orbiting out there."

"GEA tells us we need to be nice to the Nibirans."

"Oh yeah, because *they're* real nice to them, aren't they?" After the initial shock, most people had taken the discovery of Planet Nibiru more or less in stride, helped along by an extensive GEA PR campaign with the message that humanity needed to accept their long-lost Nibiran siblings with open arms...all while GEA-partnered corporations quietly moved in and began extracting their planet's resources.

"What are you getting at, anyway?" she asked him.

He glanced over his shoulder and spotted a security bot twenty meters away, which for them was well within hearing distance. "Never mind." He paid for his noodles and left, ignoring the wiry man pleading for crypto from behind a ragged blanket he'd hung over a cooling duct next to the stall.

He headed for the upper levels, to catch a magtrain to Cylinder 22. As he ascended, his step grew noticeably lighter. Nothing past Level 5 was rated safe for permanent human occupancy. The low-gravity levels higher than that were used mostly for transport, manufacturing, and hydroponics. Plants didn't much care about how strong the gravity was, beyond having enough of it to orient themselves.

Po arrived at his habitation module at last and presented his face to the scanner, while placing his palm on the reader underneath. The hatch slid sideways, and he continued into the narrow hall within.

From here, he could see straight through into the kitchen/living room, which occupied a cramped cube at the back. Everything in the module was cramped, and growing up, Po had often felt claustrophobic here—though he mostly attributed that to having nowhere to hide from his father.

Four rooms abutted the hall from here to there: three bedrooms and a bathroom. That was it.

As he passed by, Lorenzo walked out of the bedroom he shared with him and Marco. Without warning, he socked Po in the shoulder, hard.

Po resisted the urge to rub the spot he'd been punched. Instead, he shoved Lorenzo—or tried to. The older boy was bigger, and he barely budged.

The push did have some effect, though. It brought a grin to Lorenzo's face as he brought his forearm up to place against Po's neck, walking him backward until he was pinned against the wall between his mother's room and Nicole's.

"We doing this?" Lorenzo asked, his breath hot on Po's face. "We doing this right now? We doing this?"

Po gritted his teeth, glaring at his older brother, but otherwise not moving.

"That's what I thought." Lorenzo applied some extra pressure to Po's trachea, then slammed a hand against the wall near his head as he pushed away. He shot Po a grin, then turned toward the bathroom.

"No fighting," their mother called from the living room, without much enthusiasm.

With their father gone, Lorenzo seemed to consider himself the man of the house, a role he tried to enforce in much the same way Luca Abbato had. He wasn't as bad as Luca had been—not nearly—and he never raised a hand toward Rosa, Marco, or Nicole. Just Po.

Which obviously wasn't pleasant, but Po could endure it. As long as he never touched the others. If he did that, Po would kill him in his sleep. And he was pretty sure Lorenzo knew it.

He turned into Nicole's room, where he found her sitting on the bed with her back against the wall, reading something on her pad. She looked up as he entered, her eyes lighting up as they fell on him. Lowering her device onto the comforter, she made to stand.

"Hey, don't get up, Nicky. That's okay. Stay right where you are."

He crossed the room, bending down to hug his sister. Her arms felt like sticks as they snaked around him. He patted her back, and it felt like he was patting bone.

"You take your meds today?" he asked, pulling away.

She nodded, her soft smile enough to light up a room all by itself. "Just the dinner ones left."

"Well, make sure you don't forget 'em."

"I'll have you there to remind me!"

"You shouldn't rely on me to do that, you goose."

"I know. But I also know you won't forget." Her grin widened. "Maybe I'll meet a real goose one day."

That took him aback for a moment. Then he remembered what waited for him in an Equipoise warehouse—the ticket to riches beyond what he could hope to make in a month, probably a year or more.

Maybe we really can *get out of here someday. Pay off our debt, leave, never look back...and hey, go meet a goose. Why not.*

He ruffled her hair. "Believe it, goose."

She giggled. It occurred to him that she hadn't mentioned hearing the tussle between him and Lorenzo. Was that because she'd been engrossed in her reading ...or because she was desensitized to violence, at this point?

He fervently hoped it was the first one.

Marco came home, and Po put him in a headlock—but a friendly one, one that had his little brother laughing and slapping Po's thigh, not the serious kind of headlock Lorenzo might have put *him* in.

After that, their mother told Marco to heat up dinner, and before long the five of them were sitting around the countertop island, which doubled as their table, forking leftover vermicelli into their mouths. Po had covered his with pepper, to mask the stale taste.

Every seat was filled, except for one—their father's seat, at the head. Rosa refused to put away their father's chair, keeping it empty instead as a constant reminder of what Po had done. That was how he interpreted it, anyway.

"Meds," he said as the meal wound down. The pill bottle rattled as he fetched it from the counter behind him and placed it on the table in front of Nicky.

She made a face, then opened the bottle, her bony fingers working the cap.

Lorenzo pointed a fork at Po, sneering. "You're always lecturing us about adding to the debt. But you shovel those expensive pills down her throat like they're candy."

Po stiffened. "She takes as many as the doctor says to take."

"Such a hypocrite."

Their mother said nothing, ignoring the exchange as she scraped the last few morsels off her plate. Nicole and Marco were staring at theirs, his sister looking sad in a way Po couldn't stand. He wanted to punch Lorenzo in his smart mouth. But that wouldn't end well, he knew.

This is life, he reflected. *And we just have to deal.* Maybe he could get them ahead with whatever he found in that container. Maybe not. But whatever he found, it wouldn't be nearly enough to erase the massive gambling debt Luca Abbato had so willingly passed on to his children.

The system had them right where it wanted them—toiling away on Psyche Station until they died. And Lorenzo had Po right where *he* wanted him. There was nothing he could do about either.

"I saw a Marine on the way home from school today," Marco said as he stood up to collect their empty plates and slot them into the washer.

Rosa looked up sharply, then returned her gaze to the table. With a sigh, she heaved herself out of her seat, then trudged to her usual spot, on the couch.

"Did you now?" Lorenzo said. "Think you're gonna join up, small fry?" He reached out to ruffle Marco's hair, who ducked out of his reach.

"No. But...." He looked at Po, his expression solemn. "You should."

"*Him?*" Lorenzo said, his lips twisted in disgust. "He'd never make it in the Marines. He'd only rack up even more debt, trying to make it back home after he washed out."

"You gonna join?" Po asked him.

A blank look crossed Lorenzo's face, but he recovered quickly. "'Course not. I have mom to look after."

Po snorted.

"What? Think that's funny?"

Saying nothing, Po got up from the table. "Thanks, Polpetto," he told Marco.

"You're welcome," his little brother answered.

"Thanks Polpetto," Lorenzo mimicked in a snide voice.

Po ignored him, heading for the bedroom he shared with his two brothers. It didn't offer him much reprieve, since Lorenzo could just follow him in there if he wanted. But it was the only other place for him to go, and if he was lucky, he'd catch a few minutes of peace while he thought through his next move.

He was about to stretch out on his bunk when he noticed a white box sitting on Lorenzo's, rimmed in black. His mouth hung open as his brain processed the information it was receiving from his optic nerves.

A Circuit. The idiot bought a Circuit.

He seized the box and spun around, marching down the hall and back into the kitchen, his vision blurred, his ears ringing.

He slammed the box in front of Lorenzo.

"Hey," his brother roared. "Be careful with that!"

"You wanna tell me what this is?" Po asked through gritted teeth. In the corner of his eye, Marco froze, standing back-on to them at the sink. Nicole still sat where she'd been, staring at the table.

"It's an implant, obviously," Lorenzo said. "Digital radio circuit."

"You bought a Circuit on our credit. A *Circuit.*"

"I didn't. Mom bought it for me."

Po whirled around to glare at his mother. "*Rosa?*"

Her eyes didn't leave the wall, where a twenty-inch screen was inset. She shrugged. "Your brother's gone through a lot, you know, Po. I paid for the surgery to get it implanted, too. He deserves this."

Po was nearly blind with rage. He'd heard that expression before, blind with rage, but he hadn't realized it was possible for anger to actually impact vision.

But what could he do? What could he do?

Afraid of saying or doing something he'd regret, he instead opted to stomp down the hall and out the front hatch, leaving it open as he stormed past the neighboring habitation modules.

Chapter 3

Po stalked through Cylinder 22, paying little attention to where he was headed. As he went, his anger didn't subside, but fed on itself instead, growing into an inferno that threatened to consume all conscious thought.

I have to go through with my plan, now. If there'd been any doubt before, Lorenzo and Rosa had obliterated it, by putting such a crazy expense through their family credit—another extravagant addition to the mountain of debt that Marco, Nicole, and Po would all have to labor under, just as Lorenzo would.

The difference was, Lorenzo didn't seem to care. Like their father, and like their great-grandfather Alessandro, Lorenzo seemed fine with being owned by Equipoise Metals. He didn't have the same desire Po did to escape...to become a free man, and to leave Psyche behind forever.

Sometimes it felt like Po's brother and mother were conspiring to make sure the Abbatos remained corporate slaves forever. They constantly charged new purchases, mostly for Lorenzo's benefit. Like the time he'd gotten depressed and Rosa had sent him for a week on a passing Carnival Ship to cheer him up. That had set back Po's efforts to pay off the family debt by years.

His aunts and uncles were no help, either. Rosa's only sister, Vittoria, was an assistant to a GEA administrator stationed on Psyche, and the two had barely spoken since she'd taken the job. As for his father's siblings, as far as Po knew they'd all disowned each other the second they'd moved out of their father's habitation as teenagers, each drawing deeply on their newly individualized debt to do so.

He didn't bother activating his boots' magnets as he reached the southern hub connecting his home cylinder to the next, instead flinging himself into the zero-G space. When he drifted toward the overhead, he pushed himself angrily off of it, hard enough that he rocketed straight down, killing his forward momentum. Luckily, there was a bulkhead handle close enough to grab. He pulled himself tight to it, then flung himself forward with both hands, only to collide with another bulkhead.

He failed to catch a handle this time, instead careening away, drifting aimlessly along the passage. With a muttered curse, he scanned his immediate environment for another handle.

There. He grabbed it, then used it to right himself before stamping each boot twice against the floor, activating the magnets. The futile little episode did not serve to distract him from his emotions. Instead, it only stoked the flames of his rage higher.

He looked up at the bulkhead, imagining the millions of tons of rock between here and Psyche's surface, with interconnected cylinders spider-webbed throughout. And beyond them, the star-speckled expanse. Each star inert, without any atmosphere to make them twinkle, as they were said to do when viewed from Earth.

What did I do to deserve this? Better question: *What did* Nicole *do? Or Marco?*

Then again, he wasn't sure he'd enjoy Earth much better. The Global Equity Accord had maintained a stranglehold on humanity's home for centuries, imposing their beige uniformness on every corner of the Earth. They kept their subjects docile by tube-feeding them a diet of lab-grown meats, subsidized sim subscriptions, and mandatory novel medication interventions. Any hint of opposition to the regime was usually smothered with threats of cutting off the recalcitrant from their weekly crypto allowance.

Most likely they'd be happiest aboard one of the agrarian cyclers, where life tended to make more sense than anywhere else in the system, and where people lived as free from GEA as anyone did anywhere.

But what was the use of making any such plans? Po and his siblings were stuck on Psyche. He did what he could to keep Marco's and Nicky's spirits up—to convince them it was worthwhile to spend as little crypto as possible, to avoid increasing their generational debt needlessly. He tried every day to cheer them up, and to make them believe that one day, they would be free to go where they chose, and to do as they liked with their lives.

But how could they be expected to believe that? They had access to the same debt calculators he did. Even if Marco and Nicole both got jobs that paid as well as Po's once they were old enough, it would take over seventy-three years to pay off the Abbato debt. And that was assuming Rosa didn't find new little luxuries to splurge on for their oldest brother.

Besides, Nicole was too sick to work, and she sometimes let slip that she didn't expect to live long enough for any of this to matter. Po had forbid her to talk like that, but she sometimes did anyway, and either way, he couldn't control what she believed in her heart.

Marco was still young and naive enough to buy the dream Po was selling—but even so, sometimes Po suspected that deep down, even Marco sensed how grim their situation was.

Which is why I need more *opportunities like this one. It's our only way out of this mess.*

He emerged from the zero-G hub into Cylinder 21, which was one of the dedicated agricultural modules that were distributed more or less evenly throughout the colony. Having plenty of hydroponic gardens at regularly spaced intervals didn't only help reduce Psyche's food imports; it also helped scrub CO2 from the air, while producing fresh oxygen to supplement the colony's main source—oxides extracted from the asteroid itself.

The Abbatos paid a premium for living in a cylinder right next door to an agricultural module, but that was one expense Po didn't complain about. He wanted his sister breathing the freshest air available on Psyche.

With a frustrated sigh, he slipped his pad from his pocket and called up Messaging, selecting the Contact he wanted—an old classmate named Freddie Rodriguez.

Meet me at the fish farm on 23, level 8? It's important.

He held his breath and stared at the pad, waiting for a reply.

***

"Hey, Po," said a hesitant voice to his right as he watched salmon swimming by, pushing against the endless current that ran through the floor-to-ceiling tank. The tank circled the entirety of this level, so that the fish never ran out of 'river' to move through. Po wondered if they even realized they were prisoners.

He turned his head without shifting his cross-armed stance. "Hey, Freddie."

"It's, um, been a while."

"Yeah."

An awkward silence passed between them, long enough for Po to wonder why they'd stopped talking, exactly. They'd kept in touch for a few weeks after Po had quit school to work at the docks, but then Freddie had abruptly stopped messaging him. And since Freddie had always been the one to initiate conversations between them, their conversations had stopped.

Not that he'd spent very much time thinking about it. A lot had happened since then, and Po had other things to worry about.

His old friend's eyes were on the floor. Po stood almost a head above him, and from this angle he could see that Freddie's hair was thinning. *Seems early for that.*

"Are you a meshminder, now?" Freddie blurted out finally, lifting his eyes to meet Po's.

Po squinted. "What? No. I thought you knew me better than that."

"Well, that's the rumor going around."

"Seriously?" Po turned toward Freddie, careful not to trip in the lighter gravity of the fish farm level. "What, that I joined the Angels?"

"Yeah. You wouldn't be the first person to drop out of school to join them, right? And you stopped messaging anyone, so we all figured...you know." Freddie inhaled audibly, then continued in a rush. "We figured the Angels told you to cut off all ties, so as not to compromise the meshmind. They do that, I heard."

"I've been busy. Freddie, I'd never let anyone put anything inside my head. Ever. These things are bad enough." He rapped on his pad through his pocket.

"Right." Freddie chuckled, sounding relieved. "Okay, so you're still drinking the rad-trad Kool-Aid. That's good, I guess. At least, it means you probably aren't a meshminder."

"No, probably I'm not." Po suppressed a shudder. The idea of total submission to a group mind, of giving up all privacy and subscribing to every single belief prescribed to its members...that gave him the willies. A meshminder gave up every last scrap of individuality, and that was seen as a feature, not a bug. System-spanning criminal organizations and secret societies couldn't afford any of their members going rogue and disclosing sensitive information, or working at odds with the group's goals. The fact that meshminds were fixed in a single, unchanging will was the solution to all that. "I prefer my brain untampered-with, thanks."

"You sound like my dad. No wonder you two always got along so well, you're both rad-trads to the core." Freddie adopted an exaggerated Hispanic accent. "I'm getting this machine taken out of my head the second I retire! Can someone pass the enchilada sauce? Well, I'm off to Mariachi practice!"

Po gave a wan smile, mostly to humor Freddie. Usually trad-bashing annoyed him, but at least they seemed to have recovered some of their old banter. No one would ever accuse Freddie of being a rad-trad. He'd even had a Circuit implanted. Jailbroken, but...even so. It was still a Circuit.

"Hey, wanna see my new Cryptoferret?" Freddie asked.

"Your what?"

"Cryptoferrets, man. They're popping off right now. I got a bunch of 'em. I'm gonna start flipping them once they go up in price. Check it out."

Freddie held out an arm, crooked at the elbow, like he was waiting for a bird to land on it.

"I can't see anything."

"Oh. Right. No Circuit. Get out your pad, then."

For a moment, Po considered humoring him. "Freddie, I didn't come here to—"

"Come on, man. They've got the genetic algorithms tweaked just right, so the little guys adapt to your behavior. And when you—"

"I don't want to see your stretched-out rat," Po snapped.

Freddie blinked in surprise. "Wow, Po."

He sighed. "Sorry. It's just...you can't seriously believe there's still money in flipping crypto?" Everyone knew about the kids who'd become overnight millionaires back when crypto first became a thing, but that had been centuries ago, and the major coins had long since stabilized in price. New projects still sprang up from time to time, but the major ones had long ago established an unshakable dominance, administered as they were by GEA. If more recent history was any indication, Freddie's Cryptoferrets would probably go to zero inside of a few weeks.

When Freddie spoke again, he sounded mopey. "I don't have *that* much put into it. It's just something to do."

Just something to waste money on. "Look, I asked you to meet me here for a reason."

"You need my dad, right? You sent another container to the wrong place?"

Po narrowed his eyes. Yes, he'd done that with a nitrogen shipment once, and yes, he'd needed Freddie's father to help him relocate it to the correct warehouse without his manager finding out about it. But that had been an honest mistake, and one Po had only needed covered up because he'd been gunning for a promotion at the time. A promotion that had never materialized anyway.

"I sent this container to the right place, actually. At least, the place *I* wanted it to go." He wasn't about to tell Freddie that he hadn't been the one to route the container at all—that a member of the Obsidian Angels had routed it, and he was merely intercepting it at the destination before they had a chance to.

"But not the place it was supposed to go?" Freddie asked.

"That's right." Po leaned against the tank with his left hand pressed against the glass. "It's probably best we don't involve your dad in this. But I *do* need his access."

"That's going to be challenging, given his access is tied to his Circuit. Unless you're asking me to cut his head off and loan it to you for an evening?"

Po couldn't help but let out a bark of laughter at the gruesome image. "Don't play dumb with me. I haven't forgotten how your dad copied over his access to your Circuit, so you could run and fetch things for him he forgot in his office."

Now it was Freddie's turn to cross his arms. "Yeah, and he gave me that access because he trusts me not to abuse it. Or to lend it out to my sketchy friend."

I'm the "sketchy friend," am I? This wasn't exactly news to Po, but he *was* surprised Freddie had come out and said it. *Probably because I insulted his digi-ferret.* "There's a lot of coin to be made here, Freddie, with not much effort on your part. You get me access to that container, no questions asked, and I'll cut you in on the profits."

Light filled Freddie's eyes, just like when he'd spoken about his Cryptoferret scheme. The only difference was, this time he was trying to hide it. "How much of the profits?"

"Fifteen percent."

"Uh huh. Except, since you'll be running everything, I'll have to trust you're actually giving me fifteen percent."

"It'll be a healthy chunk. A lot more than you'll make flipping rats." Po could already tell Freddie was in, so he didn't mind throwing in another jab about that.

Freddie's lips writhed like a snake in heat. "Something about this seems too easy. How much risk are you asking me to take on, exactly?"

Po scratched his chin with the hand that wasn't leaning against the salmon tank, and thought about the Obsidian Angels. And about Tanner—how he'd already seemed to know him, and where he lived. The way he'd leered at him as he spoke.

I'm two steps ahead of him. Two steps ahead of all the Angels. There's no way they get to that container before Landing Day is over. And by the time they do, I'll be long gone, with nothing to link me to their missing goods.

"None at all," he answered.

***

Po marveled as the hatch slid open in response to Freddie's approach, without the need to punch in a code, provide fingerprints, or anything like that. The lock simply detected the access key stored on Freddie's Circuit and slid aside for them. Easy-peasy.

Of course, gangs like the Angels had taught companies like Equipoise Metals a long time ago not to lock anything important using mere biometrics. The Angels weren't above cutting off a finger or gouging out an eyeball to gain access to areas normally barred to the public, such as the warehouses in this sector, which served all of the station's subsurface mines.

Criminals *did* stop at doing anything to employees who stored security access in their Circuits, though. Like any good GEA partner, Equipoise automated everything it possibly could, going to great lengths to keep the number of actual humans it depended on at an absolute minimum. But complex automated systems required ongoing monitoring and maintenance, which meant highly trained admins were still required to keep them running. A company like Equipoise preferred these hires to be GEA true believers, which limited their pool of applicants even further—and made those suitable few even more valuable. Anyone who killed or kidnapped a GEA administrator could expect to be hotly pursued, and mercilessly prosecuted if caught.

As for Freddie's dad, he was an outlier. Someone who made a convincing show of being an Equipoise bootlicker in public, when in fact he despised them and couldn't wait to be free of them, probably to spend the rest of his days on a luxury cycler of his choosing. *He'll be able to afford it, too.* Administrators made absolute bank.

Freddie slapped a panel on the other side of the hatch, which closed it behind them.

"Crazy," Po muttered.

"What is?"

"That it just lets you in like that." His mind was spinning up with possibilities. Could this become something they regularly milked for profit? If they cut Dempsey in, to give them the heads-up whenever a suspected Angel rerouted a shipment...would Dempsey be willing to do that? "You can scrub us from the security footage, right?"

"How many times are you gonna ask me that? I can get root access to the system from dad's office. It's no problem to manipulate the feed. That surveillance is only a secondary measure, anyway—they rely way more on Circuits to keep warehouse access limited to admins, so the feeds aren't as protected as they could be."

"Right." *So the Angels must have someone on the inside, too—someone as high up as Freddie's dad.* That made Po a little nervous, but it didn't actually change anything.

Did it?

"My brother just got a Circuit," Po said, mostly to distract himself.

"Did he now?" Freddie looked at him with eyebrows raised. "You didn't like that, I bet."

Po didn't answer.

"Hey, you hear about Janus hijacking a shuttle and flying it into the mass driver they built on that mountain? Megalith? Apparently it's gonna take three months to fix."

"I don't watch the news." Janus was a Nibiran paramilitary organization that took issue with GEA partner corporations exploiting Nibiru's resources. They'd been launching these attacks for a while now, so it wasn't exactly a surprise. And for Po, Nibiru might as well have been a universe away.

They rounded a corner, and Po froze, eyes locked on the man approaching them down the passageway. *Act natural,* he told himself.

The man gave a friendly wave as he drew closer. "Heya, Freddie. What did your dad forget today?"

Po glanced at Freddie, who looked admirably relaxed as he grinned at the newcomer. "Hey, Mr. Pierce. Contacts case, this time. Dad doesn't want to sleep with them in again."

Pierce grinned, then shifted his gaze toward Po. "And your friend here? Did his dad forget something too?"

They both froze, Freddie's mouth hanging open in mid-reply. To his credit, he recovered quickly. "Dad suggested I give him a tour. He was asking him a lot of questions, and I think dad thought it'd be easier if I just showed him."

"A lot of questions, hey?" Pierce was still smiling, but Po watched his eyes. They seemed emotionless. Cold, even. "Well, then. We have a curious cat on our hands."

"Um...yeah." Freddie met Po's eyes briefly, then quickly looked away.

"Not technically consistent with company regs. But your secret's safe with me, Freddie." Pierce's grin grew a little wider, then he strode past them, cutting between them and saying nothing else.

"That guy gave me the creeps," Po said once Pierce was out of earshot. "He barely looks older than us. And you called him 'Mister?'"

Freddie shrugged. "He has the same position dad does—he's an admin for a different warehouse's picker bots."

"Do you think he'll mention anything to anyone?"

"Nah. He's cool." Freddie didn't sound totally convinced. "I'm just glad...." But he trailed off, not finishing his sentence.

"You're glad what?"

Freddie cast one last glance behind them, at the corner Pierce had disappeared around. "I'm glad your container isn't in dad's warehouse. It's not in Pierce's, either. So if this goes south, there'll be nothing to connect it to either of them. They won't get in trouble."

"Unless it gets connected to us, and they find out we used your dad's access to get in here."

That made Freddie's overgrown eyebrows bunch together. "Thanks for the reassurance."

They continued through the access cylinder, sometimes walking along it, other times cutting across its circumference. The entire thing was packed with storage space for goods that needed some level of gravity, such as livestock that got stressed in zero G, or medicines that would lose their pharmacological properties otherwise. But Po and Freddie were headed for the hub on the cylinder's other side, which connected to a dozen microgravity warehouses.

"Ever wonder what it would be like, not having to walk uphill all the time?" Po asked as they walked along a passageway that curved with the cylinder, so that the floor seemed to disappear into the ceiling ahead of them.

"Nah," Freddie said.

They came to the hub, and they both activated their boot magnets with the universal double-stomp. With that, they headed down a tunnel fixed in Psyche's rock, using one of the metal gangways that stretched its length. From here, they would drop into Warehouse 1B—the one where Tanner had sent whatever it was the Obsidian Angels were so keen to get their hands on.

The hatch didn't open at their approach. Instead, Freddie bent over and tapped twice on its surface with his fingertips. It slid open, and they peered down into a dimly lit cavern segmented by strips of light and crates stacked floor-to-ceiling.

Or wall-to-wall, depending on which way you wanted to call "down." A robotic picker would snatch any crate you wanted, depositing it onto a loading area for transport by magtrain. But each container could also be accessed simply by floating to it.

Po followed Freddie through the open hatch, reorienting himself so that the ceiling became his floor.

Freddie was waiting for him, hands on his narrow hips. "You got a location?"

"Yeah." Po already had his pad out and was double checking the routing info he'd gotten from the Brain. He checked it against a sign on one of the nearby racks. "This way."

They made their way to a stack near the middle of the warehouse, out of sight of the entrance hatch. The cave-like feel Po got from this place only increased as they surrounded themselves with endless rows of spiderweb-like racks, all dotted with LEDs that might as well have been glowing lichen.

Po had only ever seen caves in vids and sims, and the last time he'd visited one of these warehouses, with Freddie's dad, he'd remembered thinking that this must be what it felt like to explore one.

He came to a stop, peering up past the stacked containers, his eyes settling on one near the ceiling.

"You going up?" Freddie asked.

"Yeah."

"Strap on, then." He pulled a tether from its spool, passing the end of it to Po, who clipped it onto his belt.

"You're staying down here?"

Freddie nodded. "You seem to want to keep me in the dark about all this, and honestly, I'm fine with that."

"All right." Yanking the clip to make sure it was secure, he said, "Give me lots of line. I don't want to have to climb."

"Okay." Freddie jerked the line once, allowing him to pull more out. Once Po had enough to reach the top, he gave it another jerk, which made it catch. "Good?"

"Good." Po grasped the bottom rung of a ladder, crouched, then used his legs and his arms to propel himself upward, the rungs whipping past as he ascended.

Chapter 4

As he drew level with the container he wanted, he caught himself on one of the rungs, his momentum yanking on his arm with a painful jerk. He kept quiet, not wanting Freddie to know he'd used too much force to fling himself up.

At least I didn't catch on the end of the tether and bounce back like a yo-yo. That would have been embarrassing.

He used handles on the container's surface to move himself to its center, where it had a raised control interface about the size of his pad. He used it to access the cargo manifest, which he scrolled through with his thumb, scanning the container's contents.

Drugs. The legal kind—mostly pills, Po guessed, so they didn't need to be stored in gravity. That lent more weight to his guess that Tanner had been helping smuggle synthetics that weren't quite as legal as those listed here.

But there was only one way to find out for sure.

He used the interface to order the sliding doors to open, then clambered onto the top of the container using a handle that hung over the lip. As he did, the wide face of the container split apart at the middle, with two equal segments rolling back until the entire container was open to him.

Boxes on boxes waited inside, all tightly packed, floor to ceiling. None of them screamed "illegal narcotics."

Sighing, he floated down onto a lip that had extended from the bottom of the container as the doors opened. Affixing his boots to it, he began removing the boxes one by one, using magnets tucked inside their lining to stick them to the outside rim of the container.

I need to remember where each one goes, so I can fit everything back in as tightly as it was before. He was making an effort to place each box near to where he'd taken it, but even so, replacing them would be a puzzle.

He glanced down at Freddie, who was pacing the warehouse floor below. *How much time do we have?* he wondered. *Hopefully enough.*

What if the contraband was inside one of these official-looking boxes? He began reading the labels, but everything had scientific-sounding, hard-to-pronounce names. Then again, he doubted smugglers would print "illegal drugs" on the box they stored them in. Probably, whichever Angel had been assigned to collect them would know what they were labeled.

Am I going to need to tear open every one of these things? There was no way he'd be able to package them up again as professionally as they were now. Even if he took the time to go fetch some tape.

It occurred to him that he hadn't thought this through as well as he might have. But he continued pulling out boxes and sticking them to the sides of the container, moving faster now. His heart was beating against his ribcage, and the frantic fingers of panic were clawing at the edges of his thoughts.

We need to get out. We've already been here too long.

He'd changed his mind about bringing anything to replace the drugs with, to make up their mass after he took them. After all, this was Tanner's problem now, since he'd been the one to redirect the container to this warehouse. The missing mass would point back to him.

But what if they've already been here and removed the drugs? If that was true, then Po was risking arrest by some cop-bot for nothing.

He'd counted on Landing Day to keep the security bots away...but if the Angels had members planted here, with the same access Freddie's dad did....

He removed another box, and saw them: sheets of plastic sachets, taped to the container's ceiling. Each packet contained a dollop of neon-blue jelly. His heart leaping, he reached out and gently ripped them away from the metal, where they'd been held by a few strips of tape.

He recognized the gel-filled pouches as Joy—he'd even worked a couple shifts on Joy himself, though he'd stopped after he started making stupid mistakes that could get him fired.

Reaching into his pocket, he took out one of the folded-up plastic bags he'd stolen from near the algae vats in Cylinder 23, where they made most of the station's plastic. He began stuffing the sheets of Joy into the bag.

As he did, he realized he had a small fortune on his hands. His heart was pounding even harder than before, now. This could make the difference for his brother and sister. The difference between hope and despair. And for Nicole, the difference between sickness and health. Po just needed to figure out a way to sell it—preferably all in one go, to minimize the risk of attracting unwanted attention.

The bag was around two-thirds full by the time he pushed the last sheet down into it. He set about tying up the bag, then pulled out a second one, placed the first inside it, and double-knotted the outside bag.

This next part, he *had* planned out. He couldn't very well stroll out of the warehouse carrying a bag full of drugs. Instead, Po planned to use the pneumatic tube network that connected several of these warehouses to the medical center a couple cylinders over. The direct connection had been implemented when this section of the colony was built, so that doctors could get their hands on vital drugs for their patients as soon as they were processed.

There was a receiving station inside the locked ward where Luca Abbato was being kept, his body drip-fed a paralytic while he bided his time in a simulated prison. As Luca's son, Po had access to that ward, and he'd noticed that when the bottles of paralytic showed up, they could be picked up directly from the collector tray. By anyone.

He'd actually asked about that, one of the first and only times he'd visited the ward—how lax the security surrounding the medications seemed. The attendant he'd asked had shrugged, and said that a careful inventory was kept. If meds went missing, it would be looked into.

Which meant it *wouldn't* be looked into when something went missing that they didn't know had been there in the first place. Like dozens of sheets of Joy, for example.

All he had left to do was get this bag to the sending station on the far side of this warehouse, pack a few canisters full, then stroll out of here with Freddie. Easy.

He began packing the boxes back into the shipping container, trying his best to put them where they'd been when he opened it. *I should have taken a picture with my pad first. Stupid.* There was no way to know whether he was stacking them right until he had the thing just about filled again.

Only a few boxes were left to be packed when Freddie called out to him from below.

"Po?" His voice sounded at least an octave higher than it normally did.

That made Po scramble to the edge of the metal lip, grabbing onto the corner to crane his neck over the edge.

His entire body went rigid.

Two pairs of warehouse workers were headed for Freddie, coming from opposite directions. One of them was Pierce—the guy they'd met on the way in. Clearly, Freddie had been wrong about whether his suspicions had been raised.

Except, the expression on Pierce's face didn't seem to match the situation. He didn't seem angry, or stern, the way a superintendent who'd just caught a couple of trespassers might.

He looked *eager.*

Po also didn't like the way they were coming at Freddie from two directions. That seemed...tactical.

His grip on the cold metal of the container's lip tightened.

I'm looking at four Angels right now, aren't I?

***

"Run along, Freddie," Pierce said, his tone a lot rougher-sounding than when they'd encountered him in the corridor. "You're free to go—just keep quiet about today, or you'll get the same treatment we're about to give your friend Po."

A knot of tension took root at the base of Po's throat. *He knows my name, too. Why have the Angels been keeping such a close eye on me?* He tried to swallow the ball of anxiety, and failed.

Pierce was staring up at him. "This'll go a lot easier if you come down here and join us, friend."

The four Angels were getting closer to Freddie, who seemed rooted in place, and not just by his boots' magnets. One of the gangsters was headed straight for the mechanism that controlled the tether.

Po cursed under his breath, and clawed at his belt with shaking hands, desperate to unhook himself.

Seeing what he was doing, the Angel sprinted toward the mechanism—as fast as one *could* sprint, without gravity. Most people looked awkward when they tried to run in magboots, but this guy had clearly done a fair bit of it. His gait was exaggerated, but seemed natural to him.

At the last second, Po managed to unhook the tether. His mind reeling, he acted on his next impulse immediately.

The impulse to flee.

He pulled himself into a crouching position using the container's lip, deactivated his magboots, then launched into the air, sailing along the corridor between the two shelving stacks. The bag of Joy trailed along behind him from his tightly clenched fist. Shouts rose from the men below. Glancing back, Po saw two of them launch themselves after him.

I need to keep moving. Keep changing my direction.

He drew near enough the right-side racks to grab on, his body slingshotting uncomfortably around the metal beam he'd caught. With that, he squeezed himself in the gap between a shipping container and the metal skeleton holding it in place, shimmying sideways past it, and then past the container on the other side.

He'd made it to the next aisle. He pushed off, upward, toward the warehouse ceiling.

There were a number of handles up here, built into the ceiling's surface for those poor fools who neglected to use a tether and lost their grip. He used them to propel himself along one-handed, as quickly as he dared, his heart racing as he sailed between handles.

He winced as he hurtled toward the next handhold, at a speed that seemed too fast. Catching it nearly yanked his arm out of its socket. But he managed to keep his cry of pain to a whimper, and forced himself to continue moving.

I just need to reach the exit.

And then what? Jog through the warehouse complex with a bag of drugs swinging at his side?

He squeezed his eyes shut. If he was going to make away with his haul, he still needed to reach the pneumatic sending station. A glance to his left showed him the exit hatch, just twenty meters away. *I can escape. But what will I have to show for it?*

After this, the Angels would be gunning for him either way. So was he really going to end today empty-handed?

With a grunt, he used the handle he clung to to fling himself sideways, to the right. He flew past the warehouse's aisles, their contents blurring in his peripheral vision.

But his attention was on the far wall.

They won't think I'm crazy enough to head for the sending station. They'll think I'm at the hatch, or nearly there. I have time. And once I send these, I just need to work my way around them and escape.

He missed the next handle, crashing painfully into the wall, and rebounding off of it.

Ugh. Did they hear that?

But he had bigger problems—he was drifting in the air, well away from any handle, and nowhere near any of the shelves, either.

His thoughts racing, he twisted around to look behind him.

He was near enough to reach the wall with his leg. *If I kick off....*

He did. Lashing out with his legs, he stretched out his body like a frog's, his fingers splayed to catch one of the racks.

Yes! He'd gripped another metal beam, and now he used it to reorient himself, pushing off to fly back toward the wall he'd crashed into.

At last, he'd reached the aisle formed by the last shelving stack and the wall. Here, he climbed along each shipping container, using the handles built into their sides, and trying to keep as quiet as he could.

His heart leapt when he saw the sending station, one-third up the wall from the floor. The area was free of Angels. *I knew it. Those idiots.*

He landed on the station's ledge, using a handle to steady himself while he stomped his magboots back on. Then he grabbed an empty canister, and holding the bag between his knees, he unknotted it with shaking hands. That done, he began rolling up sheets of Joy and stuffing them inside the plastic cylinder.

A couple of sheets made their way out of his bag, drifting aimlessly. He snatched them from midair and rolled them up, the same as their fellows.

With one canister filled, he shoved it into the transport tube's bay, used the interface to select the ward where they kept his father, and executed the command. The canister disappeared with a loud sucking sound that made him wince.

He was about to look around when something slammed into him from behind, without warning. It was a person, a man, and he was clawing at Po, trying to get a handful of his clothes, or maybe his hair. Po twisted around, using the superior stability the magboots lent him to maneuver. He managed to work both hands between himself and his assailant, and bracing himself, he shoved as hard as he could.

The man flew backward, yelling—until the back of his head hit a metal beam with a wet smack. That cut off his scream with a chilling abruptness.

But Po didn't have time to process that. The other three Angels were hurtling through the air toward him, each as silent as the grave. His heart in his throat, Po stamped twice to deactivate his boots, then pushed himself off into space, in a direction empty of Angels.

His breath was coming so fast he was afraid he might hyperventilate. His vision blurred, he felt so afraid. The decision to abandon the rest of the Joy was hardly a decision at all.

This had gotten all too real, and he needed to get out of here, now. For some reason, visions of his father flickered in his mind's eye—not of Luca unconscious in the medical center's prison ward, but of his father towering over him as a child, with his brother hiding behind him.

He flew through the aisles with reckless abandon, crashing into containers, catching handles and beams at speeds that jerked his joints and hurt his hands. But the Angels were closing on him. He needed to move faster. Faster.

Did Freddie leave? It sure seemed like it. His old friend had abandoned him at the first sign of trouble. Though that didn't surprise Po.

He reached an intersection between aisles and pushed himself through, sailing through open space. Movement flickered in his peripheral vision, drawing his gaze.

It's over. He knew it as soon as he saw the Angel—Pierce—flying at an angle and speed that would cause his path to intersect with Po's right at the mouth of the next aisle. Pierce's face was stony, his jaw set, his eyes filled with determination even from this distance.

For a few seconds, everything seemed to move in slow motion, as if they were both drifting through molasses.

Then Pierce was on him, crashing into him, sending them both careening through the shelving. Po grasped for a metal beam as they whipped past it, trying to find purchase to use against his assailant, but his fingers slipped off, and then Pierce was seizing a fistful of his shirt.

His fist smacked into Po's face, squarely on his nose, which crunched. The pain made stars explode across his vision like little supernovas, and his stomach did backflips. Tiny, wobbling globes of blood spread out through the air in front of his face.

He tried to get his hands between his body and Pierce's, to push the man away, but instead his back collided with a diagonal metal beam, bringing their flight to a halt and sending spasms of pain up Po's neck and all through his lower back.

"Stop struggling," Pierce hissed. When he didn't, Pierce headbutted him. Po managed to dodge to the left, but the Angel's forehead still connected painfully with the side of his face, mashing his ear.

Someone grabbed Po's arms from behind, wrenching them painfully behind the beam he'd collided with.

A cold grin spread across Pierce's face. "You're mine now." His fist shot forward, connecting with Po's sternum, and the air fled his lungs in a whoosh.

Chapter 5

Pierce still had a hold of Po's shirt at the collar, and he was grinning at him like a wolf at an injured lamb.

"You messed up, kid. We've been sizing you up for weeks. But after this stunt today—you're way too impulsive. We'll never take you now. We need way cooler heads than yours in the Angels."

Po stared at Pierce through squinted eyes, only half-comprehending. His nose felt like a ruined mess, and his arms felt like they might snap, the way the Angel behind him was wrenching them. He was still gasping to catch his breath. And his ear hurt.

"The Angels...wanted to recruit me?" he wheezed.

"That's right. You could've had it made. Not now, though." Pierce grabbed him by the belt, then brought a knee into his groin.

Agony flashed through Po. The world became made of pain.

The third Angel still in the fight landed nearby, catching himself on the container.

"Pierce," he said. "We got a problem."

"What?"

"That other kid musta called the cop-bots. Just got the word. They're almost here."

Pierce cursed. "You check on Morty?"

"Yeah. He's still breathing."

"Go get him, and let's get out of here. Rol, head right to your office and get to work scrubbing the security feeds."

"What about the kid?" asked the Angel who still held Po from behind.

Pierce's gaze settled on him once more. "Easy. Obviously, he takes the fall for this." With that, he seized Po by the hair and slammed his head back against the metal beam.

Everything went dark.

***

Po woke with a monstrous headache, which warred with the dull ache in his groin for attention—not to mention his throbbing, ruined nose.

He tried to orient himself and couldn't. Panic took over. He flailed wildly, trying to find something solid to connect with, to grab onto. There was nothing.

Gasping for breath, he realized he was still floating in the warehouse, trailing shimmering globules of scarlet. Blood. His blood.

He brought a shaking hand to the back of his head, inhaling sharply when it made contact with the raw wound Pierce had opened when he'd slammed Po's head into the metal beam.

I'm a mess.

He floated between two shelving units, out of reach of both. The Angels had apparently set him slowly adrift in this direction, probably so he wouldn't reach a shelf, or the ceiling or floor, in time to push off and make his way to the exit hatch. To escape.

But I have to get out. If the cop-bots found him in here, he really would take the fall for all this, just as Pierce had wanted. There'd be no hope of freeing himself from the Abbato debt, then. Probably none for Marco or Nicky, either. Not without him there to egg them on, and keep them moving in the right direction.

I don't want to end up in the same simjail as Luca.

Think, Po.

The Angels had set him floating with just enough momentum that the air circulating through the cavernous warehouse probably wouldn't be of any help. His momentum would take him to the far wall long before an air current might push him to one of the shelves. And the cop-bots would appear well before that. So, not an option.

Instead, he breathed in as slowly as he could, his breath ragged and shaky. Then he pursed his lips to exhale in a concentrated whoosh. He did it again. And again.

He combined his asymmetric breathing with something like the backstroke he'd learned at the colony pool at four years old—pushing against the air with the flat of his palms, then turning his hands to slice back through it before pushing with his palms again.

It's working!

His heart hammering in his chest, he pushed against the air, and blew into it. Inch by inch, he drifted toward the shelving behind him. His pace felt excruciatingly slow. But he'd get there. In less than a minute, he wagered.

Then the hatch opened with a resounding echo, and his pulse spiked, which caused his head wound and nose to push out spherical globs of blood at an even faster pace.

Don't stop, he ordered himself, and he didn't. The cop-bots still had the entire warehouse to search. Their sensors were good, but that didn't make them omniscient. If Po could find the right hiding place, and maybe relocate at some point during the cop-bots' search, there was a chance he'd escape their notice. If he did, they might assume everyone involved had fled the warehouse before their arrival.

His journey across the gap between shelving stacks seemed to take an eternity, punctuated by the truncated hissing of the bots' thrusters as they maneuvered through the warehouse, systematically searching it, aisle by aisle. He tried to make his exhalations as quiet as he could—which was challenging, since maneuvering meant also making them as sharp as he could.

At last, his back bumped into a metal column between two containers, and he reached back to grab it. Then, with excruciating slowness, he turned himself around, grabbing onto the nearest handle jutting out from the container's surface. He used the handles to walk himself around to the other side, where he would be concealed from most viewing angles.

At last, he reached the dead center of the container's inward side—just a couple meters away from the one nestled in the other half of this shelving unit. He tried to slow his breathing, to steady his heartbeat. He raised a shaking hand to his forehead and found it slick with sweat.

It was hard to believe, but the blood rushing through his ears was actually interfering with his ability to hear the bots' jets. *Calm down, Po. Calm down.*

He kept perfectly still, straining to hear.

There. The closest bot was jetting slowly along one of the aisles—maybe two, three aisles away from him. And its sound was getting farther away. Soon, it would likely turn the corner and loop back.

I need to get closer to it. The thought terrified him, but he knew it was true. *I can push off across the next aisle while it's rounding the corner. Keep doing that, and eventually we'll pass each other.*

Hopefully without it spotting him first.

He reached for the nearest handle, and his hand slipped off it, so slick was his palm with sweat. He moaned, then nearly cursed himself for making noise. Wiping his hand off a pant leg, and then the other, he tried again.

This time, his grip was a little firmer, and he worked his way back around the container, toward the gap between aisles.

Pushing straight through is the best way. The less contact he made with surfaces, the less sound he would make. But even if he launched from the back corner of this container, he wouldn't be able to make a straight shot for the shelving on the other side. To do that, he'd need to launch himself toward the next container's corner, then slingshot himself around the handle there to sail across the aisle, and then through a gap on the other side.

Can I make that?

As a kid, he'd spent plenty of time in the zero-G playground at the center of Cylinder 15, playing tag with whatever other kids happened to be there that day, all of them blissfully unaware they were being raised as their parents' debt donkeys. He'd learned to swing around the metal structures—to control his movement and avoid colliding with anything at too high a speed.

His mother had even taken him into the mines she serviced once. That had been one of the few times he ever remembered getting along with Lorenzo. They'd had a blast bouncing off the rock faces, the beams from their headlamps swinging wildly, every which way. Their mother calling for them not to stray too far.

But this was a little different from those childhood larks. He wondered what little Po's reaction might have been, if someone had told him that one day he'd be creeping through a zero-G warehouse, trying to avoid a search party of cop-bots.

He probably would have thought it was cool.

But it was proving difficult to tap into little Po just now. His body was covered in sweat, little beads that pooled together, their surface tension making sure they stayed on him like an extra layer of damp skin. And he was trembling.

That's enough. He threw himself at the next container's corner, the air playing coldly over his exposed skin as he crossed the small gap.

His fingers closed around the handle, and he flung himself around it...

...only to lose his grip a split-second too early, the metal escaping his sweaty grasp.

The angle of his trajectory was wrong. It saw him out of this shelving unit fine, but he could already tell his path would not bring him to the gap he'd been aiming at. Instead, he hurtled straight toward a vertical beam, much too quickly to alter his course in time.

His heart hammered in his chest as he flew across the aisle, and his lower stomach clenched in anticipation of the coming impact. Flailing his arms in a desperate attempt to alter his course would be useless, so instead he held his limbs straight out, doing what he could to brace for the crash.

And crash he did. His attempt to absorb it with his limbs resulted instead in wrenching his shoulder, followed by the side of his face smushing against the metal. Stars burst across his vision as he bounced off the pillar noisily, rebounding back into the aisle.

A piercing *whoop* sounded from a cop-bot a couple aisles away, no doubt alerting the others to the sudden noise.

Po exhaled as hard as he could, then inhaled, trying to do so more softly, which was hard when he felt like he was hyperventilating. He waved his hands against the air, desperately trying to return to the shelving he'd launched from. But he was drifting again, and this time the bots knew where he was. There wasn't enough time to cross the gap.

A cop-bot appeared at the end of the aisle, its thrusters firing with algorithmic precision, allowing it to arc smoothly between the shelves.

Po could tell from the way the thing's can-shaped head snapped toward him that it had spotted him.

How could it not? He was floating in plain sight, and the bot was far from blind.

So he let himself go limp, knowing to struggle had become pointless, and would only invite more pain.

He submitted to whatever might happen next.

***

For the first time in his life, Po found himself shepherded into one of the cop-bots' holding cells.

Sure, he'd done illegal things before. But this was the first time he'd ever been caught.

The bot that escorted him in, its silicon gripper like a steel band around his bicep, had said nothing to him since they left the warehouse.

It had been a little more talkative while arresting him. "Do not resist," it had said. "If you do resist, your safety cannot be guaranteed."

The words had been chilling enough that Po hadn't second-guessed his decision to go along with whatever the bots were planning for him.

Now that they'd arrived at the cell, the bot keyed in a security code with a lump that served as a makeshift finger. The transparent plastic door hissed open, and the bot shoved him inside, hard enough that Po stumbled forward, catching himself on the far wall.

"Stand back," the bot commanded, unnecessarily. It punched in another command, and the door hissed closed.

With that, it turned to leave.

"Wait!" Po shouted. "What's going to happen to me?"

The bot ignored him, continuing down the aisle between cells.

Cursing, Po took in his surroundings—the other cells on his level, as well as those above and below. The holding cells were constructed so that they could all be physically monitored simultaneously, by anyone standing anywhere within the complex.

Everything was perfectly transparent: each cell's walls, floor, and ceiling, along with the floors and ceilings of the aisles that ran between the rows of cells. A human would be hopelessly lost in this endless tangle of nothing, but the cop-bots just followed their preprogrammed routes through the confusing plastic warren.

Looking up, Po could see the dirty feet of the guy in the cell above him. Across the aisle, a green-haired girl sat on a narrow cot. When their eyes met, she screwed up her face at him. His mouth twisting, he turned away from her to study the rest of the complex.

Right now, he felt more like a farm animal than a person.

In old movies from Earth, the characters were always going on about something called a Miranda warning, where the police—who were always people, even though bots had replaced human cops over a century ago—explained that you had the right to stay quiet so you didn't say anything incriminating, the right to a lawyer, that kind of thing.

Po wasn't even sure he would get a lawyer. As far as he understood, he'd probably be in more trouble for breaking the contract Alessandro Abbato had signed three generations ago than breaking the actual law. At least, that's what he'd always heard growing up, playing with other kids in the public tubes. But kids also liked to sound tough by pretending they knew about crime, so he wasn't totally convinced his childhood memories were the best source of legal advice.

He slammed the side of the cell with his palm, sending a shock up through his forearm and surprising even himself. A dull ache settled into his wrist, but he felt too embarrassed to nurse it with his other hand, not wanting to give the girl across the aisle the satisfaction of witnessing his weakness.

You can pummel these walls all you want, a voice inside him said. *They're made for it. Sprain your wrist and bloody your knuckles. It won't get you anywhere.*

He hated that voice. Hated it all the more for speaking the truth.

Most of the cells were full. From his vantage point, he could only spot a handful that lacked an occupant. Why so many prisoners?

Then the words of the cop-bot came back to him—the one he'd run into just after work, in the dockside market: *Heightened security measures are being implemented...an expected spike in illegal activity during the holiday.*

Well, they'd certainly capitalized on that, hadn't they? This was their harvest, during a bumper crop year.

But what now? Did getting arrested mean the terms of his contract would get worse, or would they simply make him a slave in name as well as fact?

They made him wait for answers. At some point, hours into his stay, the lights dimmed, signaling nighttime throughout the colony. The only illumination came from softly glowing purple strips set into the aisles between cells, but it was enough light to see that the green-haired girl still had her eyes on him. As much as he felt like a caged animal, she *looked* like one. And she leered at him like one, too.

Not feeling up to a staring contest, he laid back on the cot, which was shoved up against the corner of his cell and barely wide enough for him to fit. His feet dangled off the end, and so he lay on his side and got as close to a fetal position as the narrow bed would allow, which brought his feet back onto the paper-thin mattress. This was as comfortable as it was possible for him to get, it seemed.

He barely slept, unable to stop thinking about his family, and whether he'd ever see them again.

No one had offered him a phone call. That was another staple from Earth movies, but it wasn't a thing here on Psyche, apparently. He wondered if his family knew where he was, and if they did, whether they had a way to reach him.

He wondered if Lorenzo or his mother would even care he'd been arrested. Nicky and Marco would, but Marco was too young to do anything about it, and Nicole was too sick.

The more he thought about it, the hotter with shame his cheeks grew, until he was weeping into the crook of his arm, trying not to let his body shake. He didn't want the other inmates to notice him crying.

He'd failed his younger siblings. There was no doubt about that, now. No matter what happened to him in the morning, one thing seemed certain: his dream had died, of helping them escape the crippling debt their father had burdened them with.

His dream had died by his own hand.

Chapter 6

Sleep came in fragments, with nightmares and half-wakeful fugue states in which he propped himself up on one elbow and stared intensely at his surroundings from the cramped cot, wondering what bizarre dream he was having now. Then he remembered that the endless network of transparent cells was in fact his reality, and he lowered himself to the wafer-like mattress once more, to snatch what rest he could.

He'd been awake for hours by the time the bot came for him, and he watched it approach for the better part of a minute before it finally arrived. They'd deactivated his pad somehow, and he had no idea what time it was—just that he somehow felt less rested than before he'd slept. There were far fewer empty cells, now, and bots had been coming and going since he'd woken. They'd dragged away dozens of prisoners, but overall the inmate population was growing rapidly.

"Do not resist," the bot said once it keyed open the door. "If you do resist, your safety cannot be guaranteed."

Po's body was way too sore to resist, and he didn't bother asking where it planned to take him, knowing it wouldn't answer. As the bot yanked him out of the cell, its extendable silicon gripper like iron around his arm, Po noticed the girl with emerald hair sleeping soundly, her palms pressed angelically together beneath her cheek.

Probably this isn't her first rodeo. He had no idea what a rodeo actually was, but he knew the expression came from Earth's past, and he'd always liked it.

The bot whisked him through the see-through labyrinth, and like yesterday, it held Po high enough that he had to scurry on his tiptoes to keep up with its quick, precise strides. Sullen faces leered at him from a few of the cells they passed, and while the facts of their situation naturally lent them something of a sinister appearance, they didn't actually look like the hardened criminals he might have expected. Actually, Po felt sure if he'd ran across them in the tubes, they would have looked just like regular people. It was their presence in this faceless jail that dehumanized them.

He wasn't sure where the insight had come from. Self-pity, maybe. It rang true nonetheless.

The warren of plastic cubes gave way at last to a passageway that ran parallel to this cylinder's length—he could tell because it was wide enough that it curved noticeably, but otherwise he didn't feel like they were walking uphill to traverse it, and the path ahead didn't curl up till it was swallowed by the ceiling.

This wasn't the route last night's bot had used to take him to the prison. Other bot-human pairs dotted the long passage ahead, and Po even spotted a couple cop-bots dragging two humans at once. Maybe they were couples who'd been arrested together. There were also plenty of lone bots heading in both directions.

This is weird. Not even the bots' "expected spike in illegal activity" for Landing Day could account for the sheer number of colonists Po had seen here. *Something else is going on, isn't it?*

They rounded a corner, and now they were heading uphill, along a corridor that wrapped around the cylinder. It also seemed to trend slightly to the left, and Po imagined a corkscrew shape that covered the whole level. He couldn't see as many bots escorting people now, since the ceiling blocked them from view, but he caught glimpses of bots stopping at hatches that yawned open for them, through which they unceremoniously shoved their charges.

His own bot stopped without warning, jerking him forward and nearly giving him whiplash. A hatch hissed down into its casing, and the bot pushed him. He should have been ready for it, but he wasn't. He stumbled forward and caught himself on the edge of a narrow desk. Behind him, the hatch hissed shut.

The desktop lit up beneath his fingers, becoming a display that showed a bright green button labeled "YES" and a scarlet button labeled "NO."

The wall above the desk came alive a second later, showing black text on a white background. "DO YOU CONSENT TO AN AUTOMATED TRIAL? Y/N."

Po stared at the question with narrowed eyes, then looked down at the two options available to him. He looked back at the question.

"No," he said, not expecting it to do anything without him actually pressing the button—he figured the button would take his fingerprint if he pressed it, to serve as his legal signature, and if there was any way to avoid that he would.

But to his surprise the question disappeared, to be replaced by more text.

"THE CURRENT WAIT TIME FOR A HUMAN-ADMINISTERED TRIAL IS SEVEN MONTHS AND FOURTEEN DAYS. DO YOU WISH TO RETURN TO THE HOLDING FACILITY? Y/N."

This time, he kept his mouth shut, and swallowed. Would they really keep him in that cell for over seven months? Thinking of the bots' coldness, it wasn't hard to imagine they might. *Does any human even know I'm here?*

He wanted to speak to a human lawyer. But Psyche only had around forty of those—the GEA-mandated minimum was 0.4% of the population, for stations with more than a thousand people. Clearly, those forty lawyers were going to be busy for a long time given all the Landing Day arrests. And a trial conducted remotely by human lawyers on Earth wasn't feasible, given the thirty-minutes-plus it took messages to travel between Psyche and Earth. That time delay meant even a lousy lawyer would cost a fortune.

With a trembling hand, he reached out and touched the "NO." He definitely *didn't* want to go back to the cell, he knew that much.

The text disappeared, and the question from before returned. "DO YOU CONSENT TO AN AUTOMATED TRIAL? Y/N."

He sighed. "Yes."

"PLEASE PRESS THE BUTTON LABELED *YES*."

He pressed it.

"YOUR RESPONSE AND BIOMETRIC SIGNATURE HAVE BEEN RECORDED. PLEASE STAND BY."

"Stand" was about all he could do, given the room lacked anything to sit on. The display kept him waiting for what felt like an hour, but might have been only ten minutes—his pad still wouldn't work, and there was no other way to track time in the tiny room.

The text disappeared, replaced by a man with his hands folded in front of him atop an oak desk. He wore an expensive-looking suit and leaned forward slightly, grinning toothily at the camera. Behind him stretched a vast metropolis glimpsed between buildings that towered even higher than the man's office.

Po spent a moment fighting off vertigo. He'd visited cities inside sims, but even so, a lifetime in sealed environments meant large open spaces still caused his anxiety to spike.

"Mr...Abbato." The suit lifted a stack of papers into camera view, squinted at them, then put them down again. "Mr. Po Angelo Abbato. Do I have that right?"

"Yeah."

"Excellent. My name is Cory Stein, but you can call me Cory. I'll be your advocate in the upcoming proceedings."

"You're a bot."

"To be more precise, I'm a tailored artificial intelligence, trained on a dataset comprised of Mr. Stein's mannerisms, personality, diction, and most importantly his expertise. I am authorized to act as Mr. Stein in his professional capacity, and he will review a transcript of our conversation before your trial to ensure you have been given all necessary information and guidance."

Po sniffed. "You *sound* like a bot."

"I am trained to emulate Mr. Stein's mode of speech. And so, Po, if I sound like a bot, it's because Mr. Stein must sound like one! I hope he won't take too much offense to that when he reads the transcript." The bot's grin widened. "That was a joke, by the way."

The bot's smile faded a little as it seemed to realize Po wasn't likely to laugh. Stein-bot cleared its throat, and continued. "Po, I want to assure you that just as our conversation will be carefully reviewed by Mr. Stein, so will your trial be reviewed by a human judge. Every effort is being made to ensure your rights are upheld, and that you receive a fair hearing. As for the particulars of your case, you're being charged with breaking into a private facility owned by Equipoise Metals and possession of narcotics with intent to sell. But I'd like to start with you telling me exactly what happened."

Po drew a deep breath. He'd spent much of the night fretting over what his story would be, and had come to the conclusion that his only hope was Freddie. If Freddie had made good on his word to scrub the security footage, Po might have a chance. If not, he was hosed.

Freddie had to be the one who called the bots. And Po was glad he had—who knew what the Angels might have done to him, otherwise? His old friend had had his back, there. But had he been smart enough to doctor the footage showing Po stuffing drugs into that sending station's feeder?

"I sent a container to the wrong warehouse, and I didn't want to get in trouble with my boss. So I got in with a friend's help, and I was about to reroute the container to the right place when a bunch of criminals showed up. The footage probably doesn't show them, because they were talking about scrubbing it. But they're the ones who pulled the packets of Joy from the container." He shrugged. "Bad luck on my part, I guess. Wrong place, wrong time."

Stein-bot's grin had completely vanished, replaced with an expression of mild concern. "Po, I should inform you that lying to your legal representative is completely counterproductive."

"What do you mean, lying?" His heart skipped a beat.

"You're lying to me. Po, the prosecution have video of you racing your coworker to be the one to reach that same container first, when it was first unloaded from the freighter it came from. They have eye-witness footage taken from the Circuit of one Aidan Dempsey, showing you pressuring him into letting you access proprietary Equipoise Metals records. And they also have Circuit footage from the Equipoise employees who caught you inserting packets of narcotics into a pneumatic feeding station, with the presumed intent to collect them from the same ward where your father is kept imprisoned." Stein-bot shook its head, with the affect of a parent disappointed in a toddler. "I have to be honest with you, Po, this really doesn't look good for you. They're after a sentence of twenty-five years, and that might actually be a mercy. You'll almost certainly be unemployable, going forward, and I'm aware you have a substantial debt to repay. Someone in your position might be inclined to hope for the maximum sentence."

Quite a thing for my lawyer to say. Po's heart was hammering against his ribcage. "What about the footage of those same employees beating me bloody?"

The bot blinked. "There is no such footage."

"They scrubbed it, then!"

"The footage of you inserting packets of narcotics into a pneumatic feeding station shows no evidence of doctoring. That's what's relevant here, I'm afraid."

"So what's the point of this meeting, then?" Po's vision had blurred, and a high-pitched whine crescendoed in his right ear.

"If you are found guilty—which it seems certain you will be—I can tell you that it does seem likely you'll be offered an alternative to simulated imprisonment."

"Which is?"

"Enlistment with the GEA Marines. Three terms of service would be considered proportionate for the charges laid against you, but I've had recent success in similar situations with negotiating that down to two terms, especially when my clients are cooperative and plead guilty." Stein winked at him. "And you wouldn't have long to wait to begin serving out your sentence! As luck should have it, the Marines have a platoon inside your colony right now."

As luck should have it. Everything was clicking into place in Po's mind. The Marines' arrival on Psyche, just in time for Landing Day. The spate of arrests. The countless colonists being dragged into these cramped cubes for processing, like lambs to the slaughter.

This isn't justice. It's a GEA recruitment drive.

***

Po wasn't sure what he'd expected his trial to look like—a simulated courtroom, maybe, with each bot acting out the role of its human counterpart, presenting evidence, calling witnesses to the stand, making impassioned arguments, all with the drama and gravity of a legal thriller made by an Earth-based studio.

Instead, he got a court transcript generated by bots on the fly—each sentence typed by an invisible hand, just slowly enough for him to read.

COURT

Call the case.

CLERK OF COURT

People of the Global Equity Accord Vs. Po Angelo Abbato

Criminal Case 1125401589 for: Trespassing in relation to Concord Act (CA) 35983 Prowling on Corporate Property without a Lawful Excuse and Drug Trafficking in relation to CA 5682 Controlled Drugs and Substances.

This is for arraignment.

COURT

Appearance for prosecution.

ATTY. LOPEZ

Attorney Juan Lopez, counsel for the complainant.

ATTY. STEIN

Attorney Cory Stein, counsel for the defendant.

COURT

Is the accused present?

ATTY LOPEZ:

The accused is present.

COURT

Arraign the accused.

CLERK

People of the Global Equity Accord Vs. Po Angelo Abbato

Criminal Case 1125401589

Accused **Po Angelo Abbato** commits a crime of Trespassing, in relation to CA 35983, and Drug Trafficking, in relation to CA 5682, committed as follows:

That on or about three o'clock in the morning of August 9th, 2271 in the Colony of Psyche, within the jurisdiction of this court, the said accused, did then and there willfully, unlawfully, and feloniously break into an Equipoise Metals facility with the intent to recover illegal narcotics whose transit he himself had directed there, and then to sell them to his fellow colonists.

COURT

Do you understand the allegations of the facts?

Po stared numbly at the wall of text for a few more seconds, then realized it was waiting for his response. The green "YES" had reappeared, alongside the red "NO."

He tapped the "YES."

ACCUSED

Yes, your Honor.

COURT

What is your plea?

The green and red buttons flashed once more from the desktop, but this time they were labeled "GUILTY" and "NOT GUILTY." "GUILTY" was the one labeled green. Po frowned, and hammered "NOT GUILTY" with two fingers.

ACCUSED

Not guilty, your Honor.

COURT

Was there a proposal for an amicable settlement?

ATTY. LOPEZ & ATTY. STEIN

None, your Honor.

COURT

Let's proceed with the Marking of Exhibits. Prosecution?

ATTY. LOPEZ

We request that the eyewitness Circuit footage of Aidan Dempsey be marked "Exhibit A."

COURT

Mark it.

ATTY. LOPEZ

We request that the eyewitness Circuit footage of Gregory Pierce be marked "Exhibit B."

COURT

Mark it.

As the tailored AIs scrawled the words of his fate across the wall display, it seemed to Po that he was falling through layers of gauze. His head swam, and the abyss yawned beneath him, and there was nothing he could do. He felt artificial himself—and dysfunctional, like a line of broken code that wouldn't run because someone had forgotten a closing bracket.

The blocks of text grew increasingly large, until the scrolling transcript became a heaving digital beast, black on white, smashing against the walls of its digital cage again and again, roaring for release.

Soon, AIs programmed to behave like Dempsey and Pierce showed up in the scrolling text and gave answers based on their Circuit footage, but also on their past interactions with Po.

They *were* AIs, weren't they? Their answers to the lawyers' questions unspooled at the same speed as everything else, so they couldn't have been input in real time. *Maybe they were ordered to submit their answers beforehand. Or maybe not.* Po couldn't tell what was real anymore.

Eventually, he stopped paying attention to his trial altogether. The AIs didn't seem to care. The room could easily have been equipped with concealed sensors capable of picking up on his lack of attention, but if it was, no one was making use of them.

And what did it matter whether he paid attention? The algorithms debating his innocence or guilt were running all on their own. They weren't asking for his input, not since he'd selected "NOT GUILTY" from the two options given him.

This is just a formality, anyway. He'd already consented to the outcome of this trial. It was no different from every other agreement he'd thoughtlessly tapped through in his seventeen years, in order to use the countless apps, sims, and services essential to life in the twenty-third century. Equipoise Metals had owned him long before today, which meant it owned his future, too. And now it would discard him, like one would discard any malfunctioning part.

The hatch behind him hissed open, and before he could turn, a bot's silicon gripper closed around his bicep.

It took the thing less than a second to yank him bodily from the room, but before it did, it dawned on Po that his trial had ended. He even managed to read the final output shown on the screen before he was whisked away to wherever the bot would take him next:

COURT

Po Angelo Abbato, I sentence you to three terms of service with the Global Equity Accord Marines.

Chapter 7

Be careful what you wish for.

Po had no idea who'd said that first, but the phrase was still kicking around from Earth's history, after all these centuries. And right now, it seemed to fit.

Sitting in a waiting room chair, deep inside the Psyche Medical Center, with a cop-bot standing nearby to ensure his compliance, it occurred to Po that he'd gotten everything he'd wanted.

He'd planned to come to the medical center after finishing at the warehouse, hadn't he? And now here he was—though he'd taken a different route than expected, and he doubted he'd get any joy from the visit, synthetic or otherwise.

And soon he'd be leaving Psyche, possibly forever. He didn't know what the survival rate was after three service terms with the GEA Marines, but with unrest brewing on Nibiru, it was probably about to go down. Even if he lived through the three terms, how would he ever make it back here? System travel cost crypto, money nobody was likely to put up for him to get back to Psyche. Equipoise Metals basically *was* Psyche, and they certainly wouldn't touch him again.

They owned his sister and brother. But they didn't want him. Not after what he'd done. As far as Marco and Nicole were concerned, Po might as well be dead.

I'll probably never see them again. His next breath came out choppy, and his eyes stung, but he refused to let the bot see him cry. It wouldn't care whether he did or not, but he still refused to let his emotions get the better of him in front of the thing. He wouldn't have been able to explain why.

The bot seized his forearm without warning and jerked him out of the chair and toward a hatch leading deeper into the medical center. It had likely received a command that it was Po's turn to be seen, but whereas a regular visitor might be called in by a human, Po was instead dragged inside bodily without warning.

A Marine in a dappled blue utility uniform stood just inside the hatch, tapping his fingers against his rifle's stock as the bot yanked him past. He met Po's glance with an impassive expression.

They took a left and a right, and then the bot brought him to a halt in front of a broad window, through which a bored-looking woman studied him from behind a desk.

"Deposit your cPad into the receptacle," the bot ordered.

A funnel extended from the wall, awaiting his device. It was connected to a tube that twisted out of sight, and would take his pad who knew where.

A sign above the funnel read "PLEASE DEPOSIT ALL PIERCINGS, HATS, cDEVICES, JEWELRY, AND WEARABLE TAPS INTO THE FUNNEL. YOUR BELONGINGS WILL BE ASSOCIATED WITH YOUR BIOMETRICS." The bot had only asked him to put his pad in—it would know he didn't have anything else on him, thanks to the search Po had been subjected to by the one who'd thrown him in a see-through cell the night before.

He noticed the sign said nothing about his pad ever being returned to him. But what choice did he have? He dropped the device into the funnel, and it vanished.

"You're late," the woman said the instant the bot pulled Po into the room. They were the first words spoken to Po by an actual human in what felt like an eternity.

"The bot's late, you mean," Po shot back. "I've been getting dragged around Psyche by these metal goons for the last twenty-four hours."

"No, I mean *you're* late. And the correct response is 'Yes, Sergeant.'" She tapped the triple chevrons on her shoulder.

Po said nothing, but it didn't seem to bother the sergeant in the slightest. Instead, she actually chuckled. "In the military, everything that happens on your watch is your fault, and you'll do a lot better if you take responsibility for all of it. Even the things that aren't really your fault are your fault."

She studied him a few moments more wearing a wry smile, then shrugged. "It's not my job to teach you that. But I can still take satisfaction in knowing you'll get your little-punk attitude beaten out of you very, very soon. Hey, maybe I'll even get to watch some of it." She tapped a cSheet lying on the desktop, then flicked a finger across it, scrolling through what looked like a list of names. "Punk after punk on this station. A lot like the last one we visited. Ah, here you are. Po Abbato." A frown replaced the wry grin. "No Circuit, I see. Let me guess, the Abbatos are a clan of rabid traditionalists who somehow wound up living on an asteroid hundreds of thousands of kilometers from Earth, through no fault of their own."

Not exactly, Po thought but didn't say.

The sergeant looked up from the cSheet. "You do realize we'll be implanting a Circuit?"

It didn't come as a total surprise, but the idea still made Po's lip curl involuntarily. "What about nanoinjections?"

"What about them?"

"I'm officially GEA property now, aren't I?" The anger in Po's voice surprised even him. "Which means I get the full slew of all the latest barely tested pharma wonder-products. Just like an Earther."

"Why would we do that?"

"Why wouldn't you?"

The sergeant paused, glanced at the bot, then locked eyes with Po again. "Why do you think we're all the way out here recruiting, Abbato? Why go to all the extra expense and effort? Don't you think it'd be easier to limit our recruiting to Earth's vast and compliant population?"

Po narrowed his eyes, unsure where she was going with this.

"Think about why that might be," she said meaningfully, with a final glance at the bot. With that, she checked something off on his file with a tap. "The med tech's ready to implant you now. Good news is, with your implant in, we'll have tabs on you at all times. That's good news, because you'll be free to wander Psyche at your leisure, other than your scheduled appointments here at MIPS. You know what MIPS is?"

"Mobile Induction and Processing Station."

"So you're not completely clueless. More good news—with your new implant, you'll be able to achieve full immersion during a final visit with your dear old dad. Your file says you haven't visited him since his incarceration in simjail. Let me give you a piece of honest advice. Do that, Po. No matter how much you hate him. Visit your father before you go."

The sergeant seemed to be looking at him with real compassion, which was another thing Po hadn't anticipated. The tears he'd refused to shed in the waiting room threatened once more, and he willed his chin to stop wobbling.

"Go on in," she said, returning to her former curtness. "Down the hall, third hatch on your right." When he didn't move, she raised her eyebrows. "If you move fast enough, the bot won't have to drag you."

***

Po wandered through the crowded food court on Cylinder 14, fingering the adhesive stitch the med tech had told him not to touch, just past the crown of his skull. The incision didn't hurt as much as he would have expected, even as the local anesthetic wore off.

It had surprised him that the military was willing to spring for an implant before he even began basic training, not to mention the surgery to install it. That was, until he realized that it effectively turned him into a GEA spy. Even if he washed out of basic and ended up spending the twenty-five years in simjail his lawyer had talked about, after that he'd still have an implant in his brain that agents could tap into at any time. For GEA, it was merely a long-term investment.

It all made even more sense when the med tech told him that, down the road, if he wanted to get rid of the Circuit as a civilian, he'd need to pay for the surgery to remove it himself. Once it was out, he'd be required by law to send it back to the military—all at his own expense.

Yeah. Probably not happening. And so, barring a miracle, he'd have to make peace with carrying this thing around in his head for the rest of his life.

He'd been in custody long enough that it also felt strange to go anywhere without a bot's gripper clamped around his arm. But his restored ability to choose where he went didn't mean he was any more free than he had been in that cramped, transparent cell. Not really. The implant was smart enough to notify his new overseers if he went anywhere or did anything that wasn't perfectly compliant with both GEA law and the military's Code of Values and Ethics.

As for the implant itself, the med tech had explained that it would have limited functionality until he began basic training. It could still do just about everything a civilian Circuit could do, and probably more—but Po wanted nothing to do with any of it. He did his best to pretend it wasn't there, refusing to access its overlays or give it any mental commands.

His eyes played over the glowing signs and flashing menus as he tried to decide what he'd like to have as one of his last meals on Psyche. Most of the options were system-spanning chains with food that would taste exactly the same no matter what station he was on.

Normally he wouldn't dream of spending crypto on eating out, but he was hungry, and he still hadn't worked up the courage to return to his habitation module and face his family.

Lorenzo would call him an idiot, and probably hit him. His mother would acknowledge the news with the same resigned grimace that was her reaction to all bad news. For Rosa Abbato, the universe was made of bad news, and therefore it was only to be expected when a fresh batch of it was presented to her in some novel permutation.

His greatest fear was that Marco and Nicky would understand and accept what he'd done and continue loving him just as much as they had before. He wasn't sure he could handle that. In fact, it seemed likely to kill him.

"Abbato," someone growled from behind him. He recognized the voice, but not the aggressive tone.

He turned, eyebrows raised. "Demps," he asked, with genuine surprise in his voice. The look of pure animal rage on Dempsey's face seemed incredibly out of place.

Dempsey planted two spindly-fingered hands on Po's chest and shoved him with surprising force. Po staggered backward, and would have fallen flat if he hadn't managed to catch himself on the lip of a nearby table, whose base was planted sturdily in the metal floor.

But Dempsey wasn't finished. He stalked after Po, seized him by the collar, and shook him with his scrawny arms. The murderous leer that contorted the man's birdlike face would have been funny if it hadn't been so terrifying.

"My wife is going to kill me," Dempsey hissed under his breath, as if he wanted to avoid drawing attention by speaking too loudly. Never mind that half the food court was already gawking at them. "Do you understand me? My wife is going to kill me." Dempsey punctuated each word by shaking Po.

Po worked his fingers under Dempsey's grip and managed to pry the man's trembling hands off of him. He kept his hands raised defensively for a few seconds, but he didn't *think* Dempsey was going to lunge at him again. He risked lowering his defense to grip his shirt by the lower hem and pull, in an effort to straighten it. "They, uh—they arrested you too?"

"They did," Dempsey said, with abundant indignation. "Thanks to you."

"They're making you become a Marine too? Aren't you a little old?"

"I'm right at the cut-off."

Po studied Dempsey with skepticism. Then he shrugged. "Well, probably your wife won't kill you after all, Demps. Probably aliens will kill you."

Dempsey's eyes went wider than Po would have thought possible, and for a moment it seemed a sure thing that he was going to attack him again. Instead, he seemed to notice the hundred or so people staring at them, turned on his heel, and stormed away.

Po dropped into a chair and stared at the tabletop, his cheeks burning. Gradually, the silence was replaced by the renewed buzz of the colonists' chatter.

***

Years ago, Po had actually considered the military as an option for getting off of Psyche, and he'd looked into it enough that he knew at least some of what to expect over the coming days. Back then, he'd decided against it, since it would mean leaving his sister and brother behind, with no one to look out for them except Lorenzo and Rosa. Just as it would now.

He knew that most volunteer recruits went to *Military Entrance* Processing Stations, where they took an aptitude test and, based on their results, were then presented with a list to choose from, of the branches they were qualified to join.

But Po wasn't a volunteer, and he didn't get to choose. The appointments he was made to attend in the week before he left Psyche were all at a *Mobile Induction* Processing Station. GEA legally owned him before the process even began, and so the induction team helped themselves to all of his personal data—including everything they could scrape from his pad, his medical data, the tests he'd taken before dropping out of school, behavior reports...everything.

Based on that, they already knew exactly what branch he was best suited for, but they still made him take the GASVAT—the GEA Armed Services Vocational Aptitude Test. Why? Well, probably because at some point a general had needed a pointless initiative to earn himself another star, and so he'd mandated that even conscripts who the military already knew everything about would take the test.

Or maybe it was just to drive Po crazy. Who knew?

The inductors did him the courtesy of giving him two days to study for the test. Unfortunately, finding peace and quiet to do that was proving difficult. That had begun with finally coming home to break the news about his conscription to his family.

Their reactions weren't what he'd expected. Rosa had stood abruptly from the couch only to drop onto it again and break down crying, her hands covering her face. Nicole had run past Po into her room and locked the door behind her, refusing to come out. Marco pushed past him and fled out the front hatch, leaving his pad behind, as well as his shoes.

As for Lorenzo, he'd turned from the eggs he was frying to put his hands in his pockets, lean back against the counter next to the stove, and study Po wearing a strange expression. "Really," he said, his tone as unreadable as his face. After a long moment, he turned slowly back to his eggs.

None of them seemed up to contending with the reality that Marco had apparently run away from home, and so it fell to Po to scour Cylinder 22 for him, and when he failed to find his brother on any of its levels, to scour the adjacent cylinders. He was about to extend his search even farther out when a memory came back to him of chasing a three-year-old Marco through the algae vats on Cylinder 23, loudly announcing his intention to catch and tickle his brother, who was already screaming and giggling wildly as he fled.

Why that occurred to Po now, he didn't know. And actually, he'd already checked the algae production facility.

But not thoroughly enough, apparently. He found Marco sitting with his back against one of the CO2 tanks and glowering at the bright-green sludge inside the vat across from him.

His little brother was pointedly avoiding eye contact, so Po just lowered himself into the space beside Marco and waited him out.

It only took a few minutes.

"You ruined *everything.*"

Po laughed, and now his brother did turn his way—to glare at him.

"Weren't you saying just the other day I should join the Marines?"

"Yeah, but...not right now," Marco said. "And not like this."

"I didn't ruin everything, Polpetto. Because you're the man of the house, now. And you're going to take care of things."

"Me? What about Lorenzo?"

Po pulled a face at him, and Marco laughed in spite of himself.

"Like I said. You're the man of the house, now."

His brother's smile faded as quickly as it had appeared. "Will you be able to come back and visit?"

Po sighed, returning his gaze to the algae vat. "What do you think? Do you have the crypto for me to hitch a cycler back?"

"No."

"Me neither."

"I'll come and find you, then. I'll become a Marine too."

"No, you won't."

"Why not? What else is there for me to do, Po?"

"You have to stay here and look after Nicky. Make sure she's taking her meds. Help her get healthy again."

Marco's voice dropped, until it was barely audible. "She told me she's not *going* to get better."

The words were like a dagger through Po's heart, and suddenly it felt like he was sinking through the metal floor. "She *will* get better. She has to."

"What if she doesn't?"

"She has to. Now cut that out, Polpetto."

Chapter 8

Nicky was still holed up in her room by the time Po wrote the GASVAT. If she came out for food at all, then he wasn't there when she did. Every so often he would pound on her door till he got a response, and till she told him that she'd taken her meds. Other than that, he couldn't entice her into any more contact.

His mother spent all her time in the cramped room at the back that held the module's kitchen and living room. Before his conscription, he'd usually find her totally absorbed in some mindless vid about love and heartbreak aboard a cycler, or maybe upper-class drama in one of Venus' cloud cities. But now, she seemed to have fallen into a different type of stupor. She sat leaned slightly forward on the couch, staring into nothing, with errant strands of hair obscuring parts of her face. It was...creepy.

Po snapped his fingers a few inches from her nose. "Rosa. I need your attention."

"What is it." She didn't look up at him, so he crouched in front of her, to stare up into her eyes.

"If I ever find out you're buying Lorenzo luxury massages and premium sims while Nicole isn't getting her meds, I'll come back and kill him."

"What?"

"Lorenzo. I'll kill Lorenzo. Do you understand me?"

Her eyes went wider than they already were, which told him that she did. Satisfied, he stood and left.

***

Accessing the locked prison ward to visit his father was as simple as strolling toward the hatch, which unlocked and opened for him automatically. There'd been no one at the medical center's front desk, which before had meant he'd have to sit in the waiting room until someone showed up to let him in.

This time, on a hunch, he walked toward the first of a series of hatches that would take him to the ward. It opened. So did the next one, and the next.

Another person—an eager recipient of a Circuit, for instance—might have called that convenient. But what did the convenience truly gain him? The same effect was achieved: he accessed the locked ward, just as he eventually would have gotten in by waiting for the receptionist. Yes, it "saved time," but time to do what? Wait for his next medical exam at MIPS? Enjoy the domestic desolation that prevailed back in his family's habitation module? Wander Psyche aimlessly, saying goodbye to the metal prison that had held him these last seventeen years?

Even in his old life, the prospect of saving time wouldn't have excited him. He wouldn't have considered it an advantage to get home sooner, or to show up at work earlier than he had to.

And in exchange for the "time" the Circuit "saved" him, he gave up his freedom and privacy—to GEA, to Equipoise Metals, and to any other governmental or corporate entity that cared to take a peek into his whereabouts or personal data. At any given moment, EMF signals were liable, even likely, to be passing in and out of his skull, without his knowledge or consent. And there wasn't a thing he could do about it.

As for why his implant was already installed with automatic access to his father's prison ward, he wasn't actually sure. That level of human empathy seemed inconsistent with GEA, and with the way he'd been treated since his arrest. The thought had crossed his mind that the sergeant he'd encountered at MIPS had seen to it, especially considering she'd been the one to suggest he visit his father before leaving Psyche. But he didn't like the idea that anyone who belonged to the machine currently grinding him up and spitting him out had shown him a kindness, and so he swept it away.

The prisoners in the locked ward were all laid out on sustentation racks, which lined the walls in stacked rows. The setup reminded Po of a twenty-first century server room...or a morgue. Each prisoner lay feet-out, with the rack above him mere centimeters from his nose. Regular mealtimes were kept via an intravenous nutrient feed, and an acceptable level of physical function was maintained by electrodes that stimulated each inmate's muscles periodically. They'd still probably need to relearn to walk at the end of their sentence, but such was life.

Other than the electrodes and IV lines, along with another line devoted to bodily function, the inmates were completely untethered from their racks. There was nothing to stop visitors from hoisting one of the unconscious prisoners over one's shoulder and leaving...except that the prisoner's implant would trigger an alarm the moment it passed through the hatch.

His gaze hitched on the break in the sustentation racks caused by the pneumatic receiving station where he'd planned to collect the packets of Joy. He shook his head, marveling at how stupid his plan seemed now.

The next thing he noticed was how many empty racks there were, compared to the last time he'd been in here. Narrowing his eyes, he walked to his father's rack, and was relieved to find him still there. For a moment he'd been haunted by visions of going through bootcamp alongside Luca Abbato. The Marines' recruitment drive—or rather, their conscription drive—was the only explanation for the sharp reduction in inmates that Po could think of.

His father had completely lost his gut since his incarceration, and his double chin had also receded, leaving a lined and wrinkled neck. *The wonders of an electrostimulation-and-nutrient-sludge regimen.* Luca's chest rose and fell with a steady rhythm, as with someone experiencing a deep and restful sleep.

Technically he was always asleep, but his breathing rate *was* a reflection of what was happening to him inside the prison sim. Whatever he was doing right now, Po's father appeared to be at peace.

You don't deserve it.

Po crossed the room lengthwise, to the visitor racks, which were better-padded and much less claustrophobic. There were six of them in total, two rows of three, and apparently that was more than enough to accommodate demand. He'd never actually seen them in use.

Until today. A man wearing a simset over his head and long, black, robes lay on the top left visitor rack.

There were a couple odd things about that. One was that he would have had to climb the short ladder to access that rack, when it would have been easier to roll into one of the lower racks. Po supposed it was possible that all three bottom racks had been in use when the man had arrived, but it seemed unlikely.

He frowned, and it took him a few more seconds to realize the man was a priest. His frown deepened. What was he doing here, of all places?

Po got into the lower-right rack, the one opposite the priest, and stared at the convex bottom of the rack above him for the better part of a minute. This next part scared him a little, if he was being honest with himself. But his new life meant he'd have to get used to using his Circuit sooner or later. Probably sooner.

The military surgeons who'd implanted the Circuit had also outfitted him with subcutaneous sensory taps—audio, visual, and tactile, including a specialized tap that could hijack his sense of proprioception to simulate falling, changes in gravity's direction, that sort of thing. Po couldn't begin to imagine how much all that had cost, but crypto was apparently no object when it came to outfitting a new recruit for war. He'd already been assured that every tap would be unceremoniously ripped out of him should he wash out of basic, leaving only his implant. And while that held its own appeal, it would also mean he'd end up in a ward like this one. He'd rather die in some far-flung Nibiran waste than wind up like one of these vegetables.

Screwing up his features, he willed his new Circuit's interface to open for the first time. A burnished-looking gray rectangle appeared in the center of his field of vision, the edge of which gleamed exactly where it should given the ward's light sources—including the soft blue lights that illuminated the visitor rack from its head.

Po had to admit, it looked smart. He could scroll through the options using his gaze alone, but when he reached out to touch the menu's edge, he found it firm and unyielding. The corners even felt sharp, though not enough to cut him...not that it actually could cut him, even if it had been sharp enough.

The menu's tangibility was the combined work of his new tactile and proprioception taps, and he guessed he could probably turn the feature off from some submenu, but for now he liked it too much to do that. In spite of himself.

I'd better turn it off before I reach an actual battlefield. He pictured the muzzle of his rifle tapping against the interface's side as he tried to point it at an enemy about to shoot at him. *Yep. Definitely need to find that submenu.*

The "SIMS" submenu wasn't far from the top, and when he tapped the long, rectangular button it depressed with a satisfying click—as though the interface had real depth. When he released it, the submenu he'd chosen appeared.

Currently, only one sim was available to him: the prison sim. He selected it.

"ARE YOU SURE YOU WANT TO INITIATE THIS SIM? ENSURE THAT YOUR BODY IS SECURELY POSITIONED. A SUPINE POSITION IS RECOMMENDED."

Po didn't know what "supine" meant, but he settled his head back against the nylon pillow, and checked on both sides to make sure he was well away from the rack's edges.

He checked the box not to show the warning again and then tapped the green "INITIATE" button.

The prison ward disappeared. He found himself standing before the entrance of a building that stretched into the distance to his right and to his left, until its grayness collapsed into a single point. It was impossible to make out where the building ended—or whether it ended at all. Dark, granite blocks made up its facade, but its broad entrance was accented by thick, blue crystal formations that exploded from the ground on both sides. The crystals seemed to glow from within, pulsating slowly enough that the effect almost wasn't noticeable. Behind him stretched a flat and endless grassy expanse, perfectly manicured. Above, a white, featureless void passed for sky.

Eager to escape the agoraphobic anxiety brought on by the miles of open space that pressed down on him from above, he hurried between the twin crystal patches. There was no actual door, probably because there was no weather to keep out of the prison. The inside felt just as climate-controlled as the outside, and Po found it just slightly chilly, with goose pimples raising on his bare forearms.

In real life he'd worn a jumpsuit that covered almost every inch of skin, but here he wore a t-shirt and slacks. He had no idea how to change that, and he didn't feel inclined to stop in the middle of this strange place to paw through menus.

This was *way* more immersive than any sim he'd used a simset and wearable taps to access. The wearable kind had come a long way, but they had nothing on the implanted ones, which were jacked right into Po's nervous system. And with a simset, you were constantly aware of something foreign clamped onto your head...but his new brain implant simply took over his optic nerves, just as the audio taps co-opted his cochlear nerves, with the ability to completely block out what his eyes and ears should actually be seeing and hearing.

Only, the proprioception taps were the real game-changer. They made it so he really felt like he was walking into a prison, instead of lying in a visitor rack back on Psyche. This sim *was* real life, or at least it might as well be. And if the Circuit's interface ever malfunctioned, he'd be stuck in here until someone from MIPS came looking for him.

The entrance gave way to a cavernous lobby, where his footsteps echoed ominously. A human-looking guard nodded to him from a semi-circular desk, as white as the rest of the lobby, but he made no effort to stop Po as he skirted the desk and continued on into the prison proper.

Maybe I should have stopped to ask for directions, he reflected as he entered a corridor that stretched into infinity, with six-way intersections at regular intervals. The bottom half of the walls were wood-paneled, the upper half the same blinding white as the lobby he'd just left. So was the ceiling.

Instead of returning to speak to the guard, he continued walking. The guard was almost certainly a bot, and this place already felt too weird and alienating for him to want to have a conversation with a bot about anything, not even how to navigate the prison.

That quickly began to seem like a mistake. Especially as he turned down corridor after corridor, following signs that suggested where a given prisoner might be located based on his last initial. The first one had read "PRISONERS WITH SURNAMES A-E", and the next, "PRISONERS WITH SURNAMES A." Then had come "AB," and "ABB," and "ABBA." By then it had occurred to Po that someone had designed the sim to be a sick joke, especially when he came to the end of a corridor that terminated in double doors with the sign "AUDITORIUM" over them, with nowhere else to go. Opening one of the doors sent metallic echoes into a vast and unlit space, the bright rectangle cast by the hallway's lights the only illumination. Po released the door, and it swung slowly shut.

He started retracing his steps, sure he'd never make it back to the lobby, but faintly hopeful he might at least figure out where he'd made a wrong turn. Somehow, he winded up amidst cell blocks containing prisoners whose surnames began with "C," at least according to the signs. How could there possibly be enough inmates to justify such a large prison? Yes, it was a sim, and so the designers had been free to make it as big or small as they wanted. But...*why?* There sure weren't enough inmates to fill it from the ward that held his father's body. Would there even be enough prisoners in the entire system? Even if there were, how would it work for them to be imprisoned here, given the light-lag between planets and stations?

It was around then that he realized someone was following him. Footsteps whispered to him from around corners, as though from someone trying to conceal their presence. The first couple times, Po tried to convince himself he was imagining it, but as he plumbed the prison's depths, his eyes watering from its endless uniformity and blinding whiteness, he could only deny his ears for so long.

The next time he heard the steps, he charged toward the corner they'd come from, rounding it in time to glimpse a thick, segmented tail disappearing around a turn a dozen meters away, its owner dragging it along the floor behind him with a faint rasping noise.

Chapter 9

Po froze, his heart hammering arrythmically against his chest, making him worry he was about to have a heart attack at the age of seventeen, like an Earther. The sim might not be able to actually hurt him, but *that* sure would.

Then he wondered if his heart was actually beating this hard, or if the implant was just simulating that to match his emotional state. Wondering about that distracted him from his fear, and his heart rate slowed toward some semblance of normality.

"What *was* that thing?" he muttered under his breath. He couldn't hear any footsteps now. As for the tail he'd glimpsed, it brought his mind back to the vid he'd watched of the only time an Emplor had ever visited Earth, to deliver their Emancipation Doctrines to the Council of Hegemons. The alien had arrived in a shuttle that looked like it could have been made by humans.

The Emplor itself had reminded Po of how people in the twentieth century had often imagined aliens, during the heyday of UFO/UAV sightings. It had the same pure-black, almond-shaped eyes, set diagonally in its face, pointing down toward its slit-like nostrils. But it also had spines that protruded from its head, starting between its eyes and marching back along the center of its skull, presumably to continue underneath the burlap-looking robes it wore. And the tail that writhed behind it as it walked had resembled a larger version of an iguana's tail. Kind of like the one Po had just seen slither around a corner.

Along with delivering their Emancipation Doctrines, which some people called the aliens' gospel, the Emplor had warned humanity never to violate Emplora's orbital space, for any reason. And because of their superior technology, no one had objected very loudly. Even if their planet *had* mysteriously hurtled into the system twelve years ago, to be caught in the sun's orbit between Mars and Jupiter.

But what would an Emplor be doing here, of all places? And more importantly...*how?*

He shuddered as he thought about that tail, and willed his implant's menu back into existence. Scrolling through it with his eyes, he noticed a new option: "INMATE DIRECTORY." Selecting it, he found the alphabet, with a search bar at the top. He tapped the bar and imagined his father's name, which appeared there.

With that, a map replaced the directory, showing a bird's eye view of the impossibly vast prison. Unbidden, the map zoomed in, and text appeared: "YOU ARE HERE."

Then the map scrolled for a few seconds, before settling on a new location filled with long stretches of corridor, rectangular rooms, and other shapes. "LUCA ABBATO IS HERE. WOULD YOU LIKE TO BE TRANSPORTED THERE NOW?"

Po didn't hesitate to select "YES." The corridor he was in dissolved, to be replaced by another exactly like it. He stood facing a door, which his implant made to flash bright yellow. "CELL BLOCK 52013," it informed him. "LUCA ABBATO IS HERE."

The heavy door's metal handle felt cool to the touch, and when Po twisted it he found it unlocked. Pushing it open revealed a huge space that didn't resemble a "block" at all, but a wide cylinder that stretched upward for row after row, much taller than the prison had seemed from the outside. Cells lined each level, all along the periphery.

A man in a black cassock was nearing the door as Po passed through—the priest he'd seen using one of the visitor racks. Po held the door open for him, a little sheepishly, since he doubted it was actually necessary to do so inside the sim.

But the priest stopped and studied him, frowning slightly. He was a young man, his skin an olive shade, like Po's. He wore his dark hair cropped close, and he was clean-shaven. "Who...what's your name?" he asked.

"Po Abbato. Uh, Father."

The priest nodded slowly. "Wonders," he murmured. "I was just talking about you." He rose his left arm, pointing toward the third level. "He's in Cell 3-G. But if you got this far, then you'll have no trouble getting the rest of the way. God bless you both." The priest squinted at the air in front of him, which he tapped at. With that, he disappeared.

Po blinked, still not totally accustomed to how things worked in here. He'd only ever used a simset a handful of times, not near enough to get used to things like buildings whose corridors wouldn't end, and priests who vanished into thin air without warning.

But whoever he was, he'd been right: now that Po's implant knew who he wanted to find, it laid out the most efficient path in vibrant green. He followed it to a set of grated stairs, which he could feel through the supple leather boots the sim had given him.

Luca Abbato sat with his head in his hands, and he didn't seem to notice Po as he came into view before the cell. Po frowned, and stood observing his father silently, reluctant to draw his attention.

The cell was a little more spacious than the plastic one a bot had shoved Po into not long ago. Absurdly, a toilet took up one corner, though Po doubted the jail program simulated bodily functions. He hoped not, anyway. That seemed like a strange thing to code in.

A narrow cot took up the opposite wall, with a cot above it, though Po's father was the cell's only occupant. A cramped writing desk filled the remaining corner, only partially in view from where Po stood. It lacked a cPad, or paper, or writing implements of any kind. There wasn't even a drawer where such things might be hiding.

Po turned to scan the other cells that lined the airy cylinder, and couldn't spot a single other inmate anywhere. Luca Abbato was utterly alone.

When he turned back to the cell, Luca stood at the bars, a strange light in his bloodshot eyes. Po jumped, cursing.

Luca didn't react. He looked much the same as his body looked in the med center ward, which seemed odd. As Po understood it, an implant learned how to represent you physically by scanning you the first time you stood in front of a mirror after having it installed—the tech who'd greeted him after he woke from his own implantation had had a full-length one ready for him, and had made him stand in front of it, despite his grogginess.

But Luca looked just as thin here in the sim as he did in real life, even though he'd had a prodigious stomach the day he'd gone under. Moreover, just as the sustentation rack kept his hair trimmed and his face shaved, so was his body's digital representation neatly groomed.

Maybe the rack has a built-in scanner, to keep his image updated. It didn't really matter...but Po *was* given to picking apart the "why" of things, as a rule. And it was strange to see his father looking like this, instead of the three-month survivor of a system-wide civilizational breakdown that he normally resembled.

Luca pointed at his ear, and his mouth moved, but no sound came through the bars. It was then that Po's implant prompted him with the question, "WOULD YOU LIKE TO VISIT WITH INMATE LUCA ABBATO?"

He sighed. *I came this far, didn't I?* Before he could change his mind, he tapped "YES."

The cell block dissipated, just as the corridor had before. A cubic room replaced it, walled with painted concrete blocks. Along one wall were three chairs, all empty, and each of them sat in front of an ancient-looking display. Next to each display a black plastic object sat in a cradle. The plastic thing looked kind of like a small, lopsided dumbbell, all of one piece.

The central display flickered to life, showing Luca Abbato standing there, holding something to his face. It looked exactly like the thing sitting in the cradle. Luca gestured with the object, miming picking it up, then returned it to his face, seating one end over his ear with the other positioned near his mouth.

Eyebrows lowered, Po picked up the black dumbbell and tried to mimic his father's posture. He could hear faint murmuring, but couldn't make out any words. Then he noticed that Luca held his so that the cord projected from the bottom end, not the top. He reversed the device, and only then could he hear his father clearly.

"Po," his father's voice rasped into his ear. "It's...good to see you, son."

Po didn't answer. He just stared at the display, at his father, and tried to work through what a bizarre experience this was. He was beginning to understand why the prison was so needlessly vast—or at least, he'd come to a working theory. Everything had been done to alienate the inmates, to make them feel small and alone. Solitary confinement would eventually drive a person insane, Po knew, and maybe the prison even simulated a certain amount of daily "social" interaction to maintain some level of mental stability. But there was no escaping that any such interaction *would* be simulated. Po didn't know if he could have handled being imprisoned here. It was a sobering thought, especially considering how close he'd come to that—and considering he still might wind up here, if he failed at being a Marine.

But stranger than any of that was the fact of seeing his father again, after all this time. Already, his brain was having trouble reconciling the trim, clean-cut person before him with the train wreck of a man he'd lived with every day of his first fifteen years. The orange jumpsuit suited him, but nothing else about his appearance did. For some reason, that irritated Po.

Behind Luca, a sea of empty cafeteria tables stretched into the distance, bordered on the left side by a row of doors that marched out of sight. *More fake stuff to isolate and dehumanize anyone and everyone who ends up in this place. And to make any visitors never want to come back, even to visit. Let alone as a prisoner.*

"Po?" Luca said. "Am I coming through?"

"What was that priest doing here?"

Luca blinked, and licked his lips. He was staring at—well, Po didn't know what. Not the camera. And so to Po it appeared like he was avoiding even the simulated eye contact on offer to them. "Provisions are made for prisoners' religious—"

"What was he *doing* here?"

"He came to hear my confession."

"Why?"

His father's voice dropped to almost a whisper, and he gave a little shrug. "So...I could be forgiven."

Po shook his head, though he was actually unsure whether there was a camera on this end, picking up his image. He couldn't see one, if there was. "You nearly killed Rosa. You nearly *killed* my mother."

Luca gave a sharp nod. "I know, but God—"

"There's no forgiveness for someone like you, Luca. You're going to stay in here until you die."

"That's not—"

"No one forgives you. No one wants you. You're a wife-beating scumbag and your body's going to rot in a medical ward while you slowly go insane inside this digital cage. And that's what you *should* get. It's what you deserve. I ought to strangle you on my way out." He shook his head again. "But no. This is actually better. This is better." Po became conscious he was breathing heavily, almost panting.

A silence came over the line, and on the display Luca's shoulders slumped. He looked lost. And Po hated him all the more, for that.

"Po," Luca said at last, his voice even more strained than usual. "I *am* sorry. I want you to know that. I'm sorry. I—"

"It doesn't matter." With that, Po slammed the black thing back onto the cradle with all his might. If this was real life, it would have broken. But the sim wasn't programmed to accommodate vandalism, apparently.

The room disappeared, and he was standing once more outside Luca's cell. Tears streamed down his father's face, now, as he gazed pleadingly at Po through the invisible wall of silence separating them.

They broke him. This place broke him. He wasn't strong enough.

Po turned away, to face the cell block, and willed his implant's interface back into existence. He used it to exit the sim.

***

Po had never been to the staging area for Psyche's mass driver before. He'd never known anyone who'd left the colony, which was the only reason he would have come here—to see someone off. Every visitor got IDed at the entrance, and everyone knew coming here without a valid reason was a good way to draw the cop-bots' attention. So Po had always made a point of staying away.

He'd received an alert on his implant, just like the others he'd received that had instructed him to attend this medical exam or that evaluation. But instead of directing him to Psyche's med center, this one told him to report to the mass driver staging area at 0500 on August 21st to depart for the cycler where he'd undergo basic training. The alert had come at three o'clock the day before. "KEEP PERSONAL EFFECTS TO A MINIMUM," it said.

Rosa had been the only one home on the day before Po left, and when he asked her where Marco and Nicky were, she would only say, "Lorenzo has them." When he asked her where he'd taken them, she shrugged.

Whatever. As much as it killed him, he had to acknowledge that they weren't his responsibility. Not anymore. Their future was no longer in his hands—if it ever had been.

He went to bed early, without saying anything else to Rosa. It didn't seem to bother her.

This morning, on his way out of the habitation module, he'd knocked on Nicky's closed door. But there was no answer, and Marco and Lorenzo were still gone from their shared bedroom. Po wondered if he would ever see them again.

The staging area wasn't busy at this hour, and Po had no trouble spotting the uniformed sergeant directing the trickle of poolees—which, he'd learned, was what he was called until he left for basic—to one of four waiting shuttles.

I doubt this place ever gets very crowded, even during the launch window for Earth. Humanity's birthplace was still the most popular destination in the system, despite how many traditionalists were supposed to be living in extraplanetary colonies, and despite how often those trads harped about how happy they were to have escaped, and to have rediscovered their freedom in space. Earth yet called across the void to even the most hard-hearted space pioneer, and it was difficult to ignore the yearning that call incited. But few people had the crypto to finance a trip home. The ships that left Psyche tended to belong to Equipoise Metals, and those tended to contain cargo, crew, and little else.

"Abbato?" the sergeant said as he approached, no doubt tipped off by his own implant.

"Yeah."

"Yes, Sergeant, you mean."

Po sighed. "Yes, Sergeant."

The stocky man pointed toward the second shuttle from the right. "You're Shuttle Three. Sit wherever you like."

He nodded, then trudged toward the craft he'd been directed to, where it waited for its turn to maneuver into the mass driver's circular mouth.

"Po!" a small voice called from somewhere to his right.

He recognized the voice, and his heart leapt as he turned. There she was: Nicky, sitting with Marco and Lorenzo in a row of curved plastic seats stained yellow with age. Or rather, his brothers were sitting—Nicky stood at a metal railing, which she clutched with one hand as she waved with the other.

"We wanted to surprise you!" she called. "I love you!"

"I love you," he tried to call back, but it came out as a croak. He cleared his throat, turning back to the sergeant. "Can I go to them?"

The sergeant shook his head. "No time. We're shipping out soon. Get to the shuttle."

Po nodded, swallowing a lump that had formed in his throat. He returned his sister's wave, then continued walking. At the bottom of the waiting ramp, he looked again and saw that his sister was sitting now, beside Marco and Lorenzo. He raised a fist into the air. Marco raised his own fist in answer.

"Kill some Scourge!" Lorenzo shouted.

Po nodded, then continued up into the shuttle before his emotions could get the better of him.

Chapter 10

Po saw some familiar faces aboard the shuttle, but no one he knew personally. During seventeen years on a station of ten thousand people, you tended to run across the same people more than once, even if you never spoke to them. Their faces lodged in your mind like dirt stuck to a CO2 scrubber's filter.

He quickly chose a seat and sat down, before he could accidentally make eye contact with someone he actually knew.

Not that it matters. I'm sure we'll all have the chance to get acquainted soon enough.

A long wait followed, during which he thought about how the sergeant had hurried him aboard instead of letting him go hug his sister. He clenched and unclenched his fists a few times, until he forced himself to stop. *I definitely had time to say goodbye to her.*

Then, a uniformed man Po took to be the pilot poked his head into the cabin through a hatch in the front, scanned the seated poolees, and nodded to himself. He withdrew, closed the hatch, and less than a minute later a calm, detached-sounding voice came out of a speaker in the overhead: "Prepare for departure."

The entire shuttle thrummed as its engine spun up with a high-pitched whine. Thrusters were engaged, and Po's body swayed as the craft pitched forward.

He knew what would happen next, because he'd spent plenty of time reading about how mass drivers worked while he daydreamed about leaving Psyche forever. It would require a push from the shuttle's thrusters to get past the first couple coils of wire built into the tunnel's circumference, but then—

There it was. The shuttle shot forward, each charged coil an electromagnet that fired sequentially, accelerating them faster and faster. It pressed Po into his seat, and he soon felt like a puddle that wanted to fill every crevice between the cushions. The force only grew, the Gs mounting. He wondered if he was going to pass out, or if the Marines with them cared whether the poolees fainted.

He couldn't tell whether the people sitting on either side of him were still conscious, since his head was plastered back against the headrest, as theirs were. But just as his own vision began to swim, even as he instinctively clenched every muscle in his body in an effort not to faint, the G-force leveled out. It didn't diminish, and it wouldn't until they finally exited out the muzzle, but at least it stopped increasing.

The mass driver wrapped around Psyche's circumference over three times before finally terminating at a point along Psyche's surface over a hundred miles from the main colony. Po knew they'd exited when the force pressing him back into his chair suddenly fell away, and then it was as though they weren't moving at all. His body lifted off the seat a centimeter or two, held in place only by the restraints.

His neighbor's head lolled forward, indicating he'd passed out after all.

Hope he's all right.

"Amateur," said a voice from his other side.

Po looked at its owner, a lanky, round-faced guy he thought he recognized from one of the hydroponic farms. "You've been on a spaceship before?"

"No." He shrugged. "But I had the sense to read up on how to stay awake inside the mass driver, considering I knew I'd be going through it."

"Right. Uh...how *did* you stay awake?"

"Same way you did."

Po still wasn't exactly sure how he'd done that, but he decided he'd rather remain ignorant than look stupid, so he dropped it. Now that they'd launched into space, and their velocity was constant, it didn't seem like anything was happening at all. He might as well have been in one of the microgravity hubs that connected the cylinders on Psyche, but one filled with chairs and people who'd been told they were being conscripted into the Marines.

Since visiting his father, he'd done his best to act like his Circuit didn't exist, but he found himself calling up its interface and playing around with the options available to him now that he was aboard the shuttle. After a few minutes of poking around—using his gaze to select options instead of his fingers, to conceal what he was doing from those around him—he discovered he could tap into the shuttle's external visual sensors to open simulated "windows" along the cabin's sides. He could make them as big or small as he wanted, could skin them how he liked, and could even make an entire cabin wall disappear to reveal the star-speckled expanse beyond. You'd never find any actual windows in a spacecraft, since they introduced a major vulnerability for debris or weapons fire to punch through, regardless of what they were made of. Radiation was an issue, too. But with an implant, it seemed you could make your own fake ones.

It didn't take him long to close out all the windows he'd opened, his agoraphobia making him lightheaded from staring into that infinite black nothingness. There were a number of sims on offer that he might have immersed himself in to pass the time, but he decided just to sit there instead.

The first colonists to spread out from Earth must have felt like this. Like him, many of them had also sworn off the sims that had become so popular planetside. But those early voyages were so long and monotonous that almost all of the pilgrims had eventually succumbed to the siren call of those virtual illusions, so effective for alleviating the long stretches of blandness that characterized most everyone's life.

The colonists had been different in one respect, though. Whereas Earthers typically went in for sims that took them as far from reality as possible—many of them indulging in impossible perversions that would have gotten them arrested if they'd somehow managed to recreate them in real life—the colonists led a revival in historic simulations, which before that had served a very niche market.

Po had read an article on that once. Apparently, the boom in history sims caught sim makers off guard, and sent them scrambling to figure out the reason for this new appetite, and how best to feed it.

He probably could have explained it to them pretty well. By the end of the twenty-first century, the global monoculture had successfully bulldozed every traditional culture, replacing it with one much easier, much faster, much cheaper and flashier. Whether that was brought about naturally by technology addiction or architected by the elites who had assumed worldwide control around then in name as well as fact...well, that was a debate for historians.

Either way, morality had become a race to see who could tolerate the most the quickest, culture had been subsumed by sims so engrossing they were nearly irresistible to human willpower, and the world was generally a waste where everyone's slice of the pie had shrunk down to a sliver. That sliver was guaranteed, though—as long as you were willing to sell yourself into slavery to get it. And to accept that the sliver was laced with poison that would slowly kill you.

No wonder people had wanted to escape that if they could. And no wonder they'd gobbled up history sims like candy as they fled, absorbing countless details about whatever specific traditions had been robbed from them so long ago.

Out in the cold of space, a movement sprang up to revive those old cultures—a movement Po's great-grandfather had apparently participated in with gusto. Even three generations later, Po had still been subjected to an endless stream of pasta, pizza, Catholicism, cappuccino, and an unchallengeable household ban on white socks. Po and the few cousins they'd kept in touch with used to spend hours trying to outdo one another in how blunt they could be. And no one ever planned anything ahead of time.

But with each new generation, a little more steam had been lost, and from their parents Po and his schoolmates had picked up a budding cynicism about the traditional movement, a cynicism they'd incubated and nurtured since they were old enough to understand it. Even though Po would much sooner be a trad than anything else, he couldn't help but agree with the critics who said the history sims probably only gave a very surface-level impression of what it was actually like to be an Italian before the twenty-first century. He also personally wondered just how compromised the sim makers were by their GEA overseers. The likely answer seemed to be: very compromised. Chances were, Alessandro Abbato had been fed a cookie-cutter version of his heritage, enough to keep him happy, but nothing with enough actual power to create the sort of deep-rooted, tight-knit people that would have a hope of ever challenging the Council of Hegemons.

GEA was many things, but stupid wasn't one of them. To expand and maintain their power over humanity, they'd had to develop methods both sophisticated and subtle. Especially when it came to the farthest-flung colonies, where trust for the government was already in short supply. GEA knew that if it leaned too heavily on those populations, there'd be uprisings, and they couldn't tolerate the existence of up-system stations that were openly hostile to them. For one thing, those stations offered way too good a platform for bombing Earth.

Such hostile powers *had* arisen a couple times before, and GEA had learned its lesson from what embarrassing PR disasters those incidents had proven to be. Like the time AKB—the Allies of the Kuiper Belt—had taken over an agrarian cycler.

GEA had come to prefer passive systems of surveillance and control, quietly pitting groups against each other. They also liked feeding their enemies a watered-down version of the truth, one that tasted great but would inevitably crumble under the weight of its errors. A 'truth' that no one realized originated with the government's army of behavioral psychologists.

Po sighed. Growing up, his father had often told him he thought too much. Considering where he'd managed to wind up, he was having trouble coming up with a counterargument for that just now.

After a while, a sergeant went floating through the cabin, a canvas bag in tow. From it, he tossed boxed breakfasts to recruits. When Po opened his, he found a suspiciously durable yellow disc he assumed was meant to be egg, a highly processed-looking patty, and a rectangular hash brown, plus a plastic packet of water to wash it all down with. Once he finished eating, he found a sealable receptacle under his seat for the trash.

A few hours after that, lunch was served. He downed it too, and then tightened his restraints, shut his eyes, and did his best to fall asleep.

***

"Hey."

Something bony was jabbing Po in his ribcage, and he opened his eyes to find it was Round-Face's elbow.

"Quit doing that," Po said.

Round-Face jabbed him one more time, then pointed to the front of the shuttle. "Check it out."

Po rubbed his eyes, then blinked, still in the process of waking up. Poolees were talking excitedly all around them, and there seemed to be a lot of gesturing and craning of necks.

He stared at the blank wall. "Check what out?"

"Don't you have a window open to see where we're going?"

Frowning, Po brought up his interface again, not bothering to use his gaze this time but instead punching the floating buttons with his fingers. He took a deep breath, then opened a small window directly in front of him, wary of becoming lightheaded again.

"Whoa," he breathed.

"Right?"

His agoraphobia forgotten, he expanded the window to the entire front wall to get a better look at the behemoth looming against the stars ahead of them.

"That's a cycler."

"Sure is," Round-Face said. "Got any other brilliant insights you wanna share?"

Po ignored him. He'd seen images of cyclers before, and he'd known they were heading for one. Getting a human-occupied craft up to a speed that would allow it to catch up with most cyclers was the whole reason Psyche's mass driver was as long as it was.

But actually seeing one dead ahead, growing slowly larger in his view, and knowing that soon he would be *inside* it...

That was different.

They were approaching from the cycler's rear, at an angle wide enough that Po could see along its segmented metal length. The end was curved, like a gigantic pill, and its otherwise smooth surface was broken at its center by a vast mirror array used to reflect sunlight into the main habitation cylinder.

"Know what those are?" Round-Face asked him. "These things jutting out?" He pointed at one of the regularly spaced protrusions, then moved his finger to indicate another.

Po shook his head

"Laser projectors."

"Huh. It has a point defense system?"

Round-Face chuckled. "No, idiot. I mean, I guess you could call it that. But those things won't do much against an attacking ship. The lasers are only powerful enough to sweep space debris out of the cycler's path. Heats up one side of anything incoming, enough to change its orbit."

"That's good."

"Yeah, it is. There's a lot of drifting trash out here, these days." Round-Face waggled his eyebrows. "Like you. Right?"

Po gave a tight smile and nothing else.

"I'm Paisley, by the way." Round-Face held out his hand.

After a moment's hesitation, Po decided there wasn't much use in antagonizing him, and so he shook the offered hand. "Your name's Paisley?"

"That's my last name. First name Aiden. But we'll be going by last names, here."

"I'm Abbato, then."

"Got it."

Po's stomach interjected. He put a hand over it. "Are they serving dinner?"

"They already did. You slept through it."

Great.

As they approached the cycler, Po opened another window in the cabin wall to his right, so he could watch the surface as it flashed by. He began to feel like a flea flying past the side of a cliff—above or below, he couldn't see where the cylinder ended and space began. Not until he thought to open a window in the cabin's ceiling, anyway.

The shuttle thrummed, and Po thought he could hear the sound of water being sprayed at high pressure. He pitched forward against his restraints, and realized the sound was the craft's retrothrusters slowing them enough to match the cycler's speed.

A rectangular bay opened, dwarfed by the vast surface but big enough for the shuttle. The spraying sound came again, this time pushing them sideways. Once inside the bay, the pilot set them down more roughly than Po was expecting. As he did, gravity resumed, a fair bit heavier than he was used to.

He opened a window to his left in time to see the hatch rising again to reseal the cycler's surface. A few minutes after it had closed, an inner hatch opened, revealing a much larger area partitioned by a see-through wall Po thought might actually be glass.

"Eyes front!" someone screamed from just a meter away from Po, causing him to jump.

A stocky man wearing blue utilities stood at the front of the cabin with his hands on his hips. Crisp sleeves were rolled back to reveal thick biceps, and he glowered at them from beneath the round brim of a dark green hat that had a thin, shiny belt tightened against a second band of lighter green.

"Who thinks the Circuit that was given you is a toy?" he asked, not lowering his voice one decibel. "Anyone? *Raise—your—hand.*" He raised his own hand. Then, he pointed with it. "You are all liars. Not one of you has your hand raised, and yet every one of you insects has been messing around with his implant since we left that backwater waste you call a colony. You are not to access your implant unless given express permission by a drill instructor. Do you understand me? Say, 'Aye, sir.'"

"Aye, sir," came the ragged, disjointed reply.

"You will disembark this shuttle in an orderly fashion. Outside you will find a pair of yellow footprints and you will stand on them. You will *not* access your implant while you do so. Neither will you scratch yourself, or fidget, or look at anything other than the air directly in front of you at all times. *Do you understand me?*"

"Aye, sir!"

"Then move!"

Chapter 11

He'd never been spoken to like that before, not even by his father, and certainly not by his teachers. He could feel the blood pulsing through his carotid artery as he shuffled past the man glaring at the poolees exiting the shuttle in single file.

Outside, he bumped into one of the others when they both made for the same pair of yellow footprints, their eyes on the ground.

"Sorry," Po muttered, just as the other boy said, "Excuse me."

Everyone was being unusually polite with each other as each tried to find his own pair of yellow footprints as quickly as possible in the higher gravity. But no one had either the sense or the courtesy to fill the footprints starting with the farthest set available, which meant many of the poolees became obstacles for the others to trudge around. The result was a lot of milling around in confusion, and more collisions. No one dared raise their voice in anger, though. Not with more DIs standing nearby and glaring at them just as sternly as the one aboard the shuttle.

The same Marine from the shuttle marched off of it, observing them with a look of disgust as he approached. Thankfully, they'd all managed to get in place by the time he reached them, their formation facing the same direction as the craft that had taken them here. The Marine paced back and forth along their left side, and the silence that prevailed was absolute.

Po stood in the second rank from the front, on the side closest to the DI, and it took all his self control not to jump again when he resumed screaming just a few feet from his left ear.

"You are now aboard Marine Corps Recruit Depot Cycler 3. And you have just taken your first step to becoming a member of the system's finest fighting force, the GEA Marines. You should be standing at the position of attention—that means your heels are touching, your feet are at a forty-five degree angle, your fingers are in their natural curl, your shoulders are back, your head and eyes are straight ahead, and your mouth is shut."

The DI stalked around the front of the formation, like a poolee-seeking missile, and stood with his face inches from the kid in the third position in the front rank. "I *said* your mouth is shut," he yelled. He glared at the kid from that proximity for a few seconds, and Po felt very glad right then that he wasn't him. Finally, the DI returned to the left side of the formation to resume prowling back and forth.

"*Attention* is the only position from which you are to speak to a Marine, sailor, or civilian aboard this depot. Do we understand?"

"Yes, sir," a handful of poolees answered weakly—Po wasn't one of them.

The DI stopped right next to Po and yelled into his ear. "I said, *do we understand?*"

Po managed not to wince.

"Yes, sir!" the poolees all yelled back, more or less in unison.

"Our mission is to train every one of you to become a GEA Marine. Being a Marine means having honor, discipline, and spirit. Believe me when I tell you we have our work cut out for us with you worthless bugs. But we intend to use every tool at our disposal to accomplish our mission. And I do mean *every* tool. I promise you this: you will pass through those silver hatches you see before you once, and never again. Do we understand?"

"Yes, sir!"

"As civilians," he said, pacing again, "you are subject to GEA laws. You are now also subject to the military's code of laws. There are three articles that trainees need to be aware of, each of which is punishable according to the commanding officer's military judicial judgments or in court martial. Do we understand?"

"Yes, sir!"

"First, Article 62—Unauthorized Absence. You will be where you're supposed to be, *when* you're supposed to be there, in the appropriate uniform. Do we understand?"

"Yes, sir!"

"Second, Article 105. Disrespect. You will be respectful to all Marines, sailors, and civilians aboard this depot. Disrespect—either through words, facial expressions, or gestures—will not be tolerated. Do we understand?"

"Yes, sir!"

"Third. Article 106. Failure to obey an order. You will do what you're told to do, when you're told to do it, without question. Do we understand?"

"Yes, sir!"

"As your drill instructors, we are also subject both to civil law and the military code of law. But there's something I suggest you insects keep in mind. Out here in the deep black, things happen a little differently than they would on Earth. At any given time, we almost certainly are millions of miles away from the nearest living soul. No one in this system cares about what happens to you. GEA does not care. Earthers definitely do not care. Your mommy and daddy do not care. They're glad to finally be rid of you. Do we understand?"

"Yes, sir!"

"If you were to mysteriously go missing—as recruits have indeed gone missing in the past—nothing in this system would change. No one would notice. No one would care. Do we understand?"

"Yes, sir!"

"I told you we will use every tool at our disposal to somehow turn you sorry lot into Marines. And I meant that. If you disrespect or disobey me or *any* of my fellow DIs, you should not be surprised by what happens to you. Because absolutely anything might happen to those who disrespect either us or this depot. Do we understand?"

"*Yes, sir!*"

"From now on, the word 'I' does not exist in your vocabulary. The word 'me' does not exist in your vocabulary. Do we understand?"

"Yes, sir!"

"When I give the order you will form four straight lines, side by side, in front of those silver hatches. You will walk fast—you will not run. Do we understand?"

"Yes, sir!"

"Do we understand?"

"Yes, sir!"

"Get over there."

With that, the drill instructor began counting down loudly, starting from ten. For their part, the poolees walked toward the doors—hatches—faster than Po had ever seen anyone walk. Arms swinging rapidly back and forth, they hustled over like a flock of frightened ducks.

Po had always had trouble deciding which was worse, spending time at work in the Docks or being at home. But right then, he would have taken either of them over being where he was right now. Compared to his experience of Cycler 3 so far, and how he felt since getting here, it was hard to imagine anywhere he wouldn't rather be.

***

The DI had them stand in formation in front of the silver hatches long enough to fix flaws he found in their dress, then ordered them through.

On the other side he had them all take a chair at one of several long tables. Unbidden, an interface appeared in front of Po, and thus began a long process of filling out a series of forms and agreeing to contracts. How any of this had been missed during his frequent visits to MIPS back on Psyche, he didn't know. Maybe it was all redundant. That seemed like GEA.

The DI ordered them to read each page carefully regardless, and Po actually did do his best to skim them. In particular, he was looking for the clause that said recruits could expect to be jettisoned into space at any moment, which was how he'd interpreted the DI's words outside the shuttle. But he couldn't find anything on that.

His brother's words came back to him, about how Po would never make it as a Marine. *I'll show you,* Po vowed, as he initialed the next page without really reading it. In his mind's eye, he could see himself disembarking a shuttle in the Docks back on Psyche. Marco would be there waiting to see him, and Nicky. His little brother's face would shine with admiration and awe at the impressive figure cut by his brother, the Marine.

Po looked up, and caught the gaze of a recruit at a different table, who was staring straight at him. He lowered his eyebrows, and it took him a few seconds to realize who it was.

Freddie! A familiar face was a welcome sight...or, it would have been, if Freddie's expression wasn't so cold. After a prolonged moment of awkward eye contact, Freddie returned his attention to the air in front of him, raising a hand to tap his consent to yet another form.

He hadn't thought of Freddie once since the meeting with his sim-lawyer. A pang of guilt struck him at the realization, but he swept it away as best he could and continued to initial and sign.

Once the recruits had all reaffirmed that they signed over any and all bodily rights to GEA, while releasing GEA from any and all liability for their safety, they were taken to a large restroom where the mirror ran the length of one wall. A sergeant took them inside in groups of ten to stand at regularly spaced intervals, each of them facing themselves in the mirror.

"Look yourself in the eyes and read from the script I'm transmitting to your implants now," the sergeant said. "The script is actually an app, which will allow you to record a message to your family, and it will auto-filter out every sound that isn't your voice. So ignore everyone else's voice, and make sure your eyes don't wander. If you look at anyone else, or deviate from the script, the app will detect it and you'll have to do it again."

The script popped into Po's field of vision, directly where he was looking. The words were transparent, and he could only see a few of them at a time. The text scrolled automatically as he read from it, so that he could look himself in the eyes, through the words, while reading them.

"This is Recruit Abbato," he recited. "I have arrived safely at Cycler 3. Please do not send any food or bulky items to me. I will contact you in seven to nine days with instructions for sending me unencrypted messages. Thank you for your support. Goodbye for now."

The part about not sending bulky items seemed like a joke, since Po would bet crypto that none of the conscripts from Psyche had families rich enough to send them anything, bulky or not. *It's probably just the same script they have recruits read on Earth.*

On the other hand, he felt sure they were serious when they insisted on "unencrypted" messages. Electromagnetic signals couldn't get in or out of a cycler except through receivers and transmitters built onto its exterior. Administrators would probably just delete any message that came in encrypted, and Po had no doubt they'd read every word of every unencrypted message they passed along to the recruits—or they'd have a bot do it.

That just was part of what it meant to be owned by GEA. The entire contents of their lives were the government's now, to be dissected and analyzed, and probably even sold to profilers and advertisers and used in datasets to teach AIs. Training and equipping recruits wasn't cheap, especially considering some of them would probably wash out, so the military would seek to recoup those costs however they could. Po had already signed over permission to do that, by violating whatever of his 'rights' they cared to.

Once everyone had recorded their message home, a DI took the platoon to a long room divided by curtains, where a team of three doctors completed some final tests and checks to make sure everything lined up with the evaluations they'd undergone on Psyche. Po found himself waiting in line next to Paisley and another recruit named Navarro. His stomach was rumbling again, but it seemed he'd have to wait until morning to eat.

"Things are getting spicy on Nibiru," Paisley told them. "Everyone talks about the Scourge, but I don't think they're ever actually coming back to this system. It's the Nibirans that have GEA actually worried."

"How do you know that?" Po asked. "They haven't given us access to the cycler's network yet."

"Right. And when they do, it'll be filtered to show only need-to-know stuff—and there's very little we need to know. But I found out about this back on Psyche, the day before I left. The aliens hit two Basalt Country neodymium mines in the last week, put them both out of commission for a few days. An insurgent commander named To'sheth Rin claimed responsibility right away. With operations as big as these were, those companies lost billions for sure."

Navarro looked thoughtful. "Maybe that's why they're so hungry for new Marines."

"That's what I was thinking. The Nibirans worship Giru-Giru, who's sort of like an Earth Mother deity. And Rin belongs to a fundamentalist sect that believes anyone who comes from the sky is a soulless interloper fit only to die. These attacks are just the ones we're hearing about...chances are, Rin and his insurgents have been making trouble for GEA and their pet companies for a while."

Po blinked at him. "You know your implant monitors everything you say, right?"

"So what?" Paisley's round face scrunched into a condescending scowl. "The DIs don't care what a peon like me thinks, and neither does GEA. Get over yourself, Abbato. No one's going to bother you as long as you do everything they tell you."

By the time Po finally saw someone, he was getting pretty tired from the heightened gravity down here on the cycler's lowest level. The doctor helpfully explained that keeping them down here for so long actually provided valuable diagnostic data—his Circuit had been monitoring his body's response to the increased strain all this time, and now she could analyze the results.

"It looks like you're holding up well," she said. "I mean, you're no athlete, but I'd say there's a decent chance you'll make it through the next thirteen weeks."

"Great."

"What did you do back on Psyche?"

"Operated a W-200 in the Docks."

"Ah. Yeah, those mechs don't move themselves. That takes a fair bit out of you, physically. You're lucky you had that job. A lot of the boyos I've seen this evening spent their days stuck behind a console before they got here. Watch out for those types, by the way. They're the ones that'll earn your platoon plenty of IT."

"IT?"

"Incentive Training. Do I need to explain what that is?"

"No," Po said quickly, without thinking much about whether he actually needed her to explain it or not. He *thought* he had an idea what it was.

With the final medical exams over with, the same stocky DI who'd shouted them off the shuttle now ordered them out into a corridor, broad enough for them to form up and march along—right into what looked to Po like a freight elevator. The DI brought them to a halt, and left them standing at attention while he stood at ease alongside the formation. Po didn't see him do anything else, but the doors closed behind them, and the elevator lurched into motion. They were going up.

The ride took longer than Po would have expected, even though they seemed to be traveling at a pretty brisk speed. He became noticeably lighter as they rose, and as the elevator slowed to a stop, he almost felt *too* light, even though this was supposed to be normal gravity. The wall in front of them parted, opening wide, and the DI ordered them out. A few recruits stumbled as they adjusted to the reinstated one-G.

Metal floor became something...else. Po looked past his shoes and realized he was now walking on grass. Actual grass. It felt springy under his feet. It had give.

"*Eyes front!*" a voice screamed into his ear, and he jumped, his skin crawling.

He recovered quickly enough to escape any further rebuke. Trembling, he kept his gaze straight ahead as the DI marched them across a field, and then onto a concrete walkway, which they followed, heading toward a cluster of lights up ahead.

Even with his eyes glued to whatever was directly in front of him, Po still picked up on certain details from his surroundings. It was nighttime in Cycler 3, with the only light provided by building windows and beacons that shone from atop metal poles. Overhead, what he first took to be stars dotted the sky.

But that seemed impossible...and indeed, it was. There was no sky above him—that was merely the other side of the "surface cylinder," where there would be yet more buildings, and more lights. The surface was what everyone thought about when they pictured a station like this one, but from his reading Po knew there was much more to a cycler than that. The surface was really just a lot of soil dumped on the very top of a vast subterranean infrastructure. Other levels would hold offices, automated hydroponics, storage holds, and who knew what else.

He longed to see what the other side of the surface looked like, where the buildings would hang upside-down relative to where he now marched. But he could only look straight ahead if he wanted to avoid getting yelled at again, and besides, it was too dark to make out much of anything up there.

The DI took them to their barracks and showed them their assigned racks.

"Sleep well, insects," he told them.

But Po barely slept at all. His rack's mattress was thin and narrow, and he had the top one, so he kept worrying about falling off. Lorenzo had always slept in the top bunk, back home.

His heart wouldn't stop racing, and not only because of the height. He couldn't stop thinking about what the DIs were going to do to them tomorrow—and wondering if it might have been easier just to take the twenty-five years in simjail.

Chapter 12

Po didn't remember falling asleep, but a trumpet proved otherwise, jerking him back to consciousness with its frenetic call.

His eyes felt packed with sand, and he blinked blearily into the dimness as he tried to remember where he was and what he was doing there. Almost, he stepped off the rack into nothingness, but realized at the last second that he was a meter or so higher in the air than he was used to.

The overhead lights came on, and Po squinted into the brightness. Through slits, he saw the same sergeant from yesterday enter the barracks through the door near the foot of his rack.

"Wakey-wakey, roaches. Get out of beddy-bye and line up in front of your racks, *now.*"

During the scramble that ensued, the sergeant continued to stalk down the center aisle between the racks, shouting. "I don't believe I properly introduced myself. I am Master Sergeant Landry. We won't be friends for very long just long enough to get you maggots ready for the DIs who will be with you for the next thirteen weeks. After that, you'll be their problem."

Using Paisley's rack, Sergeant Landry demonstrated how to make up their beds, complete with what he called "hospital corners." Then, he grinned at them. "I hope you were paying attention, because now you get to do it. You have five minutes, and once you're finished there'll be an inspection."

It took a couple times for everyone to get their racks right, and Landry seemed to enjoy prowling around the barracks and ripping the sheets from the rack of anyone who got it wrong, making them do it again.

On the third inspection they all finally got it right, and the sergeant ordered them to form up outside the barracks, and then to run in formation to the mess hall. By now, Po's stomach was a cranky lion, and the mere mention of food had sent it roaring.

The surface cylinder was just as dark as it had been when they'd reached the barracks the night before, and it occurred to Po to wonder what time it was. Sergeant Landry brought them to a halt in front of the mess hall, cleaned up their formation by screaming a couple recruits into place, and then positioned himself at their head.

"You will enter chow hall single-file, in the order of your formation. There will be no pushing or cutting in line. A diet has already been designed for each of you and registered to your implant. Your meal will be served to you automatically shortly after you enter the hall, along the bulkhead to the right—look for your first initial and last name.

"You will eat no more and no less than the amount given you. Do not complain after eating that you are still hungry. Hungry is not sick. Hungry is not injured. Hungry is not dying. Hungry is hungry, and it will be the least of your concerns here on Cycler 3. Collect your meal, take it to an empty seat, and eat it. You may talk with your fellow recruits while you eat. When you hear me call Platoon Five-Oh-Five-Oh-Nine, you will stop talking, deposit your tray into the racks by the door, and form up right where you are now. Do we understand?"

"Yes, sir!"

"Then go eat."

Po didn't know if the others were as hungry as he was, but if they were, their fear of Sergeant Landry was greater than their appetites. They followed his instructions to the letter, entering the mess in an orderly line.

Just as the sergeant had promised, little doors along the right wall opened long enough for a tray to be pushed out before snapping shut again—probably so the recruits couldn't get too good a look at the squirters and tubes their food came out of.

But Po was surprised to find a burger and salad on his tray that actually looked pretty appetizing. He collected it from the metal bars where it sat with enthusiasm, and then scanned the hall for an empty seat. Paisley raised his hand as he was searching, waving to get his attention, and Po only ignored him for a couple seconds before giving up and heading over there. Who else was he going to sit with?

Navarro was on Paisley's left, so Po took the seat directly across from him.

"Hey, Abbato," Paisley said as Po lowered himself onto the bench. "Did you know Navarro here actually *volunteered?* He's gotta be the only one from Psyche."

Po appraised Navarro with raised eyebrows. "You probably are. Why'd you wanna work for GEA?" He suppressed a wince as he remembered his Circuit, listening silently to every word he said. The remark would probably cause some algorithm to elevate his "Dissidence Score" or something.

Navarro shrugged, frowning. "It's not so much I want to work for GEA...."

"What, then?" Paisley asked.

"My girlfriend got really sick a couple months ago, and her family couldn't afford treatment. But when you enlist, your wife gets free health insurance."

"Your wife?" Po said around a mouthful of the best beef he'd ever tasted in his life. "You said she was your girlfriend."

"I married her right before I enlisted. So she'd get the insurance."

Paisley lowered a forkful of pasta to his plate. "Wow, that's...."

"That's pretty cool, Navarro," Po finished for him.

"Thanks."

"You guys might wanna be careful, getting too close to this guy." It was Freddie, and he dropped onto the bench next to Po, without a tray.

Paisley stared at him. "Who are you? And where's your food?"

"Not hungry."

That was when Po noticed Dempsey standing behind Paisley, hands on his hips as he glowered across the table at Po.

Slowly, Po lowered what was left of his burger to his plate, figuring it was best not to be chewing as he tried to placate his old schoolmate. "Freddie, listen—"

"I'm not listening to you. I wouldn't trust a word that comes out of your mouth." Freddie turned back to Paisley and Navarro. "You shouldn't, either. The only reason I got conscripted is because this scumbag talked me into giving him my dad's access to an Equipoise warehouse. He didn't bother telling me he was planning to collect a massive load of Joy in there that he planned to sell."

"Whoa." Now it was Navarro's turn to study Po with raised eyebrows.

"It gets better," Freddie went on. "The Obsidian Angels show up while we're there because he's trying to steal their product, and I manage to get out. I *save his life* by calling the cop-bots, and guess what thanks I get? Nothing. He doesn't say a thing to try to get me off. And after they release him, he doesn't even bother contacting me. First time I see him is across the room while we're filling out forms down on the lower level. So just a word to the wise, if you're making nice with Po Abbato, that's the kind of friend you can expect to get." With that, Freddie stood.

"Noted," Paisley said.

"He ruined me, too," Dempsey said from behind Paisley.

Freddie nodded. "He ruined Demps, too. Let's go, Demps. There are plenty of other people here we need to warn."

After that, Paisley avoided eye contact and wouldn't speak to Po. Navarro gave him a tight smile, then focused intently on his food as he ate.

Po stared down at what was left of his burger, and the salad beside it. His appetite had vanished.

When Sergeant Landry finally called their platoon number, after what felt like an eternity, Paisley lifted his tray from the table and leaned across to whisper to Po.

"Do us a favor and don't sit with us again."

***

"Something's weird," Sergeant Landry said as he prowled back and forth past the formation. He stopped at the front and squinted at each of them in turn. "You bugs are acting different."

Po knew what it was. He'd felt the others' eyes on him as he fell in. Freddie and Demps had made good time around the mess hall, especially considering they'd only been given fifteen minutes to eat, and by now most of the platoon had heard their warning not to have anything to do with Po.

"Anyone gonna tell me what it is?"

The recruits all stayed quiet.

"Well, I'll find out," the sergeant said with a shrug. "Or your DIs will, after they take over in a few days. Recruits are terrible at keeping secrets, and there's always a snitch who'll come to us behind your backs. For example: your implants have automatically notified me that four of you failed to eat your entire meal, while three others found a way to divert that uneaten food onto your own trays." He poked a recruit in his prodigious stomach as he passed by him. "I wonder who that might have been?"

There was a snicker, and Sergeant Landry whirled in the direction of its source. "Shut *up!*" he yelled, and the laughter cut off.

"Now," the sergeant continued. "I could stand here going through the list of names your implants have provided me with, and match them to your ugly faces. But that would be boring. I have a better way to find out which of you are incapable of following simple instructions. Forward, march!"

Po was already on high alert, and his body reacted more or less automatically to the command. But a few recruits were slow to react to the sudden order, the guy in front of Po being one of them, who couldn't be more than a hundred pounds. Po nearly knocked him over as he collided with his back, but the little guy managed to recover his balance and fall into step with the others, after a brief glare over his shoulder at Po.

"You insects are from Psyche," Sergeant Landry went on, "so you'll be able to appreciate this, since you spent yours lives in spinning tubes. Think of Cycler 3 as just another tube, a really big one. Unless you walk along it lengthwise, you're always going to be walking uphill—just like you are right now. The cycler's big enough that you don't notice it much...at least, not at first. Not when you're marching at a leisurely pace, like you are right now.

"I wonder how many of you spent your time back in Psyche running uphill through those tubes of yours? Just from looking at you, I'm going to say approximately zero percent of you did that. Keep up, recruits!"

With that, Sergeant Landry broke into a jog. The pace was almost laughably slow, actually, and Po felt sure the fit Marine could handle a much faster one. In spite of his tough words, he was clearly taking it easy on them...

...except, he really wasn't.

Just as he'd said it would, the fact they were running continuously uphill quickly took its toll. The few bites Po had swallowed at chow became a jagged lump in his stomach, and he couldn't imagine what the recruits who'd eaten too much were experiencing. Raspy, ragged wheezing soon surrounded him, and their footfalls became even less in-sync than they'd been to begin with.

Either Sergeant Landry didn't care about that, or he was choosing not to take issue with it at this early stage. He seemed single-minded in his goal to make the recruits who'd overeaten vomit.

Po didn't feel like he was going to throw up. Instead, his regret mounted over missing dinner last night and skipping most of breakfast. The run was hollowing him out, his legs growing increasingly shaky. Even his arms trembled as he swung them back and forth.

What would happen if I just...fell out?

The thought was a tempting one, but he immediately discarded it. He knew what would happen. Sergeant Landry would make an example of him, and if he still didn't rally, worse things would probably happen.

If he washed out, he'd end up like his dad. That in itself was enough to motivate him to keep running.

Besides, the other recruits already thought he was a lowlife. If they came to the conclusion he was a weak lowlife, they'd eat him alive.

Just concentrate on putting one foot in front of the other. He was a running machine, he told himself. He'd been made to run. One foot forward, then the other. Arms swinging in counterpoise. This was all he knew. All he needed to know.

At last, it came—a loud, retching sound. Sergeant Landry called a halt, and ordered them to about-face, to watch the recruit on all fours throwing up by the light of a nearby lamppost.

Puking, as it turned out, was contagious. The sergeant had told them three recruits had overeaten, but five of them rushed to the grass lining the concrete path to expel the contents of their stomachs onto the ground, and onto themselves. The overweight kid Sergeant Landry had poked in the guts wasn't one of them. To his credit, he didn't look smug about it.

"You eat what we give you," the sergeant said. "No more, no less."

On the way back, two recruits fainted, and Sergeant Landry assigned four others to carry them back. Po's vision swam, but somehow he managed to stay upright. Sunlight was beginning to filter into the cylinder through its endcap, reflected by the big mirror there to simulate morning.

***

Sergeant Landry didn't bother taking them back to the barracks to let the recruits who'd vomited wash the bile out of their clothes. Instead, the rancid stench dogged the platoon all the way to gear issue, and Po's stomach didn't like that, even with as little as he'd eaten at breakfast.

Landry brought them to a halt in front of a square pad near the building, where four chairs were lined up in a row, with strange-looking headgear dangling from a metal column that rose above the back of each chair.

"All right, ladies!" the sergeant said. "Time to get your hair did. Front rank, take your seats." The front-rank recruits hurried to comply, each scurrying toward one of the four chairs. As they got into position, the DI continued. "Pull that big shiny helmet down onto your skull till you feel it clamp on nice and snug."

Unquestioning, the recruits complied. As each helmet descended on a recruit's skull, a buzzing sound arose, and the recruit's eyes widened at whatever was happening. A sucking sound soon followed. Before long, clumps of hair could be seen flying through the transparent tube affixed to each column, which disappeared into the ground.

"Human hair contains lots of nitrogen, excellent for breaking down and adding to the nutrient solution for our hydroponic crops," Sergeant Landry explained. "Thank you for your donation! This morning, you ate the hair of recruits past. Maggots feeding maggots. It's a beautiful thing."

Though he left the waiting recruits in formation, Landry didn't seem bothered with monitoring them too closely. Po took the opportunity to cast surreptitious glances around the surface cylinder, taking it in as the morning light strengthened, growing ever-closer to full daylight by virtue of the endcap mirror's gradually narrowing angle.

I'm glad I wasn't born in a cylinder colony. In principle, living in a cycler like this one wouldn't be too different from growing up in the tubes of Psyche. Both designs involved rotating cylinders generating centrifugal force to simulate gravity.

But the cycler's sheer size made all the difference. For one, privacy seemed in short supply inside a cycler. From where he stood, Po could see most points on the surface. His view along the cylinder's length was obstructed by buildings both ways, but its sweeping curve meant he could see pretty much everything else.

A broad belt of water split the surface into halves, the water wrapping all the way around to meet itself again, a giant ring of liquid. Stretches of sand bracketed the artificial river on both sides, and bridges spanned it in multiple places.

One endcap was still mostly dark, but there was enough light to see it was constructed to resemble mountain slopes, with thick-trunked trees sprouting from them, stretching toward the cylinder's axis. The treetops seemed impossibly high, and some of them intermingled, with the branches of trees that seemed right-side-up to Po tangled up with ones that looked upside-down.

A massive obstacle course had been built into the other endcap, the one sunlight streamed through. Its slopes and walls and paths were interspersed with waterfalls that cascaded from just below the axis' sunlight aperture. Po's mouth fell open as he took in what resembled a gigantic wagon wheel whose spokes were water, all of them tumbling in different directions.

Flocks of birds flew overhead, and not only that—Po was surprised to see clouds drifting back and forth along the cylinder's axis. There also seemed to be clumps of *vegetation* up there, floating among the clouds. The axis itself was marked by a thick cable that ran the entire cylinder's length, and from it hung tethers attached to swinging platforms, buildings, and elevators, all suspended in the air. Some of the platforms had vines and mosses hanging down from them.

Beyond the axis itself were other facilities, all with buildings that seemed to hang upside-down from the far surface, and mite-sized people that somehow walked around up there without falling. He wondered what those facilities were for. Were they for recruit training, too? But their layouts seemed different from what he'd seen of the base he was currently standing in.

"*Recruit Abbato!*" a voice screamed into Po's ear, and he jumped, shouting involuntarily.

It was Sergeant Landry, who'd somehow appeared at his side without him noticing.

"Are we boring you, Recruit Abbato? Do you find the infantry school more interesting than us?"

"No, sir!" Po yelled back.

"Then can you explain to me why you were gawking up at it like the slack-jawed yokel you are?"

"This recruit doesn't know, sir!"

"Oh, but I think you do know, Recruit Abbato. I think you're just being polite. We're boring you and you'd like something to keep your mind off your boredom. Isn't that right?"

"No, sir!"

"I said, isn't that right?"

Po paused. "Yes, sir!"

"That's what I thought. And actually, you've brought something important to my attention. I'll bet your waiting platoon mates are finding this just as dull as you seem to be. And that's why, thanks to you, everyone gets to drop to the ground and give me twenty push-ups *now!*"

Quietly cursing himself for his stupidity, Po fell to the ground, along with everyone else in the platoon not sitting in one of the haircut chairs. Po hadn't done many push-ups in his life, but he did his best to give Sergeant Landry what he was looking for.

Apparently, it wasn't good enough.

"*Stop!*"

Everyone stopped.

"Back on your feet and watch me!" Landry dropped to the ground himself, catching himself in push-up position. "Your push-ups are pathetic. Look. Place your hands slightly wider than your shoulders. Lower your body until your chest almost touches the ground—but *does not touch.* Pause. Then push yourself back up. Inhale going down, exhale going up. Keep your shoulder blades contracted." He bounded back to his feet like a spring coming uncoiled. "Any questions?"

"No, sir!" the recruits shouted.

"Then get down and give me twenty!"

Even with the sergeant's instructions, nearly everyone failed to give him twenty—not while meeting his expectations, anyway. He circled the platoon, singling out recruits' bad form. "On your feet!" he yelled at last.

"Are you bugs tired of doing push-ups?" he asked.

"Yes, sir!"

"Fair enough. We'll do burpees, then."

Chapter 13

Po's bare scalp felt weird. He could only describe it as "clammy." The way his fingers didn't slide across his hairless skin the way it seemed they should. He didn't like it at all.

"Hey, quit that," the recruit in front of him hissed under his breath. It was the runty kid Po had nearly knocked over at the start of their morning run.

"Quit what?"

"Touching your head like that. Are you *trying* to earn us more IT?"

"We're not in formation." The platoon was standing inside gear issue, lined up along the right-side wall of a corridor. That said, Sergeant Landry had already bawled at one of them for leaning against the wall—a recruit named Zhang who had to be at least six foot five. So Po lowered his hand and didn't finger his scalp anymore.

He found himself looking at the back of Zhang's lumpy head, clearly visible over the freshly shorn skulls of the other recruits. Something about the way the big guy reacted to things made Po think he didn't have too many active brain cells below the rolling topography of his cranium.

He sure is big, though. Po figured he must have grown up on at least Level 4 of whatever cylinder he'd lived in, probably 5. A developing body tended to stretch out more, living on those higher levels.

The line finally began to move, recruits shuffling forward as each one disappeared through double doors up ahead. Po peered through an open door on his left as he passed, and saw a bank of strange-looking control panels and monitors with chairs spaced all along it.

Wonder what all that's for.

When he reached the front of the line, he found Sergeant Landry staring him down. He'd been trying to work up the courage to ask the DI about what Navarro had said—about health insurance, and whether it might be available for Po's sister once he became a Marine. But something about the mixture of malice and glee in Landry's gleaming eyes as he looked at Po turned his guts into jelly, and he hurried past without a word.

A sprawling warehouse awaited beyond the double doors, with triple-decker shelves running perpendicular to the side the recruits entered from. Tables had been arranged in a broad rectangle that completely enclosed the entrance, and recruits were moving from station to station, collecting a new piece of gear from each table, under the gaze of bored-looking attendants.

For a moment, Po flashed back to the Equipoise Metals warehouse where all this had started—running from the Obsidian Angels, sending one of them into a metal beam, hiding from the bots. He realized it hadn't occurred to him until now to wonder whether the Angel had lived who'd gone suddenly silent when his head had connected with that beam.

Presumably he was okay, or Po would have been charged with murder on top of everything else. He even remembered one of the Angels saying he'd still been breathing—and so they must have dragged him out of there before the cop-bots arrived.

Still...something bothered Po about the fact he was only thinking of the Angel he'd injured now. Yes, his life had been completely upended in the days that had followed. But he'd also never been in a serious fight before, and that was definitely the closest he'd ever come to killing someone. How was he only wondering about this now?

Dempsey's scowling face popped into his mind, as clearly as if Po's implant was superimposing it over his vision. Dempsey, standing on the far side of the mess hall table, glaring at Po as Freddie told Paisley and Navarro about everything Po had done to him.

He'd always considered himself a good person, the kind of person who looked after his younger siblings, doing everything he could to loose the financial shackles Luca Abbato had tightened around their ankles and wrists. But was it possible he'd been *too* focused on doing that?

"You gonna take your bag or keep daydreaming about the yokel-infested rock you left yesterday?"

Po started, then realized the attendant was waiting for him to pick up the duffel bag and rucksack he'd put on the table before him.

How did he know I was thinking about Psyche? Then again, what else would he be thinking about? Other than this cycler, Psyche was the only place Po had ever been in his life.

"Sorry," he mumbled, and picked up the rumpled canvas bags.

He scuttled along after the little guy in front of him, whose name was Crotty, if he remembered right. From station to station, he filled his duffel bag with an assortment of items, while his ruck clung to his back like a starving and dessicated chimp.

Razor and shaving cream, sewing kit, and his uniform—plus swimwear, a sweatsuit, and sleepwear. A knife. Rain gear. Pouches. Adhesives stitches and bandages.

Some of the gear looked brand new, but other items looked like they'd been used by dozens of recruits before him. He'd heard the Corps prided itself on getting the most out of its gear as it possibly could, and looking at the nicked edge of what one attendant called an entrenching tool, he didn't find it hard to believe.

What surprised him was how low-tech this whole procedure was. They were standing on the inside surface of a mammoth spinning tube hurtling at unimaginable speeds through space. The size and complexity of a modern cycler would have been unimaginable to someone living just a century ago. And yet here they were picking gear off folding tables where they'd been laid out by other human beings.

It was strange to Po, who'd come from a world owned by Equipoise Metals, a company that preferred to rely on robots over humans whenever it could get away with it—even for policing. Maybe especially for policing.

So why not have bots hand out this gear? For that matter, why not deploy machine-Marines instead of human ones? Why not send robot forces to subdue the Nibirans? Why bother training humans at all?

The Marines and sailors he'd met so far seemed to enjoy mocking the recruits for being from a backwater like Psyche. But were they really all from Earth, or even Venus? So far, everyone Po had run into aboard Cycler 3 reminded him more of the people he'd grown up with than how he pictured Earthers.

Duffel bags filled, the recruits were ordered to form up outside gear issue, which from the outside reminded Po of spaceship designs from the twenty-first century. Its white top tapered to a point, and he wondered what use the upper levels might possibly have.

On the way back to the barracks, Po heard chittering coming from some bushes, and he risked looking while Sergeant Landry was facing ahead. Two squirrels were locked in combat, wrestling in the soil of a kidney-shaped garden bed. One seemed to get the upper hand, chasing the other away. The victor then set about yanking a weed from the soil, gripping the plant with its little paws and throwing its whole body back again and again until it loosened. The squirrel carried the weed to the middle of the garden and pushed it up onto a transparent pipe sticking up from the soil. With a sucking sound, the weed disappeared, and a dispenser nearby spat out an almond.

They were fighting over the weed, weren't they?

The squirrels, it seemed, had been trained to keep Cycler 3's gardens weed-free.

Back at the barracks, Sergeant Landry had them slowly and painstakingly organize everything they'd received, item by item, into lockers that sat at the foot of each rack. After that he gave them five minutes to change into their combat utilities.

Po's looked like they'd been worn by several former recruits, and when he put them on he found they were a size too big. But he wasn't about to draw attention to himself by complaining. Not after all the PT he'd earned the platoon earlier.

With their uniforms on, it was back to the chow hall for lunch. Tray in hand, he cast his gaze over the tables, and met Paisley's eye. The other recruit slowly shook his head, then returned to eating.

Sighing, Po sat at the end of a bench with recruits from a different platoon. A couple gave him strange looks, then they returned to their conversation, ignoring him. He ate his meal—all of it—in silence.

***

"Pick up the rifle from the stand," the disembodied voice ordered, coming from both everywhere and nowhere.

Po approached the table and did as he was told, gingerly lifting the weapon from the transparent plastic holder it was nestled in. It rose faster than he'd intended, since he'd expected it to be much heavier. This thing was so feather-light he wondered if it might float away.

Is the sim calibrated right? Or is that really how light rifles are?

When Sergeant Landry had taken the platoon to weapons issue, in the basement of the company building, Po hadn't expected to find himself standing in a featureless white void being bossed around by a technician. But after passing through a thick steel door into the arms locker, he'd been directed with three other recruits to lie on wafer-thin mats arranged in a row on the floor.

Before stretching out, Po couldn't help but notice that for an arms locker, this place was decidedly lacking in arms. Compartments with see-through plastic fronts lined the walls, and while the doors interspersed between them might have been hiding weapons, none were actually in sight.

Being told to lie down was weird, too—but he should have guessed they were going to put him in a sim. Unlike in the Psyche prison ward, this one didn't present any friendly interfaces asking him if he'd like to begin now. Instead, the arms locker disappeared, and he found himself standing here. In endless white nothingness.

It was disorienting to go from lying down to standing without ever actually getting up, and he stumbled a step. That was when the tech started talking to him in a detached monotone.

"Nestle the recoil pad against your dominant shoulder and look through the optic at the target."

"What target?" As soon as he finished asking, he noticed the paper target that had appeared, stylized as a goofy bearded man wearing sunglasses and a black beanie. Po guessed he was supposed to be a terrorist, as indicated chiefly by the pistol he was pointing at Po.

The tech didn't bother to repeat himself, and Po did as he'd been told. At first the rifle felt uncomfortably long, but when he settled it against his shoulder, it rapidly *shrunk*. The scope drew closer, till it was a comfortable three or four inches from his eyes, and the front of the weapon contracted till the foregrip was exactly where it needed to be for Po to grasp it with maximum control and comfort.

"How does the pistol grip feel?"

Po thought about it. "Uh...it's a bit bulky."

The grip shrunk a jot. "Now?"

"Good. Why is it so light?"

"It's made of a lightweight, high-strength composite," the tech said. "You were expecting a metal weapon?"

"Yeah."

"Most recruits do. Retail sim makers aren't allowed to include accurate details...the weapons in those are intentionally modeled after centuries-old gear. The sort of rifle you're holding right now is more durable and takes longer to corrode, especially with the titanium nitride coating...which is also non-reflective, *and* serves to reduce the noise the weapon produces."

"Cool."

The tech was being more generous with information than anyone Po had met so far on Cycler 3, by far. Despite his lofty way of talking, he seemed to enjoy his job, and Po didn't intend to let the opportunity go to waste.

"Can I shoot it?" he asked. "Is it loaded?"

"That's what we're doing next. Place the rifle's butt below your collarbone, nestled in the crease of your shoulder."

Po did. This time, when he looked through the sight, his vision was washed with dim yellow. As the rifle's barrel inched toward the target, the yellow gradually became more and more green, until finally it turned bright green when he was aligned to shoot the terrorist through the heart.

He squeezed the trigger—too much. The first round went where he wanted it, but the rest went wild. Not as wild as he would have expected, though. The rifle barely kicked at all.

A counter had appeared in the upper right of his field of vision, telling him he had twenty-one rounds left in the magazine. He'd fired way more of them than he'd intended. Still...that had felt really good.

"It's a dream to shoot," he said, remembering the clunky weapons he'd fired in the occasional sim over the years.

"The rounds we use are compact, which reduces recoil. Plus the fact that the rifle is now customized to you, that helps a lot."

"It's quiet, too."

"Yeah, they all have suppressors."

"Should keep us alive a little longer against the Nibirans," Po said, hoping it would get the tech talking about the conflict unfolding on the other side of the system. But he already seemed to have lost interest in the conversation, and without warning the sim ended. Po found himself lying on his back in the arms locker, staring at the overhead lights.

The covered recesses he'd noticed earlier were all alive with sound and motion. As he watched a nozzle jerking left and right at high speeds across a bed that shifted forward and backward, he realized what they were: UHAMs, or Ultra High-Res Additive Manufacturers. What used to be called 3D printers, before the term "3D" became passé. And they were printing custom rifles for the recruits who'd just been fitted for them.

Po tried to figure out which one was his, but he couldn't tell. Besides, it wasn't long before Sergeant Landry barked him back out into the hall, to wait at the back of the line until every member of the platoon had gone through the sim.

The last four recruits went into the arms locker. Time seemed to slow to a crawl, and Po's stomach fluttered as he waited for them to finish. He couldn't wait to get his weapon. Why hadn't the finished rifles been distributed to them yet?

At last, Landry strode through the steel door and out into the hall, cradling one of the printed weapons across his torso. He held it aloft for them, with one index finger beneath the stock and the other between the foregrip and the strap. "Behold the M37C, C for customized. While each of your weapons was printed for you in less than an hour, nothing has been spared in terms of either design or material. Every effort has been made to give you a battlefield edge over any adversary you might encounter. With proper care, there's a good chance this rifle will last you your entire career, assuming you insects actually earn your globe-and-wings. And you *will* care for your rifle. From this day forward, your rifle will be your lover, and you will treat her as such. You will never surrender your lover to another man. You will never drop her. You and your rifle are one. Never forget that.

"Your rifle is faithful, and she is smart. She knows your biometrics. She is synced to your implant. And she will only unjam when you pick her up. The rounds you'll fire with her will not be smart. Why? Because smart armor exists with algorithms fast enough to hack fired smart rounds on the fly, making them veer off-target. We can put enough circuitry in a round to make it smart, but not enough to introduce a robust ECM suite. Like your implant, your rifle can protect herself from hackers—your rounds cannot. And so we keep them dumb."

Sergeant Landry grabbed the rifle's pistol grip with his right hand and fished a magazine from a belt pouch with his left. He slammed the magazine into the waiting slot. "This mag holds fifty telescoped compact flechettes. I told you they're dumb rounds, and they are, but each round *does* have a tiny lens and processor capable of transmitting the footage of its flight path back to your implant, where it will be safely stored—tamper-proof, even by you. Every round you fire has a story, and it will tell us that story. So always act with the honor befitting a Marine. You are more accountable for your actions than you know." Po could have sworn the DI's eyes met his as he said that, but maybe he'd just imagined it.

"I told you never to surrender your rifle to another man, and I meant it. But while you're in training, you will only touch your weapon when instructed, and you will only see live ammunition on the rifle range. If you handle your rifle out of turn, your implant will tattle to your DIs, and you will be harshly disciplined. You will also never aim your rifle at another human unless expressly instructed to do so—*even* if you're certain it isn't loaded. Do we understand?"

"Yes, sir!"

"Good. Also, never call your rifle a gun in front of me or any DI, or you'll live to regret it until your dying day. You will refer to your M37C either as your *rifle* or your *weapon*. Now collect your rifle from the attendant, sling it over your right shoulder, and form up outside for the march back to barracks."

Chapter 14

After he took them back to the barracks and had them place their rifles in the brackets inside their lockers, Sergeant Landry ordered them to attention in front of their racks.

"This is where I say goodbye, ladies," he told them. "You probably don't like me very much, but here's a word to the wise—I've been going easy on you. After a day or two with your new DIs, you're going to miss me like you miss your mommies."

Three DIs marched crisply through the door and took up position in front of Sergeant Landry. Without a word, Landry left. Po wondered if he'd ever see him again.

"I am Staff Sergeant Mitchell," the highest-ranking DI bellowed. "On my right is Sergeant Doyle, and on my left is Sergeant Scott."

Sergeant Scott was a thin, dark-skinned man who wore a serious expression. Doyle's face was similarly neutral, though his eyes gleamed in a way that made Po feel profoundly uncomfortable. He was even shorter than Crotty.

But what Sergeant Doyle lacked in height, Mitchell made up for it, with a square jaw to go with it. All three of them looked just as lean and mean as Sergeant Landry—more, if that was possible.

"I see before me a platoon full of young men who feel unsure of themselves," Sergeant Mitchell said. "Who miss home. And who are nervous about what is to come. Well, you are right to feel nervous. Because Sergeants Doyle and Scott and I intend to stop at nothing to convert you pathetic losers into hard-eyed Marines. We only have thirteen weeks to do it. Tell me, does any one of you feel like a hard-eyed Marine right now? Say, 'yes, sir!'"

No one said anything.

"Of course you don't," Mitchell said. "There's probably nothing you feel furthest from. And that should tell you a lot about how the next few months will go. To achieve an extraordinary result, one must use extraordinary measures. As I said, and as Sergeant Landry has no doubt warned you, we will stop at none of them.

"But that all starts tomorrow morning. For now, you've reached the end of your first full day on Marine Corps Recruit Depot Cycler 3. You have plenty to think about until tomorrow." Mitchell's smile was like a cave appearing on the face of a glacier. "Recruit Crotty, you are responsible for making up the fire watch schedule, for tonight and every night, until you prove yourself unworthy of the task."

"Aye, sir!" Crotty shouted.

"Instructions for conducting fire watch are now accessible via each of your implants. Lights-out is in twenty minutes. You have twenty minutes to complete your necessaries, change into your sleepwear, and get into your racks. *Move!*"

***

Getting ready for sleep made Po realize just how exhausted he felt. His sleep the night before had seemed virtually non-existent, and he looked forward to sinking into oblivion for however many hours the DIs allowed him.

An alert popped into the middle of his vision: "YOU HAVE BEEN ASSIGNED FIRE WATCH BETWEEN 2300 AND 0100."

It took all his willpower not to groan loudly. He looked up from pulling on his sleepwear bottom and found Crotty watching him intently from where he sat on a lower bunk.

He's watching for my reaction. The little twerp had intentionally put him on the second watch, so that he'd have just long to get to sleep and start getting some actual rest before he'd need to get up again.

"WOULD YOU LIKE TO SET AN ALARM FOR 2255?" his implant offered helpfully.

With a hand as steady as he could keep it, Po reached up and tapped "YES." He wanted to give Crotty as little satisfaction for what he'd done as possible.

They'll all target you now, a voice inside him said. *You realize that, right?*

Po pursed his lips as he climbed up to his rack. That was probably true. If Freddie's campaigning against him hadn't done the trick, the fact he'd been the first to earn the platoon IT surely had. Others would no doubt mess up as badly or worse, but there was something memorable about being the first one, wasn't there?

Don't let them see you bleed. Once they smell blood in the water, you're done for.

Po grunted softly, then spent a couple minutes reviewing the instructions for being on fire watch. He was about to loosen the rack's taut sheets to crawl under them, but he paused. The barracks was climate-controlled—well, technically the entire cycler was climate-controlled. Either way, it was plenty warm enough without sleeping under the sheets, and by staying on top of them he figured he could save himself some stress in the morning.

He lowered his head to the pillow, and a second later the alarm blared into his ear. At least, it felt like no more than a second.

He bolted upright. The barracks was pitch-black, and he groped for his pad to turn off the alarm, panicking, sure the alarm would wake up half the platoon.

Then he remembered he didn't have his pad any longer. Calling up his interface, he saw the option to deactivate the alarm, and he hammered it. Though completely digital, the button's surface felt cool and smooth to the touch, thanks to the tactile taps installed in his fingertips' nerve endings.

There was only one other recruit moving—Po could only just make out his outline as his eyes adjusted to the low light. He was pretty sure it was Paisley.

Why didn't anyone else wake up?

Then, it dawned on him: of course they hadn't woken. The implant would have sent the alarm directly through his auditory taps. No one else could hear it.

At the far end of the barracks, someone rounded the corner from the restrooms—*The head,* Po corrected himself—shining a flashlight all around the room in a way Po was surprised didn't wake more recruits.

That has to be Zhang. No one else was that big, or that stupid.

Another recruit appeared at the exit, then headed for Po and Paisley. When he drew close enough, Po saw it was Navarro. Both recruits handed their flashlights over and headed for their racks, Navarro clapping Paisley on the shoulder as he did.

Po headed in the direction Zhang had come from. He had interior fire watch duty, and he felt glad he wouldn't have to memorize the eleven general orders for sentries until another night. According to his implant, a superior might demand sentries recite any of them at any time, and they'd know if he used his implant to cheat.

Although, there's nothing saying a DI won't come along and ask me to recite them too. He decided to keep them open in a transparent window that covered most of his vision, for looking over as he kept watch.

His implant also recommended using interior fire watch duty to make sure the barracks floor was swept, so he got a broom from a supply closet and started pushing it around, even though the floor already looked pretty clean.

The first hour was uneventful, which was unsurprising considering the barracks had just one outside entrance and no windows. Maybe there was a concealed entrance that would open automatically in case of a fire, but if so he couldn't tell where it was.

He made sure to record that he swept the floor in his implant's fire watch log—because the instructions told him to, but also because he wanted the credit for doing it. Other than that, a recruit whose name he didn't know yet used the head, and apparently he was supposed to record that too, so he did. Tracking when people answered nature's call felt weird, but then again, GEA would have access to that info if they wanted it, whether Po recorded it or not. He guessed that having him input the event manually was some combination of military tradition, training, and plain old convenience.

After the first hour Paisley came and found him.

"What are you doing?" Po hissed, keeping his voice as low as he could. "Is anyone watching the door?"

"You watch it. It's boring out there."

"What are you going to do?"

"This." Paisley snatched the broom from his hands and started sweeping. Actually, he was more stabbing the floor with the bristles, a technique that didn't look very effective.

"I don't think we're supposed to switch posts halfway through," Po said in a stage whisper.

"You saying you're going to tattle on me?"

"No. But what about the logs? I'm supposed to record what happens inside."

"I'll just tell you what to log when we're done. And you do the same for me."

Po closed his eyes, wanting to argue further, but also reluctant to make any member of his platoon hate him more than they already did. Finally, he shook his head and turned to head for the door, muttering the general orders to himself. He wasn't anywhere close to having them memorized. He was pretty sure he'd remember what to say if someone approached and he needed to challenge them, but there was no way he'd be able to recite any of the general orders if asked.

He grabbed his rifle from his locker—the recruit watching the entrance was supposed to have his, even though it wasn't loaded—and headed outside. Once there, he took in a lungful of the closest thing to fresh air he'd ever breathed. It tasted good...like he imagined a summer day might taste. But possibly that was due to some artificial freshener they spritzed the place with periodically. They put that kind of thing in the CO2 scrubbers every so often on Psyche, and you could always tell when it had just been added. Every breath had a slight chemical aftertaste.

This air didn't carry that acrid note, though. Maybe they could skip the artificial stuff here, because of all the vegetation. A pleasant breeze wafted past the barracks, and he drank it in with relish.

He found himself actually enjoying it out here, in spite of the sleep he was missing. *Joke's on you, Crotty.* He liked holding his M37C again, the rifle that had been made especially for him. It still felt remarkably light, and its polymer was pleasantly cool to the touch. He tapped his fingers against the pistol grip, fighting the urge to raise the weapon and sight through the optic. The only thing that stopped him was his fear that a DI would see him doing it.

It was also nice to finally get a chance to take in the sights of Cycler 3's interior without having to worry about someone screaming at him for it. Admittedly, he couldn't see much in the dark, and if his implant enabled night vision, that feature hadn't been switched on for him yet. But the clusters of lights strewn across the curved surface were beautiful in and of themselves, and as his eyes adjusted to the low dimness, he was able to make out what they illuminated. Concrete paths, parade grounds, shooting ranges, the yards of buildings. The endcaps were completely dark—he guessed they only saw use during the day. He wondered how much of the cycler he'd get to visit before his time here was up.

His agoraphobia wasn't as bad in here as he'd expected. Maybe it was knowing that just like inside Psyche's tubes, there *was* a ceiling, even if it was several kilometers above his head. It wasn't just wide open sky up there, stretching into infinity. That conferred a level of comfort, somehow.

Movement caught his eye from the opposite side, almost directly above where he stood. Someone was walking underneath a streetlight, his gait ambling, relaxed.

Who could that be? A recruit like him? A DI? What were they doing, out strolling the paths at this hour?

Po would probably never know, which he found thought-provoking. The idea that he and whoever that was up there were both living inside this enormous tin can—which was still just a speck compared to the incomprehensible vastness of space—and that they'd probably never actually meet each other...for some reason, the experience made him realize exactly how big the solar system was, in a way he'd never thought about before. It was big, and buzzing with life, and here he'd been tossed straight into that cosmic mix.

Something rustled to his left, and Po turned in that direction, clutching his M37 tighter but making sure the muzzle pointed at the ground for now. A figure was approaching across the field beyond the side of the barracks, but it was too dark to make out who it was.

He racked his mind for what he was supposed to say, but found it blank. Finally, it came to him. "Uh...halt! Who goes there?"

The figure didn't halt. It darted across the grass toward him instead, faster than seemed possible.

"Who goes there?" Po yelled, his heart hammering now, the hairs crawling on his forearms. "Halt!" Even though it wasn't loaded, he instinctively raised his rifle to peer through the sight, and discovered it had automatically switched to night vision mode.

The figure was moving nearly too fast to track, but Po managed to follow it with the scope, keeping it in sight. The word "FOCUSING" popped into his sight, and he guessed his implant was communicating with the rifle, feeding it data on what he was trying to look at, and how well he could see it. It took a fraction of a second for the figure to snap into clarity as it rushed forward, growing closer with every second.

Its midnight almond eyes. Its vertical nostrils. The spines that waved over its head as it charged, like tall grass swaying.

There was an Emplor inside Cycler 3, and it was moving on Po at top speed. Po, who only had his unloaded M37C.

It was more than he could handle. Something broke inside his brain, and he fled back inside, bellowing for help as loudly as he could.

Chapter 15

Mitchell squinted at him from beneath the brim of his campaign hat. *Campaign cover,* Po corrected himself automatically. Hats were called covers in the Marines.

"Where'd you say you saw this alien?" The DI's tone was neutral—too neutral. Po could tell he was none too pleased about being roused from his rack by the commotion.

"It was right there," Po said insistently, though he was already sure he wouldn't be believed. "An Emplor ran through that field there. It was headed straight for me. For the barracks entrance."

"Well, if anything had come inside, your fellow recruits would have seen it. Because you woke them all up." Mitchell shrugged. "Except for Zhang." Somehow, Zhang was still asleep in his rack, even as they spoke.

"I know that. Sergeant." When he'd told the others about the alien, a few of them had leapt from their racks and headed outside to confront it, still in their sleepwear. Paisley had been right behind them. But there was no alien to be seen.

"Walk with me." Mitchell started toward the field Po had indicated, and Po followed behind. "Look. The ground here is soft enough. A fully-grown Emplor weighs about fifty pounds more than a human does. If one had run through here like you claim it did, there'd be prints. And we'd recognize them. The Emplor have pretty distinct feet."

"Permission to search for footprints, sir?"

Mitchell shook his head, then waved his hand, looking resigned. "Go ahead."

Po searched frantically through the grass where he remembered the alien charging through, parting the blades with his fingers and checking the soil. His heart leapt when he found a print that looked like it had been made by a foot with five long, finger-like toes, complete with depressions at each tip that suggested claws. "Here, sir!"

The DI walked over and looked at the part of the ground where Po was pointing. "There's nothing there, recruit." His tone wasn't like the one DIs normally used—instead it was one of concern.

Po looked at the ground again and saw that Mitchell was right. The soil was perfectly smooth, totally undisturbed. But there *had* been a footprint. He'd just seen it. Where had it gone?

Sergeant Doyle approached them, from the direction of the barracks. Next to Mitchell, he looked like a dwarf—Mitchell had at least two feet on him. "Just finished skimming through his Circuit feed," he told Mitchell, with a nod toward Po. "He didn't see a thing. Reacted like he did, but his Circuit didn't pick up anything. So the kid's either a great actor, or crazy. I'm gonna go with crazy."

Mitchell was looking at Po with the sympathy he'd heard in his voice earlier. "We'll need to send him to the med clinic. They'll want to do tests."

"Sir, I just went through an entire psychiatric evaluation back on Psyche!"

"Well, they're going to need to reevaluate you." The DI shook his head. "I must say, I've never seen a recruit crack on the second night. You?" He glanced at Doyle.

"That I haven't," Doyle said, chuckling. "If they don't discharge you straight to simjail after this—or a mental ward—I'm going to start calling you Flibbertigibbety."

Mitchell broke into a grin. "I wonder which fate is worse." He slapped Po on the back. "I'll send your implant directions to the med clinic. Report there immediately and tell them what happened. I'll be monitoring you, so if you try to go anywhere else, or tell them anything about what happened other than the truth, I'll have to come set things right. And I'll be even *less* pleased than I am now. Do we understand?"

He said these last words in the usual DI voice, and Po automatically yelled back, "Yes, sir!"

What could he do? There was no defying the DIs, not unless he wanted things to get a lot worse than they already were. It seemed he'd messed up badly enough that he was now risking simjail after all, or possibly something even less desirable. But he could do nothing other than submit to the psych evaluation, and accept whatever came of it. His fate had been wrenched entirely from his hands—if indeed it had ever been within his grasp at all.

***

The evaluation ended up being both surprising and tedious at the same time. It began with a nurse sitting him down in an evaluation room and transmitting a self-assessment app to his implant, which locked out every other feature, including the ability to properly see anything, until he answered all the questions it posed him. He'd answered almost all of these during the screening process he'd undergone at MIPS, and it was annoying to have to again.

After he'd completed the self-assessment tool, and waited for what seemed like hours, a doctor wearing a sergeant's chevrons finally showed up to conduct a one-on-one interview with him, in which he asked a lot of the same questions that had been on the questionnaire—had he taken any mind-altering substances, did he have any thoughts of harming himself or others, was he hearing any voices or seeing anything that shouldn't be there right now. Po answered "no" to pretty much everything.

"All right, that's it," the doctor said after fifteen minutes or so, rising to his feet as he glanced over a large pad clutched in his right hand.

"That's...it?" Po repeated.

"You seem perfectly healthy to me. Report back to your platoon."

Po studied the doctor's face for a few seconds longer, waiting for a punchline, or a "gotcha." But the doctor just left, leaving the door open behind him. Feeling a little dazed, Po stood and walked out.

Crotty challenged him back at the barracks entrance, which Po hadn't expected. He wouldn't have guessed Crotty would give himself sentry duty, but there he was.

"Recruit Abbato," he said in answer to Crotty's challenge.

"Advance to be recognized."

Back inside, everything was dark again, and everyone seemed asleep—other than the recruit on interior fire watch, who shone his flashlight at Po as he made his way back to his rack. He wasn't sure if he should notify Sergeant Mitchell he was back, but he decided against it. Mitchell could confirm what had happened at the med clinic by accessing Po's implant, and he probably wouldn't appreciate being woken for the second time.

But if he was wrong about that, then he was sure to hear about it tomorrow. Strangely, the thought of attracting his DI's ire didn't bother him nearly as much as it would have just a few hours ago.

After all, how much worse could things possibly get?

***

Po got out of his rack the next day determined not to mess up. He was way past having any goodwill left to spend with his platoon mates: since Freddie had turned the others against him, that account had been all but depleted, and he'd probably overdrawn it by earning everyone PT and then waking them up in the middle of the night.

His standing with his platoon was bad, but not nearly as terrifying as the idea of washing out of bootcamp altogether. Last night had been a wakeup call. Becoming a Marine was all he had, now. With simjail as the only real alternative, he felt newly determined to make this work somehow.

I can't afford any more mistakes. Starting right now, I need to become a model recruit.

As for strange visions of Emplor roaming the cycler...well, maybe he was going crazy. But if he ended up at the med clinic again for hallucinations, he had a feeling they'd simply discharge him, without bothering to make him take any more stupid questionnaires. So if he saw any more aliens, or their footprints, he'd just have to pretend he didn't. No matter how real they looked.

Sergeant Mitchell gave them fifteen minutes to shower, shave, and use the head if they needed to—and then to line up in front of their racks, fully dressed in their sweatsuits. That wasn't much time, and Po could feel his heart beating in his chest as he ransacked his locker for whatever he'd need in there, sure that if he had to come back for anything he wouldn't be ready in time and he'd be singled out again.

All the showers were full by the time he reached the head, so he decided to shave first, though he'd much rather do things in the reverse order. Clearly, the other recruits all felt the same way.

Even rushing as he was, he managed to give himself only one nick, on his Adam's apple. He snagged a shower as a recruit was getting out of it, and by the time he was done washing, his throat had stopped bleeding. Some recruits were still in the shower as he finished dressing, so he figured he must be in the clear.

He exited the head to find Sergeant Doyle grinning up at him, hands extended toward Po's face as if he intended to grab it and give him a big kiss.

"Uh...sir?" Po said.

"Stay still." Doyle rubbed his hands vigorously across his cheeks. "Good. Line up in front of your rack, Flibbertigibbety."

"Yes, sir," Po said, still not sure what that had been about. Standing at attention alongside Harris, who slept in the rack below him, Po watched Sergeant Doyle through the corner of his eye as he rubbed his hands on the cheeks of every recruit who emerged from the head.

He's checking to make sure we all shaved, he realized. Would this be the routine every morning, now? Watching him reach up to each recruit's face was kind of funny. They all had at least a foot on him, except for Crotty.

Dempsey appeared, and submitted to Doyle's tactile inspection. This time, the sergeant took off his campaign hat, quick as a flash. With a snap of the wrist, he smacked poor Demps in the forehead with it, leaving a red mark. Dempsey yelped.

"Get back in there and scrape that rug off your face, recruit!" Doyle roared.

Dempsey scurried back into the head.

Harris leaned toward Po to whisper, "Are they...allowed to do that?"

Wary of getting called out for talking, Po only shrugged. But he remembered what Master Sergeant Landry had said, about the DIs using "every tool" at their disposal. Surely the talk about recruits going missing out here in the black of space had only been meant to scare them...even so, Po believed it just enough that it *did* scare him. What did GEA actually care for his wellbeing? What did anyone care? His usefulness as a Marine was his only protection. So he'd better work on becoming an extremely useful Marine.

Mitchell inspected them once they'd all lined up, along with their racks. Two recruits' hospital corners didn't meet his expectations, and so he gleefully ripped the sheets off and dumped them in a heap at their feet. "Remake them!" he roared. "If I find one more poorly made rack, *everyone* rips off their sheets and remakes them!"

He stalked up and down the barracks, but somehow, the other racks seemed to meet his standards. Once the two failed bed-makers had finished fixing their mistakes, and Mitchell checked their remade racks, he ordered the platoon to go outside and fall in.

"Time for us to get properly introduced, recruits!" he yelled, grinning at them from the front of the platoon with his hands folded behind his back. "I want you to know I understand what you must be going through. By now, you've begun to realize that life in bootcamp isn't like the spinning tin cans you grew up in. Maybe you wish the DIs were a little less mean. Maybe you'd like me to be more like your mommy."

There were a couple chuckles, which were quickly silenced by Doyle's screech to shut up.

Mitchell's smile widened. "Well, there is one thing I have in common with your mommy, recruits. I—will—never—give—up on you! Except, where your mommy might hold you close and lie to you that everything will be all right, I'm more like a hound chasing down a hare. In fact, every direction you turn, Sergeants Doyle, Scott, and I will be there to hound you, to rip a chunk from your hide, to grind you into the dust. But trust me when I say that everything we do, we do out of love for you losers! You can either crumble, stumble, and fall under the relentless pressure, or you can rise to our challenge. But mark my words: you'll leave this depot inside a body bag, or you'll leave a Marine."

Sergeant Mitchell began to pace back and forth before them, relaxed and easy. "That's my promise to you, recruits. I am a single-minded, Marine-making machine. It's all I know how to do—other than chew up recruits and spit them out. And we at Cycler 3 don't really want to spit you out. This might seem like a mean place. Sometimes it will feel like Cycler 3 is trying to kill you. And it's true, you might die here. But it's our job to make you all into Marines, and we take that job very, *very* seriously. GEA wants you to become Marines. Humanity *needs* you to become Marines. And so we're going to keep working on you maggots. Keep hammering at you. Keep tearing you down. Because the moment you feel broken, hollowed out, shattered beyond repair—that's when our real work can begin. Keep up, recruits!"

Abruptly, Sergeant Mitchell broke into a run.

"Look alive!" came the peel of Doyle's voice, like a dented bell. He jogged after the sergeant, and the platoon followed.

Po figured they'd run about five miles in Cycler 3's muggy predawn when Crotty collapsed.

Doyle called a halt, and Mitchell came back, rolling Crotty over like a cat rolling over a turd.

"Seems fine," Po heard the sergeant mutter. He rose to his full, towering height. "Pick the little wiener up and keep going."

No one else was moving, so Po stepped forward and reached under Crotty's armpits, lifting his torso off the ground. He looked around, and his eyes met Navarro's. "Get between his legs and grab them under the knees." He'd seen collapsed workers carried from the docks a couple times, so he knew what to do.

Navarro didn't hesitate, and soon, they were underway again.

Less than a mile down the path, they came across another recruit lying unconscious on the path, who'd apparently fainted and been left there by his platoon.

"You don't touch him," Mitchell barked. "You run right over him. He's not a part of your team, so he's not your concern."

And so Platoon 50509 ran on. The farther they went, the heavier Crotty seemed to get. But Po refused to complain, or ask anyone to switch out with him. Navarro didn't ask for relief, either. To distract himself, Po thought about breakfast.

Chapter 16

When Crotty came to, he stirred in Po's and Navarro's grasp, wriggling and yelling for them to put him down.

"Wiener's awake!" Doyle called cheerfully.

Crotty kicked out of Navarro's hands, found his feet, and pushed Po away. He put a hand to his head, squeezed his eyes shut, and shook himself. With a glare for Po, he took a few shaky steps, then managed to match the slow jog set by Sergeant Mitchell. Po kept a close eye on him, ready to catch him if he fell again, but he stayed upright for the rest of the run.

Breakfast followed, and Po tried his best to enjoy the peace and quiet his total social isolation afforded him. It was nice to eat alone, without having to make chitchat with anyone. That's what he tried to convince himself of, anyway.

After that came classroom time: instruction on different things their Circuits were capable of, military history, and after lunch, a session on how to march properly. Their first lesson in close order drill went better than Po expected, right up until the very end.

"The Marines pride themselves on taking marching very seriously, which means *you* will take it very seriously," Sergeant Mitchell told them. "I will show you each maneuver once, and you will reproduce it flawlessly from this day forward until the day you, retire, die, or are discharged. Mistakes will not be tolerated."

He taught them how to halt, how to mark time, how to double time—how to half step, side step, and back step. He taught them half right face. "Remember that one especially," he said. "You're going to need it a whole lot over the next three months."

From nearby, Doyle chuckled.

At the end of the hour, Mitchell had them all in formation and about to leave, when Freddie reached up to scratch his cheek as the sergeant was walking past him. Quick as a flash, the sergeant spun on his heel and punched Freddie square in his solar plexus.

"No one scratches in my formation," Sergeant Mitchell yelled down at Freddie, who was curled into the fetal position on the parade deck, wheezing for air. Mitchell looked at Paisley, who stood to Freddie's right. "Are you eyeballing me?"

"No, sir!"

"I said, are you eyeballing me?"

"No, sir!"

Mitchell loomed over Paisley for what seemed like a minute, and Po wondered if he was going to hit him too. Finally, the sergeant broke away, pacing back and forth in front of the platoon. "I told you this morning. I am not your mommy. I am also not your girlfriend, or your high school guidance counselor. You will not look at me—you will look where I tell you to look. You will not smile at me. And you *certainly* will not move in any way you have not been instructed to move. I do not care if you have an itch. I do not care if acid is eating out your eyeballs. You are to stand at attention until you are instructed to do otherwise. Is that clear?"

"Yes, sir!"

"Get up!" Mitchell bawled at Freddie. Po's old classmate dragged himself to his feet, his face red.

"Forward march!"

Po winced as they followed the sergeant toward the barracks. Their steps were still fairly out of sync, a staccato of footfalls pattering on the concrete. But either Mitchell didn't notice—which seemed doubtful—or he'd had enough of grilling them for the time being.

He didn't know whether to feel sympathetic or smug toward Freddie. It was a genuine relief to have someone else take some heat from the DIs, since for a while there Po had felt like he'd been getting all of it. If he was going to survive bootcamp, then he needed to stop being the center of attention all the time. And there was also part of him that delighted in Freddie's suffering, after his former friend had turned the entire platoon against him.

But that wasn't only uncharitable, it was also stupid. If it could happen to Freddie, it could and probably would happen to him too. He hadn't expected Sergeant Mitchell to actually follow through on his threat to use every tool at his disposal to transform them into Marines. He'd understood the DIs wanted them to *feel* as scared as possible...but he'd figured there had to be something stopping them from actually hitting recruits.

Watching Freddie gasp for air on the ground had cured him of that idea. *Sergeant Landry wasn't trying to frighten us when he told us no one in the system cares what happens to us, was he? He was simply telling the truth.*

Except, the DIs did seem to care. Not about their charges' feelings, or how comfortable they felt. But about turning as many of them into Marines as they could.

Had it always been like this aboard Cycler 3? Or had the unrest on Nibiru made GEA anxious for more fighters, as fast as possible? And if they were that desperate, why not just build and program bots to do the fighting for them?

He honestly doubted the DIs' approach to training up Marines had changed overnight, so the explanation for how hard they were on recruits probably really did come down to how far out in space Cycler 3 was, and also to GEA turning a blind eye to whatever techniques the DIs considered most effective.

But there did seem to be a certain underlying intensity that Po hadn't expected. He felt sure the DIs were under some kind of pressure from higher up. Only the Nibiran insurgency really seemed to account for that.

***

The days were starting to bleed together. Reveille came too soon, and lights-out never came soon enough. When he woke each morning, his fatigue felt like a cement body cast pinning him to his rack. Every morning, he fought through it, rubbing sand from his eyes and breathing deeply, slapping himself, trying anything he could to fully wake up.

He found it hard to adjust to sleeping in a room with so many guys, especially since he didn't trust any of them. Fire watch duty perforated what little sleep he did manage to catch, although Crotty didn't seem to be abusing his scheduling powers like Po had expected. The little guy seemed no friendlier toward Po than before, but he didn't seem to be targeting him with what watches he gave him, like he'd seemed to that first night. Maybe things had changed after Po and Navarro had carried him after he'd fainted. Or maybe Po had just been wrong.

PT seemed endless, and there were times Po was sure he'd collapse. Plus someone was always messing up and earning them IT. Usually Zhang, who was proving to be even dumber than Po had first thought. He couldn't seem to grasp the fundamentals of drill, or of how to make his rack, or anything really. One afternoon, with Sergeant Doyle putting the platoon through its paces, Zhang kept turning the wrong way. Doyle would call left face and he'd turn right, so that he stood facing the rest of the platoon wearing his usual bland expression, as uncomprehending as the side of a cliff.

It only took a few repeat incidents for Doyle to go ballistic. He advanced on Zhang, campaign cover in hand, obviously intent on smacking the recruit on the forehead with it as he seemed to enjoy doing. Except, Zhang was way too tall for Sergeant Doyle to come anywhere near his forehead.

For a long moment, the sergeant stood there fuming, glaring up at Zhang. Po was sure he'd settle for hitting him on the chest or maybe the chin. Instead, Doyle growled: "Pick me up."

"Sir?"

"I said, *pick me up!*"

So Zhang grabbed the sergeant by the sides and hoisted him up to eye level. Once there, Sergeant Doyle started whacking him with his cover again and again, leaving multiple red welts on Zhang's forehead. He seemed to get angrier the more he whacked him, until finally he socked Zhang on the chin and demanded to be put down. Once his feet were back on the ground, he marched back to the front and called "Right face, forward march," like nothing had happened.

Sergeant Mitchell had promised they'd soon learn the meaning of "Half right face," and he hadn't been lying. Anytime they heard that command, it meant someone had messed up and IT would follow. "Front leaning rest position" often came next, which meant they had to squat down, thrust their feet backward, plant their hands on the ground, and get ready to do plenty of push-ups.

More than once, the only thing that had kept Po from quitting right in the middle of a grueling PT session was the certain knowledge he'd be going straight to simjail if he did, just like his father. The doctor who'd examined him on his first day here had promised his past as a mech operator should help him get through bootcamp, but if it was helping, Po couldn't see how. He still felt woefully unprepared for this—mentally, physically, emotionally. PT left him panting, drenched in sweat. It took every ounce of willpower he had to push through what the DIs were subjecting them to. Rack time always seemed to be in the distant future, and when it finally came, it was over in an eyeblink...and he had to haul himself to his feet and go through it all over again.

Toward the end of the first week the three drill sergeants marched them to the "western" end of the base—the side closest to the endcap where sunset was simulated—and sat them down in the sand under the roof of a broad gazebo, which was big enough to shelter all of them comfortably. The shade was nice, since whoever controlled Cycler 3's weather had decided today would be a hot one.

Two long, raised wooden platforms ran parallel to each other through the gazebo, and Sergeants Doyle and Scott mounted the one closest to where the recruits were sitting.

"Time to learn pugil stick combat," Scott told them in a rich baritone. "A time-honored Marine tradition." He bent down and picked up a long object covered in pads, red on one end and black on the other. More pads sheltered his hands and wrists where he gripped the stick. "Think of this as your rifle. The red end has a bayonet affixed to it. That's why it's red. Thrust them with that end, and the red comes out." He demonstrated on Sergeant Doyle, plunging the pretend bayonet into the latter's heart. Doyle grinned.

"But don't neglect the black end—the butt of your rifle. A butt stroke can be just as effective for incapacitating an enemy, sometimes more effective." He swept the black end of the pugil stick toward Doyle's temple, stopping just shy of knocking him off the platform. Doyle stayed grinning.

"There's always some genius who pipes up at this point to let us all know that bayonets rarely ever get used in twenty-third century warfare, so let me save you the trouble. We know. But the face of war is ever-changing, and what's old has a way of becoming new again. You do not know what situations you will face as a Marine. And so the Marines still bring bayonets with them on every mission, and you will be required to qualify with the bayonet. Do we understand?"

"Yes, sir!"

"Good. Navarro and Harris, get up here."

The two named recruits leapt to their feet and rushed to the platform, where Scott and Doyle fitted them each with a mouthguard and a helmet with a cage on the front to protect their faces.

"I always start with the platoon nice guys, since they have the most pent-up rage. They just need the right encouragement to unleash it. Navarro, Harris, your job is to kill each other. If I detect that you're not trying properly to kill each other, everyone gets PT."

For the next hour, the DIs pitted the recruits against one another, shouting things like "Kill 'em. Kill 'em!" and "You kill that opponent, you understand?"

Each time a DI decided one of the combatants was incapacitated—whether stuck with the red end or hit hard enough with the black—he'd blow the whistle and set up the next match.

It was the best time Po had had in bootcamp yet. He got pitted against Crotty and another kid whose name he didn't know yet. He destroyed them both. And the matches didn't stop.

By the end, he was completely exhausted, mostly because he'd put more heart into pugil stick combat than anything he'd done since arriving on Cycler 3. His body ached, sand had found its way under his clothes, and his skin was slick with sweat. He'd pay for this for days. But he hadn't felt this alive in years.

The demands bootcamp placed on his body were only half of it. There was also the daily classroom time—hours of struggling to hold books' worth of information inside a sleep-deprived brain. Po often found himself fighting sleep during the instruction, blinking hard, biting the inside of his cheek, and doing whatever else he could to fight off the fatigue. But during a class on how to break down their rifles, it finally happened. He dozed off, only to be awakened by something bouncing off the back of his skull. He cried out, sitting stock straight, and looked down to see a helmet lying on the floor a couple feet behind his seat.

Sergeant Mitchell marched around to the front of the class, towering over Po, and he knew he was about to get chewed out. But to his surprise, Mitchel turned to Paisley, who'd somehow ended up sitting next to him.

"Did you let him fall asleep?" Mitchell yelled, with a finger jabbed in Po's direction.

"Sir, he fell asleep on his own, sir!"

"What does that mean?"

"I am not responsible for Recruit Abbato, sir!"

Mitchell raised a forefinger curled against his thumb and flicked Paisley right in the eye. "'I' is not a word I should ever hear come out of your mouth, maggot!" He made a knife hand toward Po. "This is your brother-in-arms. I hope for your sake that he does not display the same negligence toward you that you just did toward him." Mitchell adopted a mocking tone. "'Sir, he fell asleep on his own!' And what will he say about you after a Nibiran blows your skull apart because no one was watching *your* back? 'Sir, he died on his own!' Pa-the-tic." The DI took them both in with a disgusted sneer. "*Both* of you out in the hall and give me fifty push-ups. And make 'em good ones—I'll know if they're not. *Move!*"

Chapter 17

That night Po ended up with the first interior fire watch of the night, when all he wanted to do was sleep. Instead he fished the broom out of the closet and pushed it around the barracks while he went over info that had been loaded onto his implant during a class that afternoon on orbital weapons platforms.

He was trying to use every chance he got to review the material they were teaching him, including during the downtime they were given at the end of each night, to care for their uniforms and equipment. He'd discovered that he could tell his implant to read lessons to him in an AI-generated voice that only he could hear, and he used the feature to make double duty out of his ironing, polishing, and cleaning time.

Something rustled behind him as he rounded the corner toward the head—the implant's audio didn't block out any other sounds; Po wasn't sure how that worked exactly—and he turned to see who it was, ready to note in his fire watch log someone going to take a leak.

A fist collided with his right eye socket before he could raise his flashlight to see who it was. He recoiled, dropping the light as he tripped over his broom. He managed to catch himself against the wall in time for his assailant, who was little more than a silhouette, to land another punch on his jaw. Starbursts obscured Po's vision even further.

Still, he managed to duck under the next hit, and his attacker cursed when his fist hit the wall instead. It was Paisley's voice.

Paisley had at least twenty pounds on him, so tackling him took some effort. Po put everything he had into it, and the other recruit stumbled back into the wall. He heard the air go out of Paisley's lungs, and he pushed off him again to create enough distance for a swing at his face. But Paisley thrashed, and Po's fist connected with an ear instead.

His eyes were starting to adjust to the dark, and he could see two more figures closing in from his left. Someone else was sitting up from a top bunk, watching—that was Freddie's rack, wasn't it?

He tried to hit Paisley again, but the other two got between them. Po figured they were trying to break up the fight, which turned out to be an incredibly dumb assumption. Instead they each grabbed one of his arms and forced him back against the wall.

Against the bulkhead, a voice from the back of Po's brain reminded him helpfully.

"Keep still," one of the recruits holding him growled, revealing himself as Becker, a German kid who tagged along with Paisley whenever he got the chance. Po glimpsed the other kid's face, and he was sure it was Harris, his bunkmate. That surprised him—Harris always seemed so eager to please everyone. *I guess he decided he's better off pleasing Paisley than me.*

Paisley still seemed winded as he lurched forward, and the first blow he landed, on Po's solar plexus, was pretty weak. The next was harder, and the third knocked the wind out of Po's lungs.

He sagged in the other recruits' grip, but they held him firm, and Paisley kept hitting him. One blow landed on his mouth while Po was grimacing in pain, and he felt a tooth fly to the back of his throat, making him choke.

Paisley cursed again. "I'm bleeding." He cradled his hand, squinting down at it. "I gotta clean this up. Okay. We're done here."

But before he went to the head, he locked eyes with Po, who was still retching. "We've all had enough of you drawing heat from the DIs. Do it again, and next time I'll kill you."

Paisley walked away, and Harris and Becker released him. He slumped to the floor, back against the wall—*bulkhead*— feeling dazed. Becker headed back toward his rack as casually as if he really had just gone to take a leak, but Harris cast a regretful look back at Po.

"Sorry," he whispered.

"Sure you are," Po said. He finally coughed up the tooth, spitting it into his hand. He used his other hand to push himself back to his feet, wincing as he looked around for the broom.

He found it and leaned on it for a few seconds while he regained his bearings. His eyes met Freddie's, who was still sitting up in his rack.

He watched the whole thing.

His old friend broke eye contact and slowly lowered himself to his pillow, turning away and pulling the sheets over his head.

***

During inspection the next morning, Sergeant Mitchell walked past Po, stopped, then backed up till he was level with him again. He narrowed his eyes.

"What happened to you?"

"Fell out of bed, sir."

"Why are you talking funny?"

Po pulled his lips back. "Lost a tooth. Sir."

Mitchell shook his head. "Go report to Medical."

At the med clinic, the same doctor saw him that had performed his psych reevaluation. "Do you plan on making this a habit?" he asked.

"No, sir."

"Don't call me sir. I work for a living."

Po frowned. "You're a sergeant. I thought recruits were supposed to—"

"Never mind, Recruit. It was a joke."

"Oh."

"In case you do plan on making it a habit, I should warn you that it won't earn you any sympathy from your DIs. Actually, it might make them lean on you harder."

"Got it. Um, sir."

"Let me see your tooth. Or lack thereof." He snickered.

Po opened his mouth as wide as he could.

"Hmm." The sergeant prodded what was left of Po's front tooth with a gloved hand. "Well, the good news is you didn't hallucinate this one."

It took four hours for the doctor to fit Po with a pregrown tooth from the clinic's supply of them, shave it down so that it would sit snugly in the gap, and cement it in place. Po didn't like the idea of having lab-grown anything inside him, but trying to live out the alternative would have felt pretty ridiculous.

The doctor dismissed him, and Po began to leave, but he paused at the doorway. "Sir?" The anesthetic was still wearing off, and talking felt a little stiff.

"Yes, Recruit?"

"There's something I wanted to ask you."

"Go for it."

"One of the other recruits said he'd get free health insurance for his wife when he became a Marine."

"Okay."

"Does the same go for sisters?"

The doctor paused. "Is she your dependent?"

"Uh...no. I guess not."

"Then, no. I'm afraid it won't apply to your sister."

"Oh. Thank you, sir."

No one said anything when he rejoined the platoon after lunch. Surely the DIs knew exactly what had happened last night, from their implants...unless Paisley had figured out a way to hack them, and doctor their footage. But that seemed unlikely. They were military-grade, and anyway, where would he have found the time? He would have needed to edit the recordings of five different recruits' implants.

No way he managed that.

Which meant Paisley had been willing to risk getting in trouble, possibly discharged, just to put Po in his place. That seemed pretty incredible.

Do the others hate me that much? Or just Paisley?

Whatever the case, it seemed the creep's gamble had paid off. Either the DIs didn't care to review the footage, or they were content to let things lie, so long as Po didn't actively try to rat Paisley out. For all he knew, the DIs may have doctored the footage themselves, to avoid the hassle of dealing with the aftermath.

Probably it's better to let us work things out for ourselves, rather than discharge anyone over it. Especially considering how desperate GEA seems for new Marines.

Well, Po *did* plan to work things out for himself.

He bided his time throughout the afternoon—through a drill session, a prolonged IT session brought on by Zhang, and a class on first aid. He had no trouble staying alert during the class, and he actually shook Navarro awake before the DI could notice him dozing.

After the first aid class, Sergeants Mitchell and Scott took them to what they called the fitness center, where there was a boxing ring. They taught them the fundamentals, and had a couple of recruits put on head gear and gloves to get into the ring and demonstrate.

"We won't be doing any actual boxing this afternoon," Mitchell yelled. "But if any of you ever have anything you need to work out between you, there's to be no fighting anywhere except right here. If we catch you fighting in the barracks, or anywhere else, you'll be sent to Penalty Platoon, and possibly held back to graduate with the class coming after you." The DI's gaze swept over the recruits, but it seemed to linger on Paisley, Harris, Becker, and Po in particular.

Interesting.

When the time came to march to the chow hall for dinner, Po snagged himself a spot at the front of the formation, which meant he'd be one of the first to enter. But once he was inside, he didn't collect his tray. Instead, he leaned against the bulkhead and watched for Freddie to collect his.

As his old schoolmate passed by, Po took a step toward him and snagged the side of his tray, as if he was going to flip the steak and fries it held onto the floor. That made Freddie freeze, and watch Po warily, though he soon broke eye contact.

Guess he doesn't find my black eye and swollen lip too pleasant to look at.

"What do you want, Abbato?"

"You got anything to say for yourself?"

"Nothing to say to *you.*" Freddie tried to yank his tray away, but only gingerly, probably because he was afraid of his meal falling off. The tray had a vertical metal lip that was great for gripping, and Po's grasp was firm. "Let go," Freddie said.

"Not until you explain to me how you could sit in your rack and watch me get worked over like that."

"Easiest thing in the world, after what you did to me. Maybe you wanna explain *that?*"

"Freddie, look, I'm sorry for not checking on you after they let me go. I should have. I know they ruined your life, but I was kinda distracted with them ruining mine."

"It's your fault, Po. You're the one who talked me into letting you into the warehouse." Freddie yanked the tray, shifting his salad sideways and sending a cherry tomato to the floor.

But Po wasn't letting go. "And you're the one who agreed to it," he hissed. "You had to know what you were getting into."

"You're not gonna smooth talk your way out of this."

"Yeah? Like the way I smooth talked Candace into going on a date with you in ninth grade? Or when I helped you make it up to your dad after you lost his cPad? We were *friends,* Freddie. I've had your back before, just like you had mine."

"You're not gonna smooth talk your way out of this," Freddie said again. "You got what you deserved. And there's more where that came from."

Po let go of the tray, mostly out of shock. Freddie gave him a parting glare, and Po watched him cross the mess to make his way to Paisley's table, where a spot waited for him between Navarro and Harris. Paisley was watching Po through narrowed eyes.

He pressed his lips together. *There's more where that came from, is there Freddie? Well, we'll see about that.*

He turned to get his tray, and his eyes met Sergeant Mitchell's, who was sitting alone at the last table, chewing his steak and eyeballing Po with a neutral expression.

Po's heart tried to leap into his throat. But the sergeant didn't say anything—only watched him as he went to collect his tray from where it had been spat out.

"You'll want to eat fast, Recruit," Mitchell said as he walked by. "I'm almost done, and when I'm done, everyone's done."

"Yes, sir."

***

Po went through the motions of preparing his uniform for the next day and getting ready for racktime. At the moment, he had two goals in life: become a Marine, and get even with Freddie. And yesterday, Sergeant Mitchell had given him a way he could accomplish the second goal without endangering the first.

He had no fire watch that night, but he'd overheard that Freddie did, at 0300. That was all to the good. Po crawled into his rack, and while it took about an hour to overcome his paranoia over getting attacked again, once he did he got the best sleep he'd had since arriving in Cycler 3.

The next morning he sprang out of bed at reveille, already getting dressed in his sweatsuit while the trumpet still blared.

Sergeant Doyle took them on a run, and Po marveled at how easily the diminutive DI kept pace with his stubby legs. He barely seemed to break a sweat.

At breakfast, Po took his tray to where Doyle sat, and stood there waiting to be spoken to.

"What?" the DI said at last, still not looking up from his scrambled eggs.

"I want to fight Recruit Rodriguez in the ring."

Now, the sergeant did look up, a smile spreading across his face. "Do you, now?"

"Yes, sir."

"Well, I'm sure that can be arranged!" The DI's eyes bulged out of his socket, and he started eating faster, shoveling forkfuls of eggs through his grin, one after another. He washed them down his throat with big gulps of milk.

Kind of weird.

Doyle wasted no time getting them to the fitness center after breakfast. In fact, Po was pretty sure he'd cut chow short. More than one recruit had to dump what was left of their meal into the trash when the DI called their platoon number and ordered them to get outside.

Freddie, Po noticed, was one of those who had to forego part of his breakfast. *Also good.* Po had made sure to wolf his down, and while he had some heartburn, at least he wouldn't show up to the fight as tired and hungry as Freddie would.

Po wasn't above mercilessly leveraging every edge available to him, including his height advantage. He wanted to make Freddie pay.

Sergeants Mitchell and Scott met the platoon at the fitness center—Doyle had probably let them know what was about to happen with his implant. Some of the recruits seemed surprised to be back here so soon, but the sergeants looked amused, and Po noticed them exchanging glances with each other. He wondered if they were using their Circuits to place bets on the boxing match.

"Ladies and gentlemen," Sergeant Doyle said in an announcer's voice, even though everyone in the platoon was male. "Recruit Abbato has issued a challenge to one Recruit Rodriguez. Rodriguez, how do you answer? Will you box, or will you scurry away like a frightened rat?"

All eyes were on Freddie, while he glowered at Po. "I'll box. Sir."

Of course you will. How could he refuse Po's challenge in front of the others? He'd never live that down—kind of like how Po would probably never live down Freddie's smear campaign against him.

Doyle handed him a mouthguard, and then headgear and gloves. Po tapped the sides of the gloves together, going over in his head everything the DIs had taught them yesterday, along with everything he'd had his implant read to him during downtime in the barracks the night before, and during breakfast today. Since they'd visited the ring yesterday, a boxing manual had been accessible from his Circuit, and he'd taken full advantage of that.

While Freddie put on his gear, Po stepped into the ring and practiced the stance he'd seen Sergeant Mitchell use the day before, with his left toe forward and aligned with his right heel.

"This was a mistake, Po," Freddie said as he stepped into the ring.

"Yeah? You gonna ask someone to jump me after this?"

"Trust me, I don't need to."

Freddie stepped forward, gloves raised, and something about the loose way he moved seemed off to Po, who kept his fists clenched and his elbows tight to his body. A left hook came at his torso, and he bounced to the side, though not fast enough—it still grazed him under the ribs, and hurt more than he'd expected it to.

Stay moving. He bounced on his toes, shifting his position, doing his best to keep his opponent guessing. Freddie grinned at him through his gloves and shook his head.

"What?"

"You'll see."

Freddie stepped smoothly forward, jabbing then following up with a cross. Po's gloves were up—he remembered the manual stressing that—and this time he caught the jab on his elbow.

He countered with a cross, putting all his weight into it. But he overextended, and Freddie brought his shoulder forward, catching Po's punch on it and defusing much of the force. Then came a hook, which caught Po in the same place as before, on his right side just below his ribs.

The wind left Po's lungs in a whoosh, and a few of the other recruits cheered. Suddenly he couldn't jump around like he'd been doing before. His feet felt rooted to the canvas. It was everything he could do to keep standing, so he focused on defense, scuttling away from Freddie as best he could and keeping his gloves high and tight.

"This is why it doesn't pay to be a trad," Freddie said as he advanced on him. He barely sounded winded. "You swore off Circuits, but I used mine to learn how to do things. Like box."

Po gathered his strength and threw his left fist at Freddie's head, but Freddie bobbed back and to the right, dodging the punch, then surging forward with a cross of his own. It landed on Po's gloves, but it was powerful enough to send them back into his face, dazing him. Freddie pressed the attack, peppering him with two jabs in quick succession, followed by a right cross and a left hook.

Po's arms flew apart as he tried to stop the hook from connecting, but when he did, Freddie stepped into him, delivering a right uppercut to his chin.

Stars burst across his vision, and the world heaved. Blackness swallowed everything.

Chapter 18

A sound reached him, like a belt cracking against itself. No—like knuckles popping.

His eyes drifted open. Sergeant Doyle was on one knee beside him, snapping his fingers in front of his face.

"There you are, Flibbertigibbety," the sergeant said. "Do you know what you did wrong?"

"I lost."

Doyle chuckled. "True enough. Do you know *why* you lost?"

Po pushed himself to a sitting position. Ringside, the other recruits were congratulating Freddie, though a few of them were watching Po and grinning.

"Not really."

"Lots of reasons. You wouldn't stop bouncing around everywhere—you're better off keeping your feet flat on the canvas for the most part, so that you're always ready to react. You even lifted your body with every punch, which robbed your power. You didn't throw enough punches, either. Did you see how Rodriguez attacked in combos?"

"Yeah. Sir."

"You leaned past your knees with your head plenty, too. So your balance was all off. Anyways, there were plenty of other things, but I'm bored now." Sergeant Doyle stood up and walked off to talk to the other DIs, leaving Po to pick himself up and exit the ring to join the rest of the platoon. It was everything he could do not to hang his head as the others smirked. But soon enough, they were in formation again and marching off to class.

***

That evening in the barracks, Sergeant Scott came around with letters that had arrived from Psyche. To Po's surprise, one was for him. He'd given up on getting any messages a while ago, figuring that either the DIs were withholding them for some reason or his family had already forgotten about him.

The letter was inside a sealed envelope that was addressed to him, which seemed ridiculous since it had definitely come in the form of data beamed to one of Cycler 3's antennae. Someone in a subsurface administrative office must have printed it off and stuffed it in an envelope for him. Just another tradition the Corps refused to let go of, Po guessed.

That every word had already been read by multiple people was beyond doubt, probably including the DIs. Po just hoped that whoever had sent it to him had figured that out, too. The last thing he needed was for something in the letter to get him into even hotter water than he already seemed to be swimming in.

He climbed onto his rack and sat with his legs crossed to open the letter carefully, even though it was only a printout. His heart leapt when he saw the name at the bottom: Nicky. The message was disappointingly short, but getting one from his sister at all was good. It made him feel a little lighter. He'd been worried that she'd gone back to being upset with him after seeing him off at the mass driver staging area.

Po,

I'm sorry I didn't talk to you, the last few days before you left Psyche. I was so mad at you. I'm still mad. But I already feel bad about ignoring you, and I'm happy I at least came to see you before you left.

We might not ever see each other again. I can't believe it, and I hate it. But it's true, isn't it? How will you ever get back here? And how could I ever leave? Especially with me being sick....

I've been taking my meds every day, even without you here to remind me. I wanted you to know that.

Things are strange since you left. The colony feels empty, and not just because you're gone. They took a lot of people, and they put a bunch of others in jail. Lorenzo says GEA was cleaning house.

Po winced as he read that, imagining what whoever read this letter first might have thought about it.

He thinks one reason they arrested so many is because they wanted there to be fewer people for the Obsidian Angels to recruit. According to him, GEA is worried about how powerful the Angels have been getting. But on another day, he said the Angels have members planted high up in GEA, so I don't really know. Lorenzo is hard to understand.

Mom seems even more out of it, with you gone. Marco is Marco. He doesn't say much, but I know he misses you too.

Lorenzo is planning something. Some things he says makes me think he's going to try to cause trouble for you. I don't know how he would do that, but you know how he is. When he gets set on something, he doesn't stop thinking about it till it's done.

I don't think he likes how much I talk about you. And I think he can tell how much Marco misses you too. He keeps saying how he should have been the Marine, not you. I'm sure they would have taken him if he'd volunteered, so I don't know what he's so mad about.

Anyway, I don't trust him. Watch out, Po.

I had to warn you.

Love you. Miss you.

Nicky

Po quickly folded the letter again, wanting to make sure no one else caught a glimpse of its contents. He briefly considered destroying it, but realized there was no way he could bring himself to do that. Instead, he slipped it under his pillow, with the intention of sneaking it into his locker when the others were asleep.

It was a risk, to chance anyone else in the platoon getting a hold of it. He didn't need to feed Paisley or Freddie or anyone else more information about him or his situation, especially not about his own brother apparently plotting against him. But he wasn't going to destroy that letter. In a way, it felt like all he had.

He went over his uniform, looking for any loose threads. He'd seen Sergeant Scott rip a button clean off of another recruit who'd had a thread sticking out of it, and he'd needed to sew another one on that night. Po didn't want that to happen to him.

Doyle appeared at the entrance and began stalking past the recruits, sizing each of them up wearing the same look he'd had when Po had told him he wanted to box Freddie. Eyes bugged out, grin stretched unsettlingly wide across his narrow face. His eyes met Po's, and the DI waggled his red eyebrows at him.

He's looking for a target. Hope I'm not it.

He wasn't. The target ended up being Zhang, who Doyle caught leaning against the corner of his rack while the others shined their boots, ironed their uniforms, and checked over their equipment.

"Are you comfy, Recruit Zhang?" Doyle shouted, loud enough for the entire platoon to hear and probably seven other platoons besides.

Zhang sprang to an upright position. Much too late, Po expected.

He was right. Doyle ordered Zhang to get his pillow and prop it between his back and the rack post, while yelling "*I am comfy! I am comfy!*" again and again as loudly as he could.

"Keep it up, Recruit Zhang!" Doyle barked over the oaf's bellowing. "If I hear you stop, or if that pillow falls, the entire platoon will be doing PT till Reveille. You don't want that, do you? I'll be monitoring your Circuit." With that, Doyle strolled out of the barracks.

"*I am comfy!*" Zhang yelled. "*I am comfy! I am comfy!*"

He yelled it for what seemed like hours. The other recruits mostly ignored him, though the phenomenon did lend a certain awkward tension to the barracks, and chitchat was a lot more subdued during Zhang's torment.

Eventually, Zhang started to cry, sobbing wretchedly between exclamations. Tears streamed down his face. But he didn't stop shouting the words.

"*I am comfy!*" His voice hitched piteously. "*I am comfy!*"

Sergeant Doyle left him there screaming and weeping until an hour after lights-out.

***

Po's plan to keep his head down and become the best recruit he could didn't seem to be working out very well.

Things were steadily deteriorating, his standing with his platoonmates falling even further than it already was. Other recruits kept bumping into him during morning runs, "accidentally." They always apologized, but their sorries usually carried a note of sarcasm, to Po's ears.

Or, a hospital corner he'd finished folding and double checked minutes ago was found mysteriously yanked out come inspection time, and more than once his bedding was yanked off his rack by a DI and dumped unceremoniously onto the deck, for him to gather up and remake. He took to standing guard next to his rack until the last second, when one of the sergeants called them all to attention in front of their lockers.

Then someone—or multiple someones—took to flicking him in the temple while he slept. But by the time he came fully awake, there was no one to be seen. Of course, there was also the genuine worry that he was hallucinating that.

Either way, the pranks and little attacks on him seemed to be escalating, and he sensed they were building up to something. He didn't feel very eager to find out what that might be. As for the DIs, either they didn't notice anything or they chose to ignore it.

Then were the cracks during evening downtime, the others asking when he was going to challenge Rodriguez to a rematch in the boxing ring. But he could handle those.

I can handle all of it. They won't make me quit, and they won't make me do something that gets me washed out. I can't afford to.

The letter from Nicky had given him a new well of resolve to draw from. Sure, becoming a Marine wouldn't mean free health insurance for her, but there was still his salary. The military would feed, clothe, and house him, so what money would he actually need as a Marine? He could make the minimum required payments on his personal debt and send the rest to Psyche, for Nicky to get better. The only other use he could think of for it was a visit back to Psyche at some point, but that seemed like an extravagant expense, even if he could manage to save up enough. Especially when sending crypto to pay her medical bills was a much better use.

I need to get in touch with someone on Psyche who can keep an eye on things for me, he decided. *Make sure Rosa is using the money I send the way I want it used.* He could ask Nicky, except he had no guarantee his letters wouldn't be intercepted and either changed or discarded before they reached her. He also wasn't confident Nicky would tell him if Rosa was misusing the funds.

But before he could enjoy having that problem, he needed to get through the remaining eleven weeks of bootcamp. Considering how the first couple weeks had gone, that seemed like kind of a daunting prospect.

It was the day after Nicky's letter and the "I am comfy" incident—or maybe it was a couple days, they blurred together too much now to properly keep track of—at dinner-time, when Navarro sat across from him in the chow hall with a plateful of bean salad, rice, and chicken breast.

Po had already been devouring his, but when the other recruit sat he paused mid-chew, fork and knife hovering over his own steaming chicken on the verge of plunging into the meat.

His gaze flicked to three tables down, on the other side of the hall, where Paisley sat perfectly erect, staring at Navarro's back with wide, burning eyes.

"You sure you want to sit here?" Po asked him.

Navarro shrugged, grinning. "Don't worry about me. I'll only be here for a second. I'll just tell Paisley I sat here to make fun of you."

"That's a relief." But Po was still studying Navarro's face, not sure if he was joking or not. Either way, sitting here took guts. He already liked Navarro, even though he'd buddied up with Paisley from the get-go. His reason for joining the Marines, to get health insurance for his sick girlfriend—now wife—that was pretty classy. "So...why are you here?"

"You know what today is?"

"Uh...no, actually."

"It's Saturday. Which makes tomorrow Sunday."

"Hmm. That is the day that follows Saturday, yeah."

"Sure is, wise guy. You know what happens on Sunday?"

"What?"

"Religious services."

Po paused, waiting for Navarro to continue. When he didn't, he said, "And?"

"You should go to one."

"Why?"

"Because it gets you out of the barracks for an hour. Longer, if you opt to take advantage of a one-on-one direction session with the chaplain. You seem like you could use a break."

Po nodded slowly. "Do you go?"

Navarro acted like he was wounded, but this time Po was pretty sure he was joking. "What, you didn't notice me go missing every week? You hurt me, Abbato. You hurt me deeply."

"Who else goes?"

"No one." Navarro shrugged. "I'm the only one."

"That sounds great. Do I have to sign up for it, or something?"

"Just ask one of the DIs after chow. Then be at the parade ground for eleven forty-five hours tomorrow morning."

"All right. Thanks."

"You got it." With that, Navarro stood up and reached for his tray. Then he stopped, grinned, and sat back down to tear into the chicken with his teeth. He stood again with his tray. "There," he said around a mouthful of meat. "Now you can say someone ate with you at bootcamp."

Then he headed for Paisley's table, where he would no doubt have some explaining to do.

Chapter 19

Of his three DIs, Sergeant Scott seemed the most approachable—though "approachable" wasn't a word he'd really use to describe any of them. Still, Po was glad that Scott was the one with the platoon when he asked about going to a religious service.

The sergeant narrowed his eyes. "You didn't go last week."

Po shrugged.

"Well, I can't deny you. What denomination?"

"Uh...Catholic." That was what he'd been baptized, and he'd been confirmed Catholic too, though his family had stopped going to Mass pretty much immediately after. GEA would know all that, so it'd be foolish to say anything different.

Sergeant Doyle was in the barracks the next day, and while the rest of the platoon stayed to practise assembling and disassembling their rifles under his watchful, bug-eyed gaze, Po followed Navarro to the parade ground's south side.

Instantly upon stepping outside, Po felt a sense of freedom that made him realize just how suffocating and constricting he was finding bootcamp life. Big, fluffy clouds obscured the upside-down terrain overhead, and a flock of what he thought were geese was flying through them in a V, from one end of the cylinder to the other. More birds chirped from a line of trees that stood just north of the field where he'd seen an Emplor running at him, and nearby two crows fought over a crumpled piece of foil.

I guess even the birds have been trained to pick up litter. He wondered if he'd see a fight between a squirrel and a goose before he finally left Cycler 3, whenever that would be. *The goose would probably win.* Unless a squad of squirrels attacked it together....

There was a light breeze blowing across the surface, and Po paused for a second just to breathe it in.

"You look more chipper already," Navarro said, grinning back at Po from where he'd paused a few meters ahead.

"This was a great idea." Po frowned. "Did Paisley give you any trouble for sitting with me last night?"

"Not too much. I have the advantage of being a lot better liked than you. That gives me pretty good protection."

Po had heard there were five training battalions garrisoned in Cycler 3 at any given time, totaling over five thousand recruits. So he was surprised when they reached the parade ground and found little more than a hundred waiting to march to where the various chapels were found.

Aren't most recruits from extraplanetary colonies? The colonists in places like Psyche and Vesta had reputations for being mostly traditionalists, which included religious tradition. But judging from this sparse group, their parents' generation had done an even worse job at passing that on than Po had thought.

To him, it only went to show how shallow those traditions were to begin with—or at least, how shallow the versions of them were that they'd been fed by the historical sims.

Real tradition holds for thousands of years. When you think about how our ancestors really lived, us colonists might as well be playing house.

The recruit chapel stood on the southern end of the training base. It was technically several chapels, each a shallow triangle connected to the others at the base, all pointing at the cylinder's other side. Po wondered if there were chapels over there pointing in the opposite direction.

He and Navarro filed into the third one from the left, along with the forty or so other recruits attending Catholic Mass. Navarro headed for the front, disappearing through a door behind the altar, but Po sat at the very back. He already knew what to expect from the service, having gone to enough of them as a kid. He'd never gotten very much from them, despite how hard the priest seemed to try to keep the congregation engaged, with homilies he peppered with jokes and performances from the youth band led by the most promising talents. That had been Father Ramos, a different priest from the one Po had run into outside his father's simjail cell. He'd never seen that priest before.

What followed was like nothing he'd expected or experienced before.

The chaplain started by proceeding up the center aisle, then down again, this time using a golden shaker to sprinkle everyone with a sweet-smelling liquid while some people in the back sang in a language that tugged at Po's memory. He felt like he should understand the words, and in some ways they reminded him of the snatches of Italian he'd picked up from his father growing up. But whatever language the chaplain was speaking, it remained impenetrable to Po.

So did nearly everything else that happened over the next hour. The chaplain stayed facing the altar for much of the Mass, instead of directing everything he did and said toward the attendees. Navarro didn't sit with the other recruits, in the pews—instead he stood beside the chaplain, wearing a flowing white shirt over a black cassock, and every now and then he seemed to respond to what the chaplain was saying. Many of the prayers were murmured too low for Po to hear, and for long stretches the chaplain seemed to say nothing at all.

What is this?

Po couldn't understand why anyone would attend this thing, except maybe for the same reason he had—to escape the barracks for an hour. It didn't seem like any effort was being made to keep the audience entertained. Every now and then everyone would stand up, kneel, or sit back down, and Po mimicked their actions so he didn't stand out. But the chaplain wasn't even facing them, for the most part. There was no band to keep everyone awake, and the priest didn't make a single joke when he took the pulpit to speak.

That part, at least, was in English. He started his homily by reading a story from the Bible about a guy who tried planting seeds in a bunch of rocks, and then a place where there was hardly any soil, and then in some thorns. Finally, some seeds happened to fall on good soil, and something good finally grew. But all Po could think about was all those wasted seeds from before. This guy was supposed to be a farmer, but he obviously didn't know the first thing about farming.

He's about as good a farmer as this guy is a priest. Po grinned at his own joke.

Still, after the chaplain returned to the altar to say and sing more incomprehensible prayers, something about the whole thing did start to make Po want to pay closer attention. There was some quality to what was happening that felt...*strange* to him. Strange enough for him to want to understand at least some of what was happening. He brought up his Circuit's interface and poked around for a translation function, so he could start following along, but he was surprised to find it hadn't been enabled. He was sure it must be capable of translation—even civilian implants had that feature—but it was one of the many things that hadn't been turned on yet for recruits, apparently.

Notes from one of his classes caught his eye instead, a lesson from Wednesday on the role of mechs in planetary warfare, and he called it up. He hadn't felt like he'd truly grasped the lesson on the day of, but as he reread the notes, things started to click into place for him more. It made him feel a lot more relaxed as the service wound on, distracting him from not being able to understand anything happening in the strange Mass, and from the way the singing and the unusual scents had started to make him feel. He turned the opaqueness all the way up, so that the interface blocked out his view of the chaplain and the altar. But even then, he could still hear the singing. So he hunted through the menus a little more till he found recordings of marching cadences, which he played over his auditory taps.

There. Now he was wrapped in a sensory cocoon of his own making, impenetrable to outside sights and sounds.

I can do this every Sunday, he realized. *Get away from Paisley and the DIs and everyone else while I sit here and catch up on everything from the week. This is perfect. Navarro is a genius.* Although, with whatever he was doing up at the altar, even Navarro wasn't taking advantage of this like Po was.

Eventually, after an interminable stretch of mostly kneeling, recruits began to file past his peripheral vision, which the interface didn't cover. *They're going up for Communion,* he realized. He was going to join them, but then he saw another kid was staying in his seat, kneeling with his hands folded. So Po imitated him. His knees were starting to ache from the overly firm kneeler, but something inside him told him not to go to the altar, so he didn't.

Not long after that, the chaplain himself walked through his peripheral vision, away from the altar. Navarro walked in front of him, holding a crucifix aloft on a pole.

It's over, Po realized. He closed the notes and turned off the marching cadence to see what would happen next. But nothing did. The other recruits were all still sitting or kneeling in their pews, saying nothing. And that same uncomfortable feeling from before was back. Like something was gnawing at Po's organs, slowly coring him out from the inside.

***

There was a lineup outside the chaplain's office to speak to him after Mass, and whenever someone new would come, Po let him go ahead of him. Recruits trickled in, and eventually he ran out of chairs, so that giving up his spot meant having to stand while he waited.

He didn't care. The longer this took, the longer he could stay away from the barracks. He kept expecting someone to want to keep the last spot for himself, but no one did. They all accepted his offer to go ahead of him, and most of them even thanked him.

It took the better part of two hours to see the chaplain, and he used the time to review more class notes.

This is great. He was already feeling way more on top of the material. Getting to do this every week was going to be a huge leg up, and not having to watch his back every second felt amazing. He just wished he'd discovered this was possible in his first week.

The moment when the recruit ahead of him was admitted into the office came way too soon, and he only stayed in there for a few minutes. The door swung open again, and with a twinge of regret, Po rose to enter.

The priest stood as Po came in, hand extended. During the Mass, he'd worn colorful vestments, but now he was dressed in the more recognizable black cassock. Po shook the offered hand.

"I'm Father Campbell. And you are?"

"Recruit Po Abbato, sir."

"Have a seat. You don't have to call me sir."

Po frowned as he sat. "Aren't chaplains considered colonels?"

"Yes, but it's a bit different." The chaplain settled into his own chair. "You can call me Father Campbell if you like, or just Father."

"I already have a father. He's in jail." Po wasn't totally sure why he'd said it—he'd always called Father Ramos "Father" as a kid attending Mass. But those were the words that had come out.

The chaplain blinked at him, and a moment of silence passed between them. "Are you a Catholic?" he said at last.

"If I'm anything, I am. That's the church my parents dragged me to as a kid. Sir."

"Who dragged you here today?"

Po didn't have a good answer for that, so he gave none.

"I have to admit, this is the first time a recruit has attended Mass and then come to office hours afterward not wanting to say Father. But I won't make you say it. You'll have to enlighten me, though, as to why you're here. Did you come to make a confession? Receive spiritual guidance?"

It was the first time Po had considered that he might need an actual reason for being here. *Idiot.* They needed something to talk about, didn't they? Otherwise the session would end pretty quickly.

"Why do they let you offer Mass at all?" Po asked, stalling for time as he cast about for a reason he'd come to see the chaplain. "GEA hates religion. I'm surprised there are any chaplains here."

"The Marines have always had chaplains, and they insisted on keeping them. They're very aware that many recruits would never make it through bootcamp, without spiritual support."

"But what *was* that Mass, anyway? That was nothing like Father Ramos' Mass."

The chaplain smiled. "*Father* Ramos?"

He'd caught Po out a second time, and for the second time, Po had no answer.

"That was the Tridentine Mass," Campbell continued, "and it's much older than the one you went to as a child. It dates back to the 1500s, though many parts of it go all the way back to the first century."

"Why don't you just do a normal Mass? Why this one, that's impossible to follow?"

"Because I love it. And it's not impossible to follow. Didn't you see the basket of pamphlets at the front, as you came in?"

"No. *Paper* pamphlets?"

"That's right. You can take one as you leave, if you like. It's called a missal, and it has the English translation alongside the Latin. It'll be a big help to you, the next time you 'drag' yourself here. It'll take a while to get the hang of, but you'll get there." The chaplain was still smiling. "You didn't come here to discuss liturgical history, I'm sure. Why *did* you come here, Po?"

"I came...." Po began, but trailed off. He swallowed. What could he say? He'd have to act out any lie he told. The priest would have follow up questions, and Po would need to keep on inventing answers. Then he'd have to keep track of them all for future sessions, which he definitely planned to attend, if only for the extra free time it would buy him while waiting in the hall outside the office.

He'd never hesitated to lie before. But lately, his lies had landed him in a lot more hot water than usual, hadn't they? It was a lie that had bought him the favor Dempsey had done, in letting him access the Dock's Brain in order to track down that shipping container. The lie he'd told Mrs. Dempsey, about her husband being at work all day, when really he'd been out drinking.

Ultimately, that was why Po was here on Cycler 3, wasn't it? And lying to his AI lawyer hadn't done him much to get him out of it.

But that wasn't all. As annoying as he found the chaplain, he'd treated him kindly this whole time, and honestly. Po couldn't remember the last time someone had acted like that toward him. Except maybe Navarro, but even he wasn't really on Po's side—he was on Paisley's.

Either way, he didn't feel like lying to the chaplain. He sighed. "I came to get out of the barracks for a while."

The chaplain nodded, not missing a beat. "And why did you want to get away from the barracks?"

Po closed his eyes, almost wishing he'd lied. "Because they...." His voice had begun to waver, and so he stopped talking for a moment, to collect himself. *Don't cry, you wuss. Don't cry.* "They all hate me."

"Do you know who else was hated?"

Po studied the chaplain's face. He'd expected him to say something else. "Who?" he asked at last.

"Jesus Christ."

"Huh."

"*If the world hates you, remember that it hated me first.* Do you remember that line? Have you ever read the gospels?"

"No. I think I've heard that before, though."

He was pretty sure Father Ramos had read it to them one Sunday, from the pulpit. The words hadn't struck him at the time, and anyway, Po knew that he'd earned most, if not all of the hatred directed at him. But somehow, thinking on the words made Po feel a little better. If people had hated Jesus, who'd done nothing wrong, then probably it wasn't so surprising that they hated Po.

Chapter 20

The next day, Sergeant Scott pulled him out of a particularly brutal drill session overseen by Sergeant Doyle. It was the first time they'd drilled with rifles, and Doyle was scrutinizing them with his popped-out eyes and manic grin. Whenever a mistake was made, Doyle would call a halt and order the recruit who'd messed up to the front of the platoon...to stand there and watch as everyone *else* was forced to do push-ups while holding their rifles.

Po's knuckles were already bloody from being ground into the asphalt, and it didn't help that Sergeant Doyle was patrolling the ranks, looking for anyone doing sub-par push-ups so he could step on their hands as they pumped up and down. He couldn't weigh all that much, but even so, Po doubted it was pleasant, and he'd prefer it didn't happen to him.

"*Recruit Flibbertigibbety!*"

Oh, no.

"Sir, yes, sir!" he called between gasping for breath.

"Are you the Sydney Harbor Bridge?"

Po didn't know what the Sydney Harbor Bridge was, but he felt fairly confident he wasn't it. "No, this recruit is not the Sydney Harbor Bridge, sir!"

"Then why is your back arched just like the Sydney Harbor Bridge?"

"This recruit doesn't know, sir!"

He knew those words were a mistake as soon as he spoke them. But it was too late to take them back now.

"You don't know, Recruit Flibbertigibbety? You don't *know?* Well then, why don't you stand at the front of the platoon with Recruit Zhang and observe the others until you *do* know? I'll get them to do thirty extra push-ups just so you can *figure it out.* Go on, get up! The push-ups they do while you take your time to get to the front don't count!"

Po leapt to his feet and dashed to where Zhang was standing, his heart already sinking toward his boots. *I'm doomed,* he reflected miserably. Who knew what Paisley and his goons were going to do to him after this?

No one was looking at him—everyone was staring at the asphalt as they struggled through the remaining push-ups—but Po was sure he could *feel* their rage toward him building. Something was going to come of this, something bad, and probably as soon as tonight. And the DIs had so far shown zero interest in doing anything to prevent the others from targeting him. In fact, Po felt pretty sure Sergeant Doyle was egging them on.

Does he want me to die?

"Recruit Abbato!"

Po looked to his right to see Sergeant Scott beckoning him over. Relief flooded through him...but it didn't last long.

"Come with me," the DI said once Po reached him.

"Yes, sir." He trailed behind the sergeant, headed back toward the barracks. Escaping the grueling drill session was one thing, but he couldn't escape the fact that he'd been the one responsible for the platoon doing even more push-ups than Zhang's latest flub had earned them. And anyway, being singled out and called away by Sergeant Scott couldn't possibly bode well either. For a while now, Po's plan had been to blend in with the others as well as he could, to keep his head down, and to get through the rest of training as quietly and inconspicuously as he could.

He couldn't think of anything he'd failed at more thoroughly in his entire life.

Scott led him to Sergeant Mitchell's office, at the back of the barracks. Mitchell was staring into space when they entered, probably doing something with his implant, but he focused on Po as Sergeant Scott sat him in a chair and then circled the desk to stand next to the head DI.

They both studied him wearing expressions that Po couldn't quite place, at first. He'd seen the DIs exhibit a lot of emotions in their interactions with recruits—amusement, anger, sadistic glee—but he didn't recognize this one.

Then, it clicked. They looked...*sympathetic.*

"Recruit Abbato...." Mitchell said, speaking gently. "Are you retarded?"

Po blinked, and Sergeant Scott cleared his throat.

"Well, not *retarded,*" the DI went on. "That's not the right word. Sorry." He shrugged apologetically. "I'm from Vesta Station."

"What Sergeant Mitchell means to say," Scott intervened, "is, do you have an actual mental defect of some kind?"

"Um," Po answered. "No, sir. Not to my knowledge."

"That's what your psych eval said," Mitchell mused. "And so did your second psych eval. But I've gotta tell you, Abbato, I've never seen a recruit manage to turn everyone against him like you have. It really has been something to behold."

"You probably think we don't monitor recruits' implants all that closely," Scott said. "Because of the things that have gotten past us, like when Paisley and his friends—"

Mitchell cut him off with a hand gesture. "We don't need to get into specifics. Look, Abbato, we're in a little bit of a situation, here. GEA has been breathing down the Brigadier General's neck, and so he's been breathing down *our* necks. They really don't want us to wash out any recruits, not if it can be at all avoided. Things are getting...spicy, out there in the system. It all seems far away from us here on Cycler 3, and well, you don't really know anything about any of that, do you?"

"No, sir."

"That's fine. You don't need to know. Just be aware that we've never seen this amount of pressure from the higher-ups to make as many Marines as we possibly can, as quickly as we can. So there are certain things we're overlooking that in normal times would have gotten a recruit discharged. Such as, just as a hypothetical, if a recruit were to get attacked in the middle of the night while on fire watch. We'd know about something like that right away, because the implants are smart enough to alert us to basically anything out of the ordinary."

Mitchell paused, studying Po, as if waiting for him to react in some way.

"Of course," Sergeant Scott put in, "nobody's implant holds a recording of something like that happening, because it *didn't* happen. But if it *did* happen, that's the sort of thing a DI might overlook, in the environment we find ourselves in."

"That's right," Sergeant Mitchell said. "And I'm actually glad Sergeant Scott mentioned that, because this little powwow we're having is *another* thing that didn't happen, and which no one's implant will have any record of. But if such a powwow *did* happen, I'd use it to warn you that under these unusual circumstances, *you're* the one who's actually in danger of washing out."

"*Me,* sir?"

"*You don't know the word 'me!'*" Mitchell roared, slamming his palms down on the desk and causing Po to jump backward, so that he nearly toppled out of his chair.

"Yes, sir!" he yelled, louder than he meant to.

"But like I was saying," the staff sergeant went on. "Your talent for getting your fellow recruits to completely despise you is such that, given our pressing need for Marines, it seems better to discharge you than them."

"But we don't want to do that," Scott cut in.

"No," Mitchell said. "We don't. But we will if we have to. Listen, Abbato, we're sympathetic to your retar—uh, your mental deficiencies. I know your repeated psychiatric evaluations say you don't actually have any, but I'm sure there are things they must miss every now and then. We could hold you back to join the next class, but our fear is that you'll manage to make yourself into just as much of a whipping-boy as you have in your current platoon. And we want to help you. We really do. Because we care."

As he said that last, Mitchell actually held a hand over his heart.

After a few seconds, both he and Scott burst out laughing.

"All right," Mitchell said, waving at Scott with one hand as he wiped his eye with the other. "Okay. Seriously, though. What we're going to do is put you in Motivation Camp for three days."

"Motivation Camp, sir?" He'd heard about that—it was for recruits with attitude problems, and apparently designed to be even more punishing than regular bootcamp. If Motivation Camp didn't cure those recruits of their attitudes, they were held back to graduate with the class coming after. But from what Sergeant Mitchell had just said, there was a real danger that they'd simply discharge him.

"Motivation Camp," Mitchell repeated firmly. "You're probably too...deficient to understand this, but it's actually the best thing we could do for you in this situation."

Scott nodded. "That's because it's clearly unfair for us to put you in Motivation Camp. You haven't done anything to earn it, and by now all the recruits have heard how brutal it is."

"It'll earn you some sympathy." Mitchell shrugged. "That's the hope, anyway. But it really is all we can do for you, Abbato. We'll keep you there for the full three days, but after that, you're on your own. If you can't figure out a way to make it work with your platoon then, we probably will just discharge you. We can't continue risking that your hateability will lead the others into doing something to you that'll get them discharged. Hopefully that all makes sense."

Po stared at the DI. He didn't want to get held back to graduate with the next class—but he wanted to get discharged even less. So he had to say something. "Sir, the reason the other recruits hate me is because of a history I have with two of my platoonmates. They turned everyone against me. It wouldn't be like that with another class."

"We were thinking the same thing," Mitchell said. "Then we got this letter from your brother."

Po narrowed his eyes as the DI opened a drawer, removed a single-page printout, and placed it on the desk in front of him.

"It's addressed to 'the delicate hands of 50509th platoon's DIs,'" Mitchell continued. "You don't need to read it, honestly—it's just a bunch of jokes at the expense of Marines, mixed in with pro-EPA jokes. You know what the EPA is, right?"

"Earth Planetary Army."

"Correct."

Sergeant Scott spoke up. "Your brother was trying to get you smoked, and smoked bad. Normally, it would have worked. If you were any other recruit, you'd be in for it right now. But like Sergeant Mitchell said...we actually feel bad for you. Since this is the only letter your brother's sent since you got here, it doesn't seem like a good-natured prank, like a buddy might try to pull. So it isn't just your platoonmates that hate you, Abbato." He gestured toward the letter. "Even the people back home want you to suffer."

"And you *are* going to suffer," Mitchell added. "Motivation Camp is no joke. But like I said, we're doing you a favor."

Po had nothing left to say. He was pretty much dumbfounded by the entire situation.

"Any questions?" Sergeant Mitchell asked.

"No, sir."

"Fantastic. Sergeant Scott will take you directly to Motivation Camp from here. Best of luck, Recruit Abbato. We'll see you in three days."

***

The Motivation Camp DI, Sergeant Shenton, paused at the foot of his rack. "You're Abbato, right?"

"Yes, sir."

The DI flicked an envelope at him from the top of a stack. It hit Po's chest and bounced onto the blanket. With that, Shenton continued along the aisle that ran along the center of the dimly lit subsurface barracks where the recruits sent to Motivation Camp were whiling away the hours before lights-out. Some went sluggishly through the motions of straightening away combat utilities fresh from the dryer, others sat against the bulkhead or lay staring at the overhead as they waited for theirs to dry, or for the washer to suds away the slime that had built up over the course of the day. Sergeant Shenton had made clear he expected their uniforms to appear immaculate come morning inspection, even though they'd be subjected to the exact same treatment tomorrow.

No one had much energy left for the task, but they all knew showing up to morning inspection with algae on their uniform would only make things worse.

Po peeled open the envelope and extracted the printout, fighting to keep heavy eyelids open as he reads it.

Po,

I haven't gotten anything back from you. Are you mad at me for not speaking with you before you left? Please don't be mad, Po. Don't just ignore me. I don't want to lose you, so let's keep in touch, okay?

Or maybe they're keeping your letters from me. I hope that's not it. We need to be able to communicate with each other.

I'm writing this right after Lorenzo told me what he did. He sent a letter of his own, but not to say hello—he sent his to your instructors. He's trying to make them go as hard on you as possible. Hopefully you get this letter first, so you're at least ready for it, but his will probably get there before mine. I'm sorry. Hopefully it wasn't too bad.

Things are getting worse on Psyche. The bots have started searching people's homes, looking for anything tying them to the AKB. Lorenzo says GEA is worried about the AKB building ties with the Angels here. If they got a foothold on Psyche, they'd be a lot closer to Earth than their outposts farther out in the Belt. Lorenzo said that some people even believe the AKB are involved somehow in the [REDACTED].

Love,

Nicky

Po carefully refolded the letter and stuffed it under his pillow, in the hopes of taking it back to his regular platoon's barracks. With that, he lay back and stared at the bottom of the rack above him, going over what Nicky had written in his mind.

Her talk about the AKB worried him. They were the Allies of the Kuiper Belt, and they'd been designated a terrorist group by GEA soon after they'd formed, decades ago. The AKB was the main reason GEA was so paranoid to lose control of any up-system stations.

If they keep sending bots into people's homes, they will *lose control.* Colonists were only willing to let GEA push them so far. The government had always seemed aware of that, before this, but the way they were acting now reeked of desperation.

Something was causing that desperation—probably the same thing making them lean on the DIs to push as many recruits through as they could.

The Nibirans. It didn't take a genius to guess that was what the censors had redacted from Nicky's letter. They were obviously trying to keep a tight lid on what they allowed recruits to learn about the political situation, but some things were still getting through. Enough scraps that Po at least had managed to piece together a blurry picture, and it didn't seem like a pretty one.

He could at least understand why GEA was so jumpy about the Nibiru situation. It wasn't just the threat the aliens represented—it was also the effect any unrest would have on public confidence in GEA. For years, the system nets had been awash with conspiracy theories about the Nibirans showing up around the same time in human history as the Emplor and the Scourge. A lot of people believed it was all part of a slow-moving, multi-pronged invasion of humanity's home system, coordinated in secret by the three species' leaders.

That seemed like a stretch to Po. Then again, all three species appearing around the same time *did* seem like a pretty big coincidence.

I need to write Nicky back. It hadn't been resentment that had made him delay this long, but tiredness, and a fear that his sadness would spill onto the page and bring her down. Except, his silence was worse than risking her realizing how bad things were for him. He saw that, now.

"Why are you here?" the recruit in the next rack over asked him. "What did you do that made them send you to Motivation Camp?"

Po returned the recruit's gaze for a few seconds as he turned the question over in his head.

"It's simpler not to get into it," he said at last. With that, he rose to fetch his cammies from the dryer.

***

"Wakey-wakey," Sergeant Shenton shouted as he strode down the barracks' center aisle. "Rise and shine, wormies. The cesspool is calling your names."

In describing where they'd spend the day as "the cesspool," the sergeant was only being accurate. It was a long and broad rectangular tank where the wastewater from one of Cycler 3's hydroponics facilities was kept while it awaited treatment. It was the job of each recruit who found himself in Motivation Camp to climb single-file down the ladder and onto the platform at one end of the tank, there to lower himself into the slimy water, and wade through the algae to the platform on the opposite end. Once there, he was to turn around and wade back to the first platform. Then he repeated the process for the rest of the day.

Why? There was no why. Or, the lack of an actual purpose for going through this *was* the why. Motivation Camp was designed to be pointless, wretched, exhausting. After his first full day of wading back and forth through the cesspit, Po had emerged wrinkled and cold, and feeling miserable.

His memory of yesterday made sliding into the gunk even harder today. The smell of burnt garlic invaded his nostrils and made him want to vomit. Apparently it smelled like that because of all the phosphorus. More than one recruit had thrown up already, but that hadn't earned any pity from Sergeant Shenton. He stood on the platform, bone-dry, and screamed all day for them to wade faster.

Motivation Camp was much closer to the cylinder's surface than the level where Po had undergone his medical exams on his first day aboard Cycler 3. Even so, the gravity was noticeably stronger than it was on the surface level. His body was more massive here, which made the cesspool all the more grueling.

Sergeant Shenton seemed to enjoy his job, and Po supposed that made him a true sadist. He couldn't understand how anyone could *like* standing in a dimly lit tank several levels underground, where the gravity was significantly higher than on the surface, yelling at recruits to push harder in a task that accomplished nothing at all. But Shenton definitely did like it. That was beyond question. His coarse voice never seemed to tire, and he seemed to enjoy hearing it bounce off the moist walls and echo back to him as he harried the recruits endlessly.

Po didn't know which was worse, the heightened gravity or his sodden clothes that dragged at him as he trudged back and forth through the tank. His lungs were on fire, and his legs felt like rubber. He had no idea how he'd made it through the first day, and as the second morning wore on, he began to seriously entertain the possibility that he was going to die.

But he couldn't stop, could he? What might happen to him if he did? Sergeant Shenton hadn't *offered* any of them a break, and somehow Po doubted he'd be keen on the idea. *Will I simply be discharged if I try to take one?*

In the end, it didn't matter. He *needed* to stop, and since his mind didn't consider it an option, his body finally had to assert itself.

His vision blurred, and the tank stretched before him, seeming far away. At the same time, everything seemed to be traveling upward. The air around his face, the water, every molecule in his body.

Then, the light went out of the world.

Chapter 21

Foul-tasting water gushed from his mouth, spilling down his cheeks and neck. Something pumped his chest rhythmically.

"Come on," a coarse voice growled.

Po opened his eyes. A scaled face peered down at him, its almond eyes narrowed, its thin nostrils flaring. The thing was on *top* of him, violently pushing against his chest with clawed hands. Spines protruded from its head, and they waved with each shove.

Terror gave Po new strength, and he pushed the alien away, screaming and managing to get his feet under him long enough to stumble back into the wall of the tank before he lost his balance and came crashing down on his rear.

"Snap out of it," Sergeant Shenton said. "Do that again and I'll come up with something worse than wading through that swamp."

Somehow, the DI had replaced the Emplor in the dim light. There'd been no discernible transition—one second there'd been an alien, the next, Shenton.

"Sorry, sir," Po wheezed, coughing. More water spilled down his chin when he did.

"Keep coughing like that. I'll give you twenty minutes to get up the rest of the water, then it's back in the pool."

"Sir, twenty minutes?"

"You heard me. Did you think it was the first time someone fainted down here? Get yourself together, then get back in."

***

It seemed Shenton had some shred of mercy in him after all. Even though he made Po get back in the wastewater, he didn't yell at him for how slow he went, nudging himself forward through the algae with trembling arms and legs.

That night Po fell into a dead sleep within seconds of crawling into his rack. His rest was dreamless...until it wasn't.

He stood wearing his combat utilities, in an endless sea of light-colored grass that towered over his head. On the horizon, mountains reared from the earth, and in the opposite direction a forest darkened the land like a tumor spreading across skin. Above, the sky yawned, an unfathomable blue chasm that made his heart pound in his chest. He sat on the ground, which shrunk the sky somewhat—the grass blocked out more of it. That made him feel a little better. He tried not to look directly at that endless blue.

Not a breath of air disturbed the grass around him. Then, something rustled in the flora just a few meters away, and he leapt to his feet.

"Hey! Who's there?"

No answer.

Am I dreaming? If he was, it was a more vivid dream than he ever remembered having. He might as well be back on Cycler 3, or Psyche—everything seemed just as detailed and immediate as it did when he was awake. And he couldn't remember ever asking himself whether he was dreaming before, not once in his life.

The sound of more rustling reached him, this time from the opposite direction. Po decided to go on the offensive. He charged toward the noise, hoping to catch whoever it was—or whatever it was—unawares.

But he found nothing. Instead, something found *him*.

Spindly fingers closed around the back of his neck. His feet left the grass, and whatever gripped him slammed him face-first into the spongy ground. A foot landed on his back, holding him firmly in place. A foot that pierced his clothes with what could only be claws.

"Stop struggling," a sibilant voice said into his ear, accompanied by breath both hot and moist. "It only gets worse the more you struggle."

"I'll kill you!" Po yelled, pushing up against his assailant, which resulted in its nails lodging in his back. He resisted the urge to cry out in pain.

"You will not. Such a thing is beyond you."

That was hard to argue. Even getting up seemed beyond Po. He decided to lie still and wait for an opportunity to counterattack. "What do you want?"

"To help you," the alien answered. Its tone sounded no less menacing than before, but maybe that was just how it talked.

"This is your idea of help?"

"This is my idea of making you to listen to me, Po Abbato."

"How do you know my name?"

The creature seemed to ignore the question. "You've been making a mess of things for some time. Because of your blindness, your sister has been left without your aid. And now just look at the disaster you've made of things in bootcamp."

"I'm working on it."

"You certainly are. Have you considered that perhaps you should *stop* working on it?"

Po sniffed. "Why don't you let me up so we can talk face to face?"

"Because you would immediately take advantage of your newly granted freedom of movement to attack me."

He didn't deny it—as it happened, the thing was right. "What did you mean, my blindness? I'm not blind."

"You might as well be. You miss much. Back on Psyche, you might have turned things to your advantage, but you missed your opportunity. Here again, there is much that you miss, which if you saw, you could leverage for your elevation."

"What does that mean?"

"Never mind. Further information will be fruitless to you until you've had time to grapple with what I've already fed you. Such is the way with your kind."

"What's that supposed to—"

The dream collapsed.

"—mean," he said to the bottom of the bunk above his. The subsurface barracks was completely dark, and thankfully, no one around him stirred, even though he'd spoken pretty loudly.

Had that been a dream? The transition from it to wakefulness had felt strangely abrupt, and he remembered every detail just as clearly as he remembered wading through the cesspool a few hours ago. More clearly, maybe.

Other than a vague shape in his peripheral vision, he hadn't laid eyes on whoever or whatever had pinned him to the ground. Even so, it seemed likely it was the same creature he'd woken to half-drowned and spewing putrid liquid after being fished out of the wastewater. The same one that had charged at him that night on exterior fire watch.

In other words, an Emplor was paying him visits.

But why? The possibility remained that he was as crazy as Sergeants Mitchell and Scott seemed to think. They'd also told him that his implant would alert them to anything unusual. This seemed to fit the bill. So, either he *was* crazy, or the alien had a way to access his implant without the DIs knowing.

There was a third possibility: he was sane, and the Emplor's appearances had nothing to do with his implant. But that was too disturbing for him to consider for long, and anyway, if it was true, then there was no chance of ever ridding himself of the visions.

Do I want to get rid of them?

The Emplor had claimed to want to help him. So far, its visits had brought nothing but trouble. But Po was desperate, and the idea of having a member of an advanced alien species secretly on his side *did* hold a certain appeal.

The thing is going to have to do better than it has been, if it's actually going to help.

One thing seemed for sure: if the DIs didn't already know about the Emplor's interference, bringing it up to them again that he was seeing aliens would probably only make them think he was crazier than they already did. And it could end up being the thing that pushed them to discharge him.

So he would keep it to himself. And he would wait.

***

Somehow Po managed to get through the third day of Motivation Camp without further incident, unless he counted becoming more exhausted than he'd ever been in his life.

Returning to his regular barracks, rejoining 50509—it felt a lot better than he expected. The DIs really had done him a favor by making him spend three days in the high-gravity hole they called Motivation Camp. It had been the worst thing he'd experienced since arriving on Cycler 3 by far, including getting jumped by Paisley, Becker, and Harris on fire watch, or having an alien charge across a field at him. It was even worse than the humiliation he'd faced in the boxing ring when he'd challenged Freddie. Compared to wading through that slimy, windowless tank for three days straight, pretty much everything else seemed like a joke.

Best of all, it had accomplished its stated purpose. It *had* motivated Po—not just to get through bootcamp so he could finally become a Marine, but even moreso to avoid ever having to go back to Motivation Camp.

But that hadn't been the reason Mitchell gave for sending him there. He'd done it to try to make the others hate Po less, so they wouldn't do something stupid and get themselves discharged. Like Paisley almost had.

As for that, things *did* seem different between Po and his platoonmates. He wouldn't say they liked him now or anything. Far from it. Mostly, they still refused to talk to him.

But the quality of what interactions he did have with them had changed. For the better, it seemed.

This is where it all turns around, isn't it? Sure, bootcamp would still be grueling. It was *bootcamp*, after all. But the DIs were clearly on his side now, and apparently they'd even managed to make him less hated. All he had to do was regular bootcamp stuff, and try not to mess up too much. Suffer through the PT when someone inevitably did mess up. Then he'd finally be a Marine.

Of course, Doyle had never showed any sign of 'being on his side.' But maybe Mitchell and Scott had talked to him while Po was down in Motivation Camp, and now they'd all be pulling for him.

It turned out he was right. The DIs *were* on his side. Just not in the way he'd expected.

His first full day back, the platoon was attending yet another class on rifle maintenance taught by Sergeant Scott when both Zhang and Dempsey—who were sitting next to each other—*both* managed to fall asleep. Po hadn't been looking in their direction when it happened, but he had to assume it happened simultaneously, since how else could it happen?

Scott was barely done whacking them both on the backs of their heads with his campaign cover when Harris dropped his rifle onto the tile floor with a loud clatter. That drew a dark look from the sergeant, like a cloud-filled horizon in the minutes before a lightning storm.

"Harris, out in the hall and give me fifty."

"Yes, sir!" Harris carefully replaced his rifle on the table in front of him, then double-timed it out of the classroom. He'd know better than to slack off with the push-ups, since his implant would give Scott a detailed report on his form as well as the number he did. Doing *more* than ordered didn't get you anywhere, though—it only earned you extra IT, accompanied by DI mockery for being an overachiever.

Ten minutes passed without incident...until two recruits decided it would be a brilliant idea to start whispering to each other in the back of the class, maybe thinking Scott wouldn't hear. One of them was Crotty, and Po couldn't remember the other's name.

Sergeant Scott stopped talking, glowering at the two chatterers from the front of the room. It took a painfully long time for them to realize the class had stopped, and by the time they were wilting under the glare they'd finally noticed, it was far, far too late.

"All right," Scott snapped. "Everyone form up outside."

It wasn't hard to tell they were in for the IT session of their lives. All the same, Po felt almost cheerful as he marched with the rest of the platoon down the asphalt path, their footfalls still an unsynchronized patter, even after weeks of drill.

Nothing Scott could do to them would possibly compare to the three days he'd just spent wading through an algae-infested tank that smelled like one of his mother's lasagnas left in for too long. Besides, it wasn't Po that had brought this on—it was Zhang, Dempsey, Harris, Crotty, and whoever that other recruit was. The focus was on *them,* not Po. Which only supported his theory that the DIs were working with him, now.

At least, it didn't contradict the theory.

Scott brought them to the sandy stretch next to the artificial river that bisected Cycler 3's surface and immediately got them doing burpees. It wasn't long before the entire platoon was breathing heavily, and sweat popped out on Po's forehead soon after that. Whoever was in charge of the cylinder's weather had made today a hot one, and soon even he found himself resenting the recruits who'd caused this.

An intrepid pigeon landed near the right side of the platoon while they were doing jumping jacks, and for whatever reason Harris charged at it in an attempt to kick it.

"Halt!" Scott barked.

Everyone stopped.

"Recruit Harris. Why did you try to kick that pigeon?"

"Because I didn't want it coming near me, sir!"

"The respect you just showed that pigeon reminds me of the respect you showed for your rifle—and the respect your fellow recruits showed for my class." Scott paused a moment, and Po could almost hear the wheels turning in his head. "Harris, you will chase that pigeon wherever it goes, saluting it and giving it the greeting of the day. If you lose track of it, you will find another pigeon and start saluting *it* and giving *it* the greeting of the day. In case you're wondering, the pigeon is a staff sergeant and should be addressed as such. Do I make myself clear?"

"Yes, sir!"

"Start chasing that pigeon, Recruit Harris!"

And so, while the rest of the platoon struggled to maintain proper form while doing push-ups in the shifting sand, Harris ran around the field nearby, saluting the pigeon wherever it landed, and shouting, "Good morning, Staff Sergeant! Good morning, Staff Sergeant!"

A laugh escaped Po's lips—he couldn't help it.

"Who laughed?"

He clamped his mouth shut and focused on making his next push-up the best one he'd ever done in his life.

"*Who laughed?*" Scott said again. He walked around to the side of the platoon. Where Po was. "It wasn't you, wasn't it Recruit Abbato?"

"Yes, sir!"

"Everyone stop doing push-ups and stand up."

Everyone complied.

"Turn to face Recruit Abbato."

They did.

"Recruit Abbato, let's see you do twenty perfect push-ups."

Po got down in the sand and did his level best.

"Your form is awful, Abbato!"

"Sir, it's difficult to do a good push-up in sand, sir!"

"Are you giving me excuses now?"

"No, sir!"

"You *are* giving me excuses!"

"Yes, sir!"

"Abbato, come with me."

Po did. He followed Sergeant Scott to a long, rectangular fountain that presumably drew its water from the artificial river nearby. Surrounding the fountain was a wide band of gravel.

"Do you know the crab walk, Recruit Abbato?"

"No, sir!"

Scott cupped his hands around his mouth. "Do any of you know the crab walk?"

After a few seconds, Navarro raised a hand hesitantly into the air.

"Come over and show Abbato how to do it, Navarro. Come on, now. Don't be shy."

Po watched as Navarro bent over backwards and 'walked' using his hands and feet across the ground, like a crab. His chest faced up toward the terrain on the opposite side of the cylinder, and he led with his feet.

"Do you think you can do that, Recruit Abbato?" Scott asked.

"Yes, sir!"

"Good. Then do it on the gravel next to that fountain. When you reach the end of the gravel, reverse direction. Do it until I tell you to stop."

And so, as the rest of the platoon did PT on the sandbar, Po crab walked back and forth along the gravel, wondering when Scott would call for him to stop. At first, the awkwardness of walking this way was the worst part, though it did give him a rare opportunity to study the other side of Cycler 3, and watch people over there going about their daily business. Soon, the ache in his shoulders, thighs, and stomach became the worst part. But after a while, the pain in his bare hands from constant contact with the gravel took over as his least favorite part of this particular experience. At first they burned, then they grew hot like the sun. Then they started to bleed.

Sergeant Scott left him crab walking along the gravel for a long time. This had now become the platoon's longest IT session—he was sure of that, even accounting for how the crab walking on rocks made it feel much longer. Po watched noon come and go, created by the slowly rotating mirrors on both ends of the cylinder. Still, the session continued.

"All right, Recruit Abbato," Scott said after what had to be at least three hours, maybe four. "I think it might be time to—"

"Hey!" Sergeant Doyle called, jogging toward them from the direction of the barracks, his short legs pumping. "Me! I'm here! Pick me!"

Scott grinned. "Actually, it looks like Sergeant Doyle might have something for you."

"Recruit Abbato," Doyle said as he pulled up beside them, barely winded. "Do you know the bear walk?"

Chapter 22

Po's palms were on fire as he marched back to the barracks, and the air felt like gasoline for that fire as he swung his arms back and forth. His hands were shredded, with strings of flesh dangling from them. The flesh-strings snapped back and forth as he marched, and tears filled his eyes, even though he wasn't actually crying.

He'd been an idiot. Because Sergeant Mitchell had acted to try to prevent his discharge from bootcamp, he'd assumed the DIs were on his side—and actually, they probably *were.*

But he'd forgotten what the principle was behind Mitchell's strategy for keeping him from washing out. The reason the sergeant sent him to Motivation Camp to begin with. The principle was to go so hard on him that his fellow recruits' hatred became pity. And Scott had advanced that strategy today.

The brutal smoke session had taken them past lunch, and after they changed into their utilities, Doyle brought them to chow hall for supper. The portions were what they normally were, and everyone ate in silence, focused on wolfing down what they'd been given as quickly as possible. No one seemed to want to risk running out of time before they finished everything on their plate.

For his part, Po made the mistake of putting salt on his fries, and when he snatched up a few, some of the granules stuck in his ripped flesh. He wanted to scream with how badly it stung, and the reaction surprised him, given what he'd already gone through this week. Either way, he powered through the pain in silence, picking up his fork to avoid making the same mistake again.

During downtime back at the barracks, he forced himself to run cold water over his palms for several long minutes each. His mangled flesh was already going to make things difficult enough, the last thing he needed was to get an infection.

He decided to use the rest of the time before lights-out to finally write his sister back. Thankfully, he was able to rest his tattered hands while he used his implant to mentally compose the note.

Nicky,

Sorry I haven't written you till now. Bootcamp has been just so busy, but I've been learning a lot. I spent the last few days getting acquainted with the wastewater management system for one of the cycler's hydroponic food production facilities. Today, we had a class on maintaining our rifles, and after that we worked out as a platoon by the artificial river that runs through the middle of the cycler.

I wish you could see Cycler 3, Nicky. It's completely huge, and has real clouds, with plants that float in the sky. There are birds here that fly free, and squirrels that are trained to pick up the trash, and these enormous trees that grow sideways out of one of the endcaps. There are even bears, but don't worry, they get shocked bad whenever they try to come into one of the bases. When you look up, you can see little ant-sized people walking around upside-down on the other side of the cylinder's surface.

You wouldn't like the bootcamp part, but the cycler itself is really something.

I love you Nicky, and I miss you. Please take all your meds at the right times. Tell Marco I miss him too, and tell Rosa. Tell her I really mean it.

As for the letter Lorenzo sent my DIs, tell him he's gonna have to try harder than that.

Po

Reading back over what he'd written, he nodded to himself. It was all true; he hadn't lied. He'd just left out a few parts.

He uploaded the letter to Platoon 50509 Outgoing Mail, just in time for lights-out. That was good timing—the DIs would have known if he tried using his implant in the dark.

***

"That's another reason the Corps insists on offering religious services, despite how much GEA hates it."

"Huh?" Po had just finished telling the chaplain about the week he'd had—the three days of Motivation Camp, followed by hours of crab- and bear-walking, then days of his palms smarting whenever he tried to grip something. He'd left out the part about an Emplor body-slamming him by the back of the neck in his dreams.

"Faith helps people get through things like that. Tough times."

"There was a kid crying in Mass today." *I wonder what his week was like.* He'd been sitting in the same pew as Po, and seemed to be trying to hide it, but Po saw him wiping his eyes with his sleeve.

"How'd you find the Mass, by the way? Did you use a missal?"

"Yeah. It was still hard to follow."

"Well, stick with it. You'll have the hang of it by the time you're a Marine."

Po shrugged. He was still only here to get a break from the platoon, and the DIs. *And that's it—I don't* want *to get any more involved than that. If I'm not careful, I'll be the next one sniveling in a pew.* "I'll keep coming, anyway."

"To get out of the barracks, right?"

"Right."

The chaplain gave a knowing smile, but changed the subject. "You suffered a lot this week."

"I guess so, yeah."

"Do you think you suffered well?"

"What does that mean?"

"Did you accept it, or did you make it worse by letting resentment fill you?"

Po shook his head. "It is what it is. No use complaining—no one would listen, anyway. And getting upset about it wouldn't do much good either. Down in the cesspool, it was just one foot in front of the other. I couldn't afford to let myself think too much, except maybe about the reason I needed to get through it."

"Which was?"

"To become a Marine. To stay out of simjail, and make some money to send home to my sister."

"Your sister needs money."

"She's sick."

The chaplain nodded. "I'm sorry, Po. Each time we suffer, it's a cross we must try to bear well. Just like Christ carried His cross to Calvary, where He suffered so much for us, we're called to suffer too—with Him, and for our neighbors."

Po didn't answer.

"You know who else is trying to teach you how to suffer for the people around you?"

"Who?"

"What do you think it means to be a Marine, Po?"

"Honor, courage, commitment." He was just rattling off what one of the DIs had taught in one of his classes. It felt like kind of a flippant answer, but he felt like he should say something, and that's what he'd been taught. "Those are the Core Values. Right?"

"They are. Except, those aren't really *values.* The word 'values' was never used like that until a certain nineteenth century philosopher came along, who thought morality could be boiled down to whatever each person thought was best at any given moment. Think about the phrase, 'do our *values* align.' The very concept of values *aligning* implies that right and wrong is just a matter of interpretation. 'Values' are fuzzy and soft. They change with the wind."

"What are they, then, if not values? Honor, courage, commitment?"

"Those are *virtues,* Po. If you want values, go to Earth, where you can change your 'truth' like you change your socks, every day until the day you die. But out here in the black—especially in the Marines—we still depend on virtues. Eternal goods that we can rely on. *Courage* is actually a necessary condition for every virtue, since consistently doing the right thing takes courage. Staying true to your principles, despite opposition from the world, takes courage. And doing that is what *commitment* means. To pay *honor* to someone is to recognize their worth. These things don't change. They're as true now as they were two thousand years ago."

Po fell silent for a few seconds. "I don't really get it."

This was the part where any teacher from his school days would have rolled their eyes, or exhaled loudly. But the chaplain didn't even blink. "Tell me something. When you become a Marine, and you're out in the middle of a Nibiran jungle with insurgents all around you, who would you rather have at your side? Someone who'd lay down their life for you, without hesitation, or someone who's only in it for himself?"

Po licked his lips, then inhaled long and slow.

The chaplain nodded slowly, as if he'd said something. "Hopefully you're starting to understand why the Marines had something to say when GEA tried to take religion out of the Corps."

***

The gauntlet of bootcamp dragged on, with the DIs continuing their campaign to win sympathy for Po by grinding him into the dust. They seemed to do it with relish—especially Sergeant Doyle. But that didn't really matter. The effect was the same. He was sorer than he needed to be, and more exhausted. And he wondered if he was going to make it.

Think of Nicky, he told himself. *Remember how much she needs this.*

On the hardest days, the thought of his sister was the only thing that kept him going.

At least the constant pranks had stopped. He hadn't been the victim of a single one since he'd returned from Motivation Camp. The DIs really were doing a great job of making his life an unending misery, and apparently the other recruits weren't sadistic enough to add more abuse on top of that.

The day was overcast and misty when the DIs marched them almost to the easternmost end of the base, to what Sergeant Mitchell called the Confidence Course. It was essentially an obstacle course whose challenges were arranged in a straight line—*following* the curve of the cylinder, naturally, meaning they'd also be moving uphill as they progressed through it.

The cloud cover was thicker than usual today, thick enough to obscure the morning sunlight filtering in through the cylinder's eastern endcap. Careful to move only his eyes and not his head, Po saw that most of the buildings suspended from the central axis cable were obscured, though a few poked out here and there. Some of the floating plants—skyweed?—also made brief appearances as their slow orbits brought them into view.

Dew covered everything, and whenever sunlight did make it through a break in the clouds, the entire cylinder glistened like a sea of diamonds.

"Today, you get to find out what you're really made of," Sergeant Mitchell told them, standing on the eastern edge of the course's beginning with his hands on his hips. "Sergeants Doyle and Scott and I already know what you're made of—dog meat. Now you'll all have the opportunity to discover the very same thing. You will move through each obstacle as fast as you can, do we understand?"

"Yes, sir!" the platoon shouted back in rough unison.

"The first event is a medium roll-over log, which you will grab in a bear hug and climb over. Do we understand?"

"Yes, sir!"

Even as the recruits were answering, Scott and Doyle ran at the first obstacle. Po watched Doyle's stubby legs pumping, and he wondered if the others were as skeptical as he was about the little man making it over. But he didn't dare look at their faces to see.

Doyle flew from the ground in a mighty leap, grabbing the hurdle's thick wooden pole in midair, his centrifugal force carrying him around it and onto the ground on the other side.

His success surprised Po, but the diminutive DI had had a running start. *There's no way he makes the next one.*

"The second event is the up and over bar," Mitchell yelled. "It is eight feet in the air. You will jump up and grab it and then either kip over like a gymnast or do a chin-up to get yourself up there. Then you'll hook an armpit over the bar like a chicken wing, get one leg over, and kick with your free leg to roll over the bar and onto the other side. Do we understand?"

"Yes, sir!"

"Observe."

It didn't seem possible: Sergeant Doyle launched himself at the bar like a monkey at a branch. He did the gymnast thing and landed gracefully on the other side.

"Marine Corps!" Doyle yelled.

Po didn't know what method Sergeant Scott used to get over, just that he did, also shouting "Marine Corps" as he landed. He'd been too fixated on watching Doyle, as he was sure every other recruit was too.

Sergeant Mitchell gave running commentary while the other two sergeants demonstrated each obstacle for the platoon, making it all look effortless, easy.

All too soon, it was their turn. The DIs had them form two lines, since each obstacle was wide enough to accommodate two recruits at once. There only being room for two also gave the DIs easy access to call them out from the sidelines.

"That's enough, Recruit Crotty," Sergeant Doyle barked gleefully after Crotty spent twenty seconds or more struggling to get over the high bar. "You fail this event. Move on."

That's gotta be embarrassing, being told you failed the high bar by the same leprechaun who flew over it a few seconds ago.

"May this recruit have one more try, sir?" Crotty said.

"What did I just say?"

"Aye, sir."

"What did I just say?"

"Aye, sir."

"Go!"

"Aye, sir!" Crotty rushed to the next obstacle.

Po ended up behind poor Dempsey, who looked like he was going to fail the medium roll-over log—the very first obstacle. But by what seemed like a miracle, he managed to wrench himself over and plop off the other side like a slug falling from someone's shoe.

Then he surprised Po by actually making the jump to grab the high bar. He started to pull himself up.

Go, Demps!

While Dempsey was fighting against gravity, Po leapt at the roll-over log, grasping it with both arms and hugging it, tumbling over without much trouble. Once he'd regained his feet, he looked up and saw Dempsey trembling with effort.

"You almost got it, Demps," he found himself calling up. "Do the chicken wing!"

"Shut up, Po."

After another second of effort, Dempsey lost his grip and fell to the ground. He turned around and glared.

"You almost had it," Po said.

"I said shut *up*."

Po nodded down the line. "Scott's coming this way. He's gonna tell you you failed this one. Give it one more try before he gets here."

Dempsey pursed his lips, turned around, and leapt for the bar.

"You got this, Demps!" Po clapped his hands. "Get it done!"

He wasn't sure why he was cheering, or bothering to encourage the old wolverine at all. *Well, a bald wolverine, now.* Dempsey had told him to shut up, and in the past that would have bothered Po. But ever since Motivation Camp, he didn't care as much about stuff like that. He'd had it in him to cheer Dempsey on, for some reason, so he'd done it. And he kept doing it.

To his surprise, Scott didn't stop him. And when Dempsey managed to hook his armpit around the bar, then a leg, and swing himself over, the sergeant didn't tell Po to quieten down as he congratulated Dempsey loudly.

The DIs never told us we couldn't *encourage each other. But none of us ever bothered to try.* Sergeant Scott even nodded at him as he passed by.

"Demps," he whispered as Scott passed out of earshot, "you didn't say 'Marine Corps.'"

"Marine Corps," Dempsey said, a little weakly.

Po leapt at the high bar, grabbed it, and pulled himself up. He knew better than to try kipping over, but he managed to get the thing under his armpit pretty easily. Hooking his opposite leg around it, he used his free leg to swing himself over.

A shock went up his right ankle as he landed. "Marine Corps," he said through gritted teeth, stuffing the pain into whatever deep-down hole he'd been shoving every experience into since he got to Cycler 3. There was no time to process anything here—it was just ignore, move on, think about it later. Preferably a long time later. Failure was not an option, not for Po, and not for most of the recruits here.

The next event was a low jump, and Po couldn't see it defeating anyone, not even Dempsey. Indeed, the old guy was already scrambling over it as Po regained his bearing after clearing the high bar.

Po joined him on the other side. Dempsey was standing with his hands dangling, just staring at the next obstacle. It was a combination event, with a high bar followed by a part where you had to hold yourself up with your legs balanced on two long, parallel bars, as you propelled yourself along them with your arms. The obstacle finished with a high roll-over log.

"There's no way," Dempsey muttered.

"Yes way," Po said, feeling pretty cheesy even as he said it.

"Po, I'm seizing up just looking at that thing. I'll fall through those bars and break my neck. If I even make it up there."

"So, you're afraid? Good. There's a lot worse threats than this waiting for us when we become Marines. And you'll have to face 'em all down, one by one, just like you're gonna face this one down."

Dempsey turned to glare at him again. "I wouldn't even be here if it wasn't for you, Po."

"I know. It makes you angry, right? That's your fuel, Demps. Use it, and crush that thing!"

His jaw set, Dempsey let loose a roar, launching himself at the high bar and pulling himself up to it in one fluid motion, swinging his legs onto the parallel bars. With that, he shimmied down them like a madman, the tendons standing out on his skinny wrists as he pushed himself along.

Dempsey failed the high roll-over log, losing his grip and falling backward, cracking his head pretty badly on one of the metal bars on his way down. Po winced, and he made sure one of the DIs was going over to check on him before he attempted the obstacle himself.

He cleared the high bar, propelled himself down the poles, and cleared the high roll over bar Dempsey had fallen from. The low jump that came after that gave him no trouble, but he was foiled by the log wall. The start of the Confidence Course had sapped the strength from his arms, and he was feeling shaky. After a couple attempts, Sergeant Mitchell came along and told him to move on.

I failed before even getting halfway through the course. Everything else he cleared okay—except the double pull over bar, and after that his performance on the rope climb was just dismal.

"Congratulations," Sergeant Mitchell said once everyone had attempted every event. "You survived the Confidence Course—though only one of you cleared every event. Good job, Recruit Paisley."

Paisley said nothing, just stood there looking smug. Dempsey was standing next to him, holding an ice pack to the back of his head—thankfully, he seemed fine, other than a little banged up.

"You'll get another shot at the Confidence Course toward the end of your training. In the meantime, you have *that* to look forward to." Mitchell pointed, and they all followed his finger to the eastern endcap, and the obstacle course built into it, all of it segmented by the waterfalls that tumbled in eight different directions.

"We call it the Swagger Course," the sergeant said. "You'll have your first encounter with it next week."

Chapter 23

The Conditioning Marches were getting longer. And actually, bootcamp in general seemed to be ramping up, even aside from the extra punishment the DIs were laying on Po.

Today they would march four miles, each recruit carrying his rifle and a backpack full of weights, to simulate carrying gear into a combat zone. They'd head for the western endcap, follow a trail that led into the woods, and then head back. Each DI walked with bear spray clipped to his belt, and Sergeant Scott toted a tranquilizer gun.

Po felt excited to be headed for the 'mountains'—or at least the closest he would get to hiking mountains while in an enclosed habitat like Cycler 3. As the marches grew longer over the next several weeks, they'd get to spend more time on the heights, following winding paths through the redwoods, under their dense canopy of interlocking branches and leaves.

Of course, having to trudge along with so much weight, on feet already covered in blisters...well, he tried to ignore that part and focus on the coming walk in the woods.

On his left, Crotty stumbled, and Harris caught him by his pack, pulling him upright again. "You're all right," Harris said. "You're all right."

"Thanks," Crotty muttered.

Po found himself stifling a grin. Since he'd offered Dempsey encouragement during the Confidence Course, more and more recruits had been doing the same thing for each other. As the practice caught on, it seemed to make things easier for everyone. Knowing you weren't just a solitary grunt trying to struggle through basic training, but that you were a member of a team, and that the others had your back—it helped, a lot.

The DIs kept quiet about it, and did nothing to discourage the recruits from helping each other out. Each recruit still had to accomplish most tasks himself, without any outside help. But urging each other on, or even giving advice—it was helping them become a cohesive unit, and the DIs didn't seem to have a problem with it.

In fact, Po was starting to suspect that this had been the point all along.

Dempsey had grudgingly thanked him, back in the barracks on the evening they'd attempted the Course. And this morning, at breakfast, Navarro had brought his tray over to where Po sat, to chat with him throughout the meal. He didn't seem to feel the need to justify anything to Paisley about it either, or to anyone else. Something had changed with the dynamics of the platoon.

Po was marching on the platoon's right side, at the very front, so he had one of the best views of the trees as they passed between the first thick trunks.

Then an alien appeared between him and the nearest tree, obscuring that view.

It was the Emplor, and he labored under a pack of his own, lumbering on his thick legs, tail dragging behind him through the leaf- and needle-strewn forest floor.

In his shock, Po almost lost his footing, which would have resulted in Zhang trampling over him from behind, and probably extra PT for everyone. But somehow, he managed to keep pace. Which was good. The last thing he needed was to sabotage himself again, just when everyone seemed to be warming up to him.

"I thought this the perfect time to appear to you again," the alien said, without bothering to look at Po. Instead, he kept pace, as though he was part of the formation—though he marched in a rank at the front, all his own. "Why, you ask? Well, it's because you can't answer back without looking insane, which I find vastly preferable to our last conversation."

They walked along in silence for several seconds, and Po focused his entire will on putting one foot in front of the other, without tripping over an errant root or becoming tangled up in his own feet. He could hear the rasp of the alien's tail as it dragged across the ground. He could see the trail it left. Why couldn't the others? That was agonizing, for some reason.

"I am Zanth," the Emplor said, "and I know you are Po Angelo Abbato. As I averred during our previous encounter, I'm here to help you, even though you're apparently too thick to grasp that. That's not totally surprising, given my experience thus far with your kind. You are ever so slow to grasp new realities. But you *will* get there—and I'll help you with that, too. I'll have to. Tedious, but there it is.

"To help you realize what an incredible boon our connection truly is, I'll provide you with some information that should prove useful, if you're keen enough to use it. To start with, you're drawing far too much attention to yourself, with this new stance of egging your fellow recruits on whenever they misstep. You may feel noble and selfless in doing so, and you may sense that it's helping the others to finally begin to harbor some vestige of positive sentiment toward you. Both may even be true. But resentment toward you is also growing. Murderous resentment, which could lead to your death."

Po furrowed his brow, the corners of his lips stretching sideways.

The Emplor still wasn't looking at him, but he seemed to sense his skepticism. "I know you don't believe me, Po. Of course you don't. That would be too sensible. You think I'm being dramatic. Well, I suppose you'll have to *experience* something dramatic in order to fully appreciate the situation you're in. And I do hope you survive the incident. It would be a pity if you died despite my forewarning you, not to mention embarrassing.

"In the meantime, I'll leave you with this final tidbit to ponder: an Obsidian Angel has followed you here, from Psyche. And before you get excited, no, he's not here *exclusively* for you. But monitoring you, and if possible neutralizing you, are both counted among his objectives. You have managed to draw the wrong sort of attention, Po, and if our Angel can take you out without too much fuss, he will. So be on guard, if indeed you possess the capacity to take any heed of my words at all."

With that, Zanth plunged into the woods, never once glancing at Po. He disappeared around an especially thick redwood, and was gone.

Po could only march on, left to contemplate the alien's words in silence.

***

During the next few days, Zanth's words replayed in Po's mind whenever he had a spare second—which wasn't often.

He needed to concentrate on everything he did. He'd flubbed too many things during his first weeks here, and earned the platoon too much extra PT. He wasn't about to sabotage his new standing by messing up again now.

Zhang was still far and away the platoon leader in earning everyone IT, which took the heat off Po even more. As for him, the DIs seemed to be easing up with their campaign of terror against him. They could probably see just as well as he could that the others were coming around, so subjecting him to extra punishment was becoming less necessary.

Not that the DIs stopped altogether, of course. Far from it. He was in bootcamp, after all.

In his quieter moments—during barracks downtime, or the meals when Navarro didn't sit with him—he thought about what Zanth had said.

Why didn't he tell me who the Angel is? Is this a test? Am I being tested by an Emplor?

Assuming he wasn't crazy after all, and simply hallucinating his encounters with Zanth, the idea that any member of an advanced alien species would take an interest in *him* seemed absurd. He was just another schmuck who'd been arrested and sent to bootcamp, a casualty of GEA's badly concealed ramp-up to make war on the Nibirans, or at least on Janus. Po was little more than a number, and if he died, he'd become a statistic.

But if Zanth was both real and telling the truth, then who was the secret Obsidian Angel? Paisley? Freddie? Becker?

What about Navarro? he asked himself as he chewed a spinach salad during lunch one afternoon. Navarro *was* unusual, Po had to admit. He was still the only one to be friendly toward Po. That made him much kinder, and less fearful then the others. Except, when was the last time anyone outside Po's family had ever shown him kindness, without some ulterior motive?

And the fact he seemed less afraid could be explained by belonging to a meshmind. A meshmind didn't care if it lost a digit or two. It could always recruit more, and an organization as powerful as the Angels could also promise, with some credibility, that if one of its members got into trouble, other Angels would be sent to extract him. That was part of how it convinced new members to join, or so Po had heard.

His story's almost too perfect. Isn't it? A good-hearted resident of Psyche, joining up with the Marines, risking his life, all for his dearly beloved girlfriend-now-wife.

But no one questioned it. And it made Navarro the last person anyone would suspect of being a meshminder.

"Hey."

Po looked up, and his skin crawled as his eyes met Navarro's. The other recruit put his tray on the table and dropped onto the bench across from Po, apparently oblivious to his discomfort.

Po looked from Navarro to the table where he normally sat—Paisley's table. "You're over here now?"

Navarro shrugged. "Paisley's annoying today."

"I see."

"How's your salad?"

"Dry."

The other recruit crunched into a bun with his teeth. "So is this."

"What was your wife's name, again?"

"Candace."

"What does her dad do?"

"Her *dad?* Why do you ask that?"

"Why'd you ask how my salad was?"

"To make conversation!"

"Well, that's why I'm asking about her dad."

"He works in a subsurface nickel mine. Any other questions?"

"What's his name?"

"Phil. What's this about, Abbato? Why are you being weird?"

"Just making conversation. Navarro."

Navarro furrowed his brow, then set about finishing his meal in silence. As he did, Po scrutinized him across the table.

Cycler 3 was essentially a giant Faraday cage, impervious to all but the signals Admin decided it wanted to let in. That meant if Navarro was an Angel, he'd be cut off from the rest of his meshmind.

Unless, of course, there were other Obsidian Angels here. Po had heard rumors they'd infiltrated the government, so why not the Marines too? If that were true, then Navarro and his fellow Angels aboard Cycler 3 would form their own little offshoot. Their implants would probably be secretly loaded with protocols and directives from the greater meshmind, but other than that there'd be a risk of deviation.

Maybe I can use that.

"When did you first have your implant installed?" he asked Navarro.

"When I was a kid."

"Did they swap it out for a military Circuit at MIPS?"

"No," Navarro answered slowly. "My old one met their spec requirements."

"I see."

Navarro rolled his eyes. "*Everyone* is annoying today." With that, he picked up his tray and moved to another platoon's table, where he sat in silence and finished his meal.

***

Po,

Wow, you're having such amazing experiences!

I'm so glad. It's weird without you here, you know. It feels wrong. I keep forgetting that I can't just go to the Docks to find you, or knock on your bedroom door. That you're as far away as you are. A few times, I thought I heard your voice coming from the kitchen...and one time, I actually did. Mom was playing a video of your birthday from a couple years back. Going out there and only finding her standing by the counter, holding her cPad and crying...it made me cry, too. It was silly to think I'd find you out there, even if I only thought it for a second. But when you weren't there, that really got to me. Stupid, I know.

At least you're learning as much as you are. I really am glad for that. And who knows, maybe with everything you're learning, you'll figure out how to get rich, and then you'll be able to come back.

Marco saw Lorenzo in the market, hanging out with some strange people. Mom's worried about what's going on with him. He doesn't tell her everything like he used to, not anymore...they aren't as close as they were before you left. It seems like she's trying everything she can to get back what they had. She's even financing taps for him. But I don't think it's going to make him treat her any nicer.

The doctors are trying me on a new med, but I've only been taking it for a week and I've already had two seizures. My next appointment isn't for a couple more weeks. I'm not sure what to do. I could stop taking it, but then I'm afraid my old symptoms will come back, and that'll be worse than the seizures. Even though the seizures are pretty scary.

There's another med they could try me on, except it's way too expensive. Apparently it causes fewer side effects. But we won't be able to afford it any time soon.

Be extra nice to Freddie Rodriguez. He's in the same platoon as you, right? His dad just died.

I have to go study for a test tomorrow. Stay safe, Po. For me, okay? I worry about you. Try to go the whole week without doing anything crazy. And then don't do anything crazy next week either, and the next, and then the one after that.

Love you.

Nicky

Po looked up from the letter from where he sat atop his rack, and it took an effort of will not to ball it up in his hands. He partly wanted to do it out of fear, and partly out of anger.

So Rosa is buying taps for that creep while Nicky has seizures. It was exactly as he feared. Without him there to keep an eye on her, Rosa was falling back on her old habits: clinging to Lorenzo by any means necessary.

Po could understand her desire to do that, to some extent. She'd always been totally dependent on his father, even as horrible as he was, and with him in jail she'd turned to the next oldest available male for support. Now that Po was gone, she'd become even more dependent on Lorenzo

But he couldn't accept it being done at Nicky's expense. That was *so* wrong, and there was nothing he could do about it, not until he became a Marine, with a Marine's pay. Even then, he'd have to figure out how to somehow make sure the crypto he sent got properly spent, from millions of miles away.

It made him want to tip his bunk over, even with Harris lying on the bottom rack. Maybe *especially* with him in it.

And Rosa's negligence wasn't all that Nicky's letter had given him to think about. There was also the mention of Diego Rodriguez's death. That was what had given Po the lump of ice that now sat in the pit of his stomach.

How did he die? That was the question burning a hole through his mind, like a lit cigarette pushed through a pile of ice shavings.

He and Freddie had used his father's security access to get inside that Equipoise warehouse, where they'd run headlong into four Obsidian Angels. If the Angels had traced their ability to be there back to Diego Rodriguez....

Po needed to know how he died. But a tiny voice piped up from the back of his mind, the one he'd tried so many times to silence for good:

Even if he died from natural causes, there'll always be a part of you that wonders if the Angels are the ones who really killed him.

His gaze drifted down the barracks, toward Freddie's rack, where he leaned against it, chatting casually with Paisley and Becker. He didn't seem very upset. Surely he'd heard about his father's death before Po had. But then, everyone processed grief differently. And Freddie might not want to appear weak in front of the others. Even if it was because his dad had died.

I should talk to him. Tell him I'm sorry about his dad. Or, I could wait till he's alone, and then say something.

It was obviously the right thing to do, Po knew. But he also knew he wasn't going to do it. A wave of self-loathing crashed over him at the realization, but even that didn't change his certainty that he wasn't going to offer a single word of consolation to Freddie about his father.

He pulled up his Circuit interface, and even his thoughts felt sluggish, weighed down with the shame of realizing that Freddie had been right all along. He really was a scumbag.

Nicky,

How did Diego Rodriguez die?

Po

He stared at it for a few seconds, wondering if he was really going to leave it at that. Then, he uploaded it to Outgoing, and opened a new document.

Rosa,

Cancel your order of taps for Lorenzo and order that new medication for Nicky or I swear to you, I'll figure out a way to return to Psyche. You may not believe that, but believe it, Rosa. I will dedicate every cell in my body to achieving it. And when I do achieve it, I'll carry out what I told you I'd do before I left. The son you're left with when I'm finished will not be the one you love.

Po

The voice was trying to say something as he uploaded that—possibly something about his thinly veiled threat on Lorenzo's life maybe not being the best idea, from the perspective of him graduating bootcamp.

Then, the words of his last sentence came back to him: *The son you're left with when I'm finished will not be the one you love.*

The way he'd phrased that...he'd completely forgotten about Marco. What if Rosa showed the letter to him? The idea of that broke his heart. The idea of Marco knowing that Po hadn't even been thinking of him.

Surely she won't do that. Not even she *would do that.* But still. He'd basically erased his little brother with what he'd written.

Maybe that was what the voice was trying to tell me. Except, the voice was quiet now, apparently choosing to remain silent the one time Po might not mind it talking.

Chapter 24

"You seem pensive."

He looked up at the chaplain. "Pensive? What does that mean?"

"Thoughtful."

Po thought about that. "Why do you think I seem pensive?"

"Because I just spoke to you twice and you didn't answer me."

Po shrugged, and returned to his study of the side of the chaplain's desk, an unbidden sigh escaping his lips. Words were knocking at the door of his mouth, clamoring to get out, but they were all out of order, and none of them seemed like the right ones.

He tried anyway. "Am I...?" He shook his head. "At what point do you become ...responsible...for someone's death, exactly?"

The chaplain blinked. "I'm not sure I'm following, Po."

"You know I'm a conscript, right? I'm here because it was this or jail."

Campbell's face didn't change. "Do you feel ready to make a confession?"

Po lowered his eyebrows. "No. I'm not here because I murdered someone, if that's what you're thinking."

"Can you explain your question, then?"

Another sigh. "I'm here because I broke into a corporate warehouse with the help of my friend, who used his dad's access to get us in there. And his dad just died."

"How did he die?"

"I don't know. But let's say he died from a heart attack. Could I have caused that?"

The chaplain frowned. "I'm still having trouble understanding. Was his son arrested? Is he in bootcamp too?"

"Yeah."

"So, you're worried the stress might have—"

"No, that's not what I'm talking about." Po tried his best to clamp down on the frustration welling up inside him, but he couldn't help feeling annoyed with Campbell.

"I'm going to need you to explain this more clearly."

"Okay, look, back on Psyche, I worked in the Docks, and the reason I broke into the warehouse was because I was sure one of the containers we unloaded held drugs. I figured out that one of the new guys was a gang member, and he rerouted the container to a different warehouse. The one I broke into. I wanted to get to the drugs before he could. To sell them."

"I see."

The words were coming all in a rush, now. "But members of the same gang found me and Freddie there. And this gang, they're really powerful. No one knows how far their reach is. Some people think they even have people placed in GEA. So what if they found out we used Freddie's dad's access to get into that warehouse? Wouldn't they want to do something about that, to avoid anything like it happening again, since it probably interfered with their operations?"

"It's possible," the chaplain said slowly.

"So, then, would I be responsible for that?"

"Well, when you talked your friend into breaking into the warehouse, and used his dad's access without his consent—I'm assuming you didn't have his permission?"

"No."

"When you did those things, and tried to steal from the gang—drugs, no less, with the intent to distribute them—those were all sins."

"Okay."

"Sin has consequences, Po. Not just for us, but for others. When we sin, it isn't just ourselves we're hurting."

Po's eyes widened, his annoyance burning hot through his veins, quickly becoming something else. "So you're saying I killed Diego Rodriguez."

"No, I'm saying that when we violate God's laws, we shouldn't be surprised when things happen that we didn't intend. Negative things, which hurt others. I know this is hard to hear, and again, I'm *not* saying you killed your friend's father. It's very possible his death had nothing to do with your actions. But this *is* part of why confession and penance are so important. Forgiveness is available to you for the sins you did commit, and as long as you're in this world, you can still make up for any negative effects of your sin."

The chaplain paused, as if waiting to see if Po had anything to say to that. When he didn't, Campbell continued. "Right now, you're undergoing Marine bootcamp, and you're doing lots of physical things, not without risk. Recruits sometimes get hurt. Some of them have died. You must know that."

"What's your point?"

"My point is that it's a very good time to get right with God. Because that's by far the greater risk, Po. If you died without reconciling with Him first."

The chaplain's little speech had only made Po's blood run hotter through his veins. All he could think about was being back in the locked ward where they kept his father, and seeing the black-robed priest lying there motionless on one of the visitor racks.

"What was that priest doing here?" he'd asked Luca Abbato.

Luca had hesitated. "Provisions are made for prisoners' religious—"

"What was he doing here?"

"He came to hear my confession."

"Why?"

"So...I could be forgiven."

All these weeks later, Po could still hear the faint note of hope his father's voice had carried as he spoke those words. Even now, it made his stomach roil, and he twisted his lips in disgust.

What Campbell was suggesting was that he buy in to the idea that someone like Luca Abbato could be forgiven. A wife- and a child-beater. An oppressor of the innocent. A tyrant.

Getting control of himself, Po rose to his feet and sketched a salute. "I'm sorry, sir," he said. "I don't know exactly who you think I am. But whatever it is, I'm not that."

He turned and saw himself out of the office, through the empty corridor, and out the chapel.

For the last time, he promised himself.

***

Navarro had stopped sitting with Po at chow, ever since Po drove him away with his interrogation about his implant, and his girlfriend's dad. That had left him on his own again.

But the next time chow rolled around, Zhang plunked into the seat across from him. He wasn't much of a conversationalist, and replied to any questions with mostly grunts, or one-syllable answers, with his broad face down near his plate as he shoveled ketchup-smothered French fries into it.

Po felt grateful for the company all the same.

Back at the barracks, Po ran into Dempsey in the head. They both exited their stalls at the same time, and their eyes met in the mirror as they washed their hands.

"Hey, Demps," Po found himself saying. "How's your wife?"

The moment the words escaped his mouth, he wished he could round them up and stuff them back in. He fully expected Dempsey to go ballistic, like he had back in the Cylinder 14 food court.

But Dempsey didn't get angry. Instead, he cast his eyes downward as he turned off the tap, flicked his fingers into the sink, and turned to the dryer. "I don't know. She isn't answering my letters."

"Ah. I'm sorry, Demps. Maybe they're getting lost."

"I doubt it. Haven't you been getting letters from home?"

"Well...yeah. From my sister."

"There you go, then." Dempsey sighed. "I'm afraid she's going to leave me."

"Leave you? No way, Demps. She wouldn't leave you, and besides, even if she did, who'd date her?"

The older recruit gave Po a sharp look. "What's that supposed to mean?"

"It means, you're gonna be a big bad Marine, now. Any man with any sense would be too afraid to date your wife, because you'd come back and beat him if he tried."

"Huh. Thanks, Po. I think." Dempsey started to leave.

"Hey...Demps?"

He turned. "Yeah?"

"Have you talked to Freddie lately?"

"Earlier today."

"How's he doing?"

"Fine...why?"

Po blinked. "You knew Diego Rodriguez died, right?"

"Diego...Rodriguez. That's his dad?"

"Yeah. He didn't mention it?"

"Not a word."

"Wow. I guess he's...does he seem off at all, to you?"

"I haven't noticed a thing. I'm kind of amazed to hear this, actually." Dempsey shook his head. "Is it ever possible no one wrote to tell him?"

"Maybe...I guess it's possible they're waiting till he finishes bootcamp. So it doesn't distract him, or interfere with him graduating."

Dempsey nodded. "If that's the case, we shouldn't tell him either. If that's what his family's decided to do, we should respect that."

"Yeah. I won't say anything."

"Me neither. Okay, Po."

"Night, Demps."

"Night."

Chapter 25

Po hadn't gotten much chance to study the giant obstacle course built into Cycler 3's eastern endcap. Standing around and gazing idly wasn't something anyone really did in bootcamp, as he'd learned on one of his first days, to his embarrassment.

But as Sergeant Mitchell marched them toward what he'd called the Swagger Course, Po was able to get an eyeful. And he didn't like what he saw. At all.

The eight waterfalls gushed from the axis, cascading in eight different directions into the ring of water that ran below the course—meant to catch any recruits that fell in, Po guessed. But considering the surface cylinder's diameter was four kilometers, and the obstacle course went all the way up to the axis, a two-kilometer fall was possible. He'd read somewhere once that if you fell far enough, landing on water was the same as falling onto concrete. He couldn't remember how high that was, but he was willing to bet it was less than two kilometers.

On the other hand, gravity fell away to almost nothing up at the axis, and Po figured it must increase by degrees on the way down. So, falling two kilometers from there wouldn't be the same as falling the same distance on Earth.

Still...even one hundred meters seemed sure to do the job of killing any recruit unlucky enough to fall that far.

As they drew near the course, parts of it started moving. Po wasn't sure what had triggered that...maybe Sergeant Mitchell had sent a command using his implant. Whatever the cause, there was now one obstacle with a long arm that swung around in a circle, another that rotated with three pegs sticking out from it, and another that looked like a giant treadmill, with huge wrecking balls swinging back and forth over it.

There were plenty of other obstacles, but they were getting too close now for him to make them all out. Sergeant Mitchell brought them to a stop, and turned to face them, standing next to the ramp used to access the first event—a net that spanned the band of water.

"In case you're wondering," he bellowed, "no planetside bootcamp has a Swagger Course. It's something only made possible by the advent of O'Neill Colonies, which is the name for the type of cycler you're in. Very few of you, if any, will make it to the cylinder's axis today, but the goal is for all of you to make it there by the time you graduate. Those that do make it today will have the opportunity to gain some valuable experience operating in microgravity. The GEA Marines form the system's primary extraplanetary force, and proficiency with microgravity maneuvers is a must."

The sergeant pointed to one of the nearby obstacles. "The events where there's any appreciable gravity all have a net below them, which you will fall into when you fail them. We call that the 'crawl of shame'—make your way back to the ladder at the beginning and attempt the event again. If you fail three times, take the walkway around and challenge the next one. If a DI tells you you failed, take the walkway. But if any recruit uses a walkway without attempting an event three times, I'll call the entire platoon down here for a fun-filled PT session before sending you back through from the start. Do we understand?"

"Yes, sir!" shouted a chorus of voices in unison.

"About halfway up, there will be no walkways. You must defeat each event to progress. If you fail, you will try again. If you fail one of those events too many times, you're done for the day. A DI will tell you when you're done. After that, make your way back down here, to join Sergeants Scott and Doyle and I for some PT while everyone else continues the Swagger Course. Do we understand?"

"Yes, sir!"

"If you make it to the microgravity section, there will be no nets underneath the event, since you'll no longer be falling. There will, however, be bars on all sides for you to catch yourself on if you fly out of bounds. If that happens, use those to work back around to the start of the event and begin again. Do we understand?"

"Yes, sir!"

"Line up and go!"

They lined up and went. Po had been in the fourth rank, so he had a while to wait while other recruits tackled the first obstacles. There was only room for one person to try an event at a time, which made sense. As they went higher up, having two people doing an event at a time would have been too risky, and anyway, the entire morning and afternoon had been set aside for running the Swagger Course.

Zhang was behind him, and just as Po was about to start, the big recruit said, "Good luck, Abbato."

He glanced over his shoulder, and gave Zhang a tight smile. "There's no luck involved here, Zhang. Just don't mess it up." With that, he took his turn at the rope net that spanned the artificial river.

After that came a rope climb onto a long boardwalk with some of the same obstacles from the Confidence Course, mostly the easier ones. Po cleared several low jumps in a row, used the chicken-wing technique to get over a high bar—which was pretty daunting even at this height, just a handful of meters off the ground—and then plodded up a long set of broad stairs with no railings. Even the stairs had netting on either side, and a ladder at the beginning in case you somehow fell off into the net.

He didn't feel any urgency to rush. The guy ahead of him wasn't much farther ahead, and glancing behind, he saw Zhang was still clambering over the low jumps. A couple recruits were already bunched up behind Zhang, waiting.

But where would haste get any of them? The faster they went, the faster they'd get to an event they couldn't beat, which would only send them back to the ground for PT with the DIs.

That wasn't Po's idea of a good time. Way better to take it slow, size up each obstacle, and come up with the best approach before tackling it as methodically as possible.

He even found himself pausing now and then to take in the view across the length of Cycler 3's surface cylinder. Doing that was a bit of a rush, and while he was challenging obstacles, he did his best to ignore the curved expanse. But standing in the middle of a flight of stairs, or halfway up a ramp, he got a kick out of looking out over the sweeping landscape, or peering up and seeing the people and buildings hanging from the megalithic habitat's "ceiling."

If any of the sergeants noticed him taking these opportunities to enjoy the grandeur of the cylinder, they didn't seem to mind. Po wondered if he'd even hear Sergeant Mitchell bawling at him, as high as he was now. The DIs probably had the ability to hijack his auditory taps and use those to yell at him, but they didn't.

It was the first time even a moment's idleness had been overlooked in the presence of DIs. But it made sense. So long as he kept moving, and stayed ahead of Zhang, there wasn't much point in trying to stay on the heels of the next recruit.

As he climbed, the drop-off in gravity was gradual but noticeable. That didn't mean the obstacles became any easier, though—the opposite, actually. Less gravity just meant the obstacles were bigger, the high bars higher, the log walks more spaced apart.

And brand new obstacles cropped up with increasing frequency the higher he went. He finished climbing what felt like an endless ladder, and a curved wooden ramp reared up before him, stretching toward the cylinder's axis. He stared incredulously at the thing's sheer height, at a complete loss for what he was supposed to do.

With the Confidence Course, the DIs had demonstrated how to navigate each obstacle before the recruits took their first crack at it. But the Swagger Course simply had too many, and most of them were too high up. It hadn't occurred to him that it would be a problem until now.

A semi-transparent window popped into his vision, showing a man in a DI's uniform running at top speed along the boardwalk that led to the curved ramp. He didn't slow as he reached it—instead, he ran up it, his momentum carrying him up the final vertical stretch. His fingers curled around the lip at the very top, and he pulled himself up. With that, the short video repeated.

Po willed the window away, then returned to sizing up the ramp. It seemed impossible, and it probably would have been in normal gravity.

I don't weigh as much here. If I run fast enough, I'll do it.

He drew a deep breath, then sprinted forward, every fiber in his body straining to propel him forward.

A shock ran through his ankles as he hit the inclined wooden surface, but he ignored it, legs pumping as he hit the part where the ramp swept upward dramatically.

The ease with which his momentum propelled him up the artificial cliff-face surprised him, and he almost missed the lip at the top. But he managed to grasp it with one hand, and then the other. After that, clearing the obstacle was as easy as doing a pull-up. Easier, in the lower gravity.

Some more recognizable obstacles followed—and then came another new one. This event featured a vertical rotating circle with three giant pegs sticking out of it. A video popped up again to instruct him, but he swiped it away, already having figured out what he was supposed to do.

The rotating circle hung in midair, at least two meters away from the end of the boardwalk he was on. He was meant to run and leap, grab one of those broad pegs, and let it carry him to the waiting ramp on the other side.

Again, it seemed impossible: weighing as much as he normally did, those pegs were too thick to grab and support his weight on. He'd have slipped off immediately.

But he was starting to realize that this high, the Swagger Course was as much about mental strength as it was physical. He had to ignore how things *looked*, and believe he could do it in spite of how impossible each new event seemed.

So he did. He timed his sprint-and-jump to catch one of the pegs as it was on the upswing, grabbing it in a bear hug and hanging on as tightly as he could, dangling from the peg as it arced up and over.

Almost, he lost his grip and fell—and then he did lose it, just as the peg swung around and started heading back in the direction he'd come. He fell past the walkway that was his destination, but managed to grip the edge of it as he did. Another pull-up brought him up and onto the wood.

Po wanted to pump his arms in the air with victory. *I got both of those things first try!* But he didn't want the others see him being cocky...and he didn't want to let himself get overconfident. So he marched toward the next obstacle, focusing on using the triumphant energy surging through him to keep progressing.

The next one was a corridor with no bottom—two sheer vertical walls, which to traverse he had to press against with his hands and feet, using a lot of force. Again, he was sure he couldn't have made it in normal gravity. Not without a lot of training and practice. But this far up Cycler 3's eastern endcap, things were different. As long as he could make himself believe it was possible, then in the reduced gravity, it probably was.

Then came the next event, and his breath caught in his throat. He'd reached the end of the walkways. Going forward, if he failed any event three times, he'd have to make his way to the ground for Sergeant Doyle's PT session.

The next one was the treadmill he'd spotted from the ground, with wrecking balls swinging over it.

Don't think. Just go.

He sucked in a big breath and held it, running through the swinging black orbs as fast as he could. Maybe he got lucky—either way, he made it through without being knocked off even once.

Yes!

After that, things got completely wild. One event made him fling himself from bar to bar, using only his hands, across huge gaps. Another made him jump *with* a bar, swinging himself forward so that both he and the bar sailed from the little divots it rested in, to another set several meters ahead. He had to repeat the feat several times.

He failed that twice, but managed to get through it on his third try, fueled by determination seasoned with fear of Sergeant Doyle.

Another event had him flinging himself from handhold to handhold along an artificial cliff, again across impossible-seeming distances. The next demanded he grip a pair of rings and fly from peg to peg, catching himself using the rings before flinging himself again.

Even he hadn't expected to get this far. Now that he'd cracked the code, and realized how much more was possible in the lower gravity, he was on a roll. But he couldn't stop. He knew if he thought too much about what he was doing, he'd be done.

Then, he came to the microgravity section, where walking became impossible. Instead of ramps and boardwalks, narrow railed tunnels led between obstacles. He pushed himself through the first one and tackled the next obstacle.

Things started pretty simply, with an event that had him pushing off of angled boards to reach the other side. After that, he swung between stationary poles, and soon he came to an event that involved launching himself at precise angles across large distances and landing on small platforms, where he had to grab onto handles and launch out again at a new angle.

Just as Sergeant Mitchell had promised, there were always padded poles to catch himself on at the perimeter of each event, where he could work his way back to the beginning if he failed. That happened more than once, but he managed to stay below the three-strikes-per-obstacle that would force him to quit the Swagger Course and head down for PT.

Soon, he again came to events where the obstacles themselves moved. Poles fixed to a rotating disc spun around and around, forcing him to time his launch to grab one of them, then use the momentum to fling himself to the next set of revolving poles.

He cleared the second ring of poles with ease. It was when he launched himself toward the third ring that it happened.

Mid-flight, everything went black. One second he was focusing on the third ring of poles as he sailed toward them, the next, his vision was just gone.

His heart immediately started to hammer, and he flailed wildly as he knew he'd hit the revolving poles at any minute. And hit them he did—but instead of grabbing one, he sailed through them, careening off the first to crash painfully into a second, which smacked into his cheek and thigh, hard.

The pole's momentum threw him off, and he again began flailing. *I have to catch one of the safety poles at the edge of the event.* If he failed to do that, he'd exit the Swagger Course altogether, careening off in a random direction through open air.

But as Po waved his hands in front of him, praying one of them connected with a pole, things got worse. A shrill ringing started up in both ears, and his hands and feet suddenly felt like they were on fire. The pain was like nothing he'd ever felt, as though he'd plunged his limbs into glowing embers, and it was intense enough to wash out all other sensation—including whether his fingers encountered a pole or not.

I missed them, didn't I?

With each passing second, it became more certain that he'd failed to catch any of the safety poles, and was now flying free, clear across the Cycler 3 sky.

Chapter 26

As he sped through that formless no-place, his fingers and feet on fire, it crossed his mind to wonder what it really meant to go 'missing' in Cycler 3. Did it mean you died and they covered up your death, or did it simply mean that no one in the system cared enough to notice you were dead?

By now, he felt pretty sure it was the second one.

Hot bile surged up his esophagus to gush from his mouth, surprising him. He collided with it, the putrid-smelling spew splashing across his face and neck.

His heart beat so hard against the inside of his chest, it felt like it could explode. Blood rushed loudly through his ears. He'd never been so scared, and he also wasn't sure he'd ever been in this much pain. The searing sensation was creeping up his arms, now, and he felt like he could vomit again.

Depending on the angle he'd left the Swagger Course, he might reenter stronger gravity at any second, which would seize him, drawing him at top speed to his certain death. Even if there was anything he might have done, he couldn't see in order to do it. His vision was still completely gone. He might as well be floating in the space between galaxies.

Neither could he hear anything, he realized. Surely his catastrophic exit from the microgravity section of the Swagger Course had been noticed. And if it had, there was a decent chance he would have heard shouting at some point—at least from the recruits who'd been doing an event close to him. He also hadn't heard himself crash into that pole.

And what about my Circuit? Sergeant Doyle had already exercised his ability to contact him directly using it. So the DIs should have been talking to him right now, trying to calm him down, maybe even giving him some advice. But there was nothing.

My implant's been compromised. That wasn't supposed to be possible. But then, neither was getting visited by Emplor in the middle of a secure Marine training facility.

Without warning, hands seized him roughly, swinging him around. For a second, he felt a pair of shoes against his chest. Then they shoved him, sending him careening even faster in a new direction.

But he could no longer devote the mental bandwidth to speculate why it had happened, or where he might be headed. The fire spreading through his body, the panic, the nausea...all of it crescendoed to a fever pitch, overloading his mind. He went to another place, escaping this unbearable pain to some primal section of his hindbrain.

***

Apparently he'd passed out at some point, because he woke up. He was lying in a bed with a single sheet pulled over him, facing a bulkhead painted a light-gray tone. Its only feature was a fixture that projected broad triangles of light above and below it.

A nurse stood over him, blinking down at him in surprise. She held a clipboard, and looked like she'd been about to leave. "Welcome back," she said. "Can you tell me your name?"

"I can see," he said wonderingly. Then, to his horror, he burst into sobbing.

The nurse, a corporal from her rank device, waited for him to regain control of himself.

"Abbato," he said at last. "Recruit Abbato."

"Your first name?"

"Po."

"Where are you from?"

"Psyche Station."

"And what's your birthday?"

"October 9th, 2254."

"Well, your memory seems fine. I'm going to take your blood pressure." She turned to open a drawer, extracting a black band connected to a bulb and a digital display.

"Shouldn't my Circuit be able to tell you my blood pressure?" he asked slowly.

She gave him a blank look. "You don't remember what happened to you?"

"I remember everything going black while I was running the Swagger Course. And then I missed the safety poles. After that, I was in a lot of pain, and—"

"Your implant isn't functioning, Abbato. But I'm going to let Sergeant Olson go over all that with you."

The corporal took his blood pressure, and then his temperature. Seeming satisfied with both readings, she left without saying anything else.

Sergeant Olson appeared five minutes later. He was about as unexpressive as the nurse had been, and didn't look much taller than Sergeant Doyle. Bushy black eyebrows overshadowed his eyes, to match the stubble-like hair that covered his head.

"Recruit Abbato," he said with a nod, his warm voice at odds with his inert facial features. "Please, no need to get up. You've had a hard day. I'm Sergeant Olson, chief software engineer in charge of Circuit firmware for everyone on Cycler 3. How are you feeling?"

"A lot better than I was, sir."

"I'm sure that's true. I spoke to the first medic to get to you once they got you down to the surface—he told me you were unresponsive. Not to mention convulsing, frothing at the mouth, and suffering from a nasty nosebleed. He sedated you on the spot."

"I don't remember any of that."

"It's unlikely that you would. What do you remember?"

"Losing my vision. And my hearing. I remember feeling like I was on fire, so much that I couldn't tell if I was making contact with the poles or not." Po paused. "That all had something to do with my implant, didn't it?"

Olson drew a deep breath, though he seemed like he might be trying to hide that Po's question had caused him any distress. "It would appear that someone was able to exploit an until-now unknown backdoor in your Circuit's firmware interface. When one of your DIs exercises administrative access to your Circuit, his implant must first complete a 'handshake' with yours in order to grant him that access. But your attacker was able to bypass the need for any sort of authentication at all, and actually the attacker managed to gain developer access. Even your DIs wouldn't be able to do what was done to you today."

"Has it occurred to anyone that it might be a bad idea to deploy Marines with implants that can be used to cripple us? Or is it just that important to monitor and control us?"

Olson's forehead wrinkled. "The platform we give Marines is about equipping them with capabilities undreamed of by their historical counterparts, not about control, Abbato. As for vulnerabilities, what you experienced today is virtually unheard of. I've never heard of a Circuit with military firmware being compromised in the field. GEA will want to know about this, of course, and I plan on recommending modifications that will render impossible the existence of a backdoor like the one used to hack your Circuit today. I expect every Circuit in the Marines will be patched to prevent it from ever happening again. That said, I don't believe this vulnerability is shared by all implants—actually, I think it's limited to just yours. And it's now been patched. So once I switch your implant back on, you'll have nothing to worry about going forward."

Po shook his head. "Sir, with all due respect, this doesn't make sense. They installed my Circuit at MIPS. How could it have a one-of-a-kind vulnerability?"

A silence passed between them as Sergeant Olson seemed to wrestle with himself mentally. "An investigation into that will need to happen as well, Abbato. Clearly, someone at MIPS was either malicious or negligent. And by negligent, I mean negligent enough to let someone malicious get access to your Circuit."

"Malicious," Po repeated, his stomach turning to ice.

Olson nodded. "The foundation for this attack was laid before you ever left Psyche."

***

Even though he hadn't noticed a difference in the gravity, Po had assumed he'd been taken to some secret subterranean facility, where sensitive work was conducted on Circuits. Probably it was only a level or two down, to allow ease of access for personnel traveling frequently back and forth between here and Cycler 3's surface cylinder.

But it turned out he wasn't anywhere more exotic than the med clinic.

My third visit. Looking back on his reasons for each trip here, he found it difficult to decide which was the most embarrassing. They all were, for different reasons. This one, mainly for the spectacle of what had happened—how much attention it must have drawn to him.

He left his room and headed down the corridor, doing his best to avoid the nurses, doctors, and other personnel working in the clinic, even though Sergeant Olson had cleared him to leave his bed as soon as they finished their conversation. Po's implant was still deactivated, and he wondered if Olson would have been quite as unconcerned about him wandering freely if it wasn't.

He guessed the sergeant probably wouldn't have let him leave his room if the implant was active, which for Po was concerning in its own right. Switching the Circuit on would mean it reconnecting to both the Cycler's intranet and who knew how many other devices. But if they still wanted to keep it siloed, then that didn't seem promising.

They still aren't sure it's secure enough yet to reconnect to anything else. Are they?

He came to an intersection of corridors, and heard footsteps approaching from around the corner. He got ready to salute, but the nurse who appeared was headed in the same direction, and she seemed to take no notice of him. So he kept walking, keeping an eye on her back in case she turned and he needed to salute after all.

As a trad, his implant's vulnerabilities came as no surprise to him. It was part of why he'd always resisted getting an implant before the Marines had forced one on him.

Though it wasn't widely advertised, GEA insisted on the ability to access any implant at any time, including civilian implants. And as long as they refused to let go of that capability, Circuits would be unsecure. The same backdoors that GEA availed itself of could be used by bad guys.

Or by aliens. Whether Zanth was a bad guy or not remained to be seen, and it had already occurred to Po to wonder whether the backdoor the attacker had used might be the same one the Emplor had been using to hack Po's implant and insert himself into the sense data it fed him. If Sergeant Olson patched the same backdoor Zanth had been using, Po might never see the alien again.

But he hadn't brought that up to Olson.

I already told the officers about Zanth's visits once, and they thought I was crazy. What was the point in bringing them up again? Besides, part of him was still banking on the possibility that his connection with the alien might bring some kind of advantage.

Zanth predicted this. Didn't he? The Emplor had warned him that there was an Obsidian Angel among his fellow recruits, and that he would try to kill Po. Well, it seemed that had borne out.

Unless Zanth was lying, and he's *the one who tried to kill me.* But what purpose would that serve?

He stopped in front of a closed door, double checking the room number. *Fourteen. That's the one Sergeant Olson said he was in, right?*

Po wasn't totally sure, but at the risk of barging in on some stranger, he opened the door anyway.

Zhang was lying in the only rack, propped up against the headrest with a couple of pillows. His right leg was elevated in a sling, and a cast covered it, running all the way to his upper thigh.

"Abbato!" the big Chinese said, grinning widely as Po shut the door behind him.

"Hey, Zhang. Sergeant Olson told me I'd find you here."

"Who is Sergeant Olson?"

"Never mind." Po made his way to Zhang's bedside, feeling a little awkward. He wasn't sure what to do with hands, so he placed them on his hips, and wondered if it made him look as dorky as he felt. "The sergeant told me what happened. What you did. Thank you, Zhang."

Zhang shrugged. "It's just what I was supposed to do."

"Huh? You risked your life for me, Zhang. You launched yourself into the sky. You didn't have to do that."

A look of confusion passed across the other recruit's face. "Yes I did. We're not here for ourselves, we're here for each other. Watching you taught me that."

Po slowly shook his head. "I'm sorry, Zhang, but I have no idea what you're talking about."

"Yes you do. You must. When Paisley and his friends beat you up, you never told the DIs. And the way you took the DIs' abuse, without complaining. And when they sent you to Motivation Camp for no reason. And that time on the gravel, crab walking and bear walking across it for hours. And then, when you were so encouraging toward Dempsey while he was doing the Confidence—"

"All right," Po said, holding up both hands. "All right. That's enough." Somehow, he couldn't bear the unending torrent of compliments. "Look, Zhang, I'm not that great, all right? If you knew half the stuff I've done—"

"But that's just it. I've done things too, Abbato. So many bad things. But when we live for each other, that doesn't matter as much. We become something more. Part of something greater. Don't you see?"

Po stared at Zhang, at a loss for words.

"That's why I had to do it. Because it's not about me. It can't be. Not anymore."

Po lowered his gaze, amazed by Zhang's words. A silence passed between them. Then, a grin crept across Po's face, and he raised his eyes to meet Zhang's once more.

"Semper Fi," he said.

Zhang reached out one of his large hands, and Po gripped it.

"Semper Fi," the other recruit said.

Po nodded at the suspended leg. "Sergeant Olson told me you saved me, but he didn't tell me how that happened. Or how you made it back down alive."

"I pushed you back toward the Swagger Course with my feet, and right after that I collided with one of the buildings suspended from the central axis. A sensor tower—Sergeant

Mitchell said they mostly use it to monitor moisture levels and air pressure. My tibia is broken, and my femur is fractured in three places."

Po winced. "That's awful."

Zhang shrugged for the second time. "It could be worse. Actually, the tower is probably what saved me. If I had not collided with it, I was headed in a direction that would have sent me to the ground. I could not have survived."

"So the tower stopped you?"

Zhang nodded. "After that I was drifting near the axis. One of the DIs shot out on a tether from a hanging garden, grabbed me. Then they reeled us back in."

Po realized his eyebrows were about as high as they could go. "Well, you're right. It could definitely be worse." Then, his heart sank again. "Wait—you won't be able to graduate with us!"

The big recruit gave a sad smile. "No. I will be held back until I'm healed. But the doctor says I will be good as new, so at least I can still be a Marine."

"I'm glad, brother. Though, I don't like that we won't be in the same graduating class."

"That's okay. Just means I'll have to kill some extra insurgents, to catch up. You'll have a head start on me."

"Well, I'll save some for you."

"I appreciate it."

It felt like a good time to go, since Po was out of things to say. "I'm gonna...." He jerked a thumb over his shoulder.

"Yeah."

Po turned and walked toward the door. Then, he turned back. "Hey, Zhang? I'm sorry I never appreciated you before. But, just...thanks, man."

"You got it, Po. Semper Fi."

"Yeah. Semper Fi."

***

"I want you to get in the habit of never waiting for your mag to be depleted before reloading," Staff Sergeant Tibbs told them in his gentle tenor. A gust of artificial wind ruffled the grass around his feet, but he took no notice of it, instead meeting each of the recruits' eyes in turn. "Instead, take advantage of any break in the fighting to recharge your mag. Of course you're going to deplete your rounds sometimes. But you want that to happen as infrequently as possible. That's why we use breaks to reload whenever possible—so that you'll have the rounds you need, when you need them."

Harris raised his hand, which under normal circumstances none of the recruits would have ever done, except during the designated time for questions at the end of each class.

But Sergeant Tibbs only nodded. "Yes, Recruit Harris?" He'd learned all of their names during grass week, his first week with them, when he'd taught them all the basics of shooting positions, adjusting their sights, and compensating for weather conditions.

"Sir, what about situations where you need to conserve ammo, sir?"

"There are exceptions that prove every rule, Harris," Tibbs said in his usual kindly tone.

"Yes, sir."

During grass week, none of the recruits had known what to make of Sergeant Tibbs. After being yelled at by the DIs for six weeks straight, spending any time at all with an authority figure who didn't scream at them for the entire class felt like an alien experience.

Tibbs was their Primary Marksmanship Instructor, or PMI, and he was a bonafide, regular Marine. While he seemed just as tough and competent as Mitchell, he was also...nice. He hadn't raised his voice once. This far into bootcamp, that seemed wrong, somehow.

But the recruits didn't take too long to get used to it, and before long they all came to love Sergeant Tibbs intensely, way more than they would have loved someone who bothered to be nice to them out in the real world. Tibbs didn't do anything spectacular, just his job, which was to teach them how to use their rifles. Sure, he did that job well. But he also talked to them like adults. That was enough to win him a platoon's worth of adorers.

"A lot of recruits, when they fire a shot—" Tibbs raised his rifle so that he was sighting downrange through the scope. He jerked the rifle up a little, suggesting a shot fired. "—they want to immediately take their eye away from their sights to see what their shot did." He craned his neck to look down the length of the barrel, toward the targets at the end of the range. "Why is that bad?"

Po found himself raising his hand.

"Go ahead, Abbato."

"Because you break sight with your target through the scope, which means you'll have to line up your shot again if another one's needed."

"That's exactly right. And another shot often *is* needed. So instead of messing up your own aim and needing to readjust, first look through the scope and see how your shot plays out. Watch the *story* of your shot. Did you hit your target? Miss? Did you neutralize your target, or does he need another round? It's rare for a single shot to neutralize the threat posed by a hostile. So before you start gawking around your weapon, first observe how your action is playing out in the world, and finish what you started."

Po nodded along as Tibbs spoke. Just as the other recruits wouldn't normally dare raise their hands in the middle of a class, in the past he wouldn't have dared to answer a question posed by an instructor. It only would have made the others hate him more.

But things had changed, hadn't they? They'd *been* changing in the days leading up to the Swagger Course, but his almost dying that day seemed to finally remove his status as everyone's favorite target for torment. For the most part, anyway.

It had been almost two weeks since then, two weeks which had proved strangely uneventful. There'd been no more visits from Zanth, which meant Sergeant Olson likely had closed the backdoor he'd been using to access Po's implant after all. And while bootcamp could never be described as relaxing, it had at least become somewhat bearable without the entire platoon aligned against him.

The DIs had only let him visit Zhang in the med clinic once, and Po got the impression they didn't intend to let him again. Zhang would be fine, and he'd graduate with another platoon. Letting Po pay him repeated visits ran the risk of distracting him from his training. At least, he figured that was their reasoning. Who really knew, when it came to the DIs?

There was a decent chance Po and Zhang would never see each other again. That brought a twinge of sadness whenever he reflected on it. But he really did need to stay focused on completing bootcamp. Too many times, he'd come within a hair's breadth of getting discharged and sent to simjail. Besides, if Zanth was right, there was an Obsidian Angel planted in his platoon, with sights set on Po. Sure, whoever it was had been inactive for a while. But Po felt sure the Angel was only waiting and watching for his next opportunity.

I need to get him before he gets me. But how?

Sergeant Tibbs ordered them to shooting stations, jolting Po from his memory.

"Don't forget to don your ear protection," Tibbs told them. "Show your weapon some respect. In the field, your helmet will cancel the noise from each shot digitally. But what if your helmet malfunctions? Or you lose it, for some reason? I'll tell you what. The concussive force from each shot will fatigue you, and degrade your performance. It could get you killed. That's why I always carry some of this with me."

He picked up a roll of toilet paper, where it had been sitting on the grass near his feet.

"You might not believe it, but a little TP rolled up and stuffed in your ears can save your life. It's done it before, and it'll do it again."

Chapter 27

Sergeant Doyle paced the front of the classroom ranting, droning on about "terrorism awareness."

His words came out in an endless monotone rush, a style of speaking that he only used while teaching. Po had wondered more than once whether Doyle reserved this special mode for the classroom out of sadism—yet another way to torture his charges. It seemed likely.

Either way, Po sat perfectly straight in his chair, not daring to slouch, or take his eyes off Doyle, or pay anything but perfect attention to everything he was saying. At any moment, he could be called on to regurgitate the last minute of what the sergeant had said. If he failed to do so, there would be IT.

"The goal of *terrorism* is simply to instill terror," Doyle said, sounding more like a computer than a computer did, with perfectly even spacing between each word. "Which means a terrorist operation doesn't necessarily require a physical attack of any kind. If terror has been instilled, then the terrorist can consider himself a success.

"Terrorist operations can be broken down into five phases," the DI continued.

"What's the *point* of this?" said a voice to Po's left.

Po stiffened, his eyes still on Doyle, waiting for the DI to explode at whoever had said it. But the sergeant just prattled on, taking no notice of the interruption.

Then, Po realized why: Sergeant Doyle hadn't heard the voice, and neither had any of the other recruits. Only Po had heard it.

As the DI turned his back to pace in the other direction, he risked a glance to his left.

Zanth was sitting at the desk one over and one back. He was large enough that he made it look like a child's toy, and if the alien had been actually, physically present, Po might have wondered how he planned to extract himself from it.

He returned his gaze to Doyle just in time for the sergeant to turn and pace back toward him. Even sitting, Po's eyes were about level with Doyle's as he patrolled the front of the room, and as the DI passed, his gaze met Po's.

Po quickly looked away. The DIs didn't tend to respond positively when you held eye contact with them.

"I mean, truly," the Emplor continued. "When was the last time any group dared to strike out at mighty GEA? The Accord sees all, knows all. Does it not? Who can defy them?" Zanth's voice carried a mocking tone.

"Oh, don't bother answering," the alien continued. "I already know you aren't *allowed* to. Speaking at a time like this would earn you a vigorous round of IT, maybe even worse than that time near the river. Hm? And as you may already have guessed, that's exactly why I'm choosing to appear to you at this moment, when you are forced to remain silent—so that I can forestall the parade of frivolous questions you'd pester me with otherwise. As before, you can take the nuggets of gold I'm giving you, or you can leave them lying in the muck. But I would remind you, the last time you ignored my counsel, it very nearly got you killed."

The alien fell silent, for long enough that Po wondered whether he was still there. The desk Zanth had chosen was beyond the periphery of his vision, and he didn't dare risk another glance. He became conscious of his heart hammering frenetically in his chest, and some of Doyle's words managed to pierce the maelstrom of thought the alien's arrival had whipped up in his brain.

"Movement to target."

Doyle swept the recruits with his shrewd eyes.

"Trade-offs."

His stubby legs seemed to pick up speed, till he was motoring back and forth along the front row of desks, even though his speech continued to plod along, bone-dry and colorless.

"Commercial and/or industrial sabotage."

The DI's eyes narrowed as they met Po's once more. Could Doyle tell he wasn't paying attention?

"IEDs."

"This pathetic runt has total power over you," Zanth spoke again at last. "And it isn't hard to see how much he enjoys it, is it? He might as well be your god. If he told you to run outside, to that fake riverbank, and scoop up damp crud with your bare hands and stuff your cheeks full with it, you'd do it without hesitation. And you'd swallow it. And you'd enjoy a second helping, if he told you to."

"Interrupting these can damage progression," Doyle said, little legs pumping.

Po's head hurt.

"It doesn't have to be this way, Po. You possess the ability to attain heights this rodent could only dream of. He'd lick your boot, then. But if you let yourself become too much their little pawn now, you'll never manage it. They'll neuter you, if you let them."

"Are there any questions?" Doyle said.

Paisley raised his hand.

"What is your question, Recruit?"

"Sir, could you share some ways we can protect an important individual who insists on behaviors that make him a soft target? Sir."

Sergeant Doyle nodded. "If you're assigned to guard a politician or businessman, your very presence hardens them as a target, since you and your brothers are operating as part of what should be a multilayered defense."

"You already know something is amiss on Cycler 3," Zanth said. "At least, I certainly hope you do. You have enemies here, and they've already tried to kill you once. If you don't get them first, then they'll get you. And as you are, you're perfectly vulnerable to them."

"Anyone else?" Doyle asked, his gaze roving around the room.

"The scales have not yet fallen fully from your eyes," Zanth said. "But I can help you. You can choose not to accept my help if you like, and you'll get what you deserve. Tonight, I will lead you to answers. You only need follow, and behold the truth for yourself. But if you remain a subservient lamb, then slaughter will be your just dessert."

***

Po got yelled at twice that afternoon for inattention, once by Sergeant Doyle. It seemed a miracle that neither incident earned the entire platoon extra PT.

Which didn't mean today wasn't grueling, like every other day. After the class on terrorism, Sergeant Doyle took them on a six-mile conditioning march, followed by a field training session with Scott. But after Zanth's return, Po's mind was all over the place. His thoughts kept wandering, to what the Emplor was planning tonight...what he might know...and what it would mean for Po if he accepted instruction from him.

Or if he didn't.

"Recruit Abbato, do you have somewhere else you need to be?" Sergeant Scott snapped at him.

"No, sir!"

"Then I suggest you start paying attention."

"Yes, sir!"

Po tried to focus on the DI's words, but instead he found himself thinking about what it was like to be a DI on Cycler 3. It was a delicate game, and one more subtle than Po would have expected. Contrary to what he'd always assumed, the job of "drill instructor" wasn't limited to standing around yelling at recruits. It also included caring about their future, and who knew, maybe even about the recruits themselves. Po was almost certain he'd felt real sympathy from the DIs, on that day in Mitchell's office.

Above all, their job was to turn their charges into Marines. And a Marine wasn't just someone who took a weapon into combat, Po had come to realize. A Marine wasn't just about looking tough, or being tough, or taking the fight to the enemy. A Marine was supposed to care, too. About integrity. Whether every Marine lived up to that standard, he didn't know. But he knew he wanted to try.

He wouldn't have expected that before coming to Cycler 3, either.

***

Po finished the day exhausted, and while the whirlwind of thought caused by Zanth's visit hadn't abated, his energy had. As evening downtime wore on, his thoughts took on a manic quality, and even seemed louder than normal, somehow.

At lights-out, he climbed into his rack with every intention of keeping his eyes open for some signal from Zanth, but instead he fell dead asleep inside of what was probably ten minutes.

An alarm blared in his ears, causing him to inhale sharply and sit up, staring blearily into the dark, groping around his rack in confusion until it finally occurred to him to call up his implant's interface and deactivate it.

It worked, which was good, but it did nothing to explain how the alarm had been set in the first place. He only set an alarm when he had fire watch, and he didn't tonight. Even if he did, according to his Circuit, it was 0147, and no fire watch shift started at that time.

His neurons gradually resumed their normal rate of fire, and he remembered what tonight was. It was the night following the day Zanth had reappeared. There was a decent chance the alarm hadn't been set at all, but triggered by the Emplor—since, why *wouldn't* he have the ability to do that?

Without warning, the barracks lit up brightly, so brightly it seemed it should hurt his eyeballs. But it didn't, of course, since no extra photons were actually hitting his corneas. This was the result of his Circuit hijacking his optic nerves.

The bulkheads and overhead had sprouted enormous, blue-and-white flowers, and wrist-thick vines adorned the racks, hanging down their sides in flowing curtains. It looked like the kind of jungle a Joy-addict might hallucinate, with thick outlines and bright, vibrant colors. Po reached out hesitantly toward one of the vines sprouting from beneath his mattress, and he found it firm and cool to the touch.

This wasn't like any jungle that ever existed on Earth. It might as well have been from a cartoon.

He clambered over the side of his bed, lowering himself gently to the deck and taking care not to depend on any part of the vision to support his weight, since it wouldn't. No one seemed disturbed by his descent from his rack, and he couldn't see the swinging beam of light that would have signified an approaching recruit on fire watch. Maybe interior fire watch was using the head?

In the direction of the head, the vines wove together to form a beautiful yet forbidding wall, even beflowered as it was. Clearly, Zanth didn't mean him to go that way.

He could, of course. If he walked to the vines and gripped one of them, the taps embedded in his skin would do a convincing job of tricking him into thinking it was really there. But they couldn't actually block him. If he tried, he'd walk right through them.

But why do that? If he was going to follow the cues the Emplor was sending him, then he should just follow them. Trying anything else seemed counterproductive.

And so, he walked toward another giant cue—an archway that had sprung up over the barracks' exit, lavishly adorned with vines and flowers, with strings of fairy lights woven throughout. They gleamed invitingly.

As aesthetically pleasing as all this was, it was also over-the-top, and Po detected a distinct note of Zanth's trademark sarcasm in all of it. It was like the alien was saying, *You wouldn't follow my advice before, and it almost led to your death. So maybe if I adorn your path with lights and flowers?*

But Po was hardly in a position to be picky, and if a sarcastic path was the only one he had to follow, he'd follow it. Glancing over his shoulder to make sure no one had stirred, and that interior fire watch had still made no appearance, he continued beneath the arch and through the door, opening and closing it behind him as silently as he could manage.

The step outside was empty. Whoever had been assigned to exterior fire watch had either abandoned his post or was kidnapped. Po didn't have access to the fire watch schedule—only Crotty did. But if he could find out who was assigned to be here right now, it might tell him a lot.

I could go back in and check which racks are empty. But he discarded the idea as soon as it occurred to him, since it would mean risking interior fire watch catching him out of his rack.

Besides, a bright golden line hung suspended in midair, leading straight as an arrow from the barracks entrance until it took a sharp right, disappearing around the gym. The brutalist rectangle that was the recruit gymnasium reared up dead ahead, made visible by the lampposts that kept Cycler 3's simulated night at bay.

I guess that's where Zanth wants me to go. So his choices were to follow the ethereal yellow ribbon, which he was sure only he could see, or return to the safety of his rack. But would that be true safety?

It came down to whether the Emplor could be trusted. *Someone* had tried to kill him, that day on the Swagger Course. No doubt that someone would make a second attempt, and maybe soon. The question was whether the alien was actually as invested in Po's survival as he pretended to be.

Po *wanted* to trust Zanth. If he could truly claim an Emplor as his ally, that promised to be an incredible advantage. It was that thought that ultimately spurred his footsteps along the golden path, after checking around the entrance to see whether the recruit missing from his post had left his rifle. It seemed he hadn't. And so Po followed the glimmering ribbon.

As he did, he took care to check all around him for anyone else walking in the dimness. This would probably go better for him if he could avoid being seen creeping through the dark after lights-out. He didn't know what he'd find at the end of Zanth's line, but one thing he was sure of was that he was supposed to be sleeping in his rack right now, and after everything that had happened since starting bootcamp, getting caught could easily lead to getting discharged.

Every now and then he found himself glancing upward, at the opposite side of the cylinder's interior, which served as his sky. Could there possibly be eyes over there, human or otherwise, that might spy him out and make his truancy known to the DIs?

More bizarrely, he found himself wondering: was there another Po on that side of the cylinder, sneaking from building to building, also having slipped out of his barracks where he should have been sleeping?

Or, maybe that version of him had chosen to remain in his rack instead, and was dreaming the quiet dreams of the righteous.

The golden thread led him along a route no stealthier than one Po could have come up with himself. It ran first along the long wall of the gym before winding behind a row of benches and then under a line of trees that marched past the barracks of another platoon.

There, a sentry stared long and hard at Po's motionless form before wandering elsewhere, apparently persuaded that Po wasn't a skulking recruit after all, but just a trick of the shadows.

His heart hammered in his chest at almost being caught, and it took him forever to inch past the sentry, terrified the other recruit would look again and realize he was someone after all.

When at last he exited the sentry's line of sight, it occurred to him to wonder whether Zanth might have played a role in him not being spotted. Tampering with implants was clearly within the alien's power, and he'd almost certainly have the resources to render Po invisible to the other recruit's eye.

The golden thread wound on, until at last it terminated next to a dumpster that stood against a supply shed on the outskirts of the base.

Po frowned. There didn't seem to be anything particularly interesting about the dumpster, and peering around from his position kneeling next to it, he couldn't see anything worth risking discharge for.

Could Zanth's appearance in his class, the flowers and the vines, the golden thread—could it all be part of some cosmic prank?

He decided to crawl around the dumpster, as quietly as he could. Then, he saw it.

Or rather, he saw *them:* two figures leaning against each other, each grasping the other by the shoulders.

They were difficult to make out in the dimness, but they both looked male, and Po's first thought was that they were kissing, or about to. Then he realized that both men stood perfectly still, with only their foreheads touching.

Something else is going on here. But what?

As his eyes adjusted to the relative lack of light behind the supply shed, he saw that one of them was a uniformed man well into adulthood, with rank epaulets on his shoulder, which Po couldn't quite make out. The other was probably around Po's age. A recruit.

Then the recruit shifted, breaking contact with the man and turning to look directly at Po.

It was Freddie Rodriguez.

Chapter 28

Freddie didn't waste any time. He snatched up his custom-printed rifle from where it leaned against the supply shed and swung the stock at Po's head.

Po tried to stand while pulling away. The blow that had been intended for his temple connected with the side of his throat instead, sending him staggering sideways into the dumpster.

A memory flashed unbidden through his mind, of Freddie making sport of him in the boxing ring—and of the uppercut that had put an end to their bout, laying Po out unconscious on the canvas.

This time he has a weapon, and I don't. Not to mention an ally.

As he pushed himself off the dumpster and raised his hands in an attempt to catch Freddie's next attack, Zanth's voice cut through his thoughts:

"Follow my instructions exactly!"

Freddie feinted another swing at Po's head, then came around at his ribs instead. He managed to drop an arm to block the attack in time, the weapon's butt cracking painfully against his forearm.

What instructions? Po asked, before realizing the Emplor probably couldn't hear his thoughts.

The ghostly image of fists materialized in front of him, pulsing bright red and distracting him. A split second later, Freddie raised the rifle horizontally to exactly where those fists were. He held the weapon with both hands, and now he shoved it against Po's chest.

Po fell backward, and Freddie came with him, releasing his rifle with one hand to seize Po's shirtfront.

A disembodied glowing hand seized the other recruit's shoulder, and an image of Po's body twisted to the right. As for the real Po, he crashed to the ground, his back hitting hard enough to knock the wind out of his lungs.

"Why aren't you doing anything?" a frustrated-sounding Zanth asked. "Follow the instructions!"

Freddie cocked his fist back, and it was at that moment Po realized the floating red body parts represented actions he was meant to be taking. Unfortunately, the puzzle didn't quite click into place for him in time to execute the head-twist that was Zanth's prescription for deflecting Freddie's punch. And so it landed squarely on his nose. Cartilage crunched, pain exploded, and bright starbursts erupted across his vision, such that he couldn't see the Emplor's next suggested move.

But he knew he had to do something, so he wrenched his right arm out from under his assailant and used it to shove himself off the ground. Freddie had him pinned pretty solidly, though, and the move didn't accomplish much, except that the next blow landed on Po's ear, which hurt a lot, too. Still, it bought some time for both his head and vision to clear a little.

"Get it together," Zanth hissed. "Pay attention to the sensations I'm feeding you."

With that, a number of things happened so quickly they seemed almost simultaneous. A pair of scarlet arms wrapped themselves around Freddie's torso, and this time, Po didn't hesitate. He tensed his abdominals, crunching rapidly upward to grab his enemy in a bear hug.

As he locked his hands together behind Freddie and pulled him backward onto the ground, the touch taps fired along his right leg. Even though he didn't have a good enough angle to see the ghostly silhouette of Zanth's next command, the alien was somehow telling him what he needed to do by pinging his touch taps and tugging on his proprioception.

Po wrapped his leg around Freddie's left foot and then freed his right arm in order to place it where yet another pulsing red arm had appeared—hooked around his opponent's left shoulder, which pinned the arm in place.

"Now, explode!" the alien barked into his ear.

Po did. He hammered his left leg against the ground and yanked on Freddie's right arm while swinging his own left hand in the direction he wanted to go. With his enemy's left arm and leg trapped, there was nothing he could do to stop from being rolled over. The rifle flew from his grasp, clattering against the back of the supply shed, and Po ended up on top of Freddie.

"*My turn,*" he growled through gritted teeth, landing an elbow against Freddie's jaw as he tried to sit up. Something cracked inside the other recruit's mouth—Po both felt it *and* heard it.

A ghostly figure surged forward from Po, and as much as he wanted to continue dishing out payback, he decided it would probably be smart to follow the prompt. He leapt, pivoting around sharply to face Freddie's companion, who had his sidearm drawn and pointed at Po's face.

"Get down on the ground or I'll kill you," the Marine barked. "Face on the dirt with your fingers interlaced over the back of your head."

"Pay him no heed," Zanth rasped. "He won't shoot. Look—the pup is trying to rise."

It was true—Freddie had flipped himself over and was getting up onto all fours. A ghostly red leg shot out from Po, suggesting he take the opportunity to soccer kick Freddie in the face.

Po trembled, partly from exertion, maybe partly from the pain and blood loss from his shattered nose, but also from fear. He'd never had a loaded firearm pointed at him before, and a panicky voice was screaming at him from inside his head to do whatever the Marine told him to.

But he forced himself to ignore the man threatening to shoot him and he soccer kicked Freddie in the face.

Something yielded under his boot with a crunch, and the other recruit jerked sideways, then collapsed.

"*Stop or I'll shoot!*" the Marine roared.

"Notice how he isn't shooting?" Zanth said. "Get the rifle."

Po darted to Freddie's M37C and seized it by the barrel and handguard, exactly where a pair of ethereal scarlet hands were already gripping it. The weapon didn't feel as good in his grasp as his own did, but it would do.

"Now get to work," Zanth said. "Don't hesitate!"

Po didn't. He swung the rifle overhead at the Marine, who raised his arms to block the blow. The man grunted in pain as the stock cracked down onto his forearm, but Po just continued to clobber him, getting him in the ribs, the base of his neck, and finally landing a blow on his head—all with the help of the red indicators, which continued to show him the most effective angles of attack.

The hit to the head dazed his opponent, allowing Po to get another in. A resounding *crack* sent the Marine to the ground in a heap.

He turned to find Freddie stirring and moaning softly. Blood streamed from his nostrils and mouth.

Po stood still clutching Freddie's rifle at the ready, his chest heaving.

"What now?" he asked Zanth.

But the alien had apparently left, along with the red floating images that had been telling him what to do.

"*Drop the rifle and get on the ground!*" a voice yelled.

A beam of light switched on, its source somewhere far above, maybe even the cylinder's axis. It hit Po dead-center. A Marine in full combat armor appeared around the dumpster Po had first crept around, his blue visor trained on Po, along with the M37C he was pointing at him.

A second Marine came around the other side of the shed, with two others closing in from different directions. All with weapons trained on him, boxing him in.

"Zanth?" Po hissed under his breath.

But the Emplor was well and truly gone. And so he tossed the rifle away, got to his stomach, and put his face on the dirt.

***

Po found his holding cell inside Recruit Depot Cycler 3's brig to be much more accommodating than the one he'd spent the night in on Psyche.

Its lack of windows denied him what might otherwise have been a breathtaking view, swinging as the brig was from the cylinder's central axis, at a rotational speed that kept it aligned with the same spot on the surface. Indeed, the cell was uniformly gray, except for the deck and overhead, which were ringed by thin bands of a slightly darker gray.

There was a cot, and a toilet in a small square chamber off of one corner, and an imposing reinforced steel door with a slot at the bottom where three square meals a day were pushed through with reassuring regularity. The food was no worse than that he'd eaten in the chow hall, and the water he drank from plastic cups was cool and refreshing, and it tasted clean.

They kept him there for the better part of two days, judging by his count of the number of meals they'd given him. Just as his stomach was growling for its sixth meal since arriving in the brig, the door opened, and two armed Marines came in to slap restraints on his wrists and march him out into the passage.

The fact they sent *two* Marines came across as a compliment, somehow. Unless Zanth had doctored his implant's recording of what had happened, they would have seen how Po had handled Freddie and his co-conspirator. Would the Emplor have left the red-tinged "instructions" in the recording for the Marines to see? Po doubted it, somehow.

As for the alien himself, he'd stayed away, and Po still couldn't figure out what he'd been hoping to accomplish by leading him to that supply shed and helping him defeat Freddie and the Marine. Had the alien wanted them exposed, and dealt with, for some reason? Had Po merely been a useful tool, used by Zanth for the purpose, and discarded as soon as that purpose was fulfilled?

It seemed more than possible. Po had never had much trust for the Emplor as a species, but he'd let Zanth convince him he was on his side. He'd even gotten excited by the idea of having such an ally secretly helping him. But as the Marines marched him down a corridor just as sterile as the cell they'd taken him from, each with a hand on one of his biceps, he considered the likelihood that following Zanth's 'guidance' had cost him his chance at becoming a Marine, along with the next two-and-a-half decades of his life, which he'd be sure to spend in simjail once discharged.

The meeting room his escorts brought him to was small, which wasn't overly surprising for a building suspended on cables. It was well-appointed, though, with wood-paneled walls and an oaken table with two pairs of chairs facing each other across it. A halogen bulb set in an old-fashioned lamp sat on a side table at one end of the room, and above it hung the GEA Marines flag, with its fist grasping the world like a softball, a banner reading "Semper Fidelis" streaming out from between two of its knuckles. Six tiny wings sprouted from the hand, which should have looked weird, but didn't.

On the other side of the table sat two men—one of them was Staff Sergeant Mitchell, the other, someone Po didn't recognize. His hair was the same silver as the leaf-shaped epaulets that said he was a lieutenant colonel.

Po swallowed.

"Take a seat, Recruit," Mitchell said.

Po complied at once, choosing the seat nearest him, his hands still restrained behind him. His fingers rested against the chair's vertical wooden slats, and he sat up straight to avoid putting pressure on his wrists. Maintaining good posture right now was probably a good idea, anyway.

The hatch closed behind him with a thud. The fact they'd left his restraints on didn't seem promising, but the fact Sergeant Mitchell was still referring to him as a recruit did.

"This is Lieutenant Colonel Albrecht," Mitchell said. "He's the Command Inspector General for Marine Corps Recruit Depot Cyclers 2 and 3."

"It's an honor to meet you, sir," Po said. "I'd salute you if I could."

"Hm," Albrecht said. "On his best behavior, I see."

Mitchell nodded. "Yes, sir."

The CIG's face remained stony. "Sergeant Mitchell here tells me you're an exceptional recruit, and that getting out of your rack in the middle of the night to abandon your barracks constitutes highly unusual behavior for you. Is that accurate, Abbato?"

Zanth appeared in the only empty chair, popping into existence like a character from the latest open-world sim being run on outdated hardware. Po managed to limit his reaction to a slight jerk, though he'd almost cried out.

He cleared his throat. "Yes, sir."

"Then I have just one question for you, son," the colonel said. "Why did you get out of your rack?"

Po hesitated.

"Lie to them," the Emplor said. "Tell them you suspected Rodriguez was an Obsidian Angel and you noticed his rack was empty. You saw he wasn't on interior fire watch—Crotty was—so you waited till Crotty went into the head and went outside to confront Rodriguez, but he wasn't there, and so you tracked him to the supply shed."

The lieutenant colonel seemed to be weighing him with his stern eyes, and Po opened his mouth to answer, but the words caught in his throat. Since he'd been consigned to bootcamp, he'd been trying not to lie, since lies were a big part of why he'd ended up here in the first place.

"Speak," Zanth insisted. "Else he won't believe anything you say."

What choice did he have?

"Sir, has Sergeant Mitchell told you about what happened with my implant while I was running the Swagger Course?"

"I'm aware of the incident."

"Well, sir, my understanding from speaking to Sergeant Olson about that incident is that a hacker caused it to happen. It so happens that I have enemies back on Psyche, enemies who are with the Obsidian Angels—and as you may know, if one Angel is your enemy, then they all are. After what happened to me on the Swagger Course, I began to suspect there were Angel meshminders aboard Cycler 3 too, who were targeting me. Recruit Rodriguez had been acting strangely for a while, and I came to believe an Angel approached him back on Psyche, asking him to join them, after his arrest but before he took the shuttle to bootcamp."

"How was Rodriguez acting strangely?"

"Well, he seemed to hate me—more than I would have expected, even after what happened between us back on Psyche. He tried to turn the rest of the platoon against me. Also, I happen to know from a letter sent to me by my sister that Freddie's father died recently. But he didn't seem affected at all. Just like an Angel wouldn't be affected, because their identity is absorbed by the meshmind, and Diego Rodriguez didn't mean anything to the Angel meshmind."

Zanth was nodding slowly, and his breath came out in a slow rasp, his lizard's mouth open slightly, his head spines bobbing in time with his breathing. "*Good,*" he said, almost too low for Po to hear.

"You still haven't told me why you left your rack," Albrecht said.

"Well, I was having trouble sleeping, so I sat up for a bit. That's when I noticed Rodriguez wasn't asleep in his rack. And since Crotty was on interior fire watch, that meant Rodriguez would be outside. I decided I'd confront him about being an Angel, so I waited for Crotty to go into the head, and then I slipped outside. Once I got there, I saw Rodriguez had abandoned his post, and so I tracked him to the supply shed where we had our...run-in."

Albrecht raised an eyebrow.

"I shouldn't have left my rack, sir. I'm sorry."

The moment he finished speaking, Zanth vanished as abruptly as he'd appeared. Po was left alone to face his DI and the CIG.

"As it happens, Recruit, you were right."

Albrecht's icy exterior finally cracked, and he favored Po with a tight smile. Relief washed over him. He also hadn't missed Albrecht's first use of the word "recruit"—just like Sergeant Mitchell was still calling him one.

Something struck him, then.

Zanth must have doctored my implant's recording to show me noticing Freddie out of his bed, and Crotty patrolling the barracks. He was sure either Albrecht or his staff would have gone over the recording with a fine-tooth comb, and if it had shown anything other than what Po had just described, Albrecht wouldn't be smiling right now.

"Rodriguez *is* an Obsidian Angel," the lieutenant colonel went on. "Or at least, he was. His implant had been tampered with before he came to Cycler 3, a fact somehow missed by our induction process. Lance Corporal Sipes, the other individual you incapacitated, was also an Angel. They've both now had their implants removed, which is causing some interesting psychological effects. Not that I have much sympathy for either of them." He glanced at Mitchell. "Sergeant?"

"Yes. It seems they had a way of transferring substantial amounts of data, at high speeds...through their foreheads. That's what they were doing when you first found them behind the shed. Sipes worked in Communications on Sublevel 2, near the eastern endcap. It seems he used his position to receive regular updates from the system-wide Angel meshmind. But since signals can't get through the hull, and any relayed wireless signals are tightly tracked and monitored, the only way Sipes could keep Rodriguez current with the broader meshmind was to meet in person and do the forehead thing." Mitchell shrugged. "I get the impression this is new territory for the Angels—infiltrating our cyclers. They took a big risk, sending Rodriguez in here. As I understand it, Angels who've gotten cut off from the others are the ones most at risk of deviating from the meshmind, and of wanting their old life back."

"Indeed," Albrecht said. "And it's worse for them than losing two Angels—the entire Corps will be on high-alert now for any more infiltrators. Your actions were of great benefit to the GEA Marine Corps, Abbato. That's why I want to apologize for the forty-one hours we kept you in a cell. That's how long it took to sort out exactly what had happened behind that supply shed. Now that we have, I'd like to personally thank you. Recruits don't receive medals, but if you were a Marine, I'd probably be able to get you at least a Bronze star. As it stands, know that your extraordinary service to the Corps will be noted, complete with a Certificate of Commendation attached to your record. Recruits don't normally get those either, but I'm confident I can make it happen."

For a long moment, Po was lost for words. Then, he found his voice. "I'm truly honored, sir. Thank you."

"Thank *you,* Recruit Abbato. And with that out of the way, I'm sending you back to your platoon, to complete your training. You'll make a fine Marine, son. Do us proud."

"Yes, sir."

But as Po followed Sergeant Mitchell through the brig, to the elevator that would take them down one of the cables to the cylinder's surface, he didn't feel proud. Instead, he felt conflicted.

I couldn't have accomplished any of that without Zanth's help.

But wasn't that what he'd wanted? To have a secret alien friend who'd give him an unfair advantage over the other recruits?

It was. But now that he was enjoying its fruits, he found they didn't taste quite as sweet as he'd expected them to.

Chapter 29

After his stint in the brig, normal life resumed—though it did strike Po as bizarre sometimes that he'd come to consider bootcamp "normal life."

With no one trying to kill him, and no one actively trying to turn the entire platoon against him, he found himself able to focus on the day-by-day rigors of fighting to become a Marine.

And fight he did. The physical trials got harder, the training more mentally and emotionally exhausting, with every day that passed.

But more than ever, the recruits of Platoon 50509 had each other's backs. Rumors ran wild through the training base about what had happened to Recruit Rodriguez, and some of them actually came close to the truth. Po had been ordered by Sergeant Mitchell not to divulge any details, and so when Paisley told him he'd heard Rodriguez had secretly been an Obsidian Angel, he just said, "Oh, yeah?" and returned to downing his mac and cheese.

The upshot for Po was that the others accepted him more and more. Gradually, his table at the chow hall filled with companions. Paisley, Becker, Navarro, Crotty, Dempsey—he enjoyed a rotating cast of tablemates every mealtime, with always at least a couple other recruits to chat with.

He wasn't untouchable any longer. And actually, the others seemed to respect him. Sure, they insulted him, gave him grief, and even pranked him every now and then. But none of it carried the maliciousness from before. They were recruits being recruits, and a few of them, he'd even call his friends.

Zanth made no further appearances. Whatever the Emplor had been trying to accomplish with Po, he apparently felt like he'd accomplished it—at least for now. Po was left to his own devices to tackle the remaining challenges of bootcamp.

The ever-lengthening Conditioning Marches. The endless classes.

Qualifying on his M37 at the rifle range. Qualifying for swimming ability.

The return to the Confidence Course, and then the Swagger Course.

Getting tear gassed—without a gas mask on. The burning sensation, the five minutes that felt like an hour. Emerging from the gas chamber with tears and mucus dripping from his chin.

And finally, the Crucible: bootcamp's final, fifty-four-hour test.

During those last three days, the DIs did everything they could to show them what they'd actually face as Marines.

They crawled through mud, in uniform, with their rifles strapped to their backs. They crawled under barbed wire, which sometimes they had to lift for the next recruit to fit under.

They advanced with rifles raised, sighting through their scopes. They took cover. They leapt over fences with 40-pound packs clinging to their backs. All the while, sounds of weapons fire, and of shelling, played through their implants' audio taps. They had to shout to be heard.

They dragged fellow recruits to safety by the armpits. They caught each other in nets made of their own interlaced arms. They conducted night movements, when any illumination at all gave up their position to the enemy, which meant they were dead.

There was barely any food given them during the Crucible. Once, when Sergeant Scott gave them an apple each from a burlap bag, Po ate the core, seeds and all, and he suggested to Crotty that he do the same. Soon, every recruit was stuffing his leftover apple core into his mouth, some of them even picking them back up off the ground. They forced themselves to chew through the tough rind, and they got it all down.

They had to operate on something.

***

And so they came to the Crucible's final trial. After a night infiltration course, and just four hours sleep, they rose at 0400 to begin a nine-mile march that would take them out of the training base, over the patchwork fields to the west, and finally through the woods that reared from the western endcap slopes.

This would be the farthest they'd delved into that woods, and their path would take them to its heights, to the point of lowest gravity and roughest terrain. There, where the redwoods loomed impossibly tall, they'd circumnavigate the endcap and return to the point where they'd entered the woods, and then march back to the training base—to become Marines.

Po didn't feel anything except numb as he dragged himself out of his rack and pulled on his utilities. After Freddie had been exposed, he'd believed bootcamp would become a lot more straightforward. He'd figured he could simply focus on its challenges, and as long as he kept his head down, he'd succeed.

But Freddie seemed like a distant memory now, and so did his platoon's hatred of him. As Po finished lacing up his boots and grabbed his 40-pound pack from his locker, he realized bootcamp had taken way more out of him than Freddie ever had. Even his near-death experience on the Swagger Course now paled in comparison with the long, grinding struggle.

Almost dying had been frightening, but it hadn't made him so tired he could feel it in his bones. And it hadn't given him the cool, detached gaze he now saw when he looked in the mirror—with eyes that hinted of the steel underneath.

At this hour of the morning, Cycler 3 was still dark, with the lights from the base on the cylinder's opposite side twinkling through the axis clouds like stars. Nothing else moved. Cycler 3 slept.

Except for the recruits, who fell in silently. All of Alpha Company was gathering on the path between the barracks—and if they made it through this final march, they'd all become Marines today.

But as their long trudge began, that seemed like an eternity away. Po's limbs were stiff and reluctant to be moved. Each step was a fight against sore muscles and inflexible tendons. The recruits kept their silence as they progressed slowly westward. Po could almost *hear* their exhaustion in the way nothing could be heard except the patter of boots on the path, which soon turned from asphalt to dirt and rock. There weren't even any birds singing.

Crotty stumbled beside him, falling to his knees. Po could have caught him—*should* have caught him. There'd been enough time, and the other recruit had been marching right beside him. But his reaction time had dwindled to nothing. He observed everything dumbly, insensate, as if watching a pointless dream unfold.

He reached down and grabbed Crotty's hand, and helped him regain his feet.

"Thanks," Crotty muttered, though there wasn't much gratitude in his voice.

And Po found he didn't care. They were both clearly too exhausted to feel anything. Empty formalities were all that could be expected.

Several of the recruits were limping, including Po himself. He'd half-twisted his ankle during the night infiltration last night, and while it had swollen some over night, he could still walk on it. Sort of.

Despite how many limpers there were, no one fell out. Everyone refused to quit, so close to the end. Even though this slog had only just begun.

At first, corn fields and wheat fields hemmed in the broad path on both sides. Gradually, though, those became grasslands, which gave way to a barren terrain to match the path they marched on.

Structures dotted the land here and there, which Po guessed were used for power supply, communications, or storage. Maybe all three at once.

Reaching the woods and passing between the first trees put him in mind of the time Zanth had visited him, on an earlier march. Then he thought about how he'd essentially dismantled not just Freddie in hand-to-hand combat, but also a Marine. Followed by two days in the brig.

"You haven't exactly had a typical bootcamp experience," Navarro had said the next day at chow. "Have you?"

Navarro was right. Po had faced down challenges well beyond what was expected of the typical recruit. And he was still here. And that felt good. It made him proud.

But he never would have been able to face down Freddie, let alone a Marine, if it hadn't been for Zanth's ethereal promptings. The Emplor had shown him exactly where to put his arms and legs, exactly how to move. If not for that, he would have been completely at their mercy.

Worse, he wouldn't have figured out there was an Obsidian Angel in their platoon if Zanth hadn't warned him.

After his first few encounters with Zanth, he'd relished the idea of a new ally that would give him an unfair edge over the others. And he still saw the advantage in that.

But as sunlight streamed from the cycler's eastern end, strengthening with each passing minute and illuminating the forest floor, Po realized he needed to be able to fend for himself. He barely knew Zanth, and he had no clue what his motives were. Sure, as long as the alien was willing to help him, he'd use that. But he needed to make sure he was ready for the day the Emplor cut him off.

The gravity dropped off as they climbed through the endcap wood's uneven trails, lightening their loads, but offering no real reprieve. True, Po's feet felt lighter as he lifted them over the thick roots that snaked across the path. But the reduction in mass only seemed to make tripping a greater likelihood, as he had to constantly recalibrate how much force he needed to propel himself forward. Beside him, Crotty fell again, landing on his face and not moving. Po wasn't sure Crotty *would* have moved if he hadn't grabbed him by his backpack and yanked him up again. This time, he offered no word of thanks, and Po didn't ask for one. They were well beyond manners, now.

The worst part of the way gravity gradually lessened its hold on him were the flashbacks to his first day on the Swagger Course, when his implant had blacked out every one of his senses, and he'd found himself hurtling through Cycler 3's artificial sky. That wouldn't happen here, he knew. Even if someone did manage to hack his implant today, colliding with one of his fellow recruits was likely the worst thing that could result—these trails didn't reach high enough for gravity to vanish altogether.

But that didn't mean Po could shake the memory, or the creeping dread it brought.

At last, they finished circumnavigating the endcap, and the DIs led them along trails that wound gradually downward, back toward the surface where they'd first entered the wood. Technically they were traveling downhill now, but even that didn't offer the reprieve it should have, since gravity was gradually reasserting itself, and they were becoming heavier and heavier.

Birds were chirping all around them, and the silence seemed heavier than their packs, when Sergeant Mitchell yelled from the front:

"Ah-1-2-3-*4!*"

"*Marine Corps!*" the recruits all roared back automatically, in unison.

"Ah-1-2-3-*4!*"

"*Marine Corps!*"

"Planetary was a-not for *me!*"

"*Marine Corps!*"

"Orbital was just a-too easy."

"*Marine Corps!*"

"What I needed was a little bit *more!*"

"*Marine Corps!*"

"I need a life that is hardcore."

"*Marine Corps!*"

"Cycler 3 is where it all be*gan.*"

"*Marine Corps!*"

"Rocks and trees packed in a flying tin can."

"*Marine Corps!*"

The marching cadence—which had grated on Po's brain more than once as he struggled through another grueling PT session—had a different effect today. They made a sense of energy and excitement crackle in his chest, coupled with a swelling pride.

I did it, he realized. *I actually did it. I made it. I'm going to be a Marine.*

"First phase it broke me down," Mitchell hollered.

"*Marine Corps!*"

"Second phase I started comin' round."

"*Marine Corps!*"

"Third phase I was lean and mean."

"*Marine Corps!*"

"Graduation standing tall in my green."

"*Marine Corps!*"

"To anybody who asked me 'why?'"

"*Marine Corps!*"

"Here's the deal, I gave my reply."

"*Marine Corps!*"

"I'll be a Marine till the day I die."

"*Marine Corps!*"

"Motivated and Semper Fi."

"*Marine Corps!*"

After they finished with that cadence, called "Marines for Me," Mitchell led them in "Fist, Globe, and Wings." They cycled through all the cadences they'd learned during the last thirteen weeks, in what felt like the greatest hits of bootcamp.

And it made a difference. It stirred Po from his stupor, and while he was still tired, he began to appreciate what today meant. This was the culmination of all his hard work. All his perseverance—through the others hating him, through the Obsidian Angels reaching across the system and trying to kill him, through the gauntlet that was bootcamp itself. It all led to this. Today. He walked with his head held high, and beside him, Crotty seemed more energetic too. The pencil-thin recruit didn't fall again.

He's not even pencil-thin anymore, is he? Crotty was still what you'd call thin and runty, but even he'd managed to put on a layer of muscle. They were all of them transformed, from a disjointed gang of Psyche delinquents into an organized fighting force—into men, ready to take on anything the system cared to throw at them.

Sergeant Mitchell led them back to the training base, and then through it, past exercise fields, barracks, the chow hall, and finally to the parade deck. They followed him across it to the far end, where sat a replica of the Marine Corps War Memorial whose original was first unveiled in the twentieth century, somewhere in the United States, if Po remembered right. It was a place to honor the memory of every Marine who'd ever fallen in combat...and also a place where new Marines were born.

Mitchell came to a halt, about-faced, and ordered them to drop their packs, come forward, and fall in.

"Aye, sir!"

All five platoons of Alpha Company fell in before the statue, each in separate formation. Once they were all in position, a color guard raised the GEA Marines flag over the memorial.

The throaty trumpets, the crashing cymbals, the steady drumbeat...none of it had gotten inside Po the way it did today. He'd never been more fatigued hearing morning colors, and it had never moved him as it did now. That triumphant music felt like it could lift him off the ground and carry him all the way up to Cycler 3's axis.

After colors, Chaplain Campbell led the company in prayer. Po hadn't anticipated seeing the chaplain here, and it was something of a shock. Campbell had some interesting things to say about Marine Corps values, and how God figured into them, but ultimately Po had decided to leave him and his chapel behind once he'd figured out his own plan for improving things with his platoonmates.

This unexpected appearance by the chaplain on what was the most momentous day since Po had arrived on Cycler 3...it was jarring, to say the least. The chaplain represented a world which Po had dipped his toe in briefly, but had decided to set aside, just as he'd followed his father in setting it aside as a young boy. Now, that world had apparently barreled headlong into regular Cycler 3 life.

Once the prayer had been prayed, Sergeant Mitchell walked along Platoon 50509's ranks carrying a black tote, which he unclasped before each recruit, pulling out a fist-and-wings insignia and placing it in each new Marine's left hand before shaking his right.

A tight grin was on the DI's lips as he reached Po.

"It's been a pleasure," Mitchell said as they shook. "I mean that. Congratulations, Marine."

"Thank you, sir," Po said, surprised at how his voice came out in a croak. It felt strange to have his hand shaken by his DI, who until now had seemed completely untouchable.

Having finally made Marines of them, Sergeant Mitchell ordered them to fall out. That was when a familiar voice called out.

"Bring it in, Alpha. Huddle close to the memorial. Nice and tight."

"Aye, sir!" the recruits all shouted back, as everyone shifted closer to the statue.

On top of the octagonal dais where the statue was mounted, Master Sergeant Landry stood waiting for them with his hands on his hips. Landry was the sergeant who'd first welcomed Po's platoon to Cycler 3, in a way that still stressed him out just thinking about it.

"How do we feel?" Landry asked.

"Good, sir!"

"So you should. I want to be the first to say it—good morning, Marines!"

"*Good morning, sir!*" roared Alpha Company.

"Everyone ready for story time?"

"*Yes, sir!*"

"Good. Now, I just want you to listen for a while."

"Aye, sir!"

"Near the end of World War 2, after the Battle of Iwo Jima—one of the bloodiest battles of that entire war—the six Marines you see immortalized in this statue raised what was then the United States colors on top of Mount Suribachi. A journalist named Rosenthal was there to take their picture, and history was made."

Landry paced slowly back and forth in front of the statue, emphasizing each turn of his speech with firm gestures.

"That photo was printed and reprinted in thousands of magazines and newspapers, and it became *the* symbol of the undying resilience of the US Marine Corps—a fighting force so indispensable that it morphed into the GEA Marines when national governments were reorganized under the Council of Hegemons. Three of the Marines who raised this flag on that mountain—fully half of them—were killed in that very same battle. Another was wounded. This wasn't some glitzy photo opportunity, Marines. This was a gesture of confident victory, even in the middle of a conflict that was still very much raging.

"The Marines shown in this statue lived hundreds of years ago, and of course none of them are alive now. But as the good chaplain can tell you, their spirits live on forever. Just as the Marine Corps will always be here, for as long as there's a humanity to defend."

Sergeant Landry stopped and pointed back at the statue. "For all those decades, these brave men have been watching over the Corps from on high." He pointed at the newly minted Marines huddled around the statue. "They've been watching *you* these past three months—especially during these last three days, as you challenged the Crucible. And right now, they're smiling. They're smiling, because they know their sacrifice was not in vain. They know that their homeworld, and their Corps, for which they bled and died, is in good hands. In *your* hands. They know their legacy is safe here in the twenty-third century."

Po knew the Marines from the statue hadn't actually fought for Earth, but instead for the US against the Japanese. Right now, the distinction didn't bother him very much. And judging by the sniffling he heard around him, it didn't much bother his fellow Marines either.

A tear tumbled from his right eye, and he let it fall. None of them raised a hand to wipe away the tears they'd no doubt deny until their dying days.

"Gentlemen, today you become full-fledged members of our family. You have paid your dues, and you have been found worthy. You have just been awarded the fist, globe, and wings, and you have become the guardians that ensure humanity's glory forever flies. Semper Fidelis."

Chapter 30

After the emblem ceremony, the sergeants took Alpha Company back to the chow hall and fed them what they called a Warrior's Breakfast.

This was not a day, apparently, for carefully measured portions calibrated to each individual's BMI and the Corps' vision for what that should be. Their meals weren't disgorged by the little doors along the first bulkhead—instead, the new Marines could select whatever they wanted from tables that had been brought out from some supply room. On them sat platters piled high with fruit, cinnamon buns, pancakes, waffles, French toast, muffins, eggs, bacon, steak, and hash browns. Interspersed between everything else were bowls filled with cereal, berries, granola, yogurt, nuts, and syrup. The centerpiece of each table was a huge bowl of what looked like whipped cream. Po's mouth was awash with saliva by the time he reached the first offering with his tray.

"Don't be shy, Marines," Master Sergeant Landry told them. "You didn't eat like this back on Psyche, and you won't again for a long time. Go back for seconds. Thirds, if you want. You've earned it."

Po felt like he'd earned it. His stomach rumbled at the aromas, and his body began to tremble, as though being presented with such a feast had made it finally ready to admit how weak the Crucible had made him.

He found himself sitting at the end of a table, next to Paisley, who was pretty chatty under normal circumstances. But neither of them was much interested in chatting, just now. Instead, they both focused on shoveling as much food into their mouths as quickly as they could.

"Private Abbato," a voice said, and only then did Po notice the uniformed figure who'd come to a stop at the end of their table.

Private. I guess that's what I am now, isn't it?

He looked up to see Chaplain Campbell standing there, his hands clasped behind his back.

Po started to stand up and salute, but Campbell waved him back into his seat. "Please, don't let me interrupt your feasting. I came to congratulate you, Marine."

"Thank you, sir." Po cut off a sizable chunk of syrup-drenched pancake, with the intention of stuffing it into his mouth, but found he couldn't quite bring himself to do it, even though he'd been invited to. Continuing to stuff his face with the chaplain standing there talking to him...it just didn't feel right.

"Sir," the chaplain repeated, chuckling. "Still won't call me Father, eh? I guess I shouldn't be surprised."

"I told you, sir. I already have a father who's rotting in a simjail."

Paisley paused eating, glanced sidelong at Po, then broke off another piece of muffin and popped it into his mouth.

The chaplain was still smiling his usual easy smile. "You have more than one father, you know. Even if you don't acknowledge it."

"You being one of them?"

"Well, since you stopped coming to my Mass and attending my office hours, I suppose you've rejected me as your spiritual father. But that's okay. I'm talking more about your heavenly father, who wills your eternal good."

"He could have fooled me," Po muttered.

"I want you to know, Private, that you're always welcome, whether at Mass or in my office. Your SOI instructors *will* let you cross the cylinder to attend, and I'm certainly willing to receive you there, just as your father in heaven is willing to receive you, at any time of the day. All that's needed is to repent—a remedy we all stand in need of."

"Yeah, I don't think that's gonna happen."

"I know you don't," Campbell said, still smiling. "But there's something I think *you* should know. God won't ever stop calling you home, nor will He stop pursuing you. In a few months, you'll leave Cycler 3, and you'll probably never see me again. But God will never leave you. He gives each of us every grace, every opportunity, to say yes to Him. Because He loves us."

During the chaplain's speech, Po tried to keep his face as neutral as possible. But when Campbell stopped speaking, he allowed his gaze to return to his breakfast, which he still hadn't resumed eating.

"Go back to your meal, Marine," the chaplain said gently. "I've said what I was sent to say. And as paltry as my words are, I'll pray for the Holy Spirit to stir them within you. God bless you."

With that, the chaplain left.

Paisley looked at him again, and stopped chewing a mouthful of bacon and hash brown to talk around it. "Why does the crazy stuff always happen to you?" he asked.

***

A modest, four-tiered set of bleachers sat at one end of the gymnasium where their graduation ceremony was held. It was where the graduating Marines' family members would have sat, if any of them had been able to make the journey across the solar system to catch up to Cycler 3 in order to attend.

The bleachers were completely empty.

"Imagine your mother is sitting there," Sergeant Mitchell encouraged them beforehand. "And march exactly as crisply as if she was. I still have the authority to subject you to a brutal smoke session."

The only spectator that ended up attending was a small camera with a wide angle that someone had perched on the top bleacher, which would record the proceedings and transmit them back to Psyche. Back to any of their family members who cared to watch them become men. To become more than just men.

To become Marines.

Po didn't picture Rosa Abbato sitting in the bleachers as he marched with the rest of his platoon into the gym—instead, he imagined Nicky there, cheering as loudly as her illness would allow, which he felt sure she would have done even if she'd been the only one present.

And he marched for his sister just as proudly as he would have for the Council of Hegemons.

Prouder. Who am I kidding? Much more proudly than that.

***

This was the part where new Marines trained Earthside would get ten days of leave, but there'd be none of that on Cycler 3. When Po returned with his platoon to the barracks for the last time, he found everything he owned already packed into his duffel bag and rucksack, waiting for him to carry halfway around the surface cylinder's more-than-twelve-kilometer circumference to Camp Williams, where he'd attend School of Infantry.

From there, if he chanced to look up, he'd see the training base upside-down where he and his fellow recruits had sweated and bled to earn their emblems. New recruits were starting there all the time, forming new training companies. And a new platoon would be moving into this barracks tomorrow.

He wished them well.

Missing out on leave didn't really bother him. What would they have done with it? More hikes through the woods? Hang around the parade ground? Haunt the chow hall?

With his ruck on his back and his duffel bag in hand, Po was glad to be headed for Camp Williams—to be getting on with learning exactly what his life was going to consist of. Bootcamp had definitely changed him, in more ways than he probably realized. But even though he was technically a Marine, and had qualified on his M37C, he still didn't feel ready to go fight Nibiran terrorists on their own world. Nor should he, he guessed. That was what SOI was for.

All the same, trudging across the artificial-yet-uneven terrain, laden with something like eighty pounds of gear, he did have to wonder if it had really been necessary for whoever controlled Cycler 3's weather to make today so hot.

SOI began almost the minute they arrived. A corporal assigned them squad bays right away, and Po found himself sharing one with Paisley, Dempsey, and ten others he didn't know. Barring something unusual, they'd probably be together for the next seven weeks, since they'd all signed up to be infantry.

"So now we get to smell just twelve other guys instead of forty," Paisley said.

Po nodded. "Moving up in the world."

Dempsey chuckled.

The day he'd arrived at Cycler 3, Po had put Rifleman as his preferred occupational specialty, since he knew the most about it from what books and vids he'd watched on the Marines. His GASVAT scores had qualified him for more advanced jobs, but this one had felt safest, and he'd apparently met the right qualifications during bootcamp for the Corps to consider him competent enough to become one.

He wasn't sure whether that was something to be proud of or not. Then again, getting through bootcamp at all felt like a minor miracle, so probably it was.

His first class was on the philosophy of war fighting, which sounded like a snooze when he first heard the topic. He expected an hour or more of airy-fairy fluff about the high and noble ideal of serving GEA in war, or maybe the metaphysical significance of getting your leg blown off for Earthers who'd sooner curse you than thank you.

But instead, the barrel-chested combat instructor who paced the front of the lecture hall held them all riveted with his words, the obvious truth of what he said gripping Po more tightly than anything he'd listened to in a long time.

"War is nothing like you've heard," Gunnery Sergeant Emery said. "Nothing like you've seen in vids or sims. Nothing like you've dreamt. If I ask you to dig a hole in rural Idaho, it might be a chore, but compared to what you just went through these last thirteen weeks, it should be relatively straightforward and stress-free. But nothing about war is stress-free. Try digging a hole in hard, rocky terrain while under enemy fire. Try digging a hole when you could die before you finish it—when failure is not an option, because your superior decided that was the best position to set up shop. Then you'll know what it's like to be a Marine.

"To be a Marine is to know chaos. To live in a reality that's constantly shifting and morphing and trying to kill you. To face an enemy who's as smart as you are, probably smarter, who'll stop at nothing to invent a parade of endlessly innovative ways to make sure you're dead before you're twenty-five. Even if he fails to kill you, he'll have a secondary goal that'll make your life so miserable you'll wish you were dead. But he won't announce his goals to you, Marines, no. You'll never know where he is or what he's doing, or even why. Sometimes you won't even know *who* he is. Make uncertainty your bedfellow. Chaos and uncertainty are your new best friends.

"Centuries ago, a Prussian officer told us no plan survives contact with the enemy. He was sugarcoating it. Every battle's natural end is complete disorder. The longer you fight, the more confused things become. Half your squad gets taken out. Your immediate superior gets killed, and then so does *his* superior. Will you be ready to step forward and take initiative when chaos reigns? Or did you learn anything about leadership since you came to this tin can?"

The combat instructor's shrewd eyes leapt from Marine to Marine, seeming to take each one's measure in turn. "People ask why we don't use bots to fight our wars for us—or, why doesn't our enemy. I'm telling you right now, after a week at war, you'll *wish* you were facing bots. A machine, you can understand. It has well-defined goals and patterns of behavior. But a human fights dirty, and he's unpredictable, even to himself. Humans will deceive you, they'll manipulate you, make you doubt your sanity. Nothing can make you wish you'd never been born like a human being can. Believe it, Marines. Mark my words."

Emery's speech had lit a fire in Po's chest, but the flame sputtered a little at this last part.

Why is he talking about fighting humans? We'll be up against Nibirans. Won't we?

Of course, over the decades there'd been no shortage of nations who'd broken with the global order imposed by GEA. The media always sided with the Council of Hegemons in those situations, and there were always enough atrocities perpetrated by the rebel government to plaster across screens and implants the world over, to drum up public support for an invasion.

Algeria had been the most recent offender—its drawn-out rebellion had finally been quashed just a few years ago.

Maybe Emery fought in that war.

***

SOI didn't have as many PT sessions, though the marches got longer and harder, and what it lacked in PT it made up for by cramming as much knowledge as possible into the new Marines' brains, as quickly as possible.

There was free time, and Po used pretty much all of his to train. He hadn't forgotten his fight with Freddie and the lance corporal, and how helpless he would have been without Zanth's ghostly prompts. And so, evening downtime almost invariably found him in the gym. While there, he'd box or spar with anyone interested, and learn from anyone willing to teach. Sometimes, learning involved getting knocked to the floor, wheezing.

Those were probably the most memorable lessons.

"Why are you obsessed with learning self defense?" Zanth asked him on one of his walks home, a half hour or so before lights-out—the first time in a good while that the Emplor had appeared in an environment that allowed Po to answer back.

He paused before answering, wanting to choose his words carefully. If he angered the alien, he risked missing out on his help in the future. "I would have been dog meat if it hadn't been for your help against Freddie and that officer," he said slowly.

"And? Do you expect me to withdraw my help at some point?"

"I don't know what to expect from you. You haven't told me why you're doing this yet."

Zanth's tail whipped across the ground behind him as he walked, suggesting irritation. "I have, actually. In the class with your old dwarven DI, Doyle. I'm here because you have the potential for greatness, however concealed it is beneath strata of stubbornness and stupidity. Humanity has a chance at a glorious future, but it will only be brought about through the efforts of individuals such as yourself...if only you will shoulder the burden that is your destiny to bear. The Emplor are here to uplift humanity, if only you screeching monkeys would cooperate."

Po sniffed. "If I'm going to have an impact like that, I should probably learn to fight. Shouldn't I?"

"I'll *show* you how to fight. Just like I did against your schoolyard chum."

"I may not always have my connection with you, Zanth. I may not always have this implant."

"Fool. How do you think Freddie bested you the first time, in the boxing ring? Even then, he had Obsidian Angel algorithms running offline, in real time. His every blow had been optimized in advance and laid out for him. All he needed to do was execute—like you did, during your Battle of the Dumpster."

"Why didn't he have those same algorithms that night?"

"He did. But you had *Emplor* help. That's a little better than help from the Obsidian Angels."

"Okay. Let's say I'll always have you. I still need to train between fights, and keep fit, don't I? Your instructions won't do much good if I go to battle with limp noodles for arms."

The Emplor was studying him with what might have been an appraising look, though it was difficult to tell from his reptilian facial expressions. His head spines waved in the gentle breeze. "For the first time since we've met, you've actually made a point." He made a cutting gesture with his clawed fingers. "But you can't fool me. The reason you're training so hard is because you don't trust me."

"Well, maybe we'll just need to work together a little longer to get there."

"Hmm. I would have thought by now you'd suffered enough on account of your blindness to be willing to accept my aid with a whole heart. But I can see you need further *instruction.*" Zanth's eyes, locked on Po's face, smoldered in their deep sockets. "We'll see how you're feeling after your next ordeal. After that, I expect you'll be *begging* for my aid."

With that, the alien vanished.

***

That night, Po dreamed it was Graduation Day again, and he was standing in formation with his fellow graduates, trying to appear competent for the camera that would beam his likeness back to Psyche for his sister. But he couldn't stop himself from grinding his teeth. Halfway through the ceremony, their enamel began to crack apart under the pressure, and then to spill out from between his lips. He raised his hand to catch them—already an obscene breach of decorum—but he couldn't get them all. Countless fragments tumbled through his fingers to clatter on the gym floor.

He woke up in a cold sweat.

I need to get a hold of myself. Just focus on getting through SOI, Po.

So he did. He threw himself into his classes, into the constant activities and field exercises. There was certainly plenty to occupy his mind. In SOI, they went beyond pointing and shooting their rifles to learning how they were actually employed in the field. They practiced using camouflage and concealment to move stealthily through contested territory. They blew stuff up.

For the first time since arriving in Cycler 3, Po came to realize what the surface cylinder's vast tracts of empty space were used for: training the new Marines. The instructors took them out weekly for field exercises, showing them how to achieve better accuracy at greater ranges and poorer conditions, teaching them how to stay mentally tough in harrowing situations, demonstrating how to navigate using the map and compass tools built into their Circuits. Getting around a cylinder's artificial terrain was a little different from navigating planetside, but the instructors covered both.

During what they called Defense Week, Po was paired with another Marine named Wyatt and sent out into the hills bordering the endcap on this side of the cylinder. There, they were told to dig a fighting hole, which they'd sleep in for the rest of the week, all the while keeping watch for hostiles and going on occasional patrols.

Paisley had raised his hand during the briefing for Defense Week. "What if a grizzly bear comes at us while we're out there, Sergeant? Charges us, I mean?"

"Then you shoot it, Marine."

"Understood, Sergeant."

With all this constant activity happening outside Camp Williams, sometimes even taking them as far as the outskirts of the training base where they'd attended bootcamp, Po had to wonder how he'd failed to notice Marines roaming all over the countryside back when he'd been a recruit. Then he remembered how being caught gazing around the cylinder would invariably earn them IT, and it all made sense.

In the fifth week, every Marine was issued a set of SERAPH armor, which an instructor named Sergeant Ibrahim described as a general purpose defense system.

"The SERAPH system integrates seamlessly with your Circuits, which will give you a readout of everything you'd care to know in combat, including available oxygen levels, internal and external temperature, available ammo, team member positions, recent intel complete with level of certainty, environmental toxicity levels, and more. The suit's covered head to toe with multiple redundant sensors, meaning you'll essentially have eyes in the back of your head, plus a whole lot more."

With that, Ibrahim demonstrated the various pouches and the expanding/contracting slots into which magazines and grenade rounds could be stowed.

"The weight distribution on these things is a dream. You'll feel like you're wearing nothing more than a heavy jacket. The armor's resistant to rifle rounds while maintaining maximum flexibility. Note that I said *resistant* to rifle rounds. That doesn't mean you're invincible. We could have made it stop armor-piercing rounds, but then the maneuverability trade-off would be unacceptable."

The time was rapidly approaching when the combat instructors would divide their students into two forces and have them fight. That was what Po was looking forward to most, and he often found himself wondering just how realistic the instructors would make it.

Would this be something close to his first taste of combat, or would it feel hokey and fake? It seemed like there was a lot of potential to use their implants to make things look, feel, and sound real. They'd done some of that during the Crucible in bootcamp, but he knew for a fact that they hadn't come anywhere close to using the Circuit's full capabilities for immersion.

He knew that from experience, actually.

Either way, he hoped they didn't shy away from fully employing the technology to simulate actual combat, and judging by conversations with a few of the others in the mess hall, he knew he wasn't alone in that.

Fully four days before the simulated fighting would begin, Po was wrenched from his dreams by a dull roar, accompanied by the squad bay shaking all around him.

"What was that?" Paisley asked.

"It sounded like...an explosion," Po said. He glanced across the bay at Dempsey, who was still fast asleep in his rack.

"No way. Do you think they're starting Fight Week early? Springing it on us now, in the middle of the night, to keep us on our toes? Just like if we were at war."

"We haven't even been assigned sides, yet."

Another explosion rocked the bay, this one closer, and louder.

Dempsey was awake, now, too. "Was that our implants?" he asked. "Or did it really happen?"

"I think we better get into our utilities," Po said.

Chapter 31

An alarm was blaring by the time they made it out of the squad bay, unloaded M37Cs in hand—unloaded, because every round was meticulously rationed and tracked by Camp Williams' armorers, helped by an automated system.

Po was pretty sure the alarm was only ringing in their auditory nerves, and couldn't be heard by anyone who wasn't a Marine or recruit with a Circuit registered to Cycler 3. *So any attackers will think they've caught us unawares.* He couldn't decide if that was a good or bad thing, to be hit by overconfident attackers. It could result in getting the jump on those attackers...or it could be a recipe for getting mowed down by an unworried fighting force.

As they exited the barracks, automatic weapons fire barked from somewhere nearby, a lot closer than Po would have expected. Sweat popped out on his forehead and began to trickle down his face. He and the other twelve Marines from his squad bay hesitated near the entrance, unsure what to do.

Then Po spotted Gunnery Sergeant Emery across the way, holding a service pistol aimed at the ground with his back to another barracks' wall. He was waving for them to stay where they were. After checking the lane both ways, he darted across it, his head constantly on the move.

"Gunny Emery," Po said, a little ashamed at how breathless he sounded. "Is this Fight Week?"

Emery shot him a skeptical look. "Is that a serious question?"

"Uh...we thought, maybe, our implants—"

"You thought we'd use your implants to make you think you were in a real fight? Is that it?"

"Kinda."

"We want you to rely on your implants like you'd rely on your own two hands. Do you think using them to trick you is conducive to that objective?"

"I guess it isn't, Gunny."

Emery cast an appraising eye over the other Marines with Po, looking like he might be regretting risking his skin to run over here. He sighed. "Let's get to the armory and get you boys some ammo for those rifles. I could use something with a little more bite than this, too." Emery gestured with his pistol, which looked like the standard-issue M18, though probably configured to the gunnery sergeant's grip.

They followed him as he hugged the barracks, staying low and checking around the corner before leading them along the next face of the building and then darting across an alley to skirt a supply shed.

Po was right behind the instructor, and he did everything Emery did, ducking where he ducked, taking cover wherever he chose to take cover. He was about to follow Emery behind a hedgerow bordering a parade deck when Paisley tapped him on the shoulder, drawing his attention back to the barracks. Marines from other squad bays were milling around the outside of the building, clearly confused, and unsure how they should be reacting to the sounds of battle that were now getting frighteningly close.

But Po shook his head sharply, turned again, and followed Emery, motioning for the others to do the same. If the gunnery sergeant wasn't concerned about corralling the other Marines, then Po wouldn't concern himself with it either. Emery was obviously trying his best to move them across the base without drawing the attention of whoever was attacking Camp Williams. How well could he do that with a platoon's worth of Marines trailing behind him? If they were seen, they'd be easy targets, especially since Emery was the only one with any ammo.

At least, Po *assumed* the M18 was loaded.

They rounded a corner and Po spotted the armory, down the lane past several more supply sheds. So far, this area seemed free from fighting. If they could reach that armory and get kitted out, they'd at least have a chance.

Emery led them toward it, darting from concealment to concealment. It felt like Po's heart hammered harder against his ribcage the closer they got. Despite everything he'd learned since starting SOI, he still felt unready for actual combat. Maybe Fight Week would have changed things, but he doubted even that could prepare him for the real thing. Could he bring himself to kill another person? Could he even kill an alien?

A memory flashed through his mind, of the Obsidian Angel who he'd sent hurtling through microgravity to crack his skull off a metal beam. *He might have died. He didn't, but he might have.* Then he thought of Diego Rodriguez, who was probably dead because of the things Po had done back on Psyche.

Oh, yeah, he told himself. *You'd kill someone if you needed to. Wouldn't you?*

They found the armory locked up and abandoned, but Emery's Circuit gave them access. Inside, he told them each to find the set of SERAPH armor they'd been assigned based on their measurements.

Po went straight to the locker where he'd left his armor and started putting it on, each piece snapping automatically into the next, suctioning together to create an air-tight seal. Unlike when he'd had his M37C printed, no one had taken him into a sim to be fitted for his SERAPH armor. But the Corps clearly already knew all his measurements. Each piece of armor fit over his body like a second skin. A thick, tough, and protective second skin that would probably save his life.

Once they were armored up, Emery began handing out weapons and ammo as the fighting outside drew ever nearer.

The gunnery sergeant spoke low and fast. "We'll deploy in three traditional fireteams. I'll lead Fireteam Alpha, Paisley will lead Bravo, and Abbato, you're team leader for Charlie. Team leaders all get MGLs."

Multi-Shot Grenade Launchers. Po had learned to use one just last week, and while he would have liked more practice operating the M320 Emery was handing him, at least he felt fresh on its manual of arms.

He began sliding the grenade launcher's bulky rounds into the expandable slots over his abdomen as he tried his best to quell his mounting anxiety and focus on what the gunnery sergeant was saying. The SERAPH's slots closed around each round as soon as he let it go, gripping it snugly.

"I've been getting updates from the other sergeants who are fighting right now to defend Camp Williams," Emery went on. "In twenty minutes or less, this base will be overrun by an overwhelming enemy force."

They all stopped what they were doing for a moment to stare at him.

"Who's hitting us, Gunny?" Dempsey asked.

"Nibirans. They nuked a hole in the side of the cycler and we're leaking atmo. Admin's already sealed off multiple sublevels, and the surface cylinder's compromised too. The air here won't be breathable for much longer. Maybe a couple hours."

"This makes no sense," Paisley said. "How'd GEA miss them coming across the system at us?"

"We have no idea, and we don't have time for any more questions. Just know that this attack shouldn't have been possible, and hence we are utterly unprepared for it. Our objective right now is to get as many as possible to gear issue, located at the training base on the other side of the cylinder."

"Why gear issue?" Po asked, then remembered Emery hadn't wanted any more questions.

But the gunnery sergeant seemed content to answer this one. "Because that building is also a spaceworthy ship. Gear issue is capable of fully detaching from the cycler and leaving in the event of an emergency like this one."

"Oh. Right," Po said. "It kind of looks like a ship."

"And yet you didn't realize it actually was one, did you?"

"No."

"Neither will the Nibirans." Emery thrust an M320 into Paisley's hands, along with six extra rounds for him to tuck into his suit. "Our mission is to support the evacuation, to help ensure as many Marines and recruits make it out of this tin can alive. Our first objective is to reach the cycler's secondary control center on Sublevel 9, which became our main control when the nuke took out the primary. There are supposed to be personnel there around the clock, even in secondary control, but none of them are responding—cameras show they asphyxiated after the nuke hit, and sensor records confirm that all the oxygen was sucked out of there pretty much instantly."

"What'll we do when we get there?" Dempsey asked.

"No more questions. Fireteam leaders, watch out for your teams. My Alpha team will be on point to engage the enemy, while Paisley's Bravo will remain ready to quickly maneuver for a better angle and engage from it. Abbato, your Charlie boys must be ready to back either of us up if we get into trouble. All clear?"

"Clear," Po and Paisley said in unison.

"Let's move."

***

Gunnery Sergeant Emery continued talking to them as his fireteam moved out from the armory, in a different direction than the one they'd arrived from. The SERAPH suits were soundproofed, capable of keeping anything below a shout from being heard by anyone nearby, even if they were standing right next to you. Which meant that as long as you weren't throwing a tantrum inside your armor, you could communicate with your team members via an encrypted channel with an expectation of complete privacy.

"Paisley and Abbato, do *not* use your M320s except as a last resort. The moment the Nibirans hear grenades exploding is the moment they descend on us like wasps on rotten meat. To make it to the freight elevator safely, we need to appear as non-threatening as possible. That means sticking to defense only. If you have an option not to engage, then do not engage. Understood?"

"Understood, Gunny," Po said.

"Got it," Paisley said.

While Emery had been talking, Po had been whipping through menus on his Circuit, trying to figure out how to create a channel that included only his fireteam. Luckily, the function was pretty intuitive, and he had it up inside of a minute.

He willed his voice not to shake as he spoke, while at the same time trying not to sound too bossy. "We're at one hundred percent alertness, Marines," he said, wincing as his voice cracked on the last syllable. He pressed on, pretending it hadn't. "If you see anything out of the ordinary, and I mean anything, hop on this channel and let me know. I'll decide whether to pass it on to Gunny Emery. But if you see what's clearly a Nibiran, don't mess around, say it on the squad-wide. Understood?"

"Got it," Dempsey said, who Emery had assigned to Po's squad.

"Yep," said Gomez.

"Taylor?"

"I got you."

"Good. And don't get distracted by your map—*I'll* watch the map. You all keep your eyes on reality, and let me know if it looks like it's about to kill us."

A map had popped up in Po's HUD seconds after he'd stepped out of the armory, updated with enemy positions which Emery was being fed by currently engaged Marines, not to mention the multitude of sensors scattered across Camp Williams. But sensors were machines, and prone to failure. Po had already had a lesson about overreliance on technology, a stern one. Those sensors were just as hackable as his implant had been, probably moreso.

All the same, the map did offer invaluable intel on the enemy's progress through Camp Williams. And that progress was alarming. He assumed the base's defenders were comprised of combat instructors and whatever new Marines they'd managed to corral and organize on the fly, and they'd been in steady retreat since Po first got access to the map. The Nibirans were hitting from the east-northeast, while the gunnery sergeant was leading them to an elevator that lay north-northwest from their position.

Po did his best to strike a balance between covertness and speed, monitoring his teammates as closely as he could to make sure they did the same. Up ahead, Paisley's fireteam was following Alpha's route as closely as they could, and so Po led his along the same path. He had no doubt it was a good one, optimized for stealth, since it had been chosen by the gunnery sergeant. But the big question would be whether they could reach the elevator undetected before the angry tide of Nibirans crashed over them. Judging how close that rifle fire sounded, he had his doubts they could.

He was expecting their position to be overrun...but even so, he was still surprised by how quickly the instructors' line collapsed. He'd just glanced at the map seconds ago, he was sure he had, but when he looked back, the line of white dots representing the base's defenders fell apart, and the red squares pushed aggressively forward.

Whatever rifles the Nibirans were using had a sharper bark than the Marines' M37s, and they sounded close enough now that Po felt like he should be able to see them.

"Get into the warehouse," Emery said. Up ahead, Po could see him holding open the door, and waving Paisley's fireteam through. "There's an exit at the north end we can use."

Po thought that was a great idea, and he urged his team to move faster toward the gunnery sergeant. He recognized that warehouse from his walks to and from the gym, and he knew it to be pretty long. As long as the Nibirans didn't think to check inside, it would offer them excellent concealment while allowing them to advance at least a couple hundred feet.

Problem is, by the time we exit the other side, the Nibirans could be anywhere. On their left, on their right, in front, or behind. Now that the Marines had scattered, there was no predicting what the aliens would do, or where they would go. The best the map could tell them was that the Nibirans were practically on top of their position, even though they apparently hadn't realized it yet.

But his job hadn't changed, so he focused on that. *Watch the map, keep your eyes peeled for flesh-and-blood Nibirans, and watch out for your team just like Emery said. You can do that,* he told himself. Then he told himself it again, and then a third time, for good measure.

His team made it into the warehouse without incident. Emery let the door close, then sprinted ahead, to catch back up with Alpha Team. As he did, they all charged through the warehouse, pounding past shelving stacked with boxes and crates, then a row of offices, then through a labyrinth made entirely of uniforms hanging from racks.

They found Emery at a long, horizontal window near the north exit, checking every which way for the enemy.

"Clear so far," he said. "Look—this pops out." He pushed a lever on the left side all the way up, then jogged to the other side and did the same with a lever there. "You just give it a shove out onto the ground. But don't do it unless you need to. My team will move across the lane to the base of that statue. Bravo, be ready to move out and hit any Nibirans that engage us. Abbato, your team stays at that window until the area is secure and we're ready to cover you."

"Aye, aye, Gunny," Po said.

He stood at the window and watched Alpha make it to the statue without incident. Emery took a moment to check all around him while his team did the same. When they'd inspected the area to their satisfaction, they ran ahead to a rectangular gazebo bracketed by benches, where they stuck close to the gazebo's pillars while they waited for Bravo to move out.

It wasn't until Paisley made it to the statue that the crack of rifle fire came from Po's right.

The angle was wrong for him to put eyes on the attackers, but Bravo team clearly could. They crouched against the broad base of the statue, returning fire.

At least, three of them did. Paisley looked frozen. He was staring through his M37's sight toward what Po took to be the enemy position, but he wasn't doing anything. He looked frozen.

"Paisley," Emery barked. "Those mutts need a grenade. Get your M320 up."

But Paisley was somewhere else. Po saw one of his team look at him sideways, but they were too busy laying down fire to get the grenade launcher off of their team leader. For Alpha's part, they clearly didn't have the right angle to launch a grenade, and there seemed to be enough Nibiran suppressive fire to keep them pinned behind the pillars they'd chosen for cover.

Cursing, Po pulled away from the window. "This position's useless," he growled over the team channel he'd set up. He pushed between two racks of clothes, ran down another row, and then rounded a corner.

There it was: a door, just where he needed it to be.

This doesn't lead outside, right? There should be another room....

Pushing it open slowly, he saw his reckoning was right. There *was* another room beyond, and at its far end was another window, about the same size as the first one.

"Keep low," he told his team, who'd followed behind him. Crouching so they couldn't be spotted through the glass, Po darted to the window's side to operate the same sort of mechanism Emery had used to loosen the other one. Then he bent low enough to pass under the window and do the same on the other side.

With the bulkhead blocking him, he rose to his full height, then stuck the end of his pinky past the window's frame. Thankfully, the suit's AI was smart enough to know what he wanted, sparing him from having to navigate menus to find the function. One of the sensors in his little finger opened a transparent box in his HUD which showed the view outside the window.

There, twelve Nibirans were taking cover behind a row of machine-cut boulders that bordered a triangular garden. They looked kind of like a genetic scientist got drunk, crossed a frog with a dog, and called it a species. They were bipedal digitigrades, and they were wearing the sort of armor the Marines had considered cutting-edge two centuries ago.

The rocks provided the Nibirans good cover against Emery's and Paisley's squads...but not against Po, whose position put him slightly behind them.

Letting his M37 hang by its strap, he readied his grenade launcher, then swung around, pushed out the window with one hand, and fired three grenades into the Nibirans' midst.

His first went long, and he adjusted his aim so that the next two landed among the aliens crouched behind the rocks.

A bullet snapped through the air over his head just before the first grenade exploded, and he pulled back behind cover. Two more shots punched holes in the wall just inches to his right, letting beams of light stream in. Then two explosions came in quick succession.

"Paisley, Abbato, take your teams to Alpha's position. We'll cover you as you come. Those grenades have them scattering, so this is our chance. We're not far from the elevator now."

Po motioned to his fireteam to hustle back the way they came. They didn't seem to need much encouragement.

"Paisley?" Emery's voice came over the squad channel again. "Are you with me?"

"I'm with you, Gunny," Paisley answered, sounding shaken but like he might be finally coming out of his trance.

Chapter 32

More Nibirans had been coming up behind the first group—those were the ones who'd returned fire on Po. According to Emery, he'd only taken out two of the newcomers with his volley.

"But it didn't matter," the gunnery sergeant said. "They didn't expect you to be there, behind their line, and it's more the boom than anything else that scares them. Having something like that detonate just a few meters from you triggers your flight-or-fight pretty bad. Our helmets dampen the sound, but their eardrums get the full effect. You threw them into complete disarray."

"Good. Thanks, Gunny."

"Son, you're a natural born leader. If we make it out of this alive, I'm recommending you for the fast track to private first class."

Po nodded in acknowledgment, unsure what to say.

"I'm impressed too," Zanth said from the corner of the freight elevator.

Po managed not to turn around, instead using his suit's rear sensors to look at the alien. Briefly, he wondered whether the fact the Emplor showed up in the sensor feed meant he was able to hack the SERAPH suits too.

Maybe not. He could use my implant to superimpose his image over the feed. Right? Po was pretty sure that made sense.

"I must admit, I expected you to choke without my aid," Zanth continued. "But then, I suppose we chose you for a reason."

With that, he vanished.

Po turned toward Paisley. "What happened to you?"

The other boot shook his head. "I don't know. I just...lost it. I seized up."

Emery slapped Paisley lightly on the back of his suit. "Everyone responds to combat differently. You just need to drill more. In the meantime, give your M320 to Gomez and swap out with him. You're under Abbato now. Gomez, you're Bravo team leader."

"Aye, aye, Gunny."

Paisley just hung his head.

The gravity was lessening as the elevator took them toward Sublevel 9, reminding Po of his time in Motivation Camp. At the time, wading through that garlic-smelling wastewater every day had seemed like the worst thing that could happen to him while in Cycler 3. Now he was fighting Nibirans on an empty stomach, Nibirans who'd nuked a hole into the side of a GEA military facility. That wasn't supposed to happen. And Po hadn't even eaten breakfast.

Why didn't I freeze up like Paisley did? he wondered. *What makes me different from him?*

He was pretty sure Paisley had had an implant before getting conscripted, which meant he probably would have played plenty of war sims. *He should have been way more ready to kill a Nibiran than me. But he froze up, and I didn't.*

There wasn't time to ruminate on it for long. The elevator rumbled to a stop, and the doors whined open.

Red light bathed the corridor outside, and the light level changed rapidly, suggesting a flickering fixture somewhere down the corridor.

"Turn your magboots on, third-lowest setting," Emery ordered them. "That'll give us a lot more maneuverability than any Nibirans we run across."

It was a good idea, but it didn't end up being relevant. They didn't find any aliens waiting for them in the cycler's lower levels, and their journey to the secondary control room proved pretty uneventful.

Which was probably just as well, Po figured. He noticed how the gunnery sergeant didn't assign the fireteams differentiated roles, instead leading them straight down each passageway. Whether that meant there was no room for them to set up a flank down here, or just that Emery wanted to prioritize speed over caution, he didn't know. But he was glad for the chance not to find out.

Once they reached the control room, he ordered Bravo team to keep watch outside, dividing themselves into pairs to keep eyes on both ends of the corridor outside. The others, he let file in after him.

The control room was a circular room, with concentric rings of terminals marching toward the center, where a single main terminal sat, accessible from four interfaces that all faced away from each other. Emery made a beeline for one of those centermost interfaces.

"What are we doing down here, Gunny?" Dempsey asked.

"Whatever we can." Emery began tapping at the interface, staring intently at the air above it as he did. Every so often his helmet moved, as if he was scanning lines of text, or examining images.

He seemed to be reacting to *something*, which told Po that the interface had opened up a window that only the gunnery sergeant could see. That made sense. All authorized personnel aboard Cycler 3 would have military-grade Circuits, so why make it any easier for intruders to access the station's control systems by providing an actual screen?

"Seems the nuke came from a passing megafreighter using the same space lane we were, orbiting in the opposite direction. The Nibirans must have come from there, too."

"I didn't know the Nibirans had freighters," Po said.

"They don't have any spacecraft. This was a human freighter." Emery tapped a couple more times on the interface, then shook his head. "Camp Williams is totally overrun. The Nibirans own it, now."

"Can you see how many of us escaped?"

"I could, but we don't have time." Another few taps. "There. I turned on the automated defenses mounted along the axis. That should change the equation of combat. At the very least, it'll buy time for more of our people to reach gear issue."

Right. Gear issue. Which is secretly a spaceship.

"Why didn't the auto-defenses start hitting the Nibirans right away?" Gomez asked.

"Because Marines don't trust AIs with that much agency when it comes to target selection. Explicit human authorization is always required." Emery was looking at Gomez flatly, his expression deadly serious.

"All right then, Gunny."

With that, Emery led them out of the control room and in the direction opposite the one they'd come from. Before long, the corridor opened up into a wide boulevard, complete with twin lines of trees marching along the sides and two pairs of parallel travolators that stretched into the distance, each pair moving in opposite directions. Po's eyes followed the moving belts as far as they could, to the inverted horizon, where they were swallowed up by the ceiling.

So we're wrapping back around the cylinder. That made sense. Traveling lengthwise wouldn't bring them any closer to the secret spaceship in the training base.

"You boys are from Psyche, right?" the gunnery sergeant asked as they jogged together toward the travolators, most of them still looking kind of goofy as they continued to adjust to the lower gravity down here. "You have these back there?" He nodded at the travolators ahead.

"In a couple places," Paisley said.

"Don't try to run on these, or even walk. I'm going to use my access to speed them up once we're all on them. Alpha Team on the left one, Bravo on the right—Charlie, you split up between the two that are going our way. Everyone keep your magboots clamped to the metal plates, keep a wide stance, and hold onto the rails. No showing off."

They did as Emery said. Taylor and Dempsey took the rightmost travolator, and Po and Paisley stepped onto the one to its left.

"Everyone clamped on?"

"Yes, Gunny," everyone answered back. Once they had, Emery sped them up. Po's grip tightened on the moving rails, and he wished he'd used a wider stance. He disengaged his rear magboot and shifted it back, then reactivated it. *That's better.*

The line of trees blurred, and intersecting avenues whipped past. Despite the foliage, this place seemed...desolate. *Was Cycler 3 always this empty?*

"Po," Dempsey asked over the team channel Po had set up. Paisley and Taylor glanced at him, maybe because he'd used Po's first name.

"Yeah, Demps?"

"What are we going to do?"

"We're going to use gear issue to get out of here, like Gunny said."

"I know, but...after that. How do we know that freighter won't nuke us too, once we decouple from the cylinder? And even if it doesn't, where are we going to *go?*"

Po shook his head. "That's all way above our pay grade, Demps. You became a Marine, like, a minute ago. Your job right now is to help your team support the squad to complete the mission. That's all. Don't waste time whining or fretting about anything else."

A silence came over the com, and when Po looked to his right, he saw Dempsey was staring at him through his helmet's faceplate.

"You know, Po, back on Psyche, I never could have imagined you saying anything like that to me. Remember when I attacked you in that food court?"

"I'm right, Demps."

"I know you are. And I needed to hear it. So, thanks."

Po didn't answer. He hadn't expected that to go half as well, and for the moment, he felt lost for words.

For that matter, he hadn't expected to kill two Nibirans today, or to be put in charge of a fireteam of his fellow boots. He'd expected today to suck—every day aboard Cycler 3 sucked—but not quite like this.

Even though he'd told Dempsey to quit thinking about it, he couldn't help asking himself the same questions. Where were they going to go? And would the attacking freighter let them leave?

That freighter's long gone, he realized. Emery had told them it was following the same orbit as Cycler 3, but in the opposite direction. Which meant it must have launched its nuke and deployed the Nibirans in passing.

Sure, in theory, it *could* decelerate then reverse course, but that would mean a significant fuel expenditure—and even if it did that, it wouldn't catch up to Cycler 3 for a while. If the freighter had started decelerating before crossing paths with the cylinder, it might have reversed course more easily, but that early deceleration would have warned Cycler 3's admin that something was up.

They fired what they had at us, and now they're gone. Po had no idea what the reason behind the attack was, but he couldn't imagine a new element coming into play. They were already dealing with the full extent of the assault, and nothing new could be added.

But what they were already dealing with was more than enough to keep them busy. As they reached the end of the travolator, Emery patched a visual feed through to their implants. Based on the angle, Po figured it must be transmitted from a sensor affixed to an elevator cable halfway between the surface and the cylinder's axis.

From it, he could see the Nibirans had reached the training base...and now they were moving on the recruit chapels, for some reason.

Po had to stop watching the feed long enough to disengage his magboots, step off the travolator, and follow the rest of the squad into a waiting elevator. At least, it looked like an elevator. But when the doors closed behind them, it jolted sideways instead of up. He spread his legs again, farther than they'd been on the travolator, to avoid getting tossed into the bulkhead.

"Doesn't seem like the defenses did a whole lot," he muttered, returning his attention to the sensor feed.

"They did, actually," Emery said. "And are."

Po started—he hadn't realized the squad channel was active, and that his words had been transmitted to the others.

"The mutts are still engaging the autoturrets, mostly from Camp Williams. The turrets have already taken out at least a couple dozen of them. But they're programmed to prioritize enemies that are actively firing on them. The group that's hitting the training base aren't doing that, so until the defenses take out the aliens that are, these ones will be left alone."

"How are they fighting the turrets?" Taylor asked.

Emery sighed. "It seems the frog-dogs brought these rinky-dink tripod-mounted guns firing rocket-assisted HE rounds. A lot of them. I was hoping they wouldn't have anything like that. If they didn't, we might actually have a shot at retaking the station. But they obviously knew what they'd be dealing with, and they came prepared."

"HE rounds?" Taylor repeated.

"High-explosive," Gomez said. "Try paying attention in class."

The other boot ignored him. "Couldn't they damage the axis, using weapons like that?"

Emery paused before answering. "The axis is made of super-strong nanomaterials, and the turrets are all situated on buildings suspended from the axis, meters away from it. So it should be fine."

"What if it's not, though? What if their aim is bad enough that some of those rockets miss and hit the axis? Enough to take it down?"

"Then that would be very bad."

Po returned his gaze to the palm-sized display floating to his left, which showed the group of Nibirans, at least a couple squads' worth, advancing on the recruit chapels. He expanded the display, and for some reason sweat popped out on his forehead as he did. His breathing was coming a little quicker, he noticed. His heart was beating harder.

"Why are they going for the chapels?" he asked the gunnery sergeant.

"Because that's where a lot of the recruits are holed up." With that, Emery zoomed in the feed, to get a clearer picture than Po would have expected, considering the action was happening two kilometers away from the sensor's position.

His breath caught.

As he watched, a lone figure emerged from one of the chapels. The same chapel Po had been inside, for a few Sundays in a row.

It was the chaplain. Campbell.

Even if the sensor Emery was letting them access had sound, it would have been too far away to pick anything up from what was happening on the ground. And yet, as the Nibirans came to a stop and one of them stepped forward, he was clearly saying *something* to the chaplain.

To Po's shock, the chaplain answered something back.

The transport they were in shuddered to a halt, then changed course—heading upward, and finally acting like an elevator. Po felt himself getting gradually heavier, and as he did, his anxiety mounted. Soon, they'd be back in the training base, where they'd need to do something about the half-platoon of aliens threatening those recruits.

"Can the Nibirans speak English?" he asked.

Emery shook his head. "Not usually."

"Then can the chaplain...?"

"Speak Nibiran? Yeah, actually. He can."

Po watched, dumbfounded, as the chaplain held up both palms toward the aliens, then pointed back at the chapel, and then upward, toward Camp Williams.

The Nibiran leader shook his head and took an aggressive step forward, gesturing with his rifle at Campbell.

"In a few seconds, we're going to come out southeast of the chapel," Emery said, his voice sounding as tense as Po felt. "It's about a couple minutes' sprint. I'm coordinating with Staff Sergeant Young, who's leading a squad from the north. If we get there before they make it into the chapel, we can pincer them. Keep your heads, Marines. Same teams as before. Same roles."

A round of nods.

"Semper Fi," Emery added.

"Semper Fi," they murmured distractedly back over the squad channel, all of them apparently fixated on the scene in front of the chapel.

It happened just as the elevator was slowing to a halt, the doors parting even before they reached the surface, probably as a result of an override triggered by Emery. Several Nibirans spread out, raising their rifles, all of them pointed at Chaplain Campbell.

"No," Po said, his voice coming out as a rasp.

The rifles barked, peppering the chaplain, who kept his feet longer than seemed possible. But the aliens' fire was unrelenting, and after several long seconds Campbell was thrown backward onto the ground.

Yet even then, his black robes were not in disarray around his supine form. Instead, they'd settled neatly around him. His hands were somehow folded peacefully over his stomach. He looked for all the world like he'd laid himself down on the grassy expanse before the chapel to have a nap.

For a moment that seemed suspended in time like a bug in amber, the Marines stood there with the doors open and the elevator halted, each of them riveted by the sensor feed showing the field in front of the row of chapels.

"Move, Marines!" Emery yelled, his voice hitching, but breaking their trance. With that, he charged out onto Cycler 3's surface, with Alpha Team hard on his heels.

Chapter 33

Working with Sergeant Young's squad, they made short work of the Nibirans who'd killed Chaplain Campbell. Young's squad hit them straight on, with the chapel as backstop, while Emery took Alpha Team around to the east and Bravo and Charlie went west.

The Nibirans were distracted by their effort to break into the chapel when the Marines hit—at least, that's what Po chalked it up to. Either way, they didn't seem to expect this level of resistance at this late stage of their incursion.

Resistance is too weak a word, Po reflected as Gunnery Sergeant Emery explained to the frightened recruits hiding inside the chapel that they could come out. His eyes wandered across the aliens' inert corpses. *That was a slaughter.*

Still, they needed to get those recruits out of there pronto, and then hustle over to gear issue. The central autoturrets were still engaging Nibirans, and those rocket-assisted rounds were launching toward the axis from closer and closer positions. Swirling debris now cluttered the central microgravity zone. As Po watched, a building whose tether had snapped departed the microgravity, accelerating toward the ground a kilometer or so outside Camp Williams. When it hit, the ground tremored, even where Po was standing.

He returned his attention to the recent firefight's aftermath. Things would have gone a lot differently here if the chaplain hadn't ordered the recruits to bar the chapel doors, before going out himself to stall the invaders. Without either of those things, Po felt sure the aliens would have already been inside the chapel by the time the Marine squads showed up. That would have been a much different fight.

"Abbato," a tortured voice called across the lawn.

Po turned to see one of Sergeant Young's Marines kneeling next to Campbell's body with his visor raised.

Po jogged over, raising his own faceplate. "How'd you know it was me?"

Navarro sighed, deep and long. "Your name and rank are hovering right over your head. You should turn on IFF tags, man. Might help you keep track of who your brothers are."

Face flushing, Po used his implant to navigate to the relevant menu and turned them on. PRIVATE LUIS NAVARRO appeared over Navarro's head.

The other boot winced as he cast his gaze across the chapel's front, which had been pockmarked by bullets during the firefight. A tear rolled down his left cheek. "You'll help me carry him, right?"

"Huh?"

"Father Campbell." Navarro took another shuddering breath. "He died to save those recruits."

Po nodded. "Yeah. I'll help you."

In the meantime, he looked around at the other Marines who'd come in Navarro's squad. He saw Crotty, and when the diminutive boot met his eyes, Po raised a clenched fist in front of his chest. He squeezed his fingers together so hard it hurt. Crotty returned the gesture.

And there was Harris, who even after everyone stopped hating him, Po had never gotten close with like he had with some of the others. They exchanged nods.

"Come on," Navarro said, standing. "The recruits are coming out. We gotta go."

"Wait." Out of nowhere, it hit him: where was Zhang? He'd thought about him a few times since graduating bootcamp, but Marines never left Camp Williams to visit the training base.

"What about Zhang?" he asked. "Do you know what happened to him? Did his leg ever heal?" Po's heart was suddenly hammering in his chest. He felt like a selfish idiot. He'd been so focused on saving his own hide that it was only now occurring to him to wonder where the recruit was who'd saved his life.

"Po," Navarro said. He'd already grabbed the chaplain's body by the upper arms. "We have who we have. *We gotta go.*"

But Po's eyes were on the recruits as they poured out of the chapel, desperately scanning their faces.

Then, a giant lumbered out of the doors.

"Zhang!"

Zhang's head turned, and his face broke out into a sunny grin. Po was already running toward him. He threw his arms around the big lout and hammered him on the back.

"Thank God you're here!" Po said, pulling back to get another look at him.

"Yeah," Zhang said, his expression solemn. "Thank God."

***

"Incoming! *Find cover!*"

The Marines moving through the training base scattered for whatever nearby doorways or overhangs were available. Something impacted the center of the lane they'd been double-timing down, and an explosion bloomed. Heat washed over Po where he and Navarro had crouched behind a bench, hunched over and protecting the chaplain's body with their suits as best they could.

Standing back up, Po counted three Marines down as the smoke dissipated. At least one of them had to be dead.

"Grab them and let's keep moving!" Sergeant Young shouted over a wide channel, his voice hoarse.

"Was that a stray shot?" Paisley asked. "Or are they targeting us, now?"

"Assume they're targeting us," Young said. "Watch out for incoming fire and maintain coms discipline, everyone."

As they ran, Po replayed the feed from a sensor on his helmet's crown. It looked like the round had come from almost the opposite side of the cylinder, passing between buildings suspended from the axis before crossing the rest of the distance to their side.

Probably a stray round. Still, he could understand why Young was so keen to stop them from speculating over the coms. If the Nibirans *were* targeting them now, then soon they'd be targeting gear issue, once the Marines made it inside there. Which would mean their chances of getting out of here would plummet. The fewer of them realized that, the better their overall performance would be.

In the end, they almost made it to their destination without incident. Almost.

Emery had given everyone in his squad access to feeds he was monitoring on the fly, and from them, Po knew more Nibirans had now reached the training base. He didn't know how long it would take for gear issue to decouple from Cycler 3 and leave, but it seemed there should be enough time: the aliens wouldn't reach them for another ten minutes at least, and they'd just rounded the last corner. Gear issue's white bulk reared from the ground at the end of the lane, its tapered peak just as white as the day Po had been fitted for his M37. He breathed a little easier, once he saw that. His fear that gear issue had been damaged—or worse, that others had already taken it and fled—had thankfully come to naught.

A deafening *crack* resounded through the cylinder, like a bullet fired from a rifle with a muzzle the size of a small asteroid. Even with the suit's automatic sound dampening, it hurt Po's ears, and he fought the urge to let go of the chaplain's legs and clamp his hands to the sides of his helmet.

He looked up in time to see the enormous axis cable whipping majestically through Cycler 3's atmosphere in slow motion, its elastic force slowed by the many buildings and depots suspended from it.

"Brace yourselves!" Emery shouted over the wide channel.

But there was no time. The axis left microgravity and slammed into the terrain just outside the training base, causing the ground to shake and Po to fall to his knees. Explosions roared, probably from fuel canisters stored in some of the suspended depots, and great clods of dirt and grass flew through the air. Debris rained down all around the Marines, pattering on the asphalt. A massive dust cloud was already rising all along the axis' line of impact.

Next came a terrifying metallic screeching and groaning—the cylinder's superstructure crying out in protest. A crashing sound came from the direction of the western endcap, and Po imagined that was probably what an avalanche sounded like. More crashing followed from the east.

"*Get to the building!*" Emery shouted.

Navarro was looking back at Po, his features drawn tight behind his faceplate. "Don't you dare drop him."

His ears ringing, Po drew a deep breath. "Let's move!"

They sprinted down the lane toward gear issue, where someone was opening the hatch for them. Whoever it was wore a SERAPH suit, but now didn't feel like the time to stop and read his IFF tag. The Marine stood outside the hatch, holding it open and waving them through. The first of Sergeant Young's squad reached the open portal and rushed through.

More crashing sounds from the east. The dust cloud swallowed gear issue, then reached Po and Navarro maybe a second later, engulfing them, and blinding them. Still they ran, even as the light streaming through the eastern endcap dimmed for some reason, making visibility even worse.

"Turn on thermal," Po said, speaking the idea over the wide channel even as it occurred to him.

With it on, he could again see the Marine waving them through the hatch. Indeed, gear issue had its own scarlet glow, much brighter than the buildings around it.

They're preparing for departure. That was good.

Po and Navarro were the last to pass through the hatch, other than the Marine who'd ushered them in—he shut the hatch and secured it behind them.

The second it was secure, the entire building lurched, nearly sending Po to his knees again.

"Hold on to a handle," the Marine said who'd welcomed them in. He was gripping one himself, which was affixed to the bulkhead beside the closed hatch. "We're leaving."

"Music to my ears," Po muttered. "Navarro, look—this way."

They both shuffled to their right, each looping an arm through one end of a long handle before grabbing hold of the chaplain again with that hand. It would have been much easier to just let Campbell go—to lower him to the deck as the ship decoupled from the cylinder. But Navarro didn't seem to want to do that yet.

As gear issue descended through the sublevels, the dull roar of explosions reached them even through multiple layers of metal and terrain. The entire building shook. But they continued their descent, and as they did, the chaplain became heavier and heavier...

...until, abruptly, he began to get lighter. Before long, he weighed nothing at all.

***

The passengers of the S.S. *Gear Issue*, which some boot had artfully dubbed their escape ship, enjoyed a brief return of close-to-normal gravity as they accelerated toward wherever it was the higher-ups planned on taking them. But microgravity resumed after a few hours, the astrogation officer having presumably reached his desired orbital velocity.

During that time, there were plenty of recruits going around with vomit bags. Most everyone on board was dealing with some degree of space sickness.

"The fact we spent so much time accelerating must mean they're in a hurry to get somewhere," Harris speculated at dinner that night. "I heard the mutts' ride was long gone by the time we left. And they probably used a shuttle or something to board Cycler 3—nothing capable of catching up with us. We didn't have to accelerate nearly as long as we did."

Paisley snorted. "We *decelerated*, you dumb jarhead."

"Huh? How do you know?"

They were sitting around a square table with high-back chairs bolted to the floor. Well, "sitting" wasn't exactly right. More like they were floating in place, prevented from drifting free by how snugly the chairs nestled them against the table. Technically it didn't matter which way they were oriented, though on the first day, a sergeant *had* yelled at one of the boots for eating pudding upside down.

Paisley plucked his spoon from where it was magnetically affixed to the side of the table and poked it into a foil bag of crumbly chicken parmigiana. "Because *accelerating* would have meant we'd overshoot the inner planets and sail back out toward the belt. The only things farther out than Mars are mining colonies like Psyche, Jupiter's moons and the few yokels crazy enough to be there, and Nibiru. I can guarantee you we're not heading for the homeworld of the dogs who just nearly killed us all."

"Not yet, anyway," Po put in.

Paisley gave him a grim nod. "Not yet." He turned back to Harris. "*De*celerating tightened up our orbit from the elliptical orbit Cycler 3 was on, for an early intercept of one of the inner planet's orbits."

"Which one?" Harris asked.

"I dunno," Paisley admitted. "They don't give us updated orbits on our implants."

"So there *is* something you don't know," Dempsey muttered into his MRE bag.

Paisley shot him a look, then shifted his gaze to Po. "You ask me, we're headed for Camp Puller on Olympus Mons. To finish our training."

"Mars?" Harris asked, sounding as amazed as he normally did when Paisley spoke. "Why not Camp Pendleton, on Earth?"

"*Why not Camp Pendleton, on Earth?*" Dempsey mimicked, but Harris seemed too enthralled by Paisley to notice.

Paisley shrugged. "Earth is for the weak. Besides, Puller has a training base too, where the recruits can earn their globe-and-wings. Mars makes the most sense."

As it turned out, everyone aboard the S.S. *Gear Issue* had a theory about where they were headed, and they were diverse enough that Po rarely heard the same one twice. The cloud cities of Venus was probably the most interesting idea, or maybe Lebanon to fight a newly installed rogue government there. He also heard Mars' moon Phobos, Earth's moon, and Mercury, of all places. The craziest idea was that they were heading to Emplora to blame the aliens *there* for everything, and to demand they reimburse the Corps in full for what the Nibirans did to Cycler 3.

The officers weren't telling them much, and the longer that silence lasted, the wilder the rumor mill got. Po was convinced that the reason no two boots had the same idea about where they were going was because they were all trying to outdo each other with how outlandish their theories were.

Which wasn't to say the officers were ignoring them. Cycler 3's CO had managed to make it aboard gear issue before it decoupled from the cylinder, and he'd put it out that he wanted the boots and recruits kept busy, with their "temporarily suspended classes and exercises" replaced by lots of PT, gear and uniform maintenance, and keeping the escape ship sparkling clean. But even with all that, they were still graced with more free time than usual.

Po used his first stretch of downtime to explore the ship, which proved a lot bigger than he'd expected. After learning gear issue was really a spaceship, he'd assumed it had been constructed over a shaft, through which it would drop in the event of an emergency evacuation.

Instead, it turned out the building had extended through every sublevel of Cycler 3, its stern flush with the great cylinder's outer hull. At least, it *had* been, before the survivors had used it to break away from the cylinder and flee.

He supposed its size made sense, intended as it was to accommodate the entire population of the cylinder in the event of an evacuation. But only a fraction of that population had made it out alive, which made the ship feel pretty empty.

Sublevels 7 through 9 had been declared Officer's country, and few boots had a reason to pass through there. Even so, it quickly became evident that a disproportionate number of officers had made it onto the escape ship, while the station's boots had fought the Nibirans, spending their lives to buy time for their superiors to escape.

Sergeants were less populous—a lot of them had fought alongside the boots, like Emery and Young. And as became clear through the same rumor mill thrumming with thoughts about where they might be going, the sergeants had done that with very little direction from the higher-ups.

As for the recruits, their training base had seen a lot less action than Camp Williams, and their sergeants had shepherded most of them into gear issue pretty early on. Among those sergeants had been Mitchell and Scott—Sergeant Doyle hadn't made it. But between their efforts and Chaplain Campbell's sacrifice, most of the recruits had.

Po wondered if news had made it back to Psyche yet about what happened to Cycler 3. His last letter from his sister had been a while ago, and now, any she did send probably wouldn't make it to him. Would Nicky think he'd died? War had descended on the system, it seemed, and in war, things were kept secret that otherwise might have been widely shared. It was possible the higher-ups wouldn't want it known that a ship had escaped Cycler 3 and was making its way toward the inner planets.

"There's gonna be a lot of funerals when we get wherever we're going," Navarro mused during their third period of downtime, over lidded coffees they'd scored from the mess. It was just him and Po, floating above opposite racks in an otherwise empty squad bay.

Navarro sighed. "They never did find Becker's body."

"Yeah. We lost half our bootcamp platoon." He snapped his fingers. "Like that."

A silence stretched between them, each staring at their coffee cup lids.

"I can't believe he's gone," Navarro muttered at last.

"Becker?"

"No. Father Campbell."

"Oh. Right."

Another silence.

Then, Navarro spoke again. "Did you know Father Campbell used to be married?"

"Huh? I thought priests couldn't get married."

"They can't. He entered the seminary after his wife died, along with his son. Both on the same day."

Po winced. "What happened?"

"Shuttle accident. They were on their way to live with him in his apartment, in a lunar colony. The colony was founded by a company mining silicon and iron in the Mare Fecunditatis. The engine failed before they cleared Earth's troposphere, and they crashed somewhere in the Carson Desert. No survivors."

"Wow."

"Yeah. He had his wedding band melted down and incorporated into the chalice he used to celebrate Mass. The ring formed part of the stem called the knop." Navarro was studying Po's face. "You have no idea what sort of man you met, do you?"

Po lifted his shoulders. "He...listen, I'm sorry, Navarro. I know he meant a lot to you."

"He was a saint, Abbato. *Is* a saint. The kind of man you haven't heard about in your entire life. But they're still around, and God blessed you enough to meet one." Navarro's eyes were glistening.

Po nodded slowly, at a loss for words. He shifted uncomfortably.

At that moment, an alert appeared in his field of vision. "ALL MARINES REPORT TO AUDITORIUM A ON SUBLEVEL 3 AT 1900."

"Did you get that?" Po asked.

"Yeah."

He pushed himself away from the bulkhead and into the aisle between the racks. "That's in forty-five minutes. I better go get my dress uniform ready."

Navarro didn't answer, so Po showed himself out and headed for his squad bay, feeling awkward.

34

From his exploring, Po knew Sublevel 3 had no fewer than four auditoriums, and there may well be others that he'd missed.

Walking into Auditorium A minutes before the briefing and seeing empty seats, even with every surviving boot from Cycler 3 present...that was sad.

It was also infuriating. But Po willed himself not to let his anger get to him—to comport himself in what Sergeant Mitchell would have called a military manner.

And well he should. Cycler 3's CO, Colonel Alfred Lee, stood in front of a blank wall in front of the auditorium, waiting with his hands folded behind his back and his magboots clamped onto the metal floor while the last Marines took their seats. In the past, before the advent of Circuits, that blank wall would probably have featured a display of some kind, or even a screen onto which a projector would throw an image. Now, it just acted as a clean backdrop for whatever maps, graphs, or photos Lee cared to make pop up in their vision, with no option to minimize, resize, or even move the window.

"We've all been through some things this week," the colonel said the second Po's implant clock ticked over to 1900. "Some historic, unprecedented things. And no one has suffered more because of them than you Marines have. Indeed, in all the Corps' history, no Marine has ever been tested so brutally, so soon after receiving their globe-and-wings, as you all have. You saw combat sooner than any of us ever expected you to, or ever wanted you to. Without warning, without proper preparation, you were hit by a foe that proved itself merciless and lethal. And yet you rose to the occasion. You stood firm, and you did your fallen brothers proud. May God bless you all for that, and may you be commended for it."

Lee cast his calm gaze around the auditorium, and despite the recent murmurings about how many officers had survived Cycler 3 versus boots and sergeants, Po could sense his fellow Marines felt just as proud and fortified under that gaze as he did.

"You've no doubt spent the days since our evacuation mourning your fallen brothers, but I also know that at the same time, you must be doing a lot of wondering. How will you complete your training, now that the Nibiran attack brought it to such an abrupt halt? *Where* will you complete it? And what does your future hold for you? What will your career look like, now?

"I can assure you, my staff and I have been experiencing that exact same uncertainty as we communicated these last days with high command, seeking guidance on what we should be doing next. I've called you to this briefing because I finally have some information to share with you—information which should grant you some much-needed certainty. First, I'd like to share with you that I have sought and been granted permission from General Arkanian himself for you Marines to use your implants' functionality to resume your interrupted training, starting tomorrow."

With the halting gait forced by magboots, Colonel Lee walked to one side of the blank wall as an image appeared before Po's eyes, of a desert landscape overshadowed by two enormous moons. A fire raged through a city near the horizon, billowing smoke into a turquoise sky.

"The Corps vastly prefers to train its Marines in the real world, in ways that hone their bodies as well as their minds. But we also have to play the hand we're dealt. As I speak these words, humanity is officially at war, and you men are needed. We can't afford to wait till we can get you to Camp Puller or Pendleton so you can conduct the remaining classes and field exercises there. Instead, we must use every second available to us, and during the weeks it takes us to reach Earth, that will mean conducting those exercises inside an immersive virtual world enabled by your implants. In the meantime, we won't be letting your bodies go soft. Expect these virtual exercises to be accompanied by lots of PT to compensate.

"The good news is that, instead of the terrain of Olympus Mons or the California coast, you'll be training on Nibiran terrain."

A Marine near the front raised his hand, even though Lee hadn't called for questions. Po wanted to wince, but the colonel was more tolerant. "Go ahead, son," he said.

"Sir, you said we're going to Earth. What good can we do against the Nibirans there?"

"I was just getting to that. First of all, our destination isn't Earth itself, but Earth's moon. Specifically, Shackleton Crater." Nibiru's landscape gave way to an image of a lunar crater cast mostly in darkness, but with a crescent of light illuminating its rightmost lip, where banks of solar panels marched in orderly rows. Pinpricks of light shone from the crater's depths, suggesting structures there. "It may not look like much, but as those of you up on your inner system history will know, Shackleton was where the first lunar colony was constructed. It's now grown to city-size, or at least, city-size by the moon's standards. Its population is thirty thousand. The colony is almost entirely underground, to take advantage of the natural radiation shielding provided by the rock.

"By the time we reach there, you will all be fully trained Marines, each of you proficient in your individual MOS, and ready to go to work. What work, you ask? Well, GEA's intelligence agencies went into overdrive after the attack on Cycler 3, and they've figured out that the Nibirans who attacked us were trained and equipped on the moon, right under their noses."

Lee paused, letting his words fully penetrate the Marines' minds. There was a lot of shifting, and a few muttered curses, which the colonel either didn't hear or chose to let slide.

"This is obviously an...*embarrassment* to the Earthen intelligence community, to say the least. What's more, right now there's a distinct lack of Marines in the inner system who can be deployed to the moon to root out and destroy whatever human elements have chosen to betray their species. That's because, as I said, war has been declared on the Nibirans, and even before the attack on Cycler 3, almost every Marine regiment within easy reach of Earth was already en route to Nibiru.

"That means we're it, Marines. I need you to work hard, learn well, and prepare for what's coming. Marines aren't trained to lounge around Venusian sky resorts, or ogle Mars' butterscotch sunsets from some high-rise executive suite—we're trained to sweat, bleed, and die. Humanity needs you, and if you don't step up, then no one will. Semper Fi."

"*Semper Fi!*" the Marines all shouted back.

And that was that.

Acknowledgments

Thank you to the Marines and other veterans who allowed me to interview them one-on-one in order to get the details of Marine life as accurate as I could. They include Dan Abbott (GySgt), Chuck Chambers (MGySgt), Douglas Glenn (PFC), Joseph Glenn (WO4), Richard Hakala (SSGT), Bill Paradis (MSgt), Steven Reneau, Dennis Whalen, and one other veteran who requested to remain anonymous.

Thank you to my Alpha Team, who have been reading this book since its earliest stage and who've provided substantial feedback along the way, which helped me develop the story with my readers' desires foremost in mind. They are Sheila Beitler, Gwen Collins, Richard Hakala, Colin Oliver, and Jeff Rudolph.

Thank you to my ARC/proofreading team, who helped eliminate scores of spelling and grammar issues. I take full responsibility for any mistakes that remain :)

Thank you to Tom Edwards for creating such stunning cover art, as always.

Thank you to my family - Mom, Dad, and Danielle - your support means everything.

Thank you to the people who read my stories. I couldn't do this without you.

Printed in Dunstable, United Kingdom